Returning Home

SAMSARA-THE FIRST SEASON

Volume One - Book Six

JL Martin

Time Travellers Publishing House PTY LTD

ALSO by JL Martin

FICTION

SAMSARA- The First Season

That Fated Night- A Short Novella of Love and Loss

The Golden Glow

Unexpected Beginnings

Torn in Two

Loss of Innocence

Unconditional Love

Returning Home

Letting go

Soul Connections

Healing the Heart

Legacy and Love

Leo- Back to me!

Lilith- Utopia

SPAWNED OF SIN- Trilogy Series

Through Windows in the Sky I Fall

Tainted Blood, Poisoned Soul

The Ties That Bind Behind Me

Returning Home

J. L. MARTIN

Published by Time Travellers Publishing House Pty Ltd 2022

The series is written in British English, as the Author is Australian and the books are based in Australia. My American friends will find U's where they have no right to be, Z replaced with S, and so many double L's you may feel like throwing the book against the wall. I apologise in advance, and hope one day we can all live in harmony...

National Library of Australia

Cataloging-in-Publication data

Martin, J L, 1971-.

Returning Home

Samsara-The First Season

ISBN Print: 978-1-925852-33-2

ISBN Ebook: 978-1-925852-32-5

Cover design by Thea Atkinson

Editing and text design by Marianne Delaforce

Printed and bound in Australia by Ingram Sparks

A Note from the Author

IN READING THE SERIES 'Samsara-The First Season', I ask you to consider the era in which this work of fiction is set. In these more enlightened times, elements of this story may be considered homophobic, racist, and outright morally corrupt—along with being barbaric and downright ignorant. However; in 19th century Australia, they were not. Themes throughout the series are reflective of the times and are an accurate account of the attitude, bias and outright hate a large majority of society held towards the LGBTQI+ Community and our First Nations Peoples. In saying this, we no longer consider it appropriate for a fifteen-year-old girl to marry—forced or not—but 130 years ago, it was not uncommon.

The character of Leo is based on a real person. As outrageous, inappropriate and politically incorrect as he is—I love this soul. It is not my intention to stigmatise him or cause offence to anyone—only to remain authentic in my best effort to honour and immortalise a very dear man who left a significant imprint on my life—and who unfortunately was born without a filter and lacks all sensibilities; and can be very, very badly behaved.

Please be aware there are themes of violence, racism, and homophobia throughout this series; however, I have been mindful to write these scenes as sensitively as possible and with the utmost care.

I truly hope you enjoy 'Samsara-The First Season' just as much as I enjoyed writing it.

Dedication

To Amarlie Jayne.

Always know your worth.
Be kind to all who cross your path,
and in everything you do, reach for the stars.
You can achieve anything, darling.

Chapter One

I T WAS MAY 1904, nearly two-years since they executed my beautiful man. I had taken to my bed in a deep melancholy after Aaron's murder, sanctioned by the State of Victoria. Weeks spent under my quilts in our bed after I buried him had turned into months. Which then became a year—rolling into many more months after that. I was still deeply grief stricken and stayed in my bedchamber most of the time, unable to function. My thoughts were only of Aaron, and I could not shut them off, not for a moment. It was his face that filled my mind, and his voice, my ears, despite no longer being by my side. He had not shown me a sign he was safe and happy as he had promised, causing my melancholy to deepen over time rather than improve.

Thomas and Emmy slept beside me nearly every night, not wanting me to be alone. I had reassured them I was all right; however, both refused to listen. I would find them in my bed by the time I returned to my bedchamber to retire for the evening after reading their nightly storybook and tucking them up in their own. I had given up putting them back in their own beds once they were asleep, and now allowed them to sleep with me when they felt the need. They would wake before dawn and lay in my arms talking of Willow Grove, often reminiscing about their father before Bessie came in to wake us. They would obediently get up within moments of her arrival, return to their rooms to ready themselves for school, then rush downstairs to the kitchen to have breakfast with Hamish, Angus, and their cousins.

Willy and Bella would come each morning to the main house with Angus, so they could all eat together before walking to school with their beloved cousins. Leo would join them most mornings, ensuring they ate a hearty breakfast, including large portions of milk, bread and fruit, alongside the more decadent dishes he prepared. He had been like a mother hen to us since Aaron had been murdered, ensuring I had a tray brought to me three times a day, along with sending up enticing morning and afternoon teas, then supper before he finished for the day. Despite my melancholy, I was eating well and had lost no weight, as Bessie had expected. I no longer had an appetite; however, I would eat what they brought me to save arguments. I was sensible enough to know I wouldn't win when it came to battling my beloved ladies' maid and friend, who hadn't taken her eye off me since I became a widow.

Each morning after breakfast, Hamish would sit by my bed for an hour every day to speak business and advise me of the day-to-day running of Willow Grove. Our conversations would often turn to Aaron, Hamish occasionally making me laugh while allowing me to cry without judgement as he told me stories of my husband I was unaware of. He was pragmatic and accepted whatever state I was in while doing everything in his power to cheer me, often distracting me with gossip from the district.

He would soon leave to run the property, and only then would I rise from my bed and ready myself to cut white roses from my garden, taking them out to the island. I would row myself over with Dingo beside me to visit with Aaron and the boys, always staying for hours at a time. I would clean their graves, tracing my finger over their names carved into the marble headstone, then place the roses into the vases with fresh water. After staying with them for a time, I would move over to our gum tree and sit where Aaron and I once talked and dreamed while looking over the water. The island was the only place I could grieve in private. No one could get across unless they fancied a swim while I had the boat tied to the pier, waiting for my return.

I was now an empty shell, a broken woman who would never recover from the loss of her first and only love; my heart completely shattered and aching for him while I sobbed for hours everyday under our tree. I would stay until I had calmed myself enough to return to the house, my mind distracted by Aaron while my body slowly trudged across the paddocks—no different from a soul cursed to wander the earth forevermore. I would swiftly return to my bedchamber and retreat to my bed, remaining there until the next morning, and then go on to spend the day repeating the day before. Unable to walk through the hallways or spend time within any of the grand rooms in my home, I had taken to my bed since the day of his funeral and refused to take part in a world without my Aaron.

Thomas and Emmy would come and visit with me after school to tell me about their day, then go off to find Hamish—always to see if he had finished work and ask if he would take them on an adventure. He was such a wonderful godfather, and would often drop what he was doing to please them. Catherine would come and collect the children when they had a day off from school and take them to Melbourne on the train. They would shop in all the popular department stores, carting home the many treasures she spoiled them with in fancy bags. Catherine enjoyed spending time with her beloved godchildren more than she enjoyed eating chocolate, and they both adored her just as much and needed her more now than they ever had.

In the evenings, Angus and Polly would bring Willy and Bella up to the main house to have dinner with the twins, along with Hamish and Leo. They would eat together in the dining room, then retreat to the sitting room where they would play games and tell stories by the fire, trying to keep everything as normal as possible for Thomas and Emmy. Given their father was dead and their mother grieving and unable to parent them alone, they appeared to be coping.

They would go to their grandparents every Friday after school and come home on Sunday, riding their horses, Rainbow and Majestic, by themselves to the corner of the property where the Cavanaughs' lived. They would return home before lunch on Sunday with their cousins, all riding their own Martarinos we had given them when they turned two from the Willow Grove stables. Mr Cavanaugh had Eric build a large stable on the property to hold his ten grandchildren's horses, along with his own, and those of my brothers and sisters. They had twenty-two of our horses, and five-years ago Aaron had sectioned off ten acres at the back of their property for them to graze. Only recently I had signed papers transferring the plot legally to Mr Cavanaugh to protect them should they outlive me.

They insisted we continue to hold family lunches here every Sunday, and everyone still attended—apart from me. Each of my sisters-in-law and friends would take turns to come and lay on the bed with me, enthusiastically filling me in on all the gossip, while stroking my head when I cried. Dana had come every day since Aaron's funeral and lay with me for hours, sometimes not talking, only holding my hand. Catherine came as often as she could, and would stay for a time to speak of anything and everything, while sweet Polly checked in on me several times a day and was doing as much as she could for Thomas and Emmy to compensate for my deficiencies.

Jenny, Amelia and Margaret visited with me daily to bring news of the village and try to brighten me up. Leo had been wonderful, sleeping in my bed with me when the twins were away and patiently holding me in his arms as I cried for my husband. They had all been so supportive and I couldn't have wished for better friends and family around me; however, it didn't help. Their kindness and care had not eased my pain or comforted my tormented mind. I could fill the entire room with my loved ones, and I still felt alone without Aaron. I was stuck in my grief, and no matter what anyone tried to do to relieve my pain, I hadn't been able to move forward since the day he died, and had lost all hope I would.

After Aaron's funeral, Cain Stephenson from the Geelong Advertiser came to visit with me. He had attended Aaron's funeral, along with thousands of others, and I was grateful to him. Over the years, he wrote many articles about us and became a dear friend. He had asked to interview me for a follow-up article about Aaron and the effect his death had on the children and myself, along with all those who knew him and the strangers that felt they had. Cain had written a heart wrenching article, taking up two pages, and printed the photo that was taken of me and the children entering the church on the day of his funeral. He also included others he took of us after Aaron had passed, and a large photo of his coffin draped in wattle with the Australian flag covering the top when he was laid to rest.

Again, *The Sun* newspaper in Melbourne picked up the story and ran it the following day, gaining an enormous response from the public. I still received hundreds of letters a week, the sight of the postal delivery officer, Patrik, causing my heart to palpitate and my throat to close. He had become a familiar face here at Willow Grove, and was never without the hessian bag he carried filled with only my correspondence. Everyone but me opened and read them, my friends and family deciding they would only allow me to see the letters they felt were supportive and kind. Hamish and Leo often spoke in hushed tones of the many marriage proposals I received and offers of courtship, a fact they held back from me, aware I had no interest in seeking affection from any man other than Aaron, while both clearly disgusted that anyone had the nerve and bad manners to ask.

Leo would choose the letters that resonated with him most, then sit down in the late afternoon at the desk in the drawing room to write back to them, treating each as if he had known them for years. I continued to be surprised at the eclectic group of people he had befriended far beyond the shores of Australia.

He referred to them as his servants, and likened his ragtag group of loyal admirers to Club des Hashischins, a group founded in 1844 in Paris known to experiment with hashish that comprised the literary and intellectual elite of the time—formed decades before Leo was even thought of. To my knowledge, although the club was no longer active, others had sprung up in its place and membership had grown significantly over the years. I was well aware Leo was not, and never had been acquainted with anyone involved; although he often still surprised me with tales of his life before we met at the most inappropriate and unexpected moments.

I had cursed Judge Murray the morning they took Aaron from us, along with every man and woman involved in his case who harboured any ill intent towards him, wishing sickness and death for them all, and had meant every word. Ten-days after Aaron was murdered, the respected judge was struck down with an illness no physician could diagnose or treat. Cain informed me he passed away three-months later in dreadful pain, alone and screaming for death to take him from the agony he endured day after day, week after week, month after month, just as he deserved.

I had felt somewhat thrilled the curse had been so effective; however, all those around me dismissed his illness as a coincidence. I didn't believe in coincidences. Along with Judge Murry, six men who had actively worked on Aaron's case had passed away from illness and disease. Their physicians were also unable to diagnose or treat them, and all were struck down without warning over the last twenty-one-months. I had been told all endured much suffering, lingering on in unbearable pain until the heavens took pity and released them to the pits of hell. They had all been healthy, powerful men, and I was acquainted with each of them on some level. I was uncertain if they were all truly corrupt; however, the fact so many had passed proved in my mind those around me were wrong. I had never cursed or wished ill on another person in my life before Maslow entered our world uninvited. Until that very moment, I never realised my capacity to hate so deeply, and by allowing that hate to fester, I was now an empty shell filled with rage, intent on dispensing my own form of justice no matter what the consequence.

Only causing me more angst, there had been a constant stream of men calling at Willow Grove in an attempt to court me, including Detective Paul O'Neill, who continued to visit the property against my wishes. During those visits, Leo or Hamish would remain in my bedchamber to keep a watchful eye on him.

I would remain under my heavy quilt, my dressing gown wrapped around me, while he sat by my bed, attempting to lift my spirits. I had no interest in keeping company with the man; however, I no longer had the strength to argue with anyone and chose to ignore him. Despite my silence, he still insisted on calling to enquire about my health, visiting me in my bedchamber no matter how inappropriate. Often, he would stay no more than a few minutes; however, it was enough to send me deeper into a melancholy that never left me, only easing at times when with my children. My day was always worse than even I had come to expect after being in his presence—although occasionally I was touched by kindness from a stranger, lifting my spirits, if only for a moment.

One particular letter I received soon after Aaron's execution resonated with me so strongly, I was forced to reply without delay to this sweet young woman. Mrs Sarah Stewart hailed from a tiny farming town called Iona, set on the flat and surrounded by the rolling hills of Gippsland. Despite travelling somewhere nearby on our journey to Heavenly Hideaway that one time to see in the new century—nearly five long years ago now—I had never heard of the place. Carrying her own grief, she had recently given birth to twins, both stillborn, and knew of the suffering Aaron and I had endured. Only just gone three-and-twenty, Sarah had not given up hope of starting a family with her husband, Lawrence. They too had emigrated from Scotland as adults, bringing their parents and siblings with them to start a new life.

They were potato farmers who struggled from month to month to make a living; however, they were hardworking, decent people who wanted something better than what their homeland had provided them, seeking to live a comfortable life in Australia and provide for the children they planned to have. Sarah wanted ten of them, and I admired her determination and strength of spirit. She was not one to give up, and was content with very little in the way of material possessions, counting family and friends as the most important to her.

I felt the same way about so many things she wrote of, and responded in kind, opening my heart to her as she had done to me. She wrote back immediately, and a friendship by mail began. I would write to her weekly, telling her of my deepest despair and the fears I held for my children, and soon after I would receive pages of beautiful comforting words that were a tonic for my heart. She would tell me of all the delightful interactions between her family and speak of the monotony of her days and her own worries. I hoped to meet her one day when I was ready, and although I questioned if that day would ever come, it was one I silently prayed for.

Tamara would still come and stay once a month with Brian, bringing a tribe of servants to care for their children separately to ours, while my sisters-in-law visited regularly, spending time with me in my bedchamber, as did Mr and Mrs Cavanaugh, who had recovered better than I thought they would despite still grieving their son. I knew they all held grave concerns for my welfare, and felt helpless and unable to comfort me.

Hamish and Angus kept an eye on the village, and from all reports, things were running along smoothly. They would make time to drink at the pub with the workers as often as they could, and would advise me of any concerns. Jen and Margaret kept me informed of the gossip kept from the menfolk, and if I felt it necessary, I would tell Hamish. He detested being called on to sort out bickering among the women and was of the firm opinion they should work out their own problems. I had explained to him how this was the way of it and had always been since the village was established, promising as soon as I was back on my feet I would take the burden from him, much to his relief.

I lay in bed waiting for the twins to wake, my gaze fixed on them as they snuggled into each of my arms. They snored softly, just like their father, causing a smile to touch my lips for a moment. Thomas stretched and screwed up his face like he had done since he was a wean, then opened his big blue eyes, the colour of the ocean, and gazed at me sleepily.

'Good mornin', Ma. Did ya sleep well?' he asked, kissing me on the forehead.

'Yes, I did. Thanks to you and Emmy.' I reached across and touched his face, his handsome features showing the first signs of impending adulthood, everything about him reminding me of Aaron. They were thirteen and maturing far too quickly for my liking. Thomas was big for his age, and his shoulders were broadening by the day. Many of the young girls in the village and those from neighbouring farms who attended school here were already seeking his attention, but he showed no interest. Emmy favoured me more and more with every passing day. Her large green eyes and long black lashes, along with her auburn hair falling to her waist in curls, drew a great deal of attention from her male counterparts. She was tall but fine-boned and possessed the most beautiful face I had ever seen. They were so grown up for their ages, I believed as a result of all they had suffered since losing their father during their tender years. My complete withdrawal from life had only hastened their first steps into adulthood, both sadly feeling a responsibility to care for me when it should have been the other way around.

'Good morning, Emmy,' I whispered as she opened her eyes and smiled. I leaned over to kiss her nose before she yawned loudly.

'Good morning, my sweet Mummy.' She smiled again and moved closer, wrapping her arms around my neck while we spoke softly between ourselves. Thomas appeared lost in his own thoughts as he gazed silently out of the window at the old gumtree, our resident kookaburra, preparing to start his early morning song. I looked forward to the time we spent together in the mornings, just like I once looked forward to spending the early morning hours with their father before they woke and joined us in our bed. The time in between daybreak and when the respectable people were obligated to rise and start the day were my favourite hours, only now my life was unrecognisable to what it once had been. I woke alone, despite having my beautiful children with me, and no one would ever fill the void Aaron had left. Our little family would never be complete again, no matter how many people surrounded us with love and good intentions.

The twins missed him dreadfully; however, they seemed to cope well enough. There were times they withdrew, unable to hide their sadness, but would soon seek Hamish or Catherine out to confide in, easing my fears they were holding everything inside and my constant worry they would carry their grief long into adulthood. They appeared to be sensible, cheerful children to everyone who crossed their path, but I noticed the confusion and pain in their eyes when they thought I was paying them no mind.

There was a soft knock at the door before little Mary swung it open and stepped into the room. Their clothes hung neatly across her outstretched arms as she hurried over to the dressing rooms to lay them out, calling out her morning greetings before singing an old Irish song that was familiar, yet I couldn't place it. Thomas had decided to use Aaron's dressing room when he slept in my bedchamber, while Emmy used mine. Little Mary bid us farewell, cheerfully waving before dashing off downstairs to organise their breakfast with Leo. She planned to spend some time in the laundry house supervising the maids while they washed the stains from their clothing before hanging it out on the line to dry in the winter sun.

'Oh, it's such a beautiful day, Mistress, and far too good to be wasting away,' Mary called out, surprising me, given the time of year. She silently beckoned the children as she smiled sympathetically in my direction.

'I will never experience another beautiful day,' I murmured to myself. Watching in silence as my bairns rose from the bed and retreated to the dressing rooms, I stretched like a stable cat in the sunshine, my joints clicking into place. They returned shortly after to kiss me goodbye for the day, and I held them close to my chest before releasing them to enjoy their time in the kitchen. I lay back on my pillows as the door closed behind them, my thoughts turning to how quickly they were growing. I frowned as I considered the possibility that, within a few years, they could marry if they so chose. I closed my eyes as Bessie marched into the room, then hurried to my side, a breakfast tray in her hands as she stood over me.

'Open your eyes, Mistress. Leo sends his love to you this fine morning and has prepared something special to brighten your mood,' she called out, placing the tray on my lap before I could sit up. I lifted the silver cover to find not only a cooked breakfast of bacon and eggs with all the trimmings, but also buttermilk pancakes. I rested back on my pillows and ate in silence, and when I finished, I lay across the bed on Aaron's side to sip my coffee while Bessie tidied the room, muttering to herself all the while.

I had never looked in his bedside table, and hesitated for only a moment before sliding open the top drawer and slipping my hand inside, my fingers gently caressing the objects he kept there unbeknownst to me. Finding a small bible, along with all the jewellery I had ever given him, a picture of us on our wedding day caught my eye while I fiddled with some odd bits and pieces I didn't recognise or have use for. The second drawer contained books, and the third, papers, along with several official documents. I took the papers out and started flicking through them as I sipped my coffee thoughtfully. He had kept every letter I had ever written to him; my fingers caressed the paper as I felt tears sting my eyes. An envelope fell out and fluttered down onto the bed next to me, my name written on the front. I placed the papers, along with the letters, back in the bottom drawer and gripped the envelope, my trembling hand bringing it up to my lips, the scent of sandalwood filling my nose as I closed my eyes. Aaron's face filled my mind, overwhelming me; his presence so strong my eyes fluttered open to check if he was sitting in front of me. I opened the envelope, my hands shaking as I breathed in his scent.

My dearest Abi,

I'm writin' ya this while laid up in bed with a broken leg, an' I'm bored 'cause ya keep insistin' I rest an' won't come to bed to play with me. You'll notice I've stolen ya good writin' paper an' envelope, so I hope ya not mad at me. Hopefully after ya read what I have to say, you'll forgive me bad manners, me Abi girl. You're the love of me life, an' there will never be another for me. Ya outer beauty, although extraordinary, is nothin' compared to the beauty ya hold inside. You've a beautiful soul that's so pure an' honest, I'm instantly drawn to ya side whenever I see ya. I can't be apart from ya, me love. You're everythin' to me an' always will be. I have the most satisfyin' life with ya by me side, an' the two nippers you've given me. I love ya. mo anamchara. There's no other woman in this life or the next for me. The day me eyes looked into yours, I felt as if half me soul had been restored to me without ever knowin' it'd been missin'. You're the other half of me, me heart an' me soul. I feel like the luckiest bastard alive to have ya as mine, an' the life you've given me is more than I ever could've wished for. I love holdin' ya in me arms an' kissin' ya sweet lips. An' touchin' that round, firm arse of yours would turn even the most decent bloke into a malingerer who refuses to leave his bed.

What I wanna say is this. I love ya more than I believed ya could ever love another, an' our love will go on forever no matter what life presents us with. Now you've read this, get into bed with me, woman, an' do ya wifely duties.

I love ya to the moon and back. An' I still reckon the nippers will fly there in their lifetime, no matter how much ya laugh at me, Abi girl.

Aaron

I sobbed as I read the words he had written so long ago now and forgot to give me, so distressed I did not notice Hamish quietly enter my bedchamber and stride over to my side. He pulled a chair over and placed it next to the bed before lowering his enormous frame down and making himself comfortable, his shoulders forward while resting his arms on his muscular thighs.

'What's wrong with ye, Abigail? Are ye havin' a hard mornin'?' He placed the cup of coffee he had brought me on my bedside table, then lifted his own to his lips and took a slow sip. I tried to compose myself, wiping my face with my handkerchief before handing him the envelope.

'I only just found it.' I sniffed again as he took the letter out and scanned it briefly.

'Aye, I understand now. How could I ferget how obsessed he was with yer backside? He'd naw shut up about it. Aaron seemed tae ferget that afore he married ye, I once had the opportunity an' privilege as a young man tae have quite a thorough feel o' that bum o' yer's. Over yer clothin', o' course.' A slow smile touched his lips as I wiped my face again, then tried to smile back. He lowered his head and read the letter again, and after he had finished, he placed it down gently on my bedside table, taking my hand in his as I broke down again and sobbed.

'I cannot cope with any of it. He was a messy swine and left everything around for me to tidy up years after he left. I need him here, Hamish.' I raised my head and stared up at him, his gaze fixed on the yellow crested cockatoos in the gumtree just outside my window. 'Look at me. I've turned into a lunatic, just like Leo always predicted. I cannot even go downstairs without making a spectacle of myself. There is not one room in the house I can spend any time in without bursting into tears and making everyone uncomfortable. I cannot stand how people look at me now. This is the only room where I can freely grieve without upsetting everyone,' I murmured through my tears.

'Weel, ye do what ye must fer now.' He stayed beside me, holding my hand in his until I had no tears left in me to shed. He told me of the new street of terraces still under construction in the village due to the increasing demand for married quarters. A number of our workers had taken wives, and the Martarino breeding program had expanded, leaving us short and acutely aware of the need to employ more able-bodied men. Willow Grove was thriving, and so was the farm account, with more than enough money in there to cover the cost of the buildings and furnishings.

'All right. I am happy to let Richard know out of courtesy that I will organise the furniture and décor; however, I do not require his consent. We have the money available from Willow Grove's own account. Promise me they will be built to the same standard and look no different from the older terraces. Only so no one can say anyone else is being favoured with the new living arrangements. You know how petty some can be.' He nodded thoughtfully, then took a small notebook from his breast pocket and scribbled something down inside with an even smaller pencil he kept tucked behind his ear. There would soon be twenty-eight terraces once completed, more than enough to accommodate the workers we now required.

'Aye, I must get tae work or Harry will be seekin' me out. Try tae take care o' yerself, Abigail. Everyone is worried about ye, includin' yer bairns. They aren't weans anymore an' they know what's goin' on. They cannae stand seein' ye like this, an' neither can anyone else. Ye must go on with yer life fer their sake. They need ye. I'm naw their mother or their father, despite lovin' 'em as me own.' I sighed deeply, while his cheeks flushed as he continued. 'Aaron'd foot ye up the arse if he were here tae see ye in this state. He's been gone nearly two-years now, an' I know ye still miss him just as much as the day he was taken from ye, but the world doesn't stop, lass. Despite ye wantin' it tae. Yer only bringin' misery tae ye own mind by lockin' yerself in here all alone with his memory. We've been friends fer a long time now. I do understand those that love as deeply as ye do, grieve just as deeply in response tae such a sudden an' tragic loss o' someone they love. I dinnae know what tae do tae help ye anymore. I've tried the soft an' gentle way with ye, but it's naw helpin'. Maybe I need tae kick ye up the backside meself so ye'll get yer act taegether an' stop bein' so bloody selfish. Yer naw the only one who lost here. Yer children lost their father, an' they have tae get on an' do their best without their mother. I dinnae want tae be hard on ye, lass, but if ye dinnae pull yerself together very soon, I'll be forced tae intervene. Yer hurtin' Thomas an' Emmy without meanin' tae bein' blinded by ye grief, but ye have an obligation tae pick yerself up an' carry on. Naw one is sayin' ye have tae remarry or even allow any man tae court ye. Just come back tae yer children before ye feel a hard kick comin' from me boot.' I snatched my hand away, while fury rose in me, some of the anger and frustration I felt so intensely directed at myself and my inability to stop the tears streaming down my face.

'How dare you? You don't know how I feel.' I spat. 'The nerve of you sitting here threatening me. Come near my arse and you will never walk again, that I promise you. And stop pattering on with me in that brogue. You're getting worse and sound more Scottish than the bloody day we arrived here.' I turned to him, a smirk touching his lips.

'Aye. Ye seem tae forget I spent most o' me time in England gettin' schooled tae speak proper afore I met ye. It's taken me some time tae put that in the past an' be proud of me heritage an' who I am. I'm naw English gentleman an' never will be, an' I'll naw longer speak like I've a mouthful o' marbles. As expected by me parents. Anyway, we're now talkin' about me. I'm worried fer the bairns, an' I want tae know ye will sort yerself out fer their sake, if naw yer own.'

'I cannot help how I feel, but I assure you, I love my children and I'm doing my very best, Hamish. How could you expect any more from me when I'm empty inside? Aaron took everything I had with him.' I blew my nose loudly into a fresh handkerchief, then picked up my barely warm coffee and finished it before turning back to him.

'Haud yer wheesht, Abigail. I've heard enough o' yer excuses. If ye can get up every mornin' an' get yerself dressed an' over tae the island where ye stay fer hours, ye can bloody well go outside after school with yer children an' do somethin' other than sit here within these four walls. Yer so blinded by ye own pain, yer too selfish tae see anyone else's. I dinnae want tae be a bastard towards ye, lass, but if I must tae make ye realise, I'm prepared tae suffer yer wrath an' bear the consequences. I'll naw have Thomas an' Emmy hold on tae memories fer the rest o' their lives o' a mother who lost all interest in livin', even though they were still here an' needin' ye. How do ye think yer makin' 'em feel? I will bloody well tell you—as if they're naw enough fer ye an' ye dinnae care enough tae be here fer 'em. Like I said, whether ye want tae take it as a threat or naw, I'll come down hard on ye if ye dinnae get yerself together.' He abruptly rose to his feet, preparing to leave. I glared up at him as he stood over me, returning my stare while refusing to budge.

No longer wanting to think of anything, nor caring what his opinion was regarding any subject he felt entitled to force on me, I pushed it to the back of my mind before making a rude gesture with my fingers, then threw myself back down onto my pillow and covered myself with the heavy quilt. I heard him snort with amusement as he crossed the room and quietly left, closing the door behind him.

Rising from my bed within moments, I slipped on a housedress, then made my way downstairs and out the front entrance, hurrying around the side of the house and out to the back garden while trying not to be seen. I collected my basket from the back verandah, the sharp knife I used to cut my roses tucked securely inside. As I went to step back out onto the grass, Wombles came waddling over to me in the way that wombats do. Angus had told me he was, in fact, female, and carried a very young joey in her pouch that had only come to his attention a week ago.

I had learnt a lot about native animals since living at Willow Grove, discovering wombats were nocturnal creatures, rarely seen during the day; however, sometimes they would venture out of their burrows and could often be seen around the property chewing bark from the trees. Dingoes were their dominant predator, and there were several that occasionally roamed the paddocks. They ranged in colour from light brown to black and were about twenty-inches high with short legs, a thick body, and an enormous head, with round ears and small eyes—which I found extremely sweet.

They were very fat and had the appearance of a badger, I had been told by Harry. Weighing around seventy pounds, they were three feet long when fully grown, with a short, stubby tail. These unusual creatures were sexually mature by eighteen-months of age, the females producing one joey a year in the spring after a twenty-one-day gestation period. What I found intriguing was instead of having their pouch facing towards the front like other Australian marsupials, wombats had a backward pouch so that when they dug their deep burrows, they didn't get dirt in their pouch or on their young.

I thought it the most remarkable thing I had ever seen watching their babies being carried around inside the pouch, almost touching the ground as the joey grew. Once mature, the babies remained in the pouch for six to seven-months before leaving to live beside its mother, then eventually weaning itself from her at fifteen-months. They lived on grasses, sedges, herbs, bark and roots, of which there were plenty here at Willow Grove.

Wombles wasn't your usual wombat. First of all, she got along well with Dingo, only because she had clawed him once when he came too close, leaving him with a warning he never forgot. She didn't join the wisdom of wombats that roamed the property, preferring to lie about during the day on our back verandah, sleeping on and off. She spent her days finding her own food and occasionally being given fresh herbs from the kitchen.

She followed me around like a dog when I was in my garden, and I would often stop what I was doing to sit down next to her on the ground for a cuddle. Wombats could be extremely aggressive when their environment was threatened, and were extremely protective of their burrows. Wombles didn't have a burrow as far as we knew. She was far too lazy to dig one or go out and live as a real wombat should.

She stopped at my feet as I leaned down to scratch her behind the ears. We had tried to release her back onto the property many times; however, she kept turning up at our back door, looking for her basket filled with soft, woollen blankets. We eventually gave up when we found her sleeping on the ground in the cold of winter, and placed her basket back outside the door. She came and went as she pleased, finding her own food while ambling around the gardens of the main house. She rarely ventured out into the paddocks; however, must have at some point given she now had a joey growing in her pouch.

Wandering slowly through the garden, I gathered a basket full of flowers, then made my way towards the island, unable to stop thinking about what Hamish so rudely said earlier. I knew I frustrated him, given he had assumed responsibility of caring for Thomas and Emmy. I understood why he was cross with me; however, his words stung more than if he had slapped me across the face without warning. It was clear he did not understand that I wasn't behaving this way on purpose. It was something I couldn't control. Like he had pointed out, grief blinded me and I couldn't think straight, but even that brought me no comfort.

I left Wombles at the edge of the back garden, waving at her as we parted and I continued on to the island, Dingo close beside me. He missed Aaron dreadfully and was unable to bond as closely with anyone else. He still stayed by the house and went to work with the men; however, he was constantly whining and looking for Aaron after all this time. He jumped in the boat before I had even placed my basket down and unhooked the rope that held the boat securely to the pier. I sat in the boat, unmoving, feeling hot tears run down my face as I thought of how mean Hamish had been to me, despite knowing deep down he was right.

I rowed myself across with the fresh roses I had collected from the garden and tied the boat to the pier, Dingo sitting up at the stern. I made my way to our gumtree, where my boys were resting underneath its sheltering branches, sprawling out across the sky, its bright green leaves the koalas so loved to eat fluttering gently in the breeze. I had only recently noticed a family of koalas living in our tree, so high up, it was sometimes hard to see them. Occasionally, when I would come here, they would walk around on the ground; however, would run towards the thick trunk of our gumtree, climbing as fast as they could when I would approach.

Bending down to remove the flowers from yesterday, I scattered them across the water, the roses still fresh and lovely as they gently floated away. Returning to Harrison and Jack's grave, I placed some roses into the crystal vases that sat under the headstone on the small, flat slab of marble that lay across my babies. I turned to sit down on Aaron's grave next to the boys and murmured to him while stroking the marble headstone, telling him how I had only found his forgotten letter, and of the gaping hole he had left here—speaking for hours of how much the twins were growing, and all about their lives without him, adding how they thought of him every day and we talked of him often.

Sobbing as I told him how I was stuck in my grief and couldn't move on with my life as he had wanted, I cried out in pain as I spoke of how my heart felt as if it had stopped beating and my body an empty shell. After the longest time, I struggled to my feet and kissed Aaron's name carved beautifully into the marble, then Harrison and Jack's headstone, before stumbling over to our gumtree and crumpling to the ground, attempting to calm my thoughts. I gazed over the water that Aaron loved so much, and I hoped he was happy resting here—just as we had been all the times we had sat here together. I blew my nose for the last time before shakily getting to my feet to find my way back to my bedchamber.

Chapter Two

I HAD ONLY RETURNED from the island an hour before when Dana entered the room. She stood beside the bed, gazing down at me intently.

'Are you awake, dear Abigail?' she whispered, leaning down to study my face.

'Yes, Dana. I'm just laying here thinking. I haven't slept since I woke at daybreak no matter how hard I've tried.' I struggled to sit up to kiss her before laying back against my pillows.

'Good,' she replied as she moved around the room, opening the heavy velvet drapes. The bedchamber suddenly filled with bright light, something it hadn't seen in a long time. 'We need to talk.' She lay down on the bed next to me, and I turned over on my side to look at her, silently waiting to hear what she wanted to say that sounded so important. 'It's time now, Abigail,' she said, stroking my face, the chirping outside from the birds on my windowsill distracting me for a moment.

'What do you mean? Time for what, Dana?'

'It's been long enough now. It is time to stop mourning and come back to us all. Especially your children. I'm not saying you need to stop feeling sad or forget about dear Aaron. I don't know how long this despair will last for you. Maybe forever, but you need to get out of this room and walk among the living. Not the dead. I made a promise to Aaron the last time I saw him I would be here for you and help you through your grief. He also made me promise that when the time came, I had to put a stop to it and force you back into the world. That time is now, Abigail. You turn thirty in less than five-months, leaving you only a matter of weeks to organise your voyage. You gave Aaron your word you would go, and for that, you must. There are things to do and plan, so as of tomorrow, you will not be staying in this room. You will get up after the children leave, as I know you cannot go into the kitchen yet, but you have to get yourself organised. You are to join them in the dining room at night to spend time with your family before you go to bed. I know this sounds harsh, dear Abigail, but this is not what Aaron wanted for you or the twins.' She waved her hand around the room, then pointed at my chest. 'You must pull yourself together for your own sake, and that of Thomas and Emmy. We all love you and are here to help in any way we can. I'm not expecting you to jump out of bed tomorrow and forget all about Aaron, but what I am trying to make you understand is we need you to come back to us. We love you and miss you dreadfully.' She gently wiped my tears away with her handkerchief, her eyes filled with tears.

'Have you and Hamish been gossiping about me? No one understands. I do not know how to go on without him, Dana,' I murmured, unable to stop the tears while feeling utter despair.

'You will never be without him. He is still with you in your heart and your mind and in your beautiful children. We are all here to help you start your life again and will support you, but you must try. Take one step at a time. Tomorrow, take the carriage to Geelong to see Catherine so she can start your wardrobe for the journey as you're not wearing black. I forbid it. Take tea with Catherine and relax, then come home to meet the twins after school and do something with them. It will become easier, I promise. As for talking to Hamish, I have not read *The Sun* for the weather report today; however, I would be one of the first to know if hell had indeed frozen over.' She held my hand in hers, a smirk touching her lips.

Deep down, I knew she was right—and so was Hamish. I couldn't go on like this, and I had promised Aaron I would take the twins to London for my birthday. I would have to push my grief to the back of my mind and try not to think about him until I was alone if I were to do what Hamish and Dana expected.

'All right, I will try,' I promised, feeling doubtful I could carry it out. I had lost all my confidence since they murdered Aaron and was now a shell of my former self.

'That's a good girl. I know you can do this. You are strong and brave, Abigail. That's the mother the children need to see.' She smiled affectionately, then wrapped her arms around me in a warm embrace as I lowered my head and cried my heart out.

After dragging myself from my bed, I slipped on one of my black dresses before slowly making my way downstairs to the dining room. My stomach knotted up as I stepped inside, all present at the table stopping to gaze over at me, the room now silent as I slowly crossed the room to take my seat.

'Oh, Mummy, it's so good to see you here,' Emmy called out excitedly, and I smiled weakly at her. Thomas stared up at me, a wide grin on his face—just like his father—and I smiled back.

'It's nice tae see ye back in the land of the livin',' Hamish said, a smile touching his lips before he turned and winked at Thomas and Emmy. I knew he hadn't meant to hurt me, or make me feel like an even worse mother than I already believed myself to be. He felt he needed to stand up for the twins, and I completely understood; however, I didn't appreciate him acting like a boss cockie and ordering me around.

We chatted through dinner, my loved ones behaving as if I dined with them every night and my seat hadn't been empty for the last two-years, and I felt the tension in my body ease. I *could* do this. I no longer saw Aaron at the dining table anymore like I once had, and it surprised me to find I enjoyed the company and conversation.

After dinner, we retired to the sitting room—a room I hadn't been in since Aaron's coffin sat within its walls—and made ourselves comfortable. Hamish poured everyone a whisky while the children sat together on the carpet and talked of school and the gossip they had overheard about those living in the village. I drank the whisky he handed to me in one swallow, then held my glass up for another. Hamish raised his eyebrows at me, but poured me a larger one this time. I drank it just as quickly before rising to my feet to retrieve the bottle and bring it to the table.

Soon after, I kissed Thomas and Emmy before they left to find their beds, while Willy and Bella departed in a whirlwind of kisses and farewells with their parents, leaving Leo, Hamish and me to our own thoughts. A heavy silence hung over the room for the longest time before Hamish leaned forward and cleared his throat.

'Do ye think ye might be drinkin' that a wee bit fast, lass?' He watched intently as I poured another, disapproval clear in his eyes.

'No, I do not. I plan to get pleasantly drunk,' I replied, already slurring my words.

'I think it will be more unpleasantly drunk.' Leo rolled his eyes as he watched me closely. 'Don't forget, sweet cheeks, I'm the one who ends up holding your hair back,' he added, then poured himself another.

'Stop being a dickhead to me, Leo. How many times have I patted your back when you have been sick from too much drinking? Do not start this scaffy with me.' I smiled affectionately across at him, and his face lit up with a grin.

'We have had some fun over the years with you and whisky. You've carried out some of the most humiliating acts I have ever seen while under the influence of it. You completely lose your mind and get me into trouble every time by convincing me to get up to mischief,' he told me, and Hamish threw back his head and howled with laughter.

'What a load o' shite that is. I've sat back an' watched ye fer close tae fifteen-years now, an' neither o' ye has changed a bit. Ye still behave like five-year-old lassies when yer taegether. Tae this day, I dinnae know who gets who in tae trouble more, but I think yer fairly even,' Hamish told him, still chuckling to himself as Leo yawned, raising his hand to delicately pat his open mouth. I sat back in the lounge sipping another whisky while feeling no pain, when Leo excused himself for bed.

'Are you able to ensure this tavern trollop gets to her bedchamber please, Hamish? I don't want her ending up in mine, as she snores when she's stonkered. Don't you go touching her anywhere you shouldn't. It won't matter how drunk she is, she will know and pound your face until it's as flat as a pancake. I tried to touch her breasts when I thought she wouldn't notice, and she grabbed me by my testicles and twisted them until I thought I would die. Oh, you were there that time and heard me screaming for my life.' Hamish nodded, howling again in laughter as Leo ignored him and continued. 'I didn't mean to wake the entire village that night. Can you believe that some of them still hold a grudge against me all these years later just for a few squeals on a Saturday night? You would think they would be over it by now, but oh no. All I hear is, *Leo is a nasty man,* or, *Leo is mean to my children. He comes to the village to tease them on purpose. He woke me up five-years ago and I missed fifteen-minutes of sleep. He is a whinger.* And on and on they go. Little do they realise I was screaming for a reason. Abigail had my balls firmly in her grip and would not let go. She is a violent little troll at times, but I do love her. Look at her. She's already had a skin full. See how sweet her face is when she isn't chasing you around and trying to hurt you? She is so lucky to have me as her best friend,' Leo said smugly, and Hamish laughed again.

We said our goodnights, and I embraced him before Hamish and I strolled out to the back garden, a full bottle of whisky in my hand. We sat side-by-side on the lounges, the sky bright with stars, the moon full and hanging low.

'What are you doing in a few weeks' time, Hamish?' I asked, trying to focus on him while everything around me seemed to move and rock as if I were in my father-in-law's boat and couldn't find my sea legs.

'Workin' here. As usual. Why?' He lifted the bottle to his lips and took a swig before passing it to me. I put it to my lips and took a deep drink, feeling it burn as it went down my throat and settled in the pit of my stomach, creating a comforting warmth that spread to every part of me as I let my worries slip away.

'Do you want to come to England with us? Then on to France and America? I have business I must attend to in London. Aaron made me promise to take you with me.' I took another swig, the cicadas' night chorus piercing the silence.

'Aaron mentioned it tae me durin' our last visit, an' asked if I'd go tae chaperone the three o' ye. I gave him me word I would,' he replied, his voice low. I reached over and took his hand, holding it in mine.

'You are a good friend, Hamish. I couldn't have asked for anyone better to come with us. I trust you completely with my children, and I know they will have a wonderful time with you there. Maybe I should ask Catherine along.' I shook my head, realising my mistake. 'Oh, that would never work. She wouldn't be able to take the time away from work. Thomas and Emmy would have loved for her to be there,' I said, so drunk I was struggling to string my words together coherently.

'When yer ready tae court again, would ye consider me?' I turned to him, shaking my head again in confusion.

'You and me? Why would you want to go and ruin such a beautiful friendship?' I closed my eyes, feeling I was drifting out to sea, the waves crashing all around me.

'Aye, ye an' me. Abigail. Ye've had me heart fer nearly fifteen-years, an' I never asked fer it back, preferrin' tae leave it safe with ye. Over the years, I've taken what ye could offer me, an' that was yer friendship—a deep, close friendship at that, an' somethin' I cherish very much. Out o' respect fer Aaron, I tried fer years tae get ye outta me mind an' I distracted meself with other women. But I never once felt anythin' fer any o' 'em like I felt fer ye. I put me love fer ye away after ye married Aaron. 'Twas naw 'till recently, I realised how I feel about ye. I'm in love with ye, Abigail. I've always loved ye, but now, I'm deeply an' completely in love with ye. I can naw stop thinkin' about ye, or worryin' meself sick over ye.'

'Please stop,' I murmured, yet he continued on as if I hadn't uttered a word.

'Och, I suppose it took me some time after Aaron died tae let meself fall back in love with ye again. Felt I was doin' somethin' sinful an' would go straight tae Hell. I'm naw, though, Abigail. I love ye fer all the right reasons. When yer ready, I want somethin' serious between us. I'm askin' ye dinnae dismiss me as a suitor in preference tae all these other blokes that keep callin' here, just 'cause ye dinnae want tae ruin our friendship.' His voice shook with emotion. Or the whisky. I couldn't tell. Gazing up at the sky while attempting to gather my thoughts, a kangaroo exploring the garden took my attention for a moment.

'Hamish, you must listen to me. I have nothing to give you. Or anyone. Not even my children. I am an empty vessel. My heart and mind remain with Aaron and always will. That wouldn't be fair to you. Or any man. I would be doing the same thing you did for all those years. Distracting myself. And that didn't make you happy, nor did it bring any joy to the girls you stepped out with. The poor things. I apologise. I'm not trying to make you feel like shit on my shoe,' I slurred, my eyes heavy as I sat up to take a long drink of whisky.

'I'm naw sayin' now, Abigail. I mean when yer ready tae love again. Aye, I know that'll be a while yet, but I'm willin' tae wait.' I looked over in his direction to find I was unable to see his face. Only the outline of his head and shoulders was visible in the darkness, the moon covered by heavy clouds.

'Hamish, I must be honest. I don't believe that will ever happen. Do not think for a minute I don't love you, because I do. You are one of my closest friends. I treasure and love you for taking care of us and always will, but I can't give you what you want. You need to find someone who will make you happy. I'm a widow now and I will never love again. It's not fair, and the last thing I would ever want for you would be to marry someone like me. I couldn't give you what you deserve. There is someone out there for you. You just have to find her.' I lowered myself down after passing the bottle back to him. We were both very drunk now and saying far too much.

'That'll never happen. Naw 'till I have ye. An' I'll wait fer as long as it takes. Ye think I dinnae remember what 'tis like tae hold ye, tae kiss ye an' feel passion I've never felt since. I've relived it over an' over in me mind a thousand times. I cannae help how I feel about ye. I've always loved ye, but now I lust after ye. I cannae be near ye without wantin' tae pick ye up an' hold ye in me arms an' tell ye everythin' will be all right. An' then bed ye. Aye, yer worth waitin' fer, Abigail. An' I'm a very patient man.' He squeezed my hand, then placed it on his broad chest, his large hand over mine. He passed the bottle back over to give me the last of the whisky.

'The way I'm going, Hamish, you would have to have the patience of a saint if you're waiting for that to happen.'

I woke in my bed, fully dressed, and feeling very much under the weather. How I got back to my bedchamber, I had not a clue. The last thing I remembered was going out to the garden to sit with Hamish. After that, everything went black. I knew I had been carrying another bottle of whisky and assumed we consumed the entire thing between us, thus the reason I had no memory since then until now. At least I somehow found my way to my bed. The twins had slept in their own rooms last night, obviously feeling they no longer needed to look after me now I had returned to the dining room. I lay still, trying to assess the damage. Soon after, I heard Thomas and Emmy deep in conversation in the hall as they approached my bedchamber. They stepped inside, laughing as they crossed the room and jumped on my bed, causing my head to pound while nausea overwhelmed me. Emmy put her face close to mine and stared at me intently.

'Mummy, you don't look well,' she said, stating the obvious as she lifted my eyelid with her finger, causing me to grimace, the light hurting my head as I slowly opened my eyes.

'No, I'm not feeling the best. Uncle Hamish and I had too much whisky to drink last night,' I told them, shutting my eyes again as they started to laugh.

'Ma, ya know ya can't drink whisky 'cause once ya start, ya can't stop 'til ya too drunk to walk, an' then ya do funny things.' Thomas chuckled as he gently kissed my cheek, and I smiled weakly at him.

'I know, I know. I should have learnt by now, but it's your Daddy's fault. He was the one who gave me my first taste of fine whisky, teaching me everything there was to know about it. From how it's made, right down to the different flavours to expect when you drink it. I blame him entirely,' I murmured, and they laughed harder.

Bessie hurried in, carrying a tray filled with breakfast, a pot of coffee, and a large silver jug. The twins quickly kissed me goodbye, hurrying off to enjoy their own breakfast in the kitchen. She handed me the jug of freshly squeezed apple juice, which I was grateful for. I placed it on my bedside table, pouring a large glass and drinking the entire thing before looking back up at Bessie. She placed the tray on my lap, then made herself comfortable on a chair kept close to my bed.

'There you are, Mistress. Hamish warned me you could be unwell this morning and would be needing extra fluid. He certainly did. And drank a whole jug by himself before he would even think about touching the food in front of him. I think he's still waiting to see if the juice stays down. I hear you're going out today. It makes my heart sing, it does, to see you back on your feet, dressed and up and about again. Once you finish eating, I will dress you and style your hair and make you look like the beautiful woman you are.' She smiled before standing to tidy the room and prepare my clothes for the day. I was so glad I didn't have to fuss around in the mornings, ensuring I bathed each night before I went down to dinner or before bed. Bessie had washed my hair last night with a new shampoo and conditioner, leaving me smelling like strawberries.

'I'm going to see Catherine. There are a few things I need to discuss with her, and I know she would love for me to pay her a visit given I haven't crossed her door in nearly two-years,' I replied as she beamed at me. I finished my breakfast, then the rest of the juice before going to the bathroom to relieve my bladder in the chamber pot. I returned and sat at my dressing table, watching Bessie in the mirror as she came up behind me, then took my hair from its braids, smiling down at me while she brushed it until it shone. She gazed at me, pride in her eyes as she wound my hair up, then secured it at the nape of my neck.

'Come then, Mistress. Let's get you dressed and back out into the world.' She kissed my cheek before helping me into one of the five black dresses I owned. They made me look small and frail despite my height, and I felt unattractive and plain in them, aware they made me look paler than I already was, given I always kept my face shaded from the harsh Australian sun. Once I was ready, I made my way out to the waiting carriage and was soon on my way to Catherine's.

I sat upstairs in my dear friend's grand apartment, enjoying a decadent morning tea. Catherine had been more than surprised to see me walk into her shop and had dropped everything, including an obviously wealthy customer who she passed off to one of her seamstresses. I had followed her upstairs, and she swiftly led me to the drawing room to visit with her in private.

'Oh, sweet Abigail. You do not know how relieved I am that you are out of your bedchamber. I have felt so helpless, not knowing what to do to help you through your grief. You are still suffering. I can see it in those lovely eyes of yours. I don't want to say what everyone else says. You know what I mean. The constant, well-meaning reassurance and words of comfort that all will be well, that Aaron is in a better place, God only takes the best, you'll get over it in time, you will meet someone else, and time heals all wounds, etcetera, etcetera. I have heard so many things said to you over the years, and I know everyone means well because it's so hard to even know what to say, but none of it is helpful. It all sounds hollow, not to mention repetitive. All I want you to know is I can see how much pain you are in, and I am here for you day and night. I will do anything for Thomas and Emmy as you know, so anything you need, my sweet friend, I am here,' Catherine said, tears in her eyes as I smiled lovingly at her, then reached across to take her hand in mine.

'Thank you. I know you are sincere, as are the others who, like you said, do not know what to say to comfort me. Who does? I don't know what to even say to myself anymore.' I smirked at her, and her pretty face lit up with a brilliant smile. We sat opposite each other in comfortable chairs, the room quiet except for the carriages travelling on the road outside at great speed. My spirits had lifted a great deal by being outside of the fences of Willow Grove, and I found her company a great distraction from my grief and worries. We chatted about her day-to-day life, and of the voyage I contemplated that would finally take me back to London and Scotland to see the Malcolm family and Sister, while allowing me to complete my business there before going on to Paris and New York.

'Now, let's talk about the gowns I will make for the voyage. I'm thrilled you will wear colour again. You still measure the same as you always have—give or take a few inches here and there—and carry my dresses so beautifully. I will have to make day and evening wear, along with casual dresses for when you are in Scotland. Are you taking anyone with you?' she asked, sipping her tea elegantly.

'I'm taking Bessie and Mary, and the twins, of course. Aaron made me promise to bring Hamish as our chaperone, but I haven't asked him yet,' I replied as she widened her eyes, then placed her cup down on the table.

'Why would he do that? Do you think Hamish will agree to accompany you?' The lace curtain fluttered gently in the breeze, the conversations down below floating up through the window.

'I'm not sure. I know he is busy around the property, so he may not be able to leave Willow Grove for such an extensive time,' I told her as she nodded.

'I'm sure something can be arranged if Aaron wanted you to take him. He obviously had a reason for such a strange request,' she said thoughtfully as I narrowed my gaze, her eyes not leaving mine for a moment.

'Yes, he did. He asked me to promise that when I was ready to love again, I would consider Hamish. He is pushing us together from beyond the grave,' I retorted, grimacing at the memory.

'You are teasing me, aren't you? You and Hamish? I cannot imagine such a thing after all this time, and the way he has behaved up until recent years has been atrocious. No, Hamish is not for you. What on earth was Aaron thinking?' she asked, shaking her head in disbelief.

'I agree with you, but Aaron refused to listen, and I had no option but to promise, as he only told me his wishes the day before the execution. It was the last time I saw him alive. How could I refuse when I knew his mind would not rest until I gave him my word? I could not stand the thought of him dying with concerns for my future tormenting him. I didn't want him to worry about me, so I gave in and agreed. It matters not, as I am unable to love any man again, of that I am certain. How could I when my heart is filled only with Aaron?' Tears stung my eyes as she reached across and placed her hand on mine.

'I know, my dearest friend, but you are doing so much better now. It will get easier, as Dana says. There is no rule that says you have to be with any man ever again if you do not wish to be. You can take lovers when you are ready and live as a free woman. No man will ever have power over you again. It's not as though you have to rely on anyone to feed you, and most of the time, they are just plain annoying, anyway. You are in a position, my friend, where you can enjoy the fruit without having to care for the tree.' She smiled at me and I smiled back, laughter bubbling up inside me.

'I cannot believe that it's you, sweet innocent wee Catherine, suggesting I take lovers. If I had said anything like that to you ten-years ago, you would have gone purple in the face and been unable to look me in the eye. Now look at you. Suggesting I do the dirty with strange men, you wicked woman.' I smirked at her as she giggled.

'Well, there is no harm in it. Abigail, you still need to have a private life behind your bedchamber door, and you should be allowed to enjoy it with whomever you choose. You aren't obligated to be seen in public with them, or ever contemplate marriage again. You are only twenty-nine, my beautiful friend. There is a lifetime full of wonderful things ahead of you. All Aaron wanted was for you to make your time here count for something. Live it for him because he didn't get the chance. I remember every word he said to me the last time I visited him in gaol. He adored you and it was you he worried for the most. He knew everyone else would grieve for a time; however, would move on with their lives as the months passed, including his own parents. He told me you would get stuck and not be able to move forward. He made me promise to ensure that you did. I cannot and will not try to force you to do anything, now or in the future. Just know you have all the time in the world to do as you please. That's what Aaron wanted for you,' she told me as she quickly wiped away a tear that had escaped her eye.

She was right. I did not have to pressure myself and could take as long as I liked. If love found me again, then well and good, but if it didn't, all would still be well and good.

'Yes, but Aaron made no plans for me to have lovers while he was mapping out my life for me, deciding that the only man I can marry is Hamish. I told him I'm not in love with him, and the poor man is no longer in love with me. Those feelings passed years ago. He loves me as a friend, just as I do him. I do not want to be with anyone other than my Aaron,' I said as I burst into tears, and she quickly rose to her feet, hurrying over to sit next to me, then slipped her arm around my trembling shoulder.

'You do not have to do anything you do not wish to do. Bloody men are ridiculous with the promises they make to each other when it comes to women and family. Hamish isn't the type to force anything on you, although he is very stubborn once he sets his mind to something; however, you say he doesn't feel like that anymore. I beg to differ, but you know him better than I do. I consider him a friend; however, not close like you are. My Colin would not approve,' she told me, and I nodded.

That was just how it was in the society in which we lived. Women had to be extremely careful with the friendships they formed—particularly with men. Even a friendly acquaintance was often taken out of context, and talk of it often resulted in blatant lies being spread, with many considering any association with a man who was not their husband as dangerous and not worth the angst of putting yourself in that situation to begin with. I was fortunate that the men who I considered friends were married to women who I also loved. And who loved me back just as fiercely. I felt so much better after talking to Catherine. She had a way about her that gave me hope and made me believe everything really would be all right again one day.

We made our way down to her storage room arm in arm, speaking in hushed tones of *The National Gallery* in Melbourne and the recent donation they received from Alfred Felton that had everyone talking. I had never met the man, but Catherine had through her parents, who were dear friends. Alfred had immigrated in 1852 to Victoria on the ship *California* seeking his fortune in the goldfields. In 1857, he started a business on Collins Street as a commission agent and dealer in merchandise, and by 1859 had added importer and general dealer to his well-respected name. He moved to Swanston Street in 1861 as a wholesale druggist but soon went into partnership with a man named Frederick Grimwade, and founded *Felton, Grimwade and Company,* a wholesale druggist and manufacturing chemist. As the business grew, the partners acquired interests in associated industries, such as the *Melbourne Glass Bottle Works* and *Cuming Smith and Company*. Alfred had also purchased two grand estates in partnership with merchant and pastoralist Charles Campbell during his time in Victoria, and on his death in January, his share in both properties were sold to Mr Campbell.

'Dear Mr Felton's wants were few, and he never married, the poor wretch. Although my understanding is he was quite happy about that,' Catherine remarked, leading me through the shop to the room out back. 'He was a generous man and gave away enormous amounts of money to charity, and formed large collections of books and pictures that threatened to push him out of his bachelor rooms at the Esplanade Hotel in St Kilda, which is where he sadly died all alone.' She opened the door with a large key she kept attached to a chain she wore on her belt, then turned to lead me into her storage room; however, I shook my head and paused outside in the hallway.

'I find it so sad. I understand he adored art just as I do, but why give everything to the gallery? Surely there was someone here that he loved?' She nodded as she went about tidying several rolls of material strewn around the room, then opened a small window to let the fresh air in.

'Oh, they did not get all of it. The dear man had no direct descendants, so decided to set up a philanthropic trust to help the poor and support the arts here in Victoria. He wanted half of his fortune to go to charities that care for women and children, and the other half he wanted used to acquire and donate art works to the National Gallery. I did hear the gallery selected a number of pieces from Mr Felton's personal collection for retention, and the remainder was sold at auction. They added the proceeds to the bequest, but...' She lowered her voice, despite the fact no one else was present. 'I heard from my mother that after payment of legacy and probate duties, the residue of his estate was valued in excess of £378,000.' She widened her eyes as I wandered over to the window to look out at the people passing down the rear laneway.

'He certainly was generous. That is a great deal of money.' I turned and made my way back to her side to look at the new fabric that had just arrived from London. I ran my fingers along several bolts of cloth before choosing, watching her cut a small corner of the fabric and place it in her pocket so she could match it later when taking the materials she needed to make my wardrobe.

'I am going to have you looking like a princess on that ship. You look awful in these black mourning dresses, but you will be exquisite wearing colour again. I am thrilled about creating gowns for you again and already have visions of the possibilities running through my mind. I cannot wait to start and help you get back on the path you fell off two-years ago. I am just so overwhelmed you're out of bed and going to try.' She embraced me warmly before calling for her assistant and politely asking her to move the fabrics to another storeroom.

Catherine enjoyed making elaborate and unique gowns, and she enjoyed dressing me more than any of her customers. I had every gown I ever owned stored under the house, and most of them were made by Catherine's own hand. I was uncertain why I was saving them, as I knew by the time they fitted Emmy they would be completely out of style. The problem was, I could not bring myself to part with even one of them, as they all meant something to me. I remembered what I was doing and where I was when I wore them whenever I looked at my stored dresses, and it brought back lovely memories. Well, most of the time.

'Will you give me a free hand? Let me be a little elaborate? Allow maybe a touch of flamboyance to some of the evening gowns?' Her voice pleading, her cheeks flushed with excitement as we strolled down the hallway towards the locked door leading to her apartment.

'All right, Catherine. I trust you. All I ask is you do not go to extremes, or dress me in gowns that would cause those around me to stare and whisper. It will be my first time wearing colour in nearly two-years, and I feel nervous.' I felt an unfamiliar tingle of excitement run up my spine as we climbed the stairs then made our way back to the drawing room.

'Would you like Thomas and Emmy fitted out? I have their most recent measurements from two-weeks ago, but because they are growing so fast, especially Thomas, I will make them a touch bigger for him,' she said, and I agreed. We sat down and chatted while her maid brought more tea and freshly baked biscuits, while losing track of time.

I felt much improved as the hours passed, and no longer felt so frightened to face the world alone. Glancing at the clock on her mantlepiece, I gathered my things, and we embraced. I thanked her sincerely for all she had done and continued to do for me and my children, before she walked me out to my carriage to head for home, with the promise of a visit from her tomorrow. I relaxed back in my seat as Harry made his way home, thinking how fortunate I was to have those around me who loved me so very deeply. Their affection did not fill the place in my heart that was now empty, but they did make me feel loved.

Chapter Three

Harry pulled up in our large, circular driveway and helped me down. I straightened up before smoothing down the skirt of my dress, Hamish catching my eye as he stood in the distance in the stable yard. I bid Harry farewell and strolled over, not wanting to go inside the house yet. He saw me coming and made his way over to the post and rail fence to greet me.

'It's grand tae see ye up an' lookin' so bonny, Abigail. If I were tae be honest, I dinnae expect it after last night. I assumed ye'd be in yer sick bed.' He smiled, a twinkle in his eye I hadn't seen in a very long time—and a look on his face as if he wanted to bed me.

'Hamish, I need to ask a favour of you. You can say no if you want and I will completely understand. It's not a small thing to ask, like borrowing a cup of sugar? It would take six-months out of your life,' I warned him as he nodded his head thoughtfully. I told him about the voyage and the reasons behind it, along with the fact Aaron had made me promise to ask him to accompany us. He remained silent for the longest time, his face thoughtful before he screwed up his nose and looked away. I had no idea what the bloody hell was wrong with him, and had not seen him like this since we were courting so long ago.

'Aye, ye dinnae remember anythin' we talked o' last night, then?' His voice low, he gazed across the paddocks and down towards the ocean—out of sight now, but the smell of the sea and taste of salt heavy in the air today.

'I do remember most of our conversation when we were in the sitting room. Once we walked outside and the fresh air hit me, the whisky must have taken over because I do not recall a thing after that. I am uncertain how I got to bed, and I'm embarrassed to admit it to anyone but you. I apologise for being such a dirty alcoholic, as the twins say.' Feeling ashamed of myself, I turned away for a moment, but not before noticing the smirk that touched his lips. He looked me in the eye as his face broke into a wide grin. However, it was clear he was hurt, leaving me baffled and failing to understand why he was behaving this way towards me.

'Ye asked me last night. An' I've agreed tae come. Angus will take over from me while we're away. If ye dinnae mind, Abigail, I must return tae me work.' He bowed ever so slightly before turning to walk away, leaving me standing alone at the fence, staring after him in confusion.

I made my way back up to the house, thinking how strange our brief exchange was. This has been the most awkward exchange between us since I had found him in bed with Charlotte. We were usually at ease and comfortable in each other's company, and without warning, he had turned on me and now treated me as an acquaintance.

As I walked through the front entrance, I bumped into Mr Masters. He gasped when he noticed I was dressed and my hair styled before regaining his composure, his face softening. He kindly escorted me to the sitting room, then made his way to the kitchen to inform Leo I had arrived home.

I sat down on the chair near the fireplace, the room silent and filled with memories of all the times I lay in Aaron's arms or sat on his lap, the friends and family who spent time here with us, the room we all felt the most comfortable in given the grandness of Willow Grove. There wasn't a day we hadn't spent time here together as a family or with our friends. My heart hurt—I missed him so. I couldn't think of him without tears coming to my eyes before breaking down. I wiped my face with my handkerchief as Leo strutted in with his kitchen maids following behind, carrying trays of food. They placed them down on the coffee table in front of me, then Leo dismissed them with a wave of his hands and settled himself down on the chair beside me.

'Oh, it's a fabulous day. You have risen from the dead and have returned to me. Glory be! It's so good to see your pretty face, Abigail. I hope you know I only tease you about being a bushpig, along with all the other things I say when you are tormenting me. I am quite aware how beautiful you really are for a woman, but I am forced to admit that compared to you, they truly are the most unfortunate looking creatures I have ever seen. Even in comparison with the village children, women are extremely unattractive. They have extra parts where you don't need them, and missing bits where you do. I don't know how anyone can walk around without their penis. Oh, my goodness, I just realised what I said.' His eyes went wide as his face flushed before he rushed to my side and knelt down in front of me, clasping my hands in his. 'I wasn't referring to Maslow, even though he is living proof you can live without one. I'm sorry, Abigail. I am not so heartless to joke about that man.' He promptly embraced me and burst into tears, his howls filling the room and out into the hallway. I smiled lovingly as I gazed into his eyes, a river of tears still flowing, then placed my arms around his neck and kissed his face.

'I know exactly what you mean, my darling. It gives me great satisfaction to know that man is suffering for what he did. You don't have to worry you will make me cry, Leo, with anything you say. It doesn't suit you to be apologising for things that come out of your mouth. Please, just treat me as you always have. Even the offensive comments and teasing about my looks makes me feel a little better. I just need everyone to stop treating me like I am a crystal glass that is about to shatter in their hand,' I explained as he nodded while I wiped away his tears with my handkerchief.

'I still miss him, you know? He was my Goliath, my fiercest protector, who loved me as his friend. He didn't care that I was normal, and he was abnormal. He treated me the same, and I will never forget his kindness. There aren't many men in the world that will laugh about another man teasing and flirting with them. Or touching their backside. But he always took it in good humour and never made me feel like a pervert or less of a human being when I was around him.

I understand why you still mourn him so very deeply, Abigail. You won't ever find anyone else who would put up with your foul temper like he did.' His eyes fixed on a portrait of Aaron that now took pride of place above the fireplace, the mantle holding several reminders of my beloved husband, I embraced him tightly before joining him on the lounge to eat a late lunch.

We talked like we used to, and my body relaxed as I listened to the intimate details of his bedchamber romps, along with the latest gossip going around on the passionfruit vine at Willow Grove, always a constant stream of new and exciting information. We didn't need our own newspaper here; you only had to ask Amelia or Leo what was happening around the property and the district, then make a pot of tea and prepare yourself for a long visit.

We finished eating, and I leaned back and sipped my coffee, his arm around my shoulder.

'I was observing Emmy this morning at breakfast as she is maturing so fast, and realised she is a smaller version of you. I have never seen a mother and daughter look so alike. You have hardly changed since you were eighteen; however, she is coming up to the age when I met you and each day she is looking more and more like you did. Even her boobies are growing. She has told me in recent weeks more than once, and in no uncertain terms, that when she is older, if I ever try to feel her up like I do to you, she will get the axe and cut off my hands. See how much like you she is. Violent and wild,' he told me proudly as I laughed out loud. I embraced him before I stood to leave.

'I will see you when I get back. I'm off to the island to see my boys,' I called out over my shoulder as he nodded sadly, waving as I stepped into the hallway. He slowly rose from his chair and made his way back to the kitchen, leaving the trays for the maids to clear.

I walked back through the front entrance, then crept around the side of the house to the back garden. Wombles stood over near my roses eating the wheatgrass that grew around the lavender. I picked up my basket from the verandah and strolled over, with Dingo walking behind me. In no way did Dingo and Wombles get along; however, they tolerated being in the same space and had a clearly defined respect for each other to stay away. I scratched her on the ears as I tried to look under her belly, unable to see her joey as it was still so tiny. I went about gathering my roses singing our song under my breath, memories of all the nights Mr Masters would sing to us at the pub filling my head as I picked just enough to place on the graves of my boys and my friend Adelaide, who I would also visit when I was there.

There were fourteen people buried on the island, not including Leroy, mostly farm workers or members of their families we had lost over the past fifteen-years. Some were infants, some small children, while husbands and wives, mothers and fathers, and daughters and sons who had died young, most under tragic circumstances, lay here in what was now a peaceful graveyard. Every single one of them had been taken before their time, including my three boys. We had seen no more or less death than any other property in the district. Despite employing a vast amount of workers, we knew each of them intimately, and every death had significantly affected me no different from a family member passing away.

I made my way to the island, leaving Wombles to return to her basket while Dingo followed at my heel. He knew where we were going. He would sit on top of the marble slab for a time, barking at the headstone, then curl up on the foot of the grave as though he were sitting at his master's feet. It still surprised me how he remained under Aaron's coffin when he was laid out in the sitting room, and then followed the coffin to the island, jumping into the boat to be next to his beloved master. On that day at the gravesite, he had remained by my side as I knelt beside Aaron's large coffin, and as they lowered him into the ground, Dingo had whined and cried, not wanting him to leave either. He had then lain at the foot of the grave and barked, refusing to leave when Patrick came to collect me hours later.

He now slept at Polly and Angus's cottage each night at the foot of Hamish's bed. Although he wasn't as attached to Hamish, he knew and trusted him, somehow sensing he too was close to his master. He would go to work with Hamish and Angus; however, could still be found looking around for Aaron during the day. There were times he would come inside the house with Hamish and suddenly raise his head, ears pricked up while barking frantically at some unseen presence in the room. I expected he could sense when Aaron was around me, as there were also times where he would be resting by the fire, groaning in bliss as if someone were stroking him.

Dingo had formed a loose attachment to me. Well, as attached as he could be given he was a one-man dog. He would accompany me to the island every day, leaving Hamish and Angus for a time. This had been our daily routine for nearly two-years, and he knew it well. He was thirteen now and had aged significantly—quite old for a dingo—and of late, he was suffering the usual aches and pains in his hips and joints that came with age. However, he was doing well for his advanced years and hadn't been sick a day in his life, only ever forcing me to attend to him when he engaged in fights with the farm workers' dogs.

I found the cattle dogs on the property to be fascinating animals, and had researched their history soon after I settled here. I had never seen one before arriving in Australia, and had not realised just how integral they were in the efficient running of a large property such as ours. My dear friend, Adelaide, was a descendant of the man who started the breed, affectionately known as *Halls Heelers*. She only confided in me weeks before she died that Thomas Simpson Hall, a pastoralist, born at Bungool on the Hawkesbury River in 1808, was, in fact, her paternal grandfather.

She went on to tell me how her great-grandparents, George Hall and his wife Mary, arrived on the *Coromandel* in 1802 with four children as members of a small group of Presbyterian immigrants who settled on the Hawkesbury. They founded the Ebenezer chapel, and were devout in their faith—hence the reason Adelaide moved to Victoria at the first opportunity that presented itself—rejecting suitors from the area and the church and seeking a husband who would take her away from the life she so hated. Her great-grandfather, George, became a powerful and wealthy pastoralist, and encouraged his sons to search for new grazing land to expand their business. They were among the first settlers in the Upper Hunter district and selected land in biblical fashion, a term I didn't understand and one Adelaide didn't explain. By 1828, her family held nearly two-thousand-acres at Dartbrook and Gungal, and employed nine convicts, eight of them Protestant.

Adelaide's grandfather, Thomas, managed the Dartbrook property and later inherited it on his father's death. He bred station horses, Durham cattle and merino sheep. He responded to the urgent need for good cattle-dogs and imported a pair of wall-eyed blue 'merles', a cross between a Scottish collie and an Italian greyhound. In 1840, he produced a merle-dingo cross that combined the speed and silence of the dingo with the collie's intelligent obedience. Over a thirty-year period, he perfected the breed, using them solely for his own purpose, and staunchly refused to allow anyone outside of his family to access them. The animals were so effective droving the cattle, he was reluctant to assist his competitors by supplying them with his unique dogs. Dogs that he believed were worth ten men on horseback when it came to droving. The man was not considered generous in nature or known for sharing his wealth or possessions, from all reports from those close.

In comparison to other breeds, his dogs were considered one of the most intelligent and agile. They didn't run in packs, preferring to stay with their owner, and were extremely protective. Spending all their time with them, they worked alongside their master during the day, while sleeping in their baskets at night near the fire after a feed. Medium in size, they possessed a short coat in brown and black distributed evenly through a white coat. Giving the appearance of either red or blue, depending which dominated, I found them all to be sweet. The Red Heeler, or Reddy's as Adelaide referred to them, were a russet red mixed with a black, brown and white coat. While the Blue Heeler had mottled colours of grey that appeared in many shades of blue, which I thought lovely. Adelaide despised the red dogs the most, a scar on her leg reminding her every day of the attack she sustained as a five-year-old bairn. I kept my distance from the dogs, not because they were nasty, but because they were working and generally responded only to their master.

When Thomas died in 1870, only a few years before dear Adelaide was born, his family home and all that was in it, along with the stock, went to auction. This allowed the breed to become available to the wider farming community, who chose them as working dogs due to their energy, active minds and independent natures. This new breed of dog caused much excitement and became famous among Hunter

Valley cattle-men, and were in high demand by landowners for station work. Soon after Adelaide's grandfather passed, a pair were taken to Sydney where the breed was improved further, primarily by the Bagust brothers, who worked on perfecting the *Hall Heeler* until the early 1890s when dear Adelaide first arrived at Willow Grove, still so young and carrying her first child, a son born not long after she moved to the village. I had always wondered why she detested dogs, shooing them away from her front porch at every opportunity, and only when she confided in me the day I carried a basket to her door containing a litter of puppies I had sternly been told to find homes for, I finally understood.

I tied the small boat to the post and stepped onto the island, hurrying over to Adelaide's grave. Bending down to place fresh roses near the marble headstone, placed there for her children so they could visit with her, tears filled my eyes. I knew Neville no longer tended her grave or stepped foot on the island after finding out at the time of her death, Adelaide had been involved in a secret affair with John, their friend and next-door neighbour. He now suspected Molly was John's child, and it tormented him every time he looked at her. She was still young, but did favour John remarkably, and I was not the only one who noticed.

It wasn't a subject gossiped about by anyone due to her tender years, and the damage it would cause should Molly find out that Neville was not her father by blood. My friend Patty, John's wife, had spoken in confidence to me about the situation, and made it clear she was willing to accept Molly should she be John's child. She had forgiven him for his affair with her friend Adelaide a decade ago, and one thing I knew for certain, Patty was a kind and decent woman who would never take out her own pain on an innocent child.

I slowly walked over to my husband's grave, our boys buried beside him. I arranged their flowers, then lowered myself down onto the marble lying over him, placed my head in my hands, and cried. Now I was no longer hiding in my room, the island was the only place I found privacy to grieve. I felt better being up again, while trying to find the strength to face the world without him. I had always depended on Aaron in every way, leaning heavily on him. Now he was gone, I had no one like him in my life, and never would again.

I talked to him about moving on with my life, and how I was unable to leave him in the past, the birds above in the gumtree singing their secret songs to each other. I knew everyone around me believed I had lost my mind, some speaking in hushed tones of how I would visit for hours each day and talk to him. They failed to understand that I knew he was listening to me. I told Aaron what had happened yesterday, and how we were taking the voyage to England just as he had wanted. I broke down and sobbed because it wasn't him who was coming with us. Slowly rising to my feet, I made my way over to our gumtree and sat down heavily, sobbing harder. I missed him so very much. I longed for his caress on my body, his lips on mine, his arms always wrapped around me. Most of all, I missed talking to him and hearing his voice and calm, wise words. He always knew what to say and do about anything and everything we were forced to face. Now he was gone, I had no one to turn to in the same way.

I remained by their graves at the base of our tree for the longest time until I had calmed enough to return home. I stood and kissed their names engraved on the headstone, then slowly returned to the boat, Dingo close behind me and my empty basket over my arm.

I returned to the sitting room and asked Mr Masters to tell the children I was home. Within minutes, they came running towards me, both excited to see I was up and dressed, waiting for them. They threw themselves into my arms and knocked me flat on the couch, both of them on top of me, laughing at my helplessness as I giggled. After calming themselves, they snuggled into me where we lay together and talked, laughing at some of the events that had occurred at school today.

'Mrs McGinty reckons Emmy an' me are her brightest students. She can't understand why our cousins aren't up to the same standard, but I heard her tell Auntie Scarlett she should be whippin' 'em for the way they behave. Do ya think we're naughty, Ma?' Thomas asked, and I tried to smother a smile.

'Yes. When you're all together. It's something to do with the Cavanaugh blood running through your veins. You are all exactly like your Daddy and his brothers were when I met them. Rowdy, funny, and always teasing each other and getting into trouble. Don't ever let anyone change that or the relationship you have with your cousins, sweetheart. It is lovely to watch, and you know that when Mrs McGinty gets something in her head, there is no changing it. You just continue on, my boy, being happy and doing well in your studies. Have you thought anymore about what you would like to do?' We had been talking about Melbourne University after Hamish had offered to take Thomas and Emmy there to look around and see if he could spark an interest.

He was determined they would go to university and have the best education possible, kindly offering to pay all costs, as he was quite wealthy in his own right. His grandfather had left him a substantial inheritance that he came into at the age of five and twenty. There had been nothing Mr Makenzie could do to take that from him, despite making attempts to do exactly that through threats of violence, which didn't seem to faze Hamish in the slightest. As far as he was concerned, his beloved grandfather had wanted him and Angus to be his beneficiaries, and had left his son and granddaughter, Jemima, out of his Will completely. Hamish and Angus had enough money to live comfortably for the rest of their lives without working another day. However, they loved what they did and enjoyed running Willow Grove.

Hamish walked in soon after and made himself comfortable on the opposite lounge to us. The twins sat up, as did I, and he passed Thomas and Emmy a chocolate milk before passing me a caramel one.

'What flavours yours?' I asked as he sat back in his chair and drank from his enormous glass.

'Strawberry, o' course. I'm enjoyin' some o' the things Leo's been makin' o' late from the fruit around the property. Some I've never even heard o'. I've formed the opinion he's naw as stupid as he looks or sounds. Barnergu has told it tae me himself o' the uses o' herbs an' plants, an' how each part has a different purpose—mostly medicine or food. He took me out in the bush an' showed me the plants we can eat if ever lost on Willow Grove an' could naw get back home fer dinner.' He chuckled to himself as the children collapsed into giggles.

Barnergu was a native man who often camped on our property. We didn't mind, and had gotten to know him and his dog well over the years. He had sent a message to me recently through Hamish telling me that Aaron's spirit was strong and always beside me, going on to say until I could let him go he was stuck here and not where he was meant to be. Aaron visited Barnergu in his dreams, and he would relay the vision to Hamish, who visited him daily when we knew he was camped here. I had listened intently to Hamish as he relayed the message and knew in my heart; he was right. He had said Aaron still watched over Willow Grove and all that stepped foot here—that he was connected to the earth, the ocean and sky—all strong elements of Willow Grove.

Angus and Hamish had befriended him, taking food down every day to supplement his diet of bush tucker and meat he had hunted and cooked over the campfire, always making sure his dog Bam-bam—meaning 'Yellow' in his native tongue—had a full stomach. It made me smile as Bambam was a dingo, and what would possibly be considered yellow.

He was such a lovely man and told me the most fascinating stories of his culture and history. I hadn't seen him since Aaron had been murdered, however; he was constantly sending word to me, and I would reply, sending Angus or Hamish back with my response and a parcel of food I knew he enjoyed. Chocolate and pineapple juice, along with freshly baked bread and a range of preserves from our own garden were some of his favourites. He knew what cranberries were used for, along with the wheatgrass Leo often raved about, telling me they were good for the body. He would work around the farm without being asked, saying it was his way of repaying us for allowing him to use the land as his own. I did not believe anyone could own the land, no matter how much money they paid to live on it. It was an energy that could not be harnessed and was impossible to capture and keep as your own.

I made myself comfortable on the lounge as we drank our delicious flavoured milk, while Emmy went to Hamish and sat beside him, putting her tiny hand in his enormous one. I sat up straight and took a deep breath, preparing myself to tell them about the voyage we were meant to take with their father. They had known about this journey ever since they were small and had always looked forward to it as we talked about it often with them over the years.

'Now I want to tell you both something very important. We are going on an adventure on a big ship that will take us to England,' Both children roared, piercing my eardrums, while Emmy jumped up and down in her seat, clapping her hands. 'Then we are going to go to Paris and New York, just like we always talked about with Daddy.' My voice broke and I felt tears prick my eyes. Thomas looked up at me excitedly, his face becoming solemn when he noticed the tears sliding down my face. He reached over and took my hand in his.

'It's gunna be all right, Ma. Daddy's still around us, an' I know he'll be with us when we travel. There's nothin' that'd stop him from bein' there as it was the one thing he'd always looked forward to. There were so many places he wanted to take us, an' never had the chance 'cause he worked so hard here. He intended to turn it into one of the largest Martarino studs in the world. I've been talkin' to Uncle Hamish 'bout Daddy's dream for Willow Grove, an' he's written everythin' down for the next fifty-years.' My son smiled up at me, and I smiled back, lovingly moving a strand of shaggy blonde hair from his eyes. Even visiting the university hadn't changed Thomas's mind. He would work at Willow Grove, running the property with Angus, Hamish and Harry—and there was nothing further to discuss. Emmy returned to my side and made herself comfortable on my lap.

'What Thomas says is true. I feel Daddy around me all the time, just as he told me I would. He said I would feel him wherever I went in the world, and I know I will. I sometimes wake and feel him kissing my cheek or gently stroking my hair. The fact is, I know it's him because my hair has actually moved from my eyes at times, like he used to do with his finger. I don't know why you don't feel him like I do, Mummy, but I'm sure you will if you relax your body and your mind. You still find it hard to concentrate on anything. Don't cry, Mummy. I'm sure the three of us will have a wonderful time going to all those places Daddy talked of, and he will be there beside us to enjoy it too,' she reassured, her little hands gently wiping the tears from my face.

'It will not only be our small family. Bessie and Mary will come to look after us, and Uncle Hamish has agreed to accompany us as our chaperone. Your Daddy wanted him to be with us and take you to all those places you talked of for so very long.' I summoned all my strength to remain calm and hide my emotions from them during what was meant to be a happy time for us all. They both jumped up, screaming and clapping their hands as they ran to Hamish and hugged him.

'I can't bloody wait. When do we leave?' Thomas asked, grinning widely, while Emmy couldn't stop smiling.

'Oh, Mummy. I am so happy. To have Uncle Hamish and Bessie and Mary with us means the world, and we will have an even better time.' I smiled through my tears as she narrowed her gaze at me. 'I don't want you wearing black anymore. It looks horrid on you and makes you look sick and pasty. Have you organised your wardrobe through Catherine? When do we leave as I have so many loose ends to tie up myself?' Hamish and I collapsed into laughter while Emmy stared silently at me, appearing confused.

'Soon enough, my darling, but you will miss school for quite a few months, so Mrs McGinty has kindly agreed to provide you with schoolwork to do while we're away. You both seem to forget you are only thirteen.' They no longer appeared as excited as I tried to smother a smile, while Hamish grinned broadly at them before fixing his gaze on me.

'Aye, 'tis a joyful day fer all o' us tae see everyone so happy. I've naw doubt 'twill be a bonny journey back tae our homeland.' He leaned forward and took my hand across the table, squeezing it gently before letting it fall softly back in my lap. It seemed all was well between us, and I was glad of it. I could not stand to have any awkwardness creep into our friendship as I loved him, just as I loved all my friends, and hated even one cross word passing between us.

That night as I lay unmoving, wedged in my bed between my beautiful bairns, I dreamed of a tall, dark, elegant and very handsome man with a golden crown on his head, a journal, and a shotgun.

Chapter Four

W E HAD ONE WEEK to get organised before we departed, and I had worked day and night to ensure we were. Catherine was a woman of her word, and the dresses she created for the voyage made me feel like a princess. Some were far too risque for my liking, and many not risque enough for her. She had included a number of skirts that required no petticoat, fitted snugly to my waist and flowing straight down, but not to the ground as we had always worn, knowing it was a sin to show our ankles. These stopped a few inches from the ground, showing off my fashionable leather boots, along with varying other forms of footwear. She had paired them with fitted shirts, some long-sleeved, while others had no sleeves at all. They were extremely snug, buttoning down the front and tucked in with a leather belt, but I found them comfortable, and had been told more than once they were popular, requiring no assistance to dress or undress. They looked wonderful with my dainty leather boots that tied up at the front with matching laces. Catherine had told me they were to wear during the day and when I wanted to dress casually, thrilling me as I would not have to be so reliant on dear Bessie to help me dress.

Bessie was unimpressed by the latest fashion and the speed in which it was changing, becoming less structured and formal given it could put her out of a job when I required no assistance at all to dress, making me smile to myself. Bessie would always have a job with me, even if I had to make up things for her to do.

Catherine had created the most magnificent evening gowns, using every fabric I had chosen, some heavy and elaborate, while others were finely made from silk, light and easy to wear. There were several in plain colours, while others were patterned with bright designs. I adored them all and was impressed how far fashion had come in the last ten-years, even though women were still expected to wear corsets. I was the only person I knew who rarely wore them unless I had a formal event to attend.

Most of the evening gowns sparkled with either diamantes, beads of all colours, and pearls sewn into them, along with matching head pieces. Catherine knew I despised hats, so had one of her assistants, a milliner by trade, make small headpieces to clip onto the side of my head. Or the back, or top—wherever Bessie decided it looked suitable. I was grateful to her that I would not be forced to wear one hat during the time I was away. What she had made for me was exquisite, and Leo had told me they looked better than hats when I first tried one on to show him. I had everything I needed for the entire journey and wouldn't need to purchase a thing. Catherine had made sure I had a wardrobe fit for a Queen on some days, and a mother on others.

My dear friend had created the most beautiful wardrobe for Emmy, taking into account she was now growing into a young woman. She had made her day wear that was comfortable and appropriate for her age, including skirts like mine that stopped inches from the ground, and Emmy loved wearing them with her new boots. My only daughter now owned a number of evening gowns, all beautiful and suitable for a girl her age. She had tried everything on and decided the skirts, shirts and tops were her favourite because she could move around freely in them and still look elegant and like a young lady—something she was determined to be. Well, her idea of a lady was me, causing me to feel terribly guilty that her expectations were so low. It touched my heart that Emmy adored me so much, she wanted to be like me in every way. She demanded to wear the same clothing, use the same hair and body products, wear the same perfume, and share my jewellery, as well as my makeup.

Thomas had his own distinctive evening attire, thanks to Colin. He had designed several styles of trousers and jackets made of formal material, some with tails, and others in casual styles and materials to be worn during the day, along with more shirts than he would wear. He looked so handsome when he had tried them all on, then paraded around my bedchamber the day he received them, just like his father. Towering over me now, he looked exactly how Aaron did at the same age in a photograph I had seen of him at fourteen. His mother kept the picture in a frame in her drawing room beside her chair, a place she spent most of her time reading or embroidering.

I only had to watch him smile or hear him talk to see my darling husband in him, so much alike in more than just looks. Thomas was calm and had an easy way about him, unlike his fiery sister. He was a true Cavanaugh, just like his daddy and uncles. His male cousins also favoured their kin and possessed the same large build; however, it was Thomas who was identical to Aaron, the resemblance so strong it often made Mrs Cavanaugh cry whenever she looked at him.

He had a lovely nature and was kind and caring; however, when upset or offended, or if he felt someone had wronged him or someone he loved, he was quick to use his fists, just like his father—a trait that had become an enormous concern for me. I did not want anything to happen to him in future if he were ever in a situation like Aaron had been. I talked to him often of not seeking vengeance when a wrong had been committed and could do no more than hope it sunk into his stubborn wee head.

He had the attention of every young girl on the property and surrounding areas who attended school here. Emmy had told me recently Beth was in love with him and followed him around like a puppy dog, but despite Thomas always being polite, he paid no attention to her. Beth had been born here, and growing up at Willow Grove, had known Thomas and Emmy their entire lives. She was a pretty little thing and had a lovely nature. I wondered if Thomas wasn't interested in her, or wasn't interested in girls at all. Maybe his interests lay elsewhere, and I didn't know about it. I would have to wait and see if he came to me in the future.

Times like these I would find the most difficult, those special milestones in a growing boy's life when his father should have been here to talk to him. I would be watching him closely on the ship to ensure he was all right, as he worried me the most out of the two of them. If Emmy was upset about something, everyone knew about it; however, Thomas would withdraw. These were the times he needed his daddy to talk about girls—or boys—whichever road he chose to take. I was unsure if he was homosexual or not, as he hadn't discussed anything with me about girls, let alone boys.

Having grown up in a house with Leo as his uncle, I was certain if he was, he would be comfortable and trust me enough to tell me when he was ready. I would love him the same and expect everyone who loved me to continue loving Thomas just because they always had. I was jumping way ahead of myself, as I didn't have any foundation to base my suspicions on regarding his preferences. He may just be a late starter, I had often thought, while gazing at my handsome boy.

Colin had fitted Hamish out with an entire new wardrobe, as most of his formal clothing no longer fitted him. He had broadened across the shoulders and arms since he was in his twenties and hadn't bothered to replace his evening suits and evening wear over the years, often stating he had no reason to wear them. He stuck to his moleskin trousers, which all the men at Willow Grove wore with a casual shirt that was easy to move around in while they worked. Colin had also updated his casual wardrobe, as we didn't want to walk around during the day appearing well-to-do once off the ship. We wanted to look respectable without standing out like dogs' balls, as Aaron used to say. And of most importance to me, as Catherine and Colin knew better than most, was comfort.

Bessie and little Mary had new uniforms and daywear made for them, and they were both thrilled. Well, Bessie was not impressed by the length, or that their uniforms were slowly creeping up just like mine and how casual fashion had become. Unlike my opinionated ladies maid, I quite liked that skirts and shirts were now the standard attire for most during the day. No matter what class. There were no longer skirts billowing out and threatening to burst into flames should the wearer get too close to a candelabra. Nor were women left exhausted from being forced to drag around heavy gowns weighing more than two men. The expectation still remained that evening attire was as elaborate as it had always been, and hemlines remained to the ankle or below.

I had taken Bessie and Mary, along with Hamish and the children, to the best cobbler in Geelong. He had measured our feet and made Bessie and little Mary a pair of fashionable boots, along with shoes to match their daywear and casual clothes. He also made them two pairs of shoes each for work, ensuring they were flat and comfortable with laces at the front, holding them securely in place. Bessie and Mary had both told me they could stand all day in them and have not one blister to show for it, thrilling me no end as I knew better than most what it was like to wear ill-fitting shoes.

Hamish possessed extremely large feet, a little larger than Aaron's. He had several pairs of new boots made with the finest leather, and shoes for walking during the day, along with several elaborate pairs for the evening. I now owned a number of flat, dainty boots made with black, brown and cream leather to match all my new skirts and day dresses. The cobbler, a Croatian immigrant by the name of John Mandich, kindly made me various shoes to match my gowns, along with several pairs to wear during the day that I could walk for miles in. It had taken us weeks; however, we were organised now and our trunks were packed.

Hamish, Bessie and little Mary were all looking forward to being aboard a ship again after almost fifteen-years. They had all met for the first time on that voyage, and been connected to each other ever since. Thomas and Emmy were over excited about travelling on a steam ship they had only ever seen in pictures. They were comfortable around boats, being Cavanaughs; however, had never been aboard a large passenger vessel. I knew they would be in awe, just as I was when I first stepped onto one in London from the docks—so many years ago now.

They had been around wealth all their lives, exposed to the lifestyle Tamara and Elizabeth lived in Melbourne, among other wealthy friends. The sisters went about their day surrounded by luxury within the walls of their mansions, while hundreds of servants catered to their every whim, always displaying their wealth for all to see. I didn't care one way or the other, as it made them happy, and that was all I wanted for my dear friends. I had noticed many years ago, Thomas and Emmy weren't comfortable in their homes given the formality and rules they would endure when there. Despite being surrounded by wealth, the twins had never experienced the splendours of a first-class ship.

I had spent an enormous amount of time with Richard, advising him of what needed to be done while I was gone. He already did so much for us, not only being our lawyer, but our accountant as well, ensuring my taxes were paid on time. He had been handling Amelia's business dealings and taxes ever since she opened the store, while overseeing the outgoing and incoming money for the pub. Given it was a non-profit business, he made sure everything was above-board, and those running it were not overcharging and profiting from their trusted position. I left it all in his capable hands, as I detested dealing with bureaucrats and money, especially with an agent from a government I now despised.

Richard would pay all the wages while I was away, as well as the bonus I paid my staff. He had agreed to keep the books for the stud and farm and intended to meet with Mr Masters once a week to ensure everything was running smoothly. We had resolved any outstanding issues. The rest he believed could wait until my return.

Once I arrived back at Willow Grove, I would sit down with Richard to discuss whether he would continue to manage my finances, or if I would withdraw the lot and manage it myself. Or fritter it away if I so chose. Soon, I would be forced to make the same decision when it came to Mr Malcolm. I had not a clue if I would merge both funds and engage only one lawyer to look after everything—the most sensible choice in my mind that would save me a lot of money in fees. It would also simplify everything and make the entire process easier, as it was complicated and confusing for me at the best of times.

I had planned our journey so we would arrive in London months before I turned thirty, allowing me to give my instructions and sign any paperwork required to be lodged with the court. It would take some time for all this to occur, and Mr Malcolm had advised me to travel earlier than I had originally planned the last time he visited us in Australia just before Aaron was arrested. I heeded him, not knowing when making the arrangements we would arrive in London on the anniversary of Aaron's death, give or take a day or two.

The last two-years of my life had been shrouded in darkness and despair, so black I could not see what was in front of me. I had been up and out of my bed for not even a full month, yet I had found a glimmer of hope somewhere far in the distance—something to hold on to as I slowly emerged from the darkness. Although everything around me was still dim, I was functioning as best I could, while finding strength I was unaware I possessed to hide my grief when around others, including my children. The only time I allowed myself to cry was when at the island alone, or in my bedchamber with the door locked. I had gone about my days doing my best to put on a brave face and only sobbed my heart out at the gravesite, or in my bed at night alone. Sometimes I felt my heart would burst, I missed him so very much.

I sat motionless at my dressing table, staring out the window but not seeing a thing while Bessie brushed my hair.

'I worry I will say the wrong words and set you off, Mistress, but I do not know what else to say. Are you well? You seem even quieter than usual. I know it's coming time to leave, and it's coming quickly, mind you. I'm wondering if that's what the problem is and causing you to be so miserable and withdrawn?' she asked gently, fixing her gaze on me in the mirror. I smiled weakly as I looked back at her, my hair shining under her hand.

'No. I don't know. Maybe. I'm really not sure. I'm missing Aaron and my mind keeps wandering off, making me think of how he should be here and coming on this journey we planned for so long. It's more than that, though, Bessie. What I've come to realise lately is as each day passes, it is another day longer since I held him in my arms, since I saw his face or heard his voice. It doesn't get easier like everyone tells you, it's harder as time goes on. I miss him more and more as the distance between that day and this grows.' She placed the silver brush down on the dressing table, then reached into her apron pocket and took a clean handkerchief, passing it to me as tears threatened to spill down my powdered face. 'I'm worried I'm going to forget him, or my memory of him will fade as time marches on. He is so clear in my mind and I can recall his voice so easily, but that is now. What about in ten-years' time? Oh, Bessie, I cannot think of anything other than him. He had so much planned for this trip with the children. I don't think I can face going to all the places Aaron and I spoke of without him.' My voice broke and I placed my head in my hands as I sobbed, while she gently rubbed my back as she spoke soothingly to me, then went to find a cold cloth to wipe my face. She returned soon after, her eyes tear-stained, as if she, too, had been crying in secret.

'There you go, Mistress. There is no shame in crying for that sweet boy. I know how hard you've been trying in the last month to get up every day and out into the garden to wait for the children to return. We understand you still cannot venture into the kitchen, but do not fret. There is no rush, and you're being so brave and strong just doing what you're doing. The time away will do you the world of good, despite feeling as sad as you do, sweetheart. You are finally going to see your Sister Josephine again. Aaron would be so pleased you are going, just for that reason alone.' She kissed my cheek, a weak smile touching my lips for only a moment. She was right. I had been apart from Sister for far too long now, and she was the best tonic for my broken heart and tormented soul. Bessie picked up the brush to finish my hair, then touched me on the back of my head and I obediently stood.

I still wore black, and intended to until I boarded the ship as my final stage of mourning Aaron publicly. I gazed across at my reflection in the gilt-edged cheval mirror standing behind my dressing table as I smoothed my dress. I looked terrible in mourning clothes, appearing so frail, tiny, and pale when wearing them. I helped Bessie stack the breakfast dishes back onto the trays I had shared this morning with the twins. Before they ran off to eat a second breakfast with Angus and Hamish in the kitchen with their cousins.

'Thank you, dear Bessie. I will return by midday and will be in the village if anyone needs me,' I called out as she stood by the window tidying a side table. She spun around to face me, her eyes wide.

'Are you certain you are up to going to *that* village today? It's like walking into a lion's den down there with those nasty women spitting their venom at anyone that'll listen.' She placed her hands on her hips, her face a mottled red as I nodded and tried to smile.

'One nasty woman. Don't go being like Leo and exaggerating. We all know who she is, and the problems she causes between everyone living at Willow Grove. There is not much I can do about any of it until I see it with my own eyes and hear it with my own ears. If she really is that badly behaved, she will not be able to keep control of herself for long before exploding in front of me.' She sighed deeply before crossing the room and embracing me warmly, calling out her well wishes as I stepped out into the hallway.

I planned to visit with Amelia this morning, and see for myself what changes had occurred in the village over the last two-years. I strolled past the stables and up the hill, stopping abruptly at the top to gaze down at the cosy terraces and buildings I hadn't seen since losing Aaron. The breeze touched my skin as I raised my face to the winter sun, warming not only my body but my heart. There was now another street backing onto the original residences and joined the town square at the end of the road, now filled with another fourteen terraces. It looked magical even from such a distance, and like a proper little town like so many I had seen in England. Eric had done a fine job, designing and building the terraces in the same fashion while going beyond what was asked of him. He had taken it on himself to refresh the older terraces inside and out, and had painted them the same colour, bringing them all up to the same standard as the new residences. Standing side-by-side elegantly with their white walls and rusty red trims, the tiled rooves the same colour as the trim around the verandah, doors and windows. If I were an artist, this was where I would choose to spend my days atop of the hill painting the perfect picture of a perfect village. Well, perfect from the outside, I reminded myself as I slowly descended the hill.

I had not laid eyes on the new buildings, despite their completion weeks ago. Although I had been out of bed for a month, up until today, I had preferred my friends to visit me at the main house. I had not the strength or inclination to face several of the women that lived in the village who clearly disliked me, never once failing to let me, or those around them, know it. Feeling frail and weak, I was unable to cope with their pettiness. Now I no longer had my husband by my side, I could only imagine how mean these women would now be if I were forced to have dealings with their husbands. They were of the firm opinion I wanted to steal them away when Aaron was alive. It would only be worse now I was alone.

Suddenly, I could no longer breathe, and I quickly sat down on the side of the hill, halfway down the well-worn path to the village. My heart raced as I gasped for air, unable to catch my breath no matter how hard I tried. I closed my eyes and slowed my breathing, placing my head between my knees. Tears poured down my face as I silently cried for Aaron. I missed him dreadfully, more and more as the days passed, and I felt wretched. When he was first murdered, I felt my own heart had died. When I realised months later it was still there—albeit shattered beyond repair—what was left was still filled only with Aaron and pained me beyond belief. I remained on the side of the hill, a flock of yellow crested cockatoos roaming nearby picking at the remnants of grain left in a small feed trough the cattle had missed. Lowering my head into my hands, I sobbed my heart out for everything I had lost. For what my babies had lost. For what my darling man had lost. So many years taken from him. So many years of happiness and love. Just gone. I tried to pull myself together as I looked down at the exquisite village, sniffing before wiping my face with a clean handkerchief embroidered with bees.

When we arrived here fifteen-years ago, we weren't confident the idea of housing our employees in separate homes of their own in a village would work, but it had blossomed into something unique and special compared to how other farm workers were forced to live. There was a sense of community here. The residents not only worked together, they raised their families alongside each other and spent their private time with their friends who lived close by. The small village was charming and a lovely place for children to grow and spend their days, despite the problems caused by only a few.

After the longest time, I rose to my feet and continued on. I took a deep breath as I stepped onto the cobblestone road and strolled down the new street, admiring the terraces standing proudly on each side of the quaint little road. Greeting several women I had never met before, some with children at their skirts, I continued on towards the town square. I had not been introduced to any of the families who had moved here over the last two-years, hearing only through Hamish and Angus a number of the couples were both working for us—the husbands labouring on the property and their wives going into service in the main house or the dining hall. Margaret now cared for so many children, I had no idea how she coped. I adored the bairns just as much as anyone; however, I was well aware I would not care well for as many as she seemed to. She adored looking after them, no matter what age, and they adored her back. Margaret was a woman who fiercely protected those she loved, going as far as using violence to do so. She had belted Leo in the head with a walking stick only last week for visiting the village with evil intent—the sole purpose of his attendance there being to find unfortunate looking children to torment.

He had returned home that day shrieking, so loud I heard him before he even passed the stable. When I entered the kitchen shortly after, he stomped through the back door and demanded I sack her immediately, citing she was a violent lunatic, while offering to arrange her transport to Ararat. I had gently reminded him Margaret was not employed by me, and if he wanted her off the property, he would lose his best gardener, Sean—who could grow anything and made certain Leo had every vegetable and fruit he demanded. Leo had paused for a time and composed himself far quicker than usual, before telling me he would tend to the situation himself. If I had realised then what he meant by *tend*, I would have locked him downstairs under the house.

That same night, he snuck down to the village under the cover of darkness and dug up her precious garden. Placing every single plant in a pot, he loaded them onto a small cart and brought them up to the house, hiding them in the cellar underneath the house. Unbeknownst to me. When Margaret had turned up to my house in a fit of rage that morning, Leo denied all knowledge, despite the dirt under his fingernails and smudges across his face. He refused to incriminate himself, despite Margaret grabbing him by the nose and pinching hard as she twisted, making him squeal and the staff snigger. I stumbled across a room full of dying plants a few days later when putting some of my dresses into storage. I had told Angus, and he and Hamish forced Leo to return every single one and replant them where he had taken them from. He had whinged and sulked the entire time, but with Angus and Hamish standing over him, he was not in a position to refuse.

I climbed several stairs to Amelia's store and pushed open the door, the bell chiming above, to find her serving a well-to-do lady I had never met, my dear friend's face lighting up at the sight of me.

'I will be with you in a moment, Abigail. I must go out to the storeroom to retrieve Lady Chirnside's order. I will not be long.' I nodded as she politely excused herself before disappearing down the small hallway.

Lady Chirnside remained where she was, her gaze fixed on me as she looked me up and down, her nose wrinkled in disdain. I strolled around the pristine shop ignoring her, delighted to see the new items Amelia had just received from France, until a look of recognition crossed her thickly painted face.

'You are *that* Abigail. I was aware you owned Willow Grove through my mother-in-law; however, I did not expect to witness you roaming around the workers' village like a peasant. I am not sorry for what happened to your husband. He broke the law and deserved to be punished.' I stood unmoving near a shelf filled with tonics for every ailment I had heard of, and many I had not, my back to her. 'I cannot understand why you felt the need to air your dirty laundry in public, Mrs Cavanaugh. If what you say of Judge Maslow is based in truth, then I would think what you claim he did to you would be the last thing you would want anyone to know. Are you not ashamed of yourself?' I could not move even if I wanted to, the tears streaming down my face unnoticed as I continued to stare at the rows and rows of brown and green bottles, my gaze stopping on one for nervous ailments. 'I could not understand at the time why so many people cared about a man who was a criminal of the worst kind, and I'm not the only one who thinks this way. All in my circle believe he was far worse than that murderer Edward Kelly and his criminal friends. I associate with many in the judicial system, including barristers and judges, and they all believe your husband deserved to swing. It's a shame he left you with small children; however, there was nothing to be done about that, and he should not have received any sympathy on their behalf. Your children now have hope of growing into decent members of our society without the influence of such a violent father, who proved he had no regard for the law of the land.' My hands clenched into fists as I slowly turned around to find her still standing near the counter, impatiently waiting for Amelia to return. Despite noting my distress, she continued. 'He played on the fact he was protecting you. Well, my dear friend, George, has not gone near you since the day he saw you in his courtroom. I believe what he says about you is true regarding your sanity. There was nothing to protect you from. You caused all this, and really, when you think about it, *you* are the reason your husband was executed. As he well deserved.' She was so calm, behaving as if we were neighbours passing pleasantries over the fence. I summoned all my strength not to scream and crumple to the floor and prove her right—only staring back into her eyes, unable to speak even if I wanted to. I could hold my emotions no longer and collapsed into a flood of tears, my body trembling as Amelia marched back into the shop carrying a box filled with luxury items. She dropped it at the door and hurried to my side, gently taking me by the shoulders, then guided me over to the table behind the counter. Sitting me down, my dear friend patted my shaking back before turning around and striding back to the woman.

'Get out of my shop now, you mean spirited old bitch! Now!' Amelia roared in her face, her finger trembling as she pointed to the door. The woman jumped in fright and gasped aloud, staring at Amelia as though she had gone mad—and she had. Never had I seen her so enraged, or prepared to act so unladylike. The woman gathered her things before turning on her heel and hurrying towards the door, Amelia close behind. 'Move your oversized backside and get out of my store. You are never to set foot on the soil of Willow Grove again, Alice Belinda, or I will take out a full page in the Geelong Advertiser airing *your* dirty laundry. Poor Robert has only been in his grave three winters past, and you have been opening your legs to all those judges and barristers you claim such familiarity with for far longer than that. So I heard at the local tavern. Go back to Carranballac Estate, paid for by your dead husband and his parents I will remind you, and stay there until you catch yourself some unsuspecting fool silly enough to marry you,' Amelia screamed from the verandah, Lady Chirnside missing a step as she tried to get into her carriage. Her driver caught her by the arm as she stumbled; however, she rudely shook him off and scrambled up on her own, slamming the door in his face. He smiled up sheepishly at Amelia, then tipped his hat to her before taking his seat up front. 'We all know your mother-in-law who haunts the hallways of Werribee Mansion will not be impressed by your morality the next time she visits her grandchildren.' I heard a muffled screech within the carriage as it moved forward and Amelia turned back, locking the door behind her then turning the sign that hung on a string over to advise she was closed. I dried my eyes as she crossed the room and joined me at the table. 'I do apologise, dear Abigail. I wanted to slap that arrogant face of hers. I'm so bloody well angry.' She bent down to embrace me before going to the stove and pouring two cups of freshly brewed coffee. She placed the mugs down on the table, then lowered herself onto the chair next to me, speaking in soothing tones until I settled myself. I knew I should not allow people to upset me with their opinions; however, she only pointed out what I already believed. Aaron would be alive if it wasn't for me. If I had kept my mouth shut that Christmas night so long ago, he would not have gone out ten-days later and assaulted Maslow. The woman was right, despite how nasty, but Amelia had been right, too. She was a mean spirited bitch to say those things to me when we were not acquainted, but I expected nothing less from a Chirnside from what I had heard over the years from Harry. I sipped my coffee then picked up a scone, still warm from the oven and smothered in strawberry jam, a dollop of thick cream on top. She returned to open the door once I calmed myself, and we had caught up on the gossip.

'Maybe she's not far wrong.'

'Now, you listen to me, Mrs Cavanaugh. It is not your fault Aaron was killed. The investigation was corrupt from the start, and still stinks to high heaven. You must stop torturing yourself, my dear friend. Oh, for God's sake, now I see Mrs Jack getting down from her carriage. I will be right back, sweetheart. She is not a pleasant woman to deal with at the best of times, and I know she will not be happy with the news I have for her,' she whispered as a well-dressed lady entered the shop, followed by two others, who did not appear to know her.

Amelia cheerfully approached the woman, while the other customers wandered around the shop. I could hear Amelia speaking in hushed tones, and from where I was sitting, the woman did not appear to be impressed.

'You told me last week it would be here by today, and now you tell me it still hasn't arrived. I've travelled all this way to a pokey little shop that wouldn't know the difference between perfume and manure when I have better things to do with my time. I am a very important woman and you have taken a significant amount of time from my day that could have been better spent,' the customer ranted, waving her hands in the air.

'I am sorry, Madam, but I cannot control when the goods arrive. I place the order and they send it. It arrives when it arrives. I am not the captain of the ship that carries the boxes over the ocean,' she replied sarcastically as I tried not to smile.

'As if I don't know that, you rude young woman. I want my perfume now,' she demanded as Amelia returned her hard stare.

'Again, I apologise, but it will get here when it does. There is nothing more I can do. I ordered your perfume weeks ago and it should be in the next delivery from France.' Amelia was so polite, far more than I would be under the circumstances. The woman continued to glare at her before slamming her hand down on the counter.

'Do not bother. I will make my purchase somewhere else. You will now be stuck with the most expensive perfume in the world, and no one else around here can afford to take it off your hands. I hope your business can withstand such a loss.' She straightened up and prepared to leave, slipping her gloves back onto her hands.

'That is your choice, Madam, but may I wish you luck in buying this particular perfume here in Victoria, as no others will stock it due to the costly outlay, as you well know it seems. I am more than happy to keep it here in stock. I have many wealthy ladies who frequent my store, and it will sell quickly; however, then there will be another lady at your gala event walking around smelling of your scent. Good day to you, madam.' Amelia dismissed the woman with a wave of her hand, then promptly returned to the table and sat down. The woman stood as if frozen, her mouth open, unable to speak. Amelia widened her eyes at her and abruptly moved forward in her chair, as if she were ready to chase her out herself. Within moments, the shop was empty, the woman making the wise decision to follow the two ladies who had only come to look out the door. 'It's good to finally see you out and about in the world,' she said, smiling as she made herself comfortable and sipped her coffee. 'And you have some colour in your cheeks again, which is so wonderful to see. You are looking very well, Abigail, I must say.' She smiled at me again, and I thanked her.

'I am feeling much improved over these last few weeks. My grief has not lessened, of course. However, I am able to function at the very bare minimum now. I'm still eating in my bedchamber in the mornings but I do join them in the dining room each evening. It's only I cannot seem to return to the kitchen. I avoid it at all costs as I know the first thing I will see is him in there as he used to be, and I cannot bear the thought of being in there without him.' I broke down and sobbed as she took my hand in hers.

'I know it is beyond difficult for you, my sweet friend, but you will feel better as time goes on. I am not suggesting for a moment you will ever get over Aaron's death, but the pain will lessen. You are the last person who ever deserved to experience such tragedy, and so was Aaron. Going back to Scotland will be the best thing for you and the children. Is Hamish still going with you?' she asked and I nodded. 'That is very kind on his behalf. I am aware he promised Aaron he would go in his place to ensure the children saw everything he had spoken to them about over the years. You have people there who love you and cannot wait to reunite with you. Focus on them, Abigail. Sister Josephine will be overjoyed to have you back in her arms, especially with Thomas and Emmy there,' she said brightly as I smiled at her.

'I am getting a little excited about seeing them all again,' I said, thinking of the Malcolms' and Sister Josephine. Hamish had suggested that because the orphanage and those living there were close to my heart, we should rent a residence close by for a week or two so I could spend time with Sister Josephine and finally meet the children I had been helping all these years. I had agreed, feeling more excitement with each passing day at the prospect of returning to show Thomas and Emmy where I grew up and to meet my dear Sister.

I knew when we were in London the Malcolms would insist on us staying with them. I also looked forward to seeing Richard's brothers and sisters-in-law again, and was curious to see how much their children had grown since I had last been in London. The older ones would be nearly adults now, I realised as I reflected on how lovely it would have been to introduce Aaron to them.

How quickly time passed, yet a lifetime full of memories were made in that short time. How my life had changed since I left the orphanage that day, feeling it was a hundred-years ago now. Never once had the thought crossed my mind that I would be left a widow at twenty-seven-years of age with two young children to care for. When I married Aaron, I thought him invincible and expected a full and happy life with him where we would die in our bed, old and content, only weeks apart. I had believed we would have a houseful of children by now; however, that dream had been cut down too, due to events beyond our control.

My vision for my life hadn't gone to plan, and I didn't have another. I did not want any other life other than the one I had before with Aaron by my side. I knew that was impossible. Although I presented myself well to everyone around me and they saw improvement, inside I was dead. My heart stopped at the very same moment Aaron's own ceased to beat.

Going through the motions for the sake of my children, not for any enjoyment for myself, I saw no joy in anything but Thomas and Emmy. I knew if I did not have them, I would no longer be on this earth and would have followed him within days. They were the anchor holding me here, grounding me and binding me to them, giving me no choice but to go on, despite how miserable and empty I felt.

After talking for the longest time about Aaron, Amelia rose to her feet to brew more coffee. We chatted of the changes that had occurred in the village, and of the families still to come in the near future. She told me how her Mathew had a crush on Emmy, as did most of the boys their age at school. I didn't think Emmy knew, or she would have told me. Mathew often played with Thomas, Willy, Bella and Emmy, and from what I knew, they had been close since infancy. Emmy was very much like me and oblivious to signs boys often gave to show they liked a girl. I had no clue when someone was flirting with me, unless blatantly obvious and inappropriate, and I hoped she, too, stayed oblivious for many, many years to come.

I bid farewell to Amelia, embracing her warmly before stepping out onto the verandah. Making my way down the street, I admired the terraces. They were all so well kept, and everyone took such pride in them. I hurried across the undulating paddock to the top of the hill and on towards the stables, stopping in to see Harry and check on Delly. I had neglected her terribly since Aaron died, but Harry had been taking good care of her for me. Just one of the many things I had been avoiding and pushing to the back of my mind. All so I could survive.

Chapter Five

I OPENED DELLY'S STALL door and held out my hand, and she whinnied as she walked towards me. I stroked her lovely face, murmuring to her.

'How's my beautiful girl? I've missed you, Delightful.' I stroked her neck, then ran my hand down her gleaming back. She was in foal to Goliath, and I was hoping to be back to welcome the new arrival into the world.

'I thought I heard someone talking to 'emselves.' Harry leaned over the stall and grinned widely at me as I turned to face him.

'I'm not talking to myself. I'm talking to Delly.' I laughed aloud as I held out my hand to give her a carrot, while Harry pulled his pipe from his pocket and lit it.

'It's good to see you back, Mistress. It's been a long time. I know very well your great-aunt Isabelle would have grieved deeply for you had she still been alive. I wish she had been here to comfort you. She was a very compassionate woman, and would have known how to help you move on from your grief.' I nodded, willing myself not to cry as he leaned comfortably on the stall door. 'She lost three husbands herself, but was alone again when I met her on the ship. Then there were the men she loved who she didn't marry.' He chuckled to himself as I went to speak but he held up his hand and rolled his eyes. 'Before you ask, I don't know any details of her marriages. Or the men she was married to. They died long before I met her. I often wondered why a woman like her was cursed to suffer so much loss and heartbreak. She had a brother she loved very much who lived in England, but he passed a few years before she did at a ripe old age of five-and-eighty. There were a couple of nephews she spoke of, one I believe is your father after what you've told me over the years. I never met any of her kin in the five-years she was here, other than a few of her women friends from the homeland she considered family. She never spoke of them, other than her brother and her nephews, one she was none too fond of. She returned to England 'cause of her daughter, who was sickly and died. That's the reason I wish she were here, 'cause she would know how to comfort you.' I nodded, my hand unconsciously stroking Delly's neck as I stared out the tiny window. 'You have her strength within you, Mistress. I know you feel weak as a kitten, but you have her courage, too. She went on to love again many times during her life, not always marrying the men she had such intense relationships with, like me. She did once say to me that after her third husband died, she vowed never to marry again, and she didn't. From the little I know, she lived in Australia in her earlier years, and came back for long periods of time during her lifetime. She hated England and didn't want to return the last time, but was obliged 'cause it involved her kin. It was only when you told me what that London lawyer said about your parents and Isabelle, I realised why she stayed so long and never returned. She helped your mother when she was carrying you and stayed until the end to see you safe. At least she got to hold you 'cause I know she would have been delighted by you. It was no surprise to me she named you Abigail.' He smiled secretly to himself but said no more on the matter. I stared at him intently, wishing I could respect his privacy but needing to hear more, regardless of whether he wanted to discuss my aunt or not.

'Imagine being married three times and losing each of them. What a terrible burden to bear. Unless she was the one who brought about their untimely demise.' He snorted, then threw back his head and roared with laughter.

'She couldn't have hurt a fly, with all respect, Mistress. Not unless they deserved it. I knew her as well as she would let me. Your aunt was a very secretive woman by the time I met her, and she trusted few. Isabelle hadn't had an easy time of it during her life, but she hid it as best she could. She may have left you a lot of money, but as you now know, it doesn't make you happy or protect you from harm and the harsh realities of this bloody world. From what I could gather during the time I spent with her, she had been beaten down all through her life and had to keep getting up and fighting back. I think by the end of it all, she was tired.' He brushed a tear from his eye before continuing. 'The one thing that brings me comfort is I know how happy she was in her final years here at Willow Grove. She named the place after all the willow trees along the rivers that run through the property. She loved this place with every part of her and had big dreams for it. When I arrived, there were remnants of a small village right here where we stand. Nothing as grand as what's here now, just huts and cottages where her friends settled for a time. Your aunt lived where young Polly and Angus now stay, and although she made plans for the main house twenty-years before she returned to England for the final time, she never got to start it and left it for me to see it done.' He grinned down at me as I shook my head, feeling confused.

'Where did all the people who once lived here go?' I sat down on a stool, Delly's head in my lap.

'Hmmm, I'm not sure. I know most who moved here in the 1840s were dead or had moved on by the time I arrived. From what I heard in town, they regarded the place as a commune filled with outcasts. Many had been convicts, some were natives your aunt befriended, while others were shunned by society for whatever reason. She never told me why people left seemingly all at once, but did say those who chose to live out their days here are buried down near the village. Your aunt didn't become serious about developing Willow Grove into what it is now until just before I met her.'

'Were Sean and Margaret here when it was considered a commune?' He snorted again and shook his head.

'Nah. They started here around the same time I did. Isabelle told me it broke her heart when her friends passed on, and those left decided it wasn't the same here and shot through. It was then she decided to hire workers and turn the property into a business rather than a home for the unwanted.'

'I've never seen a graveyard near the village or the remains of any buildings other than a few sheds,' I exclaimed as he chuckled.

'That's because it was all cleaned up in preparation for the new buildings. The huts had fallen into disrepair, so we used the wood to warm our homes. Regarding the cemetery, there were only small wooden markers placed there, never headstones, and they were eroded away by the weather. They were cleared away once we heard word of your aunt's death. Isabelle didn't want those that came after her to know who was buried there, so we made sure her last wishes were carried out.'

'Oh my. She really did have a lot of secrets if she needed to hide her friends. Even in death.' I collapsed into a fit of giggles while he chuckled to himself.

'You are very much like her, Mistress, an' it gladdens my heart she has, in some small way, left a piece of herself behind. You favour her strongly, not only in looks, but in character. You'll get through this, just as others have done before you. How you come out the other end is up to you. You can let this shape the rest of your life, leaving you angry and bitter—keeping your heart so well protected you'll never allow yourself to love again—or you can stand up and take your life back. I know it's not the same without Aaron, but you still have at least sixty-years yet to live. You don't want all that time to be taken up in misery and sorrow with a bunch of regrets thrown in. You deserve to be happy. Now how you choose to do this is completely up to you, and you'll find your own path and direction as your grief eases,' he told me kindly as I continued to stare at him. He always seemed to know what to say, not only to shock and surprise me when it came to great-aunt Isabelle, but to make me feel better.

'Three husbands?' I said incredulously as he smirked, nodding his head vigorously. 'You would think she would have learnt after the first one.' I smiled again as he grinned back.

'Yeah, it took me off guard, too. She did tell me one of her marriages was by force and she never loved the man, but she did adore the others. Not that men didn't want to marry her, as like I told you, she was a beauty, but the fact she lost three husbands and multiple lovers she cared for did sadden me to know she experienced such great misfortune and sorrow. I do know for a fact she was very young when she first came to Australia, and lived in many places, not just Geelong. And smart as a whip, she was. Could read the page of a book within seconds and have it committed to memory. Intelligent and beautiful, my Isabelle. As I said, it brings me comfort that she's left a small part of herself here.' He smiled and shifted on his feet, and I knew immediately that was the end of any talk of great-aunt Isabelle.

It was nice to know that even though my parents did not want me, I once had an aunt who cared enough to leave me everything she owned. And she was kind, providing a home and family for those who had none. I felt like I finally belonged somewhere. Now I knew where I had inherited the ability to read so fast and other small similarities family members share. I wished I had been able to meet her when she was younger as she sounded so very interesting, despite Harry's reluctance to confide too much in me about her. I never pushed him, letting him tell me things about her as they came to him and he felt like a yarn. He had obviously tired of the subject for today, although I was still of the firm belief he knew far more than he would ever speak of, to me or anyone else.

'How are you enjoying working with Hamish, Harry? Has he settled in? I know he can be hot-headed, and I wondered how he is getting along with the workers given he has such strong opinions?' I enquired, and he nodded thoughtfully, pausing for a time.

'We all miss Aaron sorely. I want you to know that, Mistress, but Hamish is doing a fine job carrying on in his place. You don't have to worry about his temper. He's fair with the workers, just like Aaron always was. I'd say he's earned their respect and admiration,' he replied as I nodded, satisfied all was well. I had worried Hamish may not be as effective doing Aaron's job due to his temper. However, my concerns seemed to have been in vain given Harry seemed satisfied, and I knew that if he wasn't, he would certainly tell me.

'That's good to hear everyone is happy. I cannot stand it when there is division amongst people.' I stood stroking Delly while we talked until Hamish strolled in and stood alongside Harry.

'What are we talkin' about?' Hamish interrupted, throwing me two more carrots, which I slipped into my pocket.

'Nothing for your ears,' I replied, smiling weakly as I fed her another carrot. Harry bid us farewell to return to his work, while Hamish stepped into Delly's stall and patted her on the rump.

'She's bonny, is she naw? Can ye imagine the foal from her an' Goliath? It'd be the champion o' Willow Grove. Are ye goin' tae sell it?' Delly nuzzled her face into my stomach, trying to get the other carrot from my skirt pocket as I giggled.

'No. I'm keeping it and will eventually ride it as mine when Delly goes to God,' I replied, still laughing as she butted me with her head in frustration while Hamish chuckled.

'Do ye want tae sit on her? Ye haven't been on her fer so long now,' he enquired as he stepped towards me. No sooner had I said yes, he lifted me up on top of her. I tried to get comfortable, allowing myself to sink into her muscular back while stroking her thick neck, then leaned down to pat her chest as he remained by the door, watching her closely. 'Have ye remembered anythin' o' what we talked o' the other night?' he asked, his arms folded across his enormous chest.

'No, I have not, and you keep asking and I do not understand why. If I said something wrong, please just tell me as you have been acting strange around me ever since. If I have said or done something to offend you, I am truly sorry.' I looked down at him enquiringly as he rolled his eyes.

'Nah, ye haven't,' he replied sharply as I rolled my eyes back at him.

'Well, tell me what it is because you are driving me bloody mad with it. I can't stand you acting all strange towards me.' I threw up my hands in frustration as he glared at me.

'If ye cannae remember, I'm naw tellin' ye,' he murmured, appearing greatly offended. I had no idea what I had said, but I promised myself to stay away from whisky for a while.

'Do you want to come and have lunch with me in the garden?' I no longer wished to discuss our drunken conversations and slipped off Delly, landing on my feet.

'Thank ye, but naw. I'll grab somethin' in the kitchen later,' he replied, avoiding my gaze as he turned and walked out without another word.

Seated beside Leo on the lounge in the sitting room, I devoured a delicious scallop pie he had made fresh this morning, taken from a large basket of seafood delivered to his kitchen by Luke before dawn.

'I could eat two of these,' I remarked while chewing a scallop, the flaky pastry melting in my mouth.

'Oh, for goodness' sake, Abigail, eat with your mouth closed. Do you know what chewed up scallop pie looks like in your mouth? Oh yes, it looks like that, you fisher wife. You eat like the mangy seagulls always flying at me for scraps. Now I think about it, you also remind me of Baboo, the gorilla I saw eating his dinner at the London zoo. The ones with the big red bums,' he told me thoughtfully.

'That's a baboon, thus the reason he was named Baboo, I suspect,' I told him as he narrowed his gaze at me.

'I don't care which one has the red bum. I haven't seen yours for a while, so lift your skirt and show us so I can compare,' he told me as I continued to eat contentedly.

'You won't be seeing my bum, thank you very much. And that reminds me. Stay out of my underwear drawer. You have stretched everything out with your fat arse so that nothing fits me anymore. I had to replace everything to go on this trip because of you. Imbecile,' I warned him as he giggled.

'I like how silky they are. They don't make men's underwear like that,' he complained as I stuffed the last of my pie in my mouth, then leaned over and poured myself a mango and banana juice. 'There is more in the kitchen. Slow down before you cause your own death here in front of us. You will never go hungry.' He laughed as I choked on the last of it, then quickly took a sip of my drink. 'I'm going to miss you when you're gone, butterball. It will be the longest time we have been apart since we met,' Leo reminded me for the thousandth time, his voice filled with emotion as I grabbed his hand.

'It will pass in no time. Think of the lovely rest you will have with Sally cooking for Angus, Polly and you, while everyone else will eat at the dining hall and won't bother you. It will be heaven, and you will have the house all to yourself. Maybe you can sneak Brian down here,' I said wickedly. A slow smirk spread across his lips.

'I never thought of that. Oh, Abigail, you're right. We could do it in every room of the house as he likes to do. Swing around from place to place and no one would ever know.' He clapped his hands together in delight while bouncing up and down on his chair. I placed my hand over his to stop him, demanding he look into my eyes.

'I am well aware of the places Brian likes to copulate, but I'm warning you now. Stay out of mine and the children's bedchambers or you will not have an appendage to be swinging around anywhere with Brian,' I warned him, and he laughed. He was still giggling when he went to get more pies. On his return, I ate another, soon feeling I could sleep.

'We are not finished yet. I made something special for you.' He lifted a silver cover to reveal chocolate mousse with a thick dollop of cream, a sprig of mint delicately placed on top. Although I was full as a boot, I could not pass it up and quickly spooned the thick creamy mess into my mouth. 'The worst part of it all is I'm forced to put up with Pollyanna thinking she's the boss of me while you're gone. You really should leave me in charge of everyone, including Angus and Harry. It is the only responsible thing to do given I know how this place runs. I tell everyone how to do their jobs properly anyway, so it wouldn't intrude on my time. Leave everything to me. I promise you can trust me.' He smiled sweetly, while I shook my head vigorously, trying to swallow as quickly as I could before he spoke again.

'If I agreed to that, I would come home to no staff, no farm workers or stable hands, and no Angus and Polly. The whole place would be a ghost town because of an Italian chef roaming through an empty mansion, throwing tantrums as he waits on my return. I could not do that to anyone with a clear conscience, so the answer is a loud and definite no. You don't have to work while I'm gone. Why don't you go on a holiday to the seaside? I know you are not short of a quid because I've never seen you spend a penny of your own. Travel around Australia for six-months. Go and see the outback, the mountains, the rivers and the ocean that surrounds our country. It's such an enormous place it would take a lifetime to see everything. You could go up north and see crocodiles in the rivers, or even right up the top of Australia where they are in the ocean. Go and do something exciting,' I encouraged him as he stared back at me, his eyes wide.

'What part of you suddenly thought, *Oh yes, Leo would make a wonderful jackaroo travelling around the outback with all the rugged blokes?* Was it my frilly pink bloomers that gave it away or my high-pitched squeals when I get overexcited? Oh yes, Abigail, I would last five-minutes out there and you know it. You are trying to send me off to be killed. You're sick of me, aren't you? You want Sally to be your chef. I knew it. I knew it. I saw you whispering to her the other day, and she made you a special cake that I don't know how to make. I hate her now. She's stealing you from me. I'm going to give her one of my famous bitch slaps,' he said crossly as I shook my head.

'What? That doesn't make sense.'

'Oh, yes it does. She's a bitch, and I'm going to slap her fucking hard. After that, I will be famous,' he replied as I collapsed into loud laughter.

'Oh, stop it! She is not, and you won't be touching a hair on her head or I will be twisting your ear and balls simultaneously on my arrival home. Now listen to me and calm yourself. I asked her to make something out of the nuts we have growing, so she created a mango and macadamia cheesecake, and it was delicious. I know you refused to try it out of spite, and even attempted to taint it by pulling one of the hairs from my head to place in a slice when no one was looking. Not very kind of you, or sensible, because Polly ended up with that piece, and is now furious. You are my chef and will always be my chef; however, Sally also has a talent when it comes to creating recipes, so stop being so jealous. She has made nut paste for the children to have on their toast from our trees, along with a sweet chestnut paste that is lovely on cakes and scones. Peanut paste, cashew paste and burnt beer nut paste for the children's toast and sandwiches is very much appreciated by the children. They adore it.' He looked away, his arms folded across his chest as he grunted angrily.

'See how irresponsible she is? Giving the children beer at their age? You need to sack her, or I will while you're gone.' I rolled my eyes in defeat, then lay back down on the lounge. We discussed how Hamish had been behaving since that night we got drunk a month ago, and I told him what he had said to me since. 'Maybe you kissed him, or even better, fornicated with him and he is offended that you don't remember.' He squealed with laughter before falling back on the lounge, kicking his legs in the air.

'All right, you exaggerator. I see what you are doing. You are trying to put things in my mind so I will be worried something has happened between us. Very funny, Leo. It's not going to work because I would remember if anything of that nature passed between us. And it did not. We no longer feel that way towards each other.' I smiled at him as he giggled.

'Well, something happened. It's clear how much in love with you he is now. He's fallen for you again in the last year. I watched it happen as he took care of you and the twins. I predicted this would happen. You're the only one who can't see it.' He straightened up in his chair, his face serious.

'That was over a long time ago, Leo. Hamish and I left that behind many years ago. I love him as my friend, but I'm not in love with him. I know he loves me too, but not in the way he once did. He looks after me and the twins out of obligation to Aaron. I know he made promises to him the last time they saw each other; however, he won't tell me what passed between them. Like I said, it's been over for a long time now,' I said as he shook his head.

'Not for Hamish. I don't think it's ever been over for him when I look back at how self-destructive he became in the years after you married Aaron. Given all the women he has been with, not once did I ever see him happy with one of them. I've seen the way he looks at you with those come-hither eyes that resemble melted chocolate. You don't have to love or marry him to have sex with him, Abigail. It's been a long time between drinks for you now. Don't you just want to climb him like a tree trunk and have your way with him?' He wiped the corner of his mouth with a napkin, then winked at me.

'No! I do not, Leonardo, and stop putting thoughts into my head.' Suddenly, my mind filled with visions of climbing gum trees, and getting shit on by the birds who nest there.

'There is nothing wrong with taking a lover, Abigail, and it may do you some good and put a smile back on your face. Just make sure you have strict rules, and are clear about what you want and don't want. If you can't love again, tell the poor man that, then no one gets hurt. It works for me and Brian, not that we have the option of ever being together anyway, but that's not the point. Find someone who accepts your terms, who you can have some fun with. I'm so jealous of you. If I were in your position, I would take ten lovers. You have them lining up at the door. It's only because you have so many people surrounding you that we manage to keep them away. You can always pick a few out of that lot. Some are fairly handsome as well, which is surprising given how unfortunate-looking you are at times.' I shook my head in astonishment as he laughed again.

'I do not want to be with anyone, in any way, ever again. Maybe in time, I will soften and take a lover, as I do miss the intimacy of having a man in my bed. I just cannot see myself doing that for a very long time, if at all. I'm not interested, and you can stop trying to push me and Hamish together. He doesn't need it, nor do I. We have a great friendship now and I rely on him heavily as it is, which makes me feel terribly guilty as he has no time to have a life of his own.' I sighed deeply. I hated feeling pressured by anyone, including well-meaning friends like Leo.

'He has plenty of time to have his own life, but he chooses to stay here from daybreak 'till midnight. There is nothing stopping him going to the pub at the end of the week to meet all the women that only go there in the hope of attracting his attention. But again, he chooses not to. He only ever turns up there with Angus after work for a couple of beers, then comes straight back here. If you don't want to do the dirty with him, let me have him. Oh, the things I could do that would make that man...' he went to say, his eyes glazed over as he stared up at the chandelier sparkling above.

'Stop! Stop it right now. Stop talking about Hamish as if he is an object to be used at will. He is our friend and we love him no matter what he looks like.' I smothered a smile, his eyes sparking mischievously.

'Yes, but I love him a hell of a lot more because he is so usable.' I laughed aloud, sending a prayer of thanks to the heavens above for this man who barrelled into my life so long ago uninvited—and never left.

Chapter Six

I SLOWLY OPENED MY eyes, the room still dark as I turned to kiss Aaron and put my arms around him. Finding his side of the bed empty, I realised all at once he was no longer here with me and never would be again. Tears slid down my face as I lay on his side of the bed and snuggled as deeply into the mattress as I could. We sailed in two-days, and I didn't want to go. I had slipped back into my melancholy the closer the day came to depart on our long-awaited voyage—a journey that had been planned and looked forward to for so many years between us. Now I would have to face it alone with only my friends for support.

This was not how my life was meant to be. I could not face this without him, and no longer had the strength to want or keep trying to go on without him. He was all that filled my thoughts, day and night. I would dream of him constantly, and it was only during these dreams I felt truly happy. Feeling so lifelike when Aaron held me close to his chest, apologising over and over for leaving me alone, I would wake to find him gone and sob for him every night more than once. I had no control over any of it, no different from every other aspect of my life. I had learnt it mattered not who you were or what you had—tragedy and suffering waited around the corner for all. There was no warning or prevention when it set its sights on you, ready to come rolling into your life like a thundercloud and destroy everything in its path.

I looked across at Leo snoring loudly beside me, then reached over and pinched his nose, cutting off the air. I waited for a few moments until I heard a familiar shriek, and released him.

'Abigail, get off me, you lunatic. You have been trying to kill me in my sleep, but I couldn't prove it 'till now, you wicked witch of Willow Grove. I wish Goliath were here with us so I could tell on you. He always took my side.' He turned over and lay his head next to mine on my pillow.

'What are you talking about? He never took your side once. He may have protected you from me when you caused me to lose my mind and attack you, but no, he was always on my side. You were a big, fat pain in his arse,' I told him as all the memories of Aaron with Leo flooded my mind, nearly all of them making me smile.

'Oh, I wish he had let me be a pain in his arse, the handsome boy that he was. Let's not get all sad and boring, though. You're not staying in bed today as I won't have you backsliding like the happy clappers do. They are no different to you, butterball. They run around during the week being wicked, then turn up to St. Mary's of the Angels in our beautiful city of Geelong on a Sunday to cleanse their black souls, say a few words in prayer, and ease their hypocritical conscience. All the while hoping the church doesn't fall down on top of them, or they get struck by lightning when they leave. After ridding their conscience of wrongdoing, they are of the firm belief they still have a foot in the gate of heaven, and continue going about being ring-holes for the rest of the week,' he announced, as if giving his own sermon to the masses. I stared at his handsome silhouette and rolled my eyes—our resident Kookaburra preparing himself in the gumtree by my window to sing his morning chorus.

'How do your ridiculous metaphors relate to me? How do people going to church on a Sunday affect my choice to remain in my bed today?' He gazed back at me before stroking my face as though I was a child who understood nothing.

'I'm not really sure, as I don't know why I went off on that subject. Oh, I was only explaining you're evil and at risk of being struck by lightning, I suppose. Anyway, back to me. You cannot lay about in bed all day as though you are the Queen of Willow Grove, like you usually do. You have friends coming to see you before you sail, so I'm certain they don't want to see you miserable and back in bed. We have all had enough of it. It's been too long, and I miss you. I know you wouldn't have survived without me, and I know you appreciate it, except for the occasions you go insane and chastise me for no reason. There is still time for you to take me with you, you know? It's not fair Hamish gets to go when I am your best friend and love Thomas and Emmy more than anyone does. I have never teased them once in their whole life. They are my babies and the most perfect specimens of human beauty I have ever seen. Well, except for myself, of course.' He sat up and continued to plead with me, while I remained where I was and shook my head.

'I cannot take you with me, even if I wanted to. That was not what Aaron and I planned; however, that's not the reason you are staying here. I would love to have you come with me, and even booked your passage as a surprise, but Bessie found out and told me in no uncertain terms that if you accompany us, she would not come, and neither would Mary. The thought of being trapped on a boat with you for weeks on end has brought back Bessie's night terrors of our journey here, and what a pain in her backside you were. You did it to yourself, my friend.' I smothered a smile as he rolled his eyes and pulled a face at me. Soon after, I heard Bessie step into my bedchamber, sighing heavily when she saw Leo sprawled out in my bed as if he owned the place.

'Good morning to you, Mistress. Not long now until we sail. I know you don't want to go, but you will. Mr Aaron gave me strict instructions the last time I saw him I was to drag you to the ship if you refused to take this journey. Don't think for a minute I won't,' she warned me as she busied herself in my wardrobe organising my clothes for the day.

'That's why you need me to come along, Bessie. I am the only one now who can control her. She will be nothing but trouble on that ship without me beside her,' he said sweetly as Bessie narrowed her gaze at him.

'Don't you go thinking for a minute I've forgotten what you two got up to on our voyage over here? You were that trouble following along behind me, Leonardo, and I still have flashes in my mind of you dangling the mistress over the side of the boat by her feet. I am looking forward to the time away as a hiatus from your antics, including the tantrums and dramatics that go along with you, and all the trouble and mischief you get her into when I'm not looking. It will be nice to be around people who have their full minds about them,' she snapped as she raised her hand, clicking her fingers while motioning us to get out of bed.

'No! You only want to see my enormous python that takes up half the bed. Ask Abigail. It's so big it has to sleep in between us and has its own pillow to rest its head on. She cuddles it sometimes because she mistakes it for me, being the same size as a fully grown man and all,' he called out, and I collapsed into giggles. She glared at both of us as she stood at the foot of the bed with her hands on her hips.

'Oh, you wish, you stupid boy! And stop being so disgusting. I am counting down the minutes, not the hours, until we leave here and you behind with it, you imbecile. Get your hairy arse out of this bed before I belt you so hard you'll have bruises for a month,' she threatened as he quickly moved to the side of the bed and pulled the covers back, standing up in his pink silk pyjamas and slipping on his matching robe. I couldn't help but smile as I struggled out of bed, pulled on my dressing gown, then obediently followed Bessie to the bathroom to wash and ready myself for the day.

I relaxed in the back garden, unable to go inside to the kitchen or face being in any of the rooms that held so many memories of my husband. I had been across to the island this morning, as was my usual habit, and had only just arrived back, deciding to rest before seeing what was for lunch. Mr Masters stepped out of the back door, and upon seeing me, walked down through the garden towards me. He seemed to always know how to find me when he needed to speak to me, as if he possessed some sort of sixth sense that could locate me no matter where I was hiding. I rested back on the sun lounge as he came and stood beside me, looking down at me formally, as was his manner.

'Good afternoon, Mistress. I have your friend, Dana, here to visit with you. Would you like to meet with her in the sitting room, or another of your choosing? If I may be so forward to say, the drawing room holds far fewer memories of your husband? It has always been under-used, in my humble opinion. It may be in your best interest for a time to entertain your friends in the drawing room,' he suggested helpfully, and I nodded, remaining silent as tears stung my eyes.

Little did he know, Aaron and I would often sneak off to my drawing room and my office, the two rooms in the house I felt truly belonged to me, to spend time alone together as no-one ever looked for us in there. I could not face being in the house at all at the moment. Feeling extremely fragile after spending the morning with Aaron and my boys, the thought of parting, even for a short time, upset me deeply. I had visited them every single day since their funerals, come rain, hail, or shine. It made me feel closer to the three of them. Aaron still hadn't shown me a sign he was around me, or safe and happy. I could feel him at times, but as for the true sign he had promised. Nothing.

'Thank you, Mr Masters. I will sit with her under the back verandah at the table. Do you mind asking Leo to send lunch out for Dana and myself?' I asked, and he nodded.

He kindly reached out his hand and offered it to me, assisting me to my feet. We walked back towards the house, my attention on the immaculate garden with its English trees and plants combined with the native flora, all beautiful when in bloom. Making myself comfortable on the enormous chair, its thick cushion comfortable on my backside, I watched Mr Masters disappear back into the house. I adored this outdoor dining set, as it was one of the last things Aaron had made for us while living under the house. I heard Dana before I saw her, calling out a cheery greeting to the kitchen staff as she passed by them and came through the back door.

'Hello, sweetheart. It's so good to see you out of bed. I'm still not used to it. I have expected to find you back there each time I visited over the last month. You look wonderful, despite being in that horrid black. I cannot wait to see you in colour again. You always look so exquisite. The fashions have changed so much in the last two-years.'

She came to my side, kissing me before making herself comfortable on the chair beside me.

'I know. I found that out when Catherine made my wardrobe,' I replied as she laughed loudly.

'You cannot go by what Catherine dresses you in as a standard. She is years ahead of everyone else. You will only have to look around when you are on the ship at how the average man and woman dress these days. It has changed through all classes of society,' she told me expertly as I smiled back at her. We chatted for a time before Sally brought out our lunch, several kitchen maids following behind her to assist. Leo was nowhere to be seen, and I assumed he had taken off and was likely down at the village tormenting the children, causing me to grimace. 'Abigail, I must ask you. Why are you taking that bloody Hamish with you? It has been gnawing at me as I do not trust him as far as I could kick him. An act I would so very much love to carry out. Many times. Hard. In the head,' she told me succinctly as I choked on my ginger beer. It took me a few moments to regain my composure.

'Aaron made me promise to ask him to come, and from what I know, he made Hamish promise to agree to it. He did not want three females and two children travelling alone to countries we have never been to before. I am forced to have an escort anyway now I'm a widow, and he has kindly agreed to join us as our chaperone. He has no underhanded plans, Dana. He is doing this for Aaron and his godchildren.' She narrowed her gaze before placing her cutlery back down on the table while I continued to eat.

'He may well be, but don't tell me he has no other motivation. He has fallen back in love with you. Not that I believe for a moment he ever stopped. Hamish may have convinced himself over the years he only cared for you as a friend, but it is all kangaroo shit. As your friend, I am only trying to warn you. Do not allow him to sweep you up in his charms or move in on you again. I'm aware he is regarded as one of the most handsome of the available men in the district; however, looks can be deceiving. As they are most definitely in his case. I know you view him as a close friend, but I do not trust him around you. You are extremely vulnerable at the moment, and I'm worried you will fall into his arms and he will hurt you like he did once before. There are hundreds of men wanting to court you when the time is right, and I beg of you to not allow him to distract you. I have no doubt there will be many available men of good character in first class seeking your time and attention. Do not waste what you have of it on Hamish,' she told me firmly as I stared at her, summoning all my strength to hide the pity I felt for her carrying a heavy load of hate for so long now.

'Dana, as you said, he is my friend and has been an excellent one at that. He has had two-years to move in on me, if what you say is true, but has not said a word out of place that would lead me to believe he would. I can think of no one else who would be a better escort for me and the children, as I am also terrified of travelling on my own. I know I have Bessie and Mary, but they are women, and as you know, we are not treated as men are. It gives me a certain amount of peace to know he will be with Thomas and Emmy. He always makes sure they have a wonderful time, whatever they do, and will always keep them safe from harm. We need him given Aaron isn't here anymore to do any of that,' I gently tried to explain as she turned to look at me, shame-faced, her cheeks turning pink.

'I apologise for what I just said. It was extremely selfish of me. I wasn't thinking of how you and the twins would be alone with two servants. Both female. Of course, you needed a chaperone. I had not given it a thought, to tell you the truth. He is a good friend to you and a wonderful godfather, which is the only praise I will give the man. I stand by what I said. He has fallen in love with you again. After the way he has treated so many women, including my poor Charlotte, he doesn't deserve a woman like you in his life. That is the honest truth of it and how I feel. He should never have happiness again, and I know if you ever became involved with him, he would have everything he has ever wanted and his life would be complete. I will only ever wish the man ill; however, I will not go on about it as I know it upsets you. There will be many wealthy, eligible bachelors on the ship, and I hope you will give them a chance rather than direct any romantic attention toward him.' She wrinkled her nose in disgust as we finished our first course, the silence between us broken only when Sally arrived with the second.

'I'm not interested in romance with anyone, especially not Hamish,' I replied, cutting into my chicken Cleopatra.

'You must bed someone on the ship. That's the whole point of taking a journey like this. I know for a fact you will have your pick of eligible men the first night you walk into the dining room. You have grown into a beautiful, confident, elegant woman now. You're not that fifteen-year-old child who was forced into adulthood so suddenly. You are more exquisite the older you become. There is a certain sensuality about you in the way you walk and hold yourself. Men notice you. Have some fun, sweetheart. Set your body free and forget about love, and all that's expected of a lady. Grab the first man you are attracted to and bed him. If he's no good at it, pick another until you find someone who makes you sweat and burn. You need to fuck someone; it doesn't matter who it is. Enjoy it, as you won't have to see him again once the ship docks. You are accountable to no one now, only yourself. Don't waste your life, as you are far too lovely to sleep alone for the next seventy-years. Take back control of your own destiny and find some happiness for yourself. You may discover it in the most unlikely of places. This is the start of a new, exciting part of your life. You can no longer look back when your feet are taking you forward—it is the way you must go. If you so choose, you never have to marry again, Abigail. You have more money than any man you will ever meet. I know you are an intelligent woman and will sort out the men who only want to be with you for your wealth. And then there is the small matter of you being the famous Mrs Aaron Cavanaugh.' She picked up her glass and sipped the ruby red wine, then picked up her cutlery to finish her meal, while I exhaled loudly, gazing out over the garden filled with birds scavenging for food.

The attention around Aaron, his trial and execution, as well as every detail of his life, was eagerly sought after by his many admirers. Many still spoke of him affectionately and had turned him into a hero after his death. It seemed people from all over the world knew our story, leaving me uncomfortable. I wished now they would leave him be and let him rest in peace.

'Leo told me the same thing. He's not as articulate or as colourful as you are in how you express yourself, but he meant the same. In all honesty, I don't miss sex at all, I miss having sex with Aaron. My body isn't interested in any form of intimacy with the first man I see. It's like I'm dead inside in all ways, including sexually. I do not believe it will ever come back now he's gone. I always felt there was more than one person on this earth who you could fall desperately and deeply in love with. That it was only a matter of compatibility when you found someone who suited you in every way, but there were a thousand others out there you could be just as happy with. I'm no longer of that opinion. I believe you only get one love and one chance. Once that has been taken from you, you live on as best you can; however, will never find the same happiness again. I used to think differently before Aaron was murdered, but now, I know I was wrong,' I said sadly as we finished our main course. The kitchen staff cleared the table, before Sally came out with a large black forest cake she had made with fresh cherries from our tree.

'Oh, sweetheart. It will come back. I know that much. All it will take is for the right man to touch you that first time. You will know he is the right one to take to your bed by the way he makes you feel. It may take some time, but it will happen.' I cut us both a large slice of cake, and we chatted for the longest time, sipping our coffee while enjoying the dessert. I noticed Hamish walking up from the stables towards the back door and cringed inside. He and Dana would cross paths, whether I liked it or not, as he would be forced to pass us to get to the back entrance leading to the kitchen. He spotted Dana before she saw him, and he stopped several yards away from the table.

'Good afternoon, ladies. 'Tis bonny tae see ye've enjoyed a decadent luncheon, as is the usual way o' it when ye dine with Mistress Abigail. I was wonderin' if ye could spare some time fer me tae have a word with ye, Abigail. Naw rush. When Dana has finished her visit 'tis soon enough,' he said politely as Dana threw her napkin on the table and abruptly stood. Despite ignoring his presence, she was furious, a range of emotions crossing her face, none of them good, as she stared down at me.

'I'm sorry, Abigail, but I will be leaving now. I cannot sit in the presence of a contemptible bastard like this, friend to you or not. I am ashamed to be making such a scene when I have come to wish you well on your voyage, and I apologise. Please remember my advice when it comes to men,' she snapped, glaring across suspiciously at him before picking up her bag, swiftly turning on her heel, and marching towards the front of the house. I quickly stood as Hamish shrugged his shoulders at me, then sat down at the table in Dana's now empty chair. I hurried along the back of the house until I caught up with her near the driveway where her elaborate carriage stood waiting. Her driver obediently remained in his seat until he saw her, then scrambled down to assist her into the carriage. She turned and took my hands in hers, tears in her lovely eyes. 'I apologise again, dear Abigail. When I look at that man, all I see is my daughter and how he treated her. It leaves me wondering what my grandchild would have been like, and what my daughter would be doing now if it wasn't for him storming into her life and taking all he could take, then abandoning her. I hate him, and will never be able to sit in the same room and have him address me as if I am a friend. I try so hard to respect your friendship with him; however, it takes all my strength not to harm him. Many a night I have lain in my bed and thought of the shotgun in my wardrobe and how I would like to use it on him. Please do not think I take any joy from feeling such hate. I wish I was able to forgive and let the past go; however; try as I might, it's not something I am able to do, nor do I believe I ever will. Please be careful around him. Now you are alone, he will do everything in his power to make you his own. That is all I will say on the matter. May you have a wonderful voyage, my darling girl, and know I will be thinking of you. I am aware how difficult this journey will be for you, and when I put my own feelings aside, I am pleased you have Hamish to support you, given he was as close as a brother to Aaron. Please take care while you are away and come back safely to us all.' She embraced me warmly before I stepped back and watched her depart, waving as the carriage turned around in the large, circular driveway then continued down the mile-long stretch, lined in oak trees, to the gatehouse leading out to the main road. Sadness overwhelmed me as I wiped away a tear, feeling confused and wretched, now knowing this was my life.

'What was so important you would risk your life to come within a few feet of Dana?' Hamish grimaced as I joined him at the table and sat back down, cutting myself another piece of cake. Sally had served his lunch outside, bringing a roasted chicken and vegetables out on a silver platter while I was gone.

'Aye, I wanted tae make sure ye weren't backin' out o' the voyage. I know what yer like, an' Aaron warned me ye'd try. He said if Bessie dinnae throw ye over her shoulder an' load ye on that ship, I was tae do it meself.' He chuckled, his mouth full as I smothered a smile, recalling a similar conversation I had with Bessie only yesterday.

'How Aaron was so confident I would agree to take you with us I will never know.' I picked up his cup and took a sip, knowing he took his coffee the same way I did, creamy and sweet.

'He made me promise if ye wouldn't, I was tae book me own passage on the same ship an' go anyway. He dinnae want ye travellin' without a man he trusted beside ye, an' given everyone else is married an' their wives unlikely tae agree tae such an arrangement, I was the chosen one.' He chuckled to himself as he picked up a chicken leg in his large hand and started to eat.

'So, you agreed? To spy on me and insert yourself into my voyage without invitation or consent whether I liked it or not?' I asked incredulously as he grinned.

'Aye. It just made it easier ye wanted me there an' asked me yerself. That alone makes me feel more comfortable tae go, knowin' ye invited me 'cause before I felt I was intrudin' on what would've been such a special time fer ye. I was forced tae listen tae Aaron spoutin' on about this journey fer years, on an' on, never shuttin' up, as usual. That was why I think he wanted me there in the end. I know of all the plans he had for ye an' the bairns, an' what he wanted 'em tae see. He had everythin' mapped out in his head, as ye know. It's bonny tae know I can contribute some o' him tae the twins while we're away. I've memorised what he told me o' certain places he wanted Thomas an' Emmy tae know about. I'll do me best tae make it a happy time fer them, an' I'll support 'em durin' the times they find difficult,' he told me kindly as I felt tears prick my eyes.

'Thank you, Hamish. You're right though. I don't want to go, but I know I must. Who will look after the boys' graves while I'm away?

Who will take flowers and keep the marble clean when the birds shit on it? I know it sounds ridiculous to all of you, but it's important to me.' I wiped tears from my face before shoving another forkful of cake in my mouth.

'I must have the ability tae read minds these days. It's all been sorted. I have yer friends from the village, Margaret an' Jenny, agreein' tae take it in turns each day an' take fresh flowers an' keep the graves tidy. They even promised they'll stay awhile an' visit with 'em. I dinnae want tae leave ye with any excuses why ye couldn't go.' He grinned at me, making me smile. At least I knew my boys would be well looked after until I could get back to them. I knew their souls weren't in their bodies anymore; however, I still felt the need to continue caring for them out of respect that these bodies had carried the essence of people I adored.

'Thank you, Hamish. Have you managed to sort all your business before we leave?' I asked him inquisitively as he cut himself a large slice of cake.

'Aye, all done. Harry, Angus, an' Sean will oversee their own areas. Harry's supervisin' the grooms an' stable hands, Angus, the farmhands, an' Sean's runnin' his team o' gardeners alongside Tommy. Mr Masters will run the house as expected, an' report directly tae Richard. It all seems tae be under control. Richard will meet with 'em once a week tae ensure everythin' is runnin' smoothly in yer absence. I dinnae believe ye have anythin' tae fash about. Weel, other than leavin' Leonardo here tae terrorise 'em all.' I laughed aloud, as did he, the wind rustling the leaves of the gumtree above.

'How is the farm going?'

'Aye, bonny. We have more foals than usual expected this spring, an' the breedin' program is doin' exceptionally well, with Goliath bein' the most requested stud when the wealthy are orderin'. Ye'll see substantial profit in the farm account by early next year.' I nodded, reaching out to pick up a picture from the table that had been left outside to dry. Hamish looked across and raised his eyebrow enquiringly.

'Oh, it's just a picture Emmy painted of the Australian flag with the changes that were made to it last year,' I explained, and he frowned as I shook my head in disbelief. 'How can you not know about your country's flag? They altered it on the 20th of February, 1903. Nearly a year-and-a-half-ago, Hamish. You should hang your head in shame,' I teased as I placed the picture back down.

'Looks exactly the same tae me.' He studied it intently while I finished the last of the coffee.

'They changed the stars of the Southern Cross. Now each one, apart from the smallest, has seven points, representing the states and territories,' I explained as I pointed to each. We chatted for a time about Emmy and her love of painting, and how I intended to take her to Geelong to buy her the art supplies she required to continue to develop her skill when we arrived back in Australia. When what seemed like five-minutes turned into an hour, I excused myself to allow him to return to his work and made my way to my room.

That night as I lay in my bed, a thousand thoughts running through my mind, I eventually drifted off into a disturbed sleep. I dreamed of many things I could not remember the following day, including a king, a rainbow lorikeet, and a pink diamond.

Chapter Seven

THE DAY OF OUR departure had finally arrived, and we waited patiently on Sandridge Railway Pier at the first-class entrance of the ship, ready to embark. We had travelled to Melbourne yesterday and stayed overnight at the Delmont to ensure we did not have to rush this morning. The children were overexcited and could not stay still, while Bessie and little Mary weren't much better. Hamish appeared happier than I had seen him in a long time as they gazed up at the enormous ship, pure excitement on their faces. I seemed to be the only one who wasn't thrilled about this voyage. It had hit me all at once this morning when we arrived at the dock and I realised Aaron should have been beside me and wasn't—and would never be again.

We walked up the platform to the entry door of the ship and stepped inside, finding it even more elaborate than the ship we had travelled on to Australia. Thomas and Emmy gazed around the reception room in awe, their mouths open. Our trunks had been loaded onto the ship over an hour ago and taken directly to our suites by a grey-haired man who seemed familiar; however, I couldn't place him, an unusual occurrence for me.

We were ushered into our suite containing three luxurious bedchambers and several main rooms elegantly decorated. Bessie and little Mary had agreed to share a cabin, as had Thomas and Emmy. I was fortunate to have a room all to myself, while the main suite consisted of a sitting room and a separate dining area, along with a private outdoor balcony where we could take our meals while enjoying the sea air. A large bathroom sat adjacent to the sitting room, a beautiful bath with decadent products to use placed in a basket near the basin. The entire suite was far more spacious and luxurious than I had expected, leaving me feeling extremely spoiled. The suite and ship itself was far more modern and extravagant than the one we had travelled to Australia on, and I reflected how at the time I thought it the most wonderful thing I had ever experienced—comparing this to a hotel that could float while carrying three times the amount of staff required to cater to every want, whim and need of the passengers able to afford such comforts.

Hamish had his own private suite next door; however, I imagined he would be in our suite the majority of the time during the day to spend time with Thomas and Emmy and take them on adventures around the ship. Grief had gnawed at my stomach ever since I woke this morning, and I knew why, as did everyone around me. Aaron lay in the soil of Willow Grove instead of standing among us ready to embark on this journey we dreamed of for so long. I stepped into my bedchamber, a tenth of the size of my own back home, yet it was cosy and welcoming. Comforting even. Lowering myself onto the bed, I lay down to see if it was comfortable and found it to be better than I expected. I stared up at the ceiling for the longest time, holding back tears while memories flooded my tormented mind. Until Emmy knocked on the door, Thomas behind her, calling out to invite me to join them out on the balcony for morning tea. Surprisingly, I accepted.

I strolled into the sitting room to find Thomas and Emmy all alone. After some discussion, I took them by the hand to enjoy afternoon tea outside, while Bessie and little Mary continued to unpack. We stumbled upon the deck by accident, where the staff cheerfully served groups of six to eight ladies sitting at each table in all their finery. I glanced around, feeling self-conscious, then relief washed over me when I saw an empty table at the back. I guided the children towards it while trying not to gain the attention of the women around me. We seated ourselves as a waiter approached and took our order, a young lady with her son pausing at our table to ask if she could join us. She was of a similar age to me, her son possibly a year or two older than my own.

She introduced herself as Maggie Millar, and her son Mark. They lived in Melbourne, and she, too, was a widow. Her husband had recently died, sustaining an injury to his head when he stepped out in front of a tram he did not see until it was upon him. Poor Maggie, lost in her grief, decided to take Mark back to England to escape the memories, feeling she had no one to support her in Melbourne after her beloved's death. She planned to stay with her parents in London for three-months before returning home to Australia. Her husband came from old money and was wealthy in his own right, leaving her a fortune. She no longer spent her time caring for her husband or bothering to run an efficient household, leaving it all to her servants while she took to her bed for a time. Her housekeeper suggested a visit home would be a tonic for her and young Mark to help them get over her husband's untimely death. And she had listened.

'I am also widowed,' I said shyly, and she nodded sympathetically.

'May I be so forward as to ask how he passed?' She was gentle and softly spoken, a true lady, it seemed, by the way she held herself and the quality of her dress, and I saw a kindness in her of the rarest kind.

'My Aaron was executed at the Melbourne Gaol the year before last,' I murmured, my eyes glazed as my mind went back to that morning. She sat back in her chair as if I had slapped her, her eyes wide while her mouth opened and closed several times without a word being spoken.

'I remember you. It was in all the papers. What you went through affected me so very deeply. I sobbed into my pillow at night and prayed every day for you and the little ones.' She opened her handbag and took out a fresh handkerchief, quickly dabbing at her eyes for a moment. 'My husband was furious about the trial and what he saw as a miscarriage of justice. He felt so strongly about it, he took us into the city to protest outside of the gaol in the days leading up to the execution. Very unlike my husband, let me assure you. We were sick in body and mind when your Aaron died.' She paused again, sniffing elegantly while smoothing her perfectly coiffed hair with her dainty hand, every finger adorned in gold and precious stones. 'To then see photographs of you and the children at the funeral procession just broke my heart.' We bonded over cups of tea and cake, the grief of losing our husbands so young, and how fortunate it was to meet on a ship carrying hundreds of passengers, while the children talked. We agreed to meet again at the same time tomorrow before gathering our things and preparing to leave. The golden glow surrounding my new friend had taken me by surprise and left me of the opinion we had met somewhere before.

'Ma, can we go an' explore the ship with Mark? Please? I'll ask nothin' else of ya,' Thomas begged, staring up at me with his father's eyes, the colour of the ocean.

'Do you know how to get back to our cabin?' I asked, my hands trembling slightly at the thought of them getting lost amongst so many strangers who would not care for their safety like I did should they get into trouble or cause mischief, as boys of that age often would.

'Yeah, I think so. If we can't find it, we'll ask someone,' he replied sensibly, while Emmy gazed up at me pleadingly, not uttering a word and allowing her brother to negotiate their freedom. I knew I would have to eventually give them room to take a few steps out into the world without me. As long as they came back after testing it, I was confident I would manage.

'All right, but be back in time to get organised for dinner,' I shouted after the three of them as they ran off before I could finish. Maggie and I laughed as we parted, again promising to meet tomorrow. I knew they were growing and there was nothing to be done to stop it, but they would always be bairns to me. They were not much younger than I was when I took ship from London to Australia, and was swept up in my first romantic tryst. I hoped the same did not happen to Thomas and Emmy. I wanted them to live out what was left of their childhood as children and grow into well-established adults before they made any serious decisions about their lives.

I returned to the suite to find my trunks unpacked and everything in its place. Crossing the room to the wardrobe, I opened the door to look at the dresses, all truly exquisite and so very beautiful. I ran my fingers over the fabrics and textures of the cloth, selecting a gown to wear tonight before undressing and climbing into bed for a nap while the children were occupied elsewhere.

I fell asleep almost immediately, only to be woken much later by the sound of Bessie barrelling into my bedchamber, bright light flooding the room as she pulled the heavy drapes back, then turned to me.

'Mistress, it's not long until dinner and I must make you presentable. Mary and I are going to eat with the other servants, so there will be no forcing me to eat in first class this time,' she grumbled, stopping near the foot of the bed. I smiled at the memory and struggled to my feet, crossing the bedchamber to my private dressing room, where a small table with an oval mirror sat. I slipped out of my nightgown and put on fresh undergarments, then Bessie assisted me into the bronze evening gown I had chosen. Low in the neckline and firm across my waist and hips, the elegant skirt fell to the floor around me, the delicate sleeves the same as the lacework covering my back and shoulders, joined at the bust with a lace rosette. I looked into the full-length mirror, deciding it would do before sitting at the dressing table for Bessie to style my hair and apply face paint.

We chatted about the ship, and the people she had already met. When she had finished with me, I no longer recognised myself. I appeared no different to how I looked all those years ago when Aaron was a free man, long before we lost our boys—so long ago now, back when we attended parties and gala events.

'You look beautiful, Mistress. I don't think any man, single or married, will be able to keep his eyes away from you. I haven't seen you look like this since before all that terrible business.' I rose to my feet, standing still as she dabbed some French perfume onto my neck and behind my ears, sadness in her eyes as she tried to smile. I patted her hand and thanked her before stepping out of the room to enquire if the children were ready. I found Hamish relaxing on the lounge with them by his side, the three of them fixing their gaze on me admiringly as I stood in the doorway.

'Mummy, you look like a princess. All I can say is thank goodness you are out of those black dresses. It was a terrible colour on you.

I have a photograph of you with your hair the same way, all piled up atop of your head with scruffy bits falling down your back and around your face. Do you know the one I mean? It was Daddy's favourite,' Emmy said, standing to embrace me.

'Yes, sweetheart, I know the one. I didn't know you had it, though,' I replied, tickling her and making her giggle. Thomas, much taller than me these days, came to my side and kissed me on the cheek, tears in his eyes.

'This is the Ma I remember. All dressed up like this, an' lookin' so lovely. I remember all the times we'd go to parties at the pub with Daddy, an' you an' he would be dancin' an' laughin' the night away while we pretended to sleep under the tables an' watched ya. Ya look beautiful, Ma.' He placed his hand on my back as he led me over to a seat. 'It's good to have ya back.' He kissed me again as Hamish looked on but said not a word.

'Are we ready to go and eat?' I asked, knowing they would be starving by now, just as I was.

'Yes,' they screamed, so loud I covered my ears, while Hamish promptly rose to his feet, smiling down affectionately at them.

We walked in companionable silence to the dining room, the twins running ahead. Bessie and little Mary had already left to dine with the other staff of the first-class guests on the ship, of which there were many. I hadn't failed to notice the looks and whispers that seemed to follow me wherever I went since embarking this morning, and my children had noticed it too.

We arrived at the frosted glass doors leading into the dining room, and Hamish politely held the door open, following us in to wait at the desk to be escorted to our table and seated. We followed the young waiter across the room, and was ecstatic to find Maggie and Mark sitting at the same table.

'Surely this cannot be a coincidence? If it is, it certainly is a lovely one at that.' I kissed her cheek, a confused smile touching her lips for a moment. I was well aware this was not the accepted practice when greeting each other in public, but Maggie beamed at me after her initial surprise.

'No, it's not a coincidence, Abigail. I requested to be seated with you. I hope you don't mind, as we are travelling alone and have no chaperone. I have not kith or kin in Australia and could find no suitable person able to travel with us, and bringing my servants would only irritate me when we have staff on board. It was so nice to meet you today, and I would truly like to get to know you better,' Maggie said, raising a glass of champagne to her lips and taking an elegant sip, before smiling warmly at me from across the table.

'I am pleased you requested to dine with us. It will be far more fun having you here. The children are already deep in their own conversations and could not care less if we are here or not. I think it's wonderful.' I introduced Hamish as my brother-in-law, causing him to grimace. Another couple soon joined us with their three children, all similar in age to my own.

They introduced themselves as Ronald and Irene Delaforce. They were returning to England after a three-month visit to Melbourne to ascertain if they wanted to start a new life in Australia. They decided after only three-days to purchase land to build a grand house, intending to immigrate as soon as they secured the property on which they wanted to settle. Mr Delaforce planned to breed merino sheep on a large scale, supplying only the highest quality wool to his customers. I was not surprised to hear they had been looking at land around the Geelong area. It seemed whenever I was aboard a ship, I made friends with people who ended up living close by.

They had been looking at a ten-thousand-acre property in Ceres, not far out of Geelong, and had signed a contract of sale only days before departing Melbourne. They appeared to be extremely wealthy; however, I didn't ask how they had made their fortune, feeling it rude. The children were introduced as Ronald Junior, who was fifteen, Hannah, a year younger, and Marianne, just thirteen. Mr Delaforce had decided to bring his family with him to see how they liked Australia, unable to be parted from them for such an extensive time. I found their children to be well mannered, sensible and kind. They had made the decision together as a family to immigrate, and I admired them very much.

Our entrees were served, and we began to eat while becoming better acquainted, the atmosphere at the table friendly and cheerful.

'Hamish, it is very kind on your behalf to chaperone your sister-in-law, given she will be travelling with the children for what will be an extensive period. I'm sure your brother, God rest him, would be extremely proud. I believe you will have a job on your hands, though, keeping the eligible bachelors away from Mrs Cavanaugh on the ship. I do not wish to be indelicate; however, I overheard many a discussion between a number of young men on board the ship today, all on the same topic. Mrs Cavanaugh. Of course, she is a well-known figure; however, that was not what was being talked about,' Ron said, flushing slightly as Maggie giggled, while Hamish narrowed his gaze at me.

'I heard similar discussions among the women. Some are green with envy because of the attention Abigail receives from the male passengers, despite many not setting eyes on her until this evening, thus the reason, no doubt, everyone is watching our table. They have seen her in the newspapers for years and admired her strength and beauty, only now they are excited they have the opportunity to meet her directly,' Irene told everyone as I groaned. I could not think of anything worse than spending my entire time on the ship having strangers approach me, wanting to talk about Aaron. I would not cope under the pressure, feeling so fragile in body and mind. We continued to eat as I became more self-conscious of the stares and whispers directed at our table.

Maggie and I invited Irene to join us for afternoon tea tomorrow, and she graciously accepted. Hamish was unusually quiet, his large shoulders tense as he sat between Emmy and Maggie. I was well aware his usual manner was to charm his dining companions with fascinating tales, while behaving as if they were the most interesting people he knew. More so when one was a widow and available. Maggie seemed overwhelmed by Hamish, her cheeks blushing pink whenever she looked at him. Or him at her. Maybe as the voyage went on, and when he was not so cantankerous and ill mannered, a spark could ignite the flame of love. And they may make a good match. In the short time I had known Maggie, it was obvious she possessed a sweet nature with a friendly and kind disposition, drawing me in immediately.

We continued talking through dinner, and by the time dessert came, the children had made us swap seats with them so they could all sit together. They appeared to be having a wonderful time, which thrilled me and brought me back to my first time on a ship, lovely memories filling my mind.

The orchestra began to play, and a gentleman I had noticed staring at our table since we arrived approached. He was tall and striking, his suit made of the finest cloth, his manner engaging, while the way he walked drew the eye of every woman present. I had seen him once in a dream not that long ago; however, I could not remember what occurred or passed between us, only his handsome face and lovely russet hair.

'Good evening, Madam. My name is Lord Reginald Harrington. I do not wish to sound overfamiliar, but I have not been able to take my eyes from you since you stepped into the room this evening. Have we met?' I shook my head; although I too felt we were acquainted. 'I noticed you wear a ring, and felt obliged to enquire if you are married. I have heard you are not; however, am uncertain what to believe given the gossip that flows so freely on a ship such as this.' He stood over me, smiling down kindly, a heavy silence hanging over our table, while all around us the guests had quietened, their gaze fixed on me, several women whispering behind their hands. 'Are you married?' He raised his eyebrows, appearing amused as my cheeks began to flush, a snigger in the distance as I frowned.

'Good evening, Lord Harrington. I can assure you the gossip is correct this time. I am married; however, I was recently widowed without warning or consent.' I smiled politely, hoping he would return to his table and all in the room would lose interest, yet he remained beside me, a respectable distance between us.

'Splendid. Not the sad news you are widowed, but the fact you are available. My deepest condolences for your loss, my dear. It seems there is nothing to prevent you having this dance with me.' He offered me his hand, while I kept mine clasped in my lap.

'Lord Harrington, I thank you for your kind offer, but I have not danced in many years.' I kicked myself I had not the time to think of a more believable excuse, leaving me flustered. I hadn't given any thought to what I would say if a man approached me to dance, or how I would rebut them without causing offence. All around me watched on, some clearly fascinated by our exchange, including my children.

'There is no need to concern yourself with such trivial details, Madam. I give you my solemn oath that I will take great care of you and return you unharmed to your companions, and I'll say nought if you step on my toes.' He winked at me, then taking my hand in his, led me to the front of the extravagant room, the orchestra playing *Sweet Adeline*. He placed his hand on my lower back, keeping a respectable distance between us. 'You have not formally introduced yourself, Madam.' He stared down into my eyes, his face breaking into a wide grin.

'No doubt if you recognise me from listening to gossip, you well know my name, Lord Harrington.' I smiled as he threw back his head and howled, his deep, musical laughter causing many to stop and stare.

'I do, Mrs Cavanaugh. I must confess, I only became aware a few hours ago you are the great-niece of Lady Isabelle Delmont and felt obliged to introduce myself. My grandmother was a very dear friend to her for many years. Since they were lassies. If I had set eyes on you before I was told of this serendipitous connection between us, I would have recognised you as one Lady Delmont's own without question. You favour her immensely.' I nodded, not surprised in the least after all I had heard from Harry over the years in regards to my aunt—but serendipitous it surely was.

'You met her then?' His eyes lit up, a smile touching his lips for a moment.

'Oh, yes. Your aunt lived at our estate for over a year. I was only a lad of four when she returned from Australia to stay with us, but my memories of her are vivid.' I nodded again, uncertain how to feel about this handsome stranger.

'I never had the opportunity, and it is deeply upsetting to me. On another note, I must apologise for my awkwardness this evening. I have not danced with anyone but my husband in fifteen-years. A terrible excuse, I know.' My nervousness eased a little as he elegantly swept me around the dance floor, his large, warm hand still firm on my lower back, his other holding mine.

'Mrs Cavanaugh, please do not worry yourself. We are family friends now thanks to your great-aunt and my grandmother. They were closer than sisters. I gave you my solemn promise I would look after you, and a man is only as good as his word.' He continued to dance me around the polished floorboards, showing himself to be a gifted dancer, and after only a few minutes, I began to relax and enjoy myself.

'Where are you going, and where did you come from?' His pale green eyes twinkled in amusement and he laughed again, an infectious sound that made me smile.

'You do get right to the point. Blessed with beauty and intelligence, I see. I dared only hope there was such a combination in one woman.' Despite him staring into my eyes, the aura surrounding him took all my attention, the golden glow only I could see radiating from his masculine frame and warming my soul. 'I live in London, and spent most of my youth there, but I have business interests in Australia that demand I travel frequently between Melbourne and my family estate in Scotland. I'm returning to an enormous house where I rattle around alone with only servants to keep me company. Then there is the dreaded fact my dear mother is doing everything in her power to have me betrothed to any young lady with aristocratic bloodlines. No matter how plain, boring and void of any sense they may be. Are you filled with pity for me yet?' His eyes twinkled as I smothered a smile, the candelabras casting a romantic light across the room while I ignored the stares and whispers from those sitting in silence watching us.

'Oh, not a drop. It appears you are in the fortunate position to choose the best wife a man could want.' He shook his head, his face now serious as he continued to dance me around the room, not once missing a step.

'I would rather see a woman across the room and instantly desire her, and on discovering she is as lovely inside as she is outside, fall deeply and immediately in love with her. I want to marry for love,' he murmured, and I felt my heart skip a beat. I had not a clue why I was reacting to this stranger as I was. He was young and handsome—and a Duke at that—but I had nothing to give this man. I felt some sympathy that he felt pushed to marry for any other reason than love; however, he was blessed compared to most. Every eye in the room was on us when the music stopped; my cheeks flushed as I thanked him for the dance and quickly returned to my table.

'Do you know *who* he is? Maggie asked, her eyes wide as she moved her chair closer to mine.

'Only his name. He seems very nice, though, from what I do know of him.' I lowered myself into the chair, relieved to be back at the table.

'He is only one of the wealthiest bachelors in England, Abigail. Lord Harrington owns a number of grand estates and holds several titles to go with it. He is young and handsome. Rare for a man with his money and power. I overheard several ladies talking of the fact he was on board and how they planned to find him and try to catch his eye, but it appears they are far too late and you already have. We all noticed how he looked at you.' She smiled as the orchestra started playing a waltz and Hamish rose to his feet, standing by my side within moments.

'Will ye dance with me, Mrs Cavanaugh?' He offered me his arm, a slight smirk touching his lips.

'Oh, I would enjoy that very much.' He took my hand in his to assist me to my feet when I felt a jolt go through my arm, no different than if struck by lightning in a summer storm. My body became warm and tingly within moments, thus the reason I had refused to let him touch me for so many years. Not even a handshake in greeting. It was only after Aaron was killed I realised I no longer reacted in that way to him, and was able to hold his hand when talking and occasionally embracing as friends. And had felt such relief. I did not understand what had changed, and snatched my hand back from his, my heart pounding hard in my chest. He had touched my arm this morning, and nothing had happened, this change leaving me startled and confused. He stared down at me, confusion in his own eyes as I remained in my seat.

'What the bloody hell is wrong with ye? I'm doin' the polite thing an' askin' ye tae dance, an' ye just acted like me hand's on fire. Hurry an' get yer backside up off that chair as yer makin' me look a fool. All these people here think I'm beggin' ye for a dance, an' yer refusin' me.' He smirked as he took my hand again and pulled me to my feet, our dining companions laughing aloud at him. He led me to the dance floor and took me in his arms, not leaving a respectable distance between us. The urge to climb him like a tree overwhelmed me, bringing Leo to mind. 'Ye look beautiful, Abigail. Every man in the room is starin' at ye. If Aaron were here with ye now, he'd be so proud. An' rightly so,' he said kindly as we continued to dance. Thomas and Emmy beamed at us from the table, and Hamish waved to them. Emmy smiled and blew kisses back to him, while Thomas waved discreetly.

'Would you walk with me on deck once the children are in their beds, just as we once did when we first met?' I asked, and he nodded, glancing at me in surprise. I had no idea what had come over me as I stared up into his brown eyes, the desire to kiss him overwhelming as I summoned all my strength not to. Hamish was my friend, and I had felt no attraction to him before he took my hand to dance. Being back on the ship was obviously reawakening long forgotten memories that were best left forgotten. He held me close against his broad chest, sending waves of warmth through every part of me. The music stopped abruptly, the musicians taking a well-earned break as we made our way back to the table. I breathed a sigh of relief as he returned to his chair, an odd look on his face I was unable to read. I never knew what he was feeling or thinking like I did with my Aaron.

Soon after, when the music commenced once again, a pleasant looking gentleman approached our table and asked Maggie to dance. She accepted, and I watched her cross the room, her arm in his, before gliding around the dance floor. She was petite and extremely pretty, her black hair perfectly styled, while her bright blue eyes sparkled, reflecting her lovely nature I had discovered in such a short time. When she returned, she sat down next to me and sighed.

'He is no Duke like you have managed to catch yourself, but he is a respectable gentleman who I may dance with again,' she whispered, her face positively glowing. I placed my hand on her shoulder and squeezed encouragingly. I knew better than most how difficult it was to return to normal life after suffering the devastating loss of a husband, and I was proud of her. We soon farewelled our companions, while Thomas and Emmy said goodnight to their new friends, planning to meet them after breakfast tomorrow before reluctantly following us back to the suite.

Chapter Eight

Hamish made himself comfortable in the sitting room of the elegant suite, while Thomas and Emmy changed into their nightclothes in their room. He poured us each a nightcap, the twins returning to kiss us goodnight before I tucked them into bed. I joined Hamish, sitting opposite while sipping the ruby red wine from the sparkling crystal glass, enjoying the flavours as they burst in my mouth, tickling my throat as I swallowed, a warmth settling in the pit of my stomach.

'Och, that Lord Harrington's an oily idjit, a real smarmie piece o' work,' he remarked as he poured me another glass of wine.

'What do you mean? He seemed perfectly nice and a genuine type of fellow from the little we spoke.' I shifted in my seat, my arms crossed as he smiled.

'Aye, he's nothin' but a womaniser. Did ye naw notice how he tried tae work his charms on ye? Did it work?' He grinned, passing me my glass.

'Maybe a little.' I laughed aloud; however, he did not, settling back down in his chair and changing the subject. We finished the bottle of wine, and I went to check if the children were asleep. I was reluctant to leave them alone in the cabin without Bessie or little Mary despite their soft snores, and returned to Hamish and opened another bottle of wine to drink while we waited.

An hour passed before Bessie opened the door and stepped inside, little Mary following, both appearing alarmed to find us waiting on them.

'I apologise for my tardiness, Mistress. Did you have somewhere to be?' She bustled around the room, picking up empty wine bottles and corks, her face flushed, while Mary went to check on the children.

'Please don't worry yourself, Bessie. Hamish and I planned to take a walk on deck before bed. We were happy to wait, as long as you enjoyed yourself,' I said, smiling up at her.

'Oh, we did, Mistress. There was dancing and drinking and so many people just like us,' little Mary interjected as she stepped back into the sitting room, her face flushed, her eyes shining with happiness. We finished the wine and Hamish stood to leave, and I quickly followed.

'I will not be long,' I called out and waved, feeling slightly drunk, the door closing behind me as they giggled. We climbed the stairs to the highest deck, as we had done the first night we met so long ago, and sat down on a bench to watch the young lovers share a private moment, unaware of our presence. Feeling relaxed from the wine. I gazed up at Hamish sitting silently beside me, the moon high in the sky, the stars twinkling like diamonds on black velvet.

'What's wrong with you? I'm the one who is meant to be walking about looking miserable. You must cheer up, or I will be forced to change back into black,' I teased and elbowed him in the ribs. He smiled and took my hand in his, a familiar jolt shooting up my arm, spreading warmth through every part of me. 'May I ask you a question, Hamish?' He looked down at me and grinned, the roar of the ocean filling my ears, the waves crashing hard against the ship.

'Aye, o' course. Ye can ask me anythin', Abigail. Ye know that.' Continuing to hold my hand firmly in his, his face showed no emotion.

'What would you say if I wanted to take you to my bed? As my lover, nothing more?' The words tumbled out before I could compose myself, and I felt the heat rise to my face. His head snapped up, his eyes wide as he let go of my hand and turned to face me.

'How can ye ask me somethin' like that, Abigail? I always thought ye were a respectable woman, an' here ye are just offerin' yerself up tae any man like it means nothin' tae ye. I'm astounded ye could even say somethin' like that tae me. An' yer a mother. Ye should be ashamed o' yerself,' he snapped, his eyes now fixed on the yellow moon in the distance, the ocean breeze touching my skin, the taste of salt on my lips. I gazed up at him in silence, realising I had not articulated myself clearly. Trying again as he stood up and walked a few feet away from me, he leaned on the polished wooden balustrade, gazing out over the sea.

'Let me explain before you go getting all Catholic on me. I'm not interested in sharing my bed with *any* man. I'm interested in sharing my body with *you*. I've been dead inside for so long now, and something has awakened in me. I need to be intimate with someone I trust, and you are one of the few men in this world I trust with my life. Most of the others are related to me, married, or only enjoy having relations with other men.' I giggled as he turned and looked back at me, narrowing his gaze and grimacing before returning to my side. He sat back down heavily, staring at me for the longest time.

'So, what yer offerin' me is yer body with naw promise o' love or marriage in the future? Tae call on me when ye feel like fornicatin' an' then kick me out o' yer bed once yer satisfied? I suppose ye also want tae keep it secret from everyone as well?' There was a note of anger in his tone, yet he appeared calm, his voice low.

'When you put it like that, it sounds really awful, but yes, that is what I'm offering you. I would never kick you out of bed.' Smirking to myself, I leaned back on the hard seat, waiting for him to respond. Surprised I had the courage to speak this way, I was well aware the wine had certainly helped loosen my tongue, but in no way made my decision for me. I knew deep down if I thought it through, I would stop anything between us going any further, but I was sick of thinking. About everything.

'I'll tell ye one last time what I told ye the night we guzzled that whisky between us. The night ye can only remember half o', Abigail. I gave ye me heart fifteen-years ago. An' ye still have it. I've loved ye since the day I met ye. When ye left me, I had tae accept 'twas over an' ye loved another. I tried tae let ye go, but there was somethin' that always bound me tae ye. When I knew I could never have ye, I took what ye offered me. Yer friendship. An' I was satisfied with that. 'Till recently. I'll make it clear tae ye now. I want all o' ye. An' I'll have ye eventually, but I'm willin' tae accept any small piece ye offer me. If it's only yer body, I'll take it. Fer now. I'll naw pressure ye, but I'll naw wait forever fer ye tae let me in tae yer heart again. I'll force me way back in if I have tae, whether ye like it or naw. I'll naw lose ye again.' He took my hand again, holding it tightly between both of his.

'Well, I disagree with you. I doubt very much I will change my mind, or want more than I have asked. There are going to be some rules before we do this, as I do not wish to hurt you.' He glanced across at me suspiciously, then stared up at the sky for the longest time before turning his face towards me and narrowing his gaze.

'What rules?'

'You cannot be overfamiliar, and must treat me the same as you always have. Except when we're alone. I do not want you to hold or kiss me after the act itself. I'm not ready for that kind of intimacy. And no talk of marriage or telling anyone about us or what happens in private. Especially the children.' My mind raced as I tried to think if I had left anything out or forgotten an important detail that would protect the both of us, while he slipped his arm around my shoulders to keep me warm.

'Aye, but I believe Thomas an' Emmy would be over the moon with it. Did ye see their faces when we were dancin' tonight?' He stared down into my eyes, the breeze stronger now, whipping around me and causing me to shiver.

'Yes, I did. They looked happy enough; however, I think they are just thrilled I'm out of bed, if I were honest. I do not believe their enthusiasm was due to foreseeing some great romance between us.' I smiled at the recollection while he chuckled to himself, his shoulders relaxed now.

'Am I allowed tae even kiss ye before, durin', or after ye take me tae yer bed?'

'Hmmm, I'm not sure. Can we just take it as we find it?' He nodded, his arm still around me while holding tight to my hand.

'Aye, but what about this Lord Idjit? Are ye goin' tae offer him yer body, too?' I looked up abruptly, and saw the laughter in his eyes.

'Hamish, that's offensive. Of course not. I explained this could only happen with someone I trust. That leaves you. It only makes my decision easier since you are handsome, and have a beautiful body that I cannot wait to get my hands on.' I smiled, and he smiled back and squeezed my hand, wisely remaining silent.

Hamish accompanied me back to my suite, then stepped inside to bid Bessie and little Mary goodnight. They were both getting ready to retire for the night as he sat down on the lounge, while I made myself comfortable opposite him.

'How was your walk?' Bessie enquired, glancing across at Hamish, who was unusually quiet, his face pale, before fixing her gaze on me.

'It was interesting.' I raised a glass to my lips and took a sip of apple juice, finding it tart and causing me to wrinkle my nose. 'Nothing tastes as good as it does at home.' I exchanged glances with Hamish, a slow smile touching his lips before he gracefully rose to his feet.

'Aye, it's gettin' on an' I must go find me bed. Goodnight, ladies. I'll see ye all at breakfast.' He crossed the room to the door and let himself out, taking his hat and coat in hand, the door quietly closing behind him.

I remained where I was, quietly chatting to Bessie and little Mary for a time before saying my own goodnights and heading to my room. Bessie followed me in and helped me out of my gown, then guided me to the dressing table and gently pushed me down onto the velvet stool, taking my hair down pin by pin as I stared into the gilded mirror, my undergarments barely keeping me warm.

'Isn't it wonderful to be out at sea again?' Bessie, brush in hand, stared out of the porthole, the waves crashing against the side of the boat as the steamship glided through the water, barely noticing.

'It is, dear Bessie, and I am so pleased you and Mary are enjoying yourselves. As you may have noticed, the twins seem to have made a number of friends already. I doubt Mary will have much to occupy her time during this voyage. She will be beside herself.' I laughed aloud as she giggled to herself, the brush whipping through my hair before she was satisfied. She plaited my shiny tresses before placing the brush down on the table, then led me over to the bed and slipped a white silk nightgown over my head. I climbed in, feigning exhaustion while settling myself under the heavy quilt to wait for my overly attentive maid and little Mary to go to sleep.

I watched the minutes tick past, the clock on the mantle similar to one in Emmy's bedchamber. It was only when I heard Bessie's muffled snore in the distance, I silently rose from my bed and slipped on my dressing gown. Creeping silently across the sitting room, I opened the door to the suite, then slipped into the hallway, tying the belt of my dressing gown as I hurried to Hamish's door. Knocking twice as I looked up and down the hallway, hoping not to be seen, he swung the door wide and grabbed my hand, pulling me inside before anyone came upon us. Shaking his head in disapproval at my state of undress and disregard of all things proper, he silently took me by the hand and led me to his comfortable sleeping quarters. Smaller than mine, but just as elaborate, he stood before me, fully dressed, his eyes fixed on mine. I felt naked despite my respectable nightclothes, and what was worse, neither of us appeared to know what to do or where to start now we were alone.

'I feel foolish now. Is this something you still wish to do?' I murmured, the confidence and bravado that had filled me only minutes before dissipating the moment I stepped inside, leaving me nervous and full of regrets for opening my mouth when we had danced.

'Aye, I've made up me mind on the matter.'

He took a step closer and paused, then reached up to caress my face with his thick, calloused fingers, his eyes fixed on mine. Slowly running his finger down my neck, I felt shivers go down my spine before he forcefully grabbed me by both arms and pulled me to his chest, his kiss full of desire as his mouth melted into mine, demanding I respond to him. Pulling me down onto the bed, he frantically fumbled with the buttons on his trousers while roughly attempting to pull my nightgown up over my head.

'Stop, Hamish. You need to slow down. We have plenty of time.' I struggled to sit up, pushing him off me as best I could. Distant conversations I had with Tamara came flooding back to me, along with her thoughts on his love making abilities during their affair. I quickly rose to my feet and took his hand, pulling him back up onto his feet. Raising my hands, I slowly unbuttoned his shirt, my lips on his, then let it fall from his broad shoulders and onto the floor before doing the same with his trousers. Once he stood before me as naked as the day he was born, I slipped out of my dressing gown, my nightgown flimsy and a little transparent. He moved closer and kissed me again, gently slipping the thin strap from my shoulder, sliding it down my arm, then doing the same with the other—my nightgown soon dropping to the floor, leaving me naked before him. He took a step back, his eyes glistening as he gazed down at me, my heart beating fast, while I was finding it hard to breathe.

'Yer far more beautiful than I ever imagined. An' I've imagined this moment fer a very long time.' He kissed me again while gently guiding me down onto the bed, then lowered his body onto mine. I shook my head and pushed hard, both hands on his chest as he rolled onto his back before I straddled him, then leaned down to kiss his lips. He slowly sat up, his arms wrapped around me, demanding more with his kiss. Setting my body on fire, I pushed him back down on his pillows and slowly lowered myself onto him. He groaned as he closed his eyes, and I bent forward to kiss him again. Straightening up, I slowly started to move my hips, his eyes fixed on mine while caressing my body with his hands.

I had lost any urge I once had to make love since Aaron was taken from me. However, it was now clear my baser nature and desires had not disappeared but lay dormant when grief sought me out, filling every part of me. Something had reawakened in me , and it took my breath away without warning. I closed my eyes, my hips instinctively moving faster, while pleasure started to build deep within my core, any inhibitions I had now forgotten, along with any guilt I carried for sharing the most intimate part of me with a man I was not in love with. He held my hips firmly, his eyes never leaving me once as he thrust deeper inside me until I could hold on no longer. My body spasmed as I cried out, pleasure pulsating through every part of me. Hamish gasped, then groaned, holding me tighter while his body shuddered. Once it had passed, I leaned forward and kissed his lips gently, my body heavy.

'Thank you,' I whispered, kissing him again before rolling over to my side of the bed. He lay beside me in silence for the longest time, his brow furrowed. I was unable to read him as I once could with Aaron, leaving me uncertain of his mood. 'Are you all right?' I already felt uneasy, as though I had just committed a mortal sin with a family member and had now condemned us both to Hell.

'Aye, far better than all right, but I have tae be honest with ye, Abigail. I'm a bit stunned. Can I ask ye a question without ye takin' offence?' He stared across at me, a sheepish grin touching his lips, while my stomach knotted up as I nodded, unsure if I wanted to hear what he had to say while laying beside him, naked and vulnerable as a newly hatched chick.

'It depends on what you want to ask.' I rolled onto my side to face him, resting my head against my hand.

'Do ye get the same feelin' as a man grippin' every part o' ye when ye bed me? 'Tis only ye seemed tae lose yerself an' naw longer noticed I was here in the room with ye.' I collapsed into giggles, and he smiled, taking my hand in his.

'Yes, I do. And I have some faint memory of you being there, however slight.'

'I've naw experienced anythin' like it in me life. Usually the women who want ye tae marry 'em play hard tae get an' make ye work fer it so ye try tae get their skirts up fast. An' get it in an' over as swiftly as possible. They normally like it tae be finished quick, but ye dinnae?' he asked as I smiled at him.

'No, I don't. You have to learn to slow down a little, that's all. I won't put up with you just sticking it into me for a few minutes and having your own fun and not concerning yourself with my pleasure.'

'Ye enjoy it? Ye truthfully like doin' it?'

'Yes, very much.' I smiled to myself at his complete lack of knowledge about women and their bodies. For a man that had lay with so many, I was more than a little surprised by him. I closed my eyes, luxuriating in the afterglow of my release as he lay deep in thought. He had awoken things in me that had been dead since Aaron passed over, and despite my conscience pointing out I should feel guilty and ashamed, I didn't in the slightest.

'I've never witnessed a lass enjoy fornicatin' as much as ye. Yer the most allurin' woman I've ever seen. I feel as if tonight was the first time I've been intimate with anyone.' He appeared thoughtful as I tried to smother a smile. 'I know I can naw hold ye, but can I hold yer hand instead?' I placed my hand in his, and he closed his fingers over mine. We talked for a time of stuff and nonsense before I sat up, preparing to rise and ready myself to return to my suite. He reached out and grabbed me by the shoulders, pulling me back to his chest before kissing me deeply. 'Yer naw goin' yet. I want tae try that again an' see what else ye can teach me.' I kissed him, letting myself melt into him, and stayed a while longer.

Hamish joined us for breakfast on our balcony. I did not have any feelings one way or another about what we did last night, seeing it for what it was—a physical release between two friends who were lonely and enjoying each other in private. No one else needed to know as far as I was concerned, and I hoped he would keep his word and remain silent.

He kissed the top of Emmy's head and squeezed Thomas's shoulder, then sat down next to me. He glanced at me, lust in his eyes as he said good morning, and I greeted him back as I usually did. The twins were off to meet their friends after breakfast to spend the morning together, and I wasn't sure how I would spend my day, only having woken not a quarter of an hour ago.

'How did you sleep, Hamish, being the first night on the ship and all?' Bessie asked cheerfully as she helped herself to several poached eggs and three rashers of bacon.

'Och, I had the best sleep I've ever had in me life,' he answered, staring across at me as I started to blush. He sent shivers up my spine the way he looked at me now. We finished breakfast, and Bessie and little Mary hurried back into the suite, while the twins rose to kiss me and Hamish goodbye, soon leaving us alone. 'I need ye back in me bed. What are ye doin' this mornin'?' He placed his hand on my thigh, my muscles tightening at his touch, a pleasant sensation running through my body.

'I haven't planned anything yet,' I replied, a smirk touching my lips as his chocolate brown eyes twinkled at me.

'Well, then, lass. I'm happy tae help fill in yer day. Come tae me room after I leave.' He stood up to go, placing his hand on my neck, tickling my collarbone with his thumb as he gazed down at me. I hoped he was seeing our tryst for what it was. I was unable to give him my heart, still so filled with Aaron. The last thing I wanted was to hurt Hamish, now knowing he loved me. He bent down and kissed my lips, despite being told not to kiss me that way, then quietly left the room.

I was reluctant to admit, even to myself, I was enjoying this new aspect of our friendship, and had surprised myself how easily I had taken him as a lover. All my life I had been taught to believe that to lay with a man, you must first love him and be married. It didn't hurt that Hamish was extremely attractive and possessed a magnificent body, along with a ruggedly handsome face. As I knew and trusted him beyond measure, the decision had been far easier to make. I felt comfortable with him having been in love with him all those years ago, and had always felt connected to him due to the golden glow that surrounded his body.

The fact I knew that deep inside he was sensitive and kind, and would treat me respectfully, had been the deciding factor in taking him as my lover. I was frightened of being intimate with men I didn't know after what Maslow had done to me. Thus the reason it had been so important to me if I were to invite a man into my bed, it would be a man I trusted and cared for.

Making love after so long had made me feel in control of my life again, especially my body. I found it exciting and liberating, despite Hamish being an extremely selfish lover. I had refused to let him act in that way with me; however, I could see he was used to having sex purely for his own benefit. It made me wonder how many women out there tolerated this type of sexual partner. Hamish was of the opinion it was normal, and how all his mates behaved as well. I again had thanked the universe for Dana and the fact that I knew better and wasn't one of those women who thought that was how sex was, is, and always would be.

Aaron and I had learnt everything together and had gone on to have an exciting and fulfilling love life. Despite the fact Hamish had been with so many women, I had experienced more sex than he, with Aaron and I making love often. Hamish's sex life had been sporadic, only making love when he could get into a woman's bed for a time. I knew he would sometimes go months without being with anyone. When he had been in relationships that appeared to be leading to marriage, Angelique and Nellie would only occasionally sleep with him when he pushed the issue.

I stood and went to Hamish's suite. No sooner had I knocked on the door, he had me inside and in his arms, his lips on mine in a passionate embrace. He brought out the lust in me, and I frantically pulled at his clothes, stripping the shirt from him within moments. I ran my hand down his chest, muscular and smooth, whereas Aaron had only a smattering of blonde hair across his.

'I can naw keep me hands off ye. Ye've released somethin' in me an' now I cannae stop wantin' tae be with ye. Thank God it was naw like this when ye were with Aaron. I would've cut me own throat.' He unbuttoned my dress, then pulled it from me impatiently before lowering me down onto the lounge. He gazed down into my eyes for a moment, then lay on top of me, pinning me down with his weight, his face only inches from mine. 'I know all about yer rules, an' I have some o' me own. When yer in me bed, I'll kiss ye however I want tae, whether ye like it or naw. I'll talk o' me love fer ye, even though ye dinnae care tae hear it. An' one day, I'll marry ye.' He lowered his head and kissed my breasts, and then my mouth for the longest time, before carrying me to his bed.

Chapter Nine

I MADE MY WAY along the first-class deck to meet Maggie for
afternoon tea, the twins following close behind. Irene had sent
her apologies as she was suffering a headache and had taken to her
bed. Maggie and Mark were waiting for us at the table, and I smiled
brightly as I hurried towards her, quickly sitting down beside her
while the children chatted excitedly.

'I have a secret,' I whispered, my mouth near her ear.

'What is it?' she asked, wide eyed as I discreetly glanced around to
ensure we were not overheard.

'I've taken a lover.'

'Oh my. Really? I knew you would find someone here on the ship
after I saw the way the men looked at you in the dining room last
night, but you work fast, my sly fox of a friend. I was considering
doing the same thing one day when I'm ready. Do you recommend
it?' She raised her cup to her mouth and took an elegant sip, her eyes
sparkling inquisitively.

'Highly recommended. It's not the best lovemaking I've ever experienced, but there is certainly potential.' I smiled at her again,
reaching across to pat her hand as she giggled. The children ate their
cucumber sandwiches, then moved on to the scones while sipping
their lemonade, their backs to us as Maggie and I talked, our voices
low. Not that they paid us any mind being so involved in their own
conversations.

'What was it like after only being with your husband?' Maggie whispered, her face flushed.

'It was different, which is good because I do not want to be reminded of Aaron while doing *that* with someone else. It was like my body had been craving him without my knowledge. At first I thought I wouldn't know what to do with someone else, but once I got over the first few minutes and passion took over, it was like nothing else in the world.' She nodded, her eyes fixed on me, while the children's rambunctious laughter filled our ears. 'It is as though he has woken my body from a long slumber, and now when he touches me even in passing, he sets me on fire. The way he kisses makes me want to crawl inside him and stay there forever,' I said dreamily, reminding myself of Polly when she first met Angus. I cringed and quickly adjusted my thoughts accordingly.

'But you don't love him?' she asked, her face falling in disappointment. I already knew dear Maggie was a romantic and believed in fairy tale endings. Unlike me, who knew better.

'No. I'm not in love with him, but I do care for him.' I realised how horrid this conversation sounded if anyone should hear. 'I'm still deeply in love with Aaron, and I cannot let him go, or allow myself to have feelings for this other man,' I explained as best I could.

'I completely understand, Abigail, and I feel the same way on the matter. I'm lonely now and long to feel a man's touch, but I am completely in love with my dead husband and do not know if I can.' Tears filled her eyes, and I felt my own threaten to spill over, knowing too well the dilemma Maggie faced. By no means was it easy after being so deeply in love with a man, then to wake up one day without them beside you, and to realise they never would be again was soul destroying. To take another man to your bed felt like a betrayal to them long after they were gone.

'I have only done this because I trust this man completely. It wouldn't have happened with anyone else. You will know when it's the right time, Maggie, and who the right person will be to share your body with.'

We chatted about Melbourne and shared acquaintances, the comfortable bond between us growing stronger the more we found we had in common. Maggie had married young like me, and was already pregnant with Mark. After they married and Mark was born, she was the happiest she had been in her life. So in love with her husband and child, she wanted a big family, and although she never had any trouble falling, she had trouble carrying them to term. She had suffered two stillbirths and seven miscarriages throughout the course of her marriage. We talked of the pain of losing a child, or children as it was in both our cases, and how it was a loss you never recovered from, and the grief of losing a beloved husband so suddenly. We held hands as we talked and shed tears together, completely understanding of each other's pain. We soon organised the children as we prepared to leave.

'Ma, can Mark please come to our cabin so we can go explorin' before dinner with the Delaforce children?' Thomas asked. I could see no harm in it if his mother agreed, as it was nice to see them all making new friends and gaining that bit of extra independence away from their parents.

'If it's all right with Maggie,' I replied. They all stared up at Maggie in silence, causing me to smother a smile.

'Oh, all right, go on with you all,' she said, kissing me goodbye and leaving the three of them to me. We walked back to our cabin, the children running ahead, before stepping inside to find Hamish waiting for the twins in the sitting room.

'I'm here tae see if ye want tae go swimmin'? Yer welcome tae bring wee Mark here,' Hamish asked, expecting howls of excitement.

'Oh, no, Uncle Hamish. We would, but we are meeting our other friends before dinner,' Emmy replied, kissing him on the cheek and waiting for my permission to go.

'All right. I know you are dying to be with your new friends so go, but if you are late back to ready yourselves for dinner, I will not allow you to go out again with them in the afternoons,' I warned as they nodded.

'Thank you, Mummy. You're the best,' Emmy squealed, both hugging me tightly. They scampered out of the room as quickly as they could, Mark behind them, waving as they went.

'They really are grown. The first attractive face that comes along, an' they get rid o' ye immediately. Drop ye like a hot potato, an' after all the time an' effort an' love ye put in tae 'em. I must admit, I feel a wee bit hurt bein' dumped like this,' Hamish remarked, his eyes twinkling, a smirk on his lips.

'That is a parent's lot in life, but I now see a godfather gets treated no different. No need to feel special.' I smiled at him as he chuckled. 'They only keep you close while they need you, and then you see them intermittently when they are older. And only then when they need something from you. Then they are gone again.' I laughed aloud as I sat down next to him and patted him on the back. 'They adore you, Hamish, but they are not your wee bairns anymore. Surely you have noticed Thomas doesn't do kisses and hugs anymore with you, and only lets you kiss him on the head when no one but us are around? He is doing that back thumping like Aaron used to do.' I smiled again at his surprise at being passed over for something better by the twins, and how Thomas was turning out to be so much like his father.

'Aye, I know I should be happy fer 'em. I've naw forgotten what it's like tae be their age, but I dinnae realise it would be this hard.' His face fell as I smothered a smile, then thumped him playfully on the back.

'You're as dreary as a winter's day. Cheer up, they will come back when they want something.' I laughed again, and he joined me, before turning to kiss me deeply, pushing me back on to the lounge, his hand on my breast over my bodice. We did not hear the door open, or Bessie and little Mary step inside, until I heard a gasp. I quickly pushed Hamish away and looked up to see Bessie staring open-mouthed at us, while little Mary had turned white and hurried off to her room, avoiding us completely. We sat up and I straightened my hair. 'Sorry, we thought you were going to be gone for a while,' I tried to explain, my cheeks on fire. Bessie stood in the centre of the room glaring down at both of us, her hands on her stout waist.

'Whether I'm gone or not should make no difference. How long has this been going on between you?' she demanded to know, her cheeks now the colour of the beetroot Leo often pickled for us.

'Only since last night, Bessie. I give ye me word,' Hamish replied, his eyes twinkling in amusement as he watched her. Bessie stared in silence at the both of us sitting side-by-side for the longest time.

'I'm going to my room. I have to think about this.' She abruptly turned on her heel, marched to her room, and slammed the door behind her.

'What does she have tae think about? Does she plan tae stop me seein' ye? Stay with ye every minute o' the day so I cannae get ye alone?' He threw back his head and howled with laughter, while I merely shrugged my shoulders as I had not a clue.

'Don't laugh because she could do any of those things and not think twice about it. She will take it out on my hair later.' I grimaced as he chuckled.

'Come tae me room? They know now so it naw matters anymore. The twins have abandoned me an' aren't interested in me company anymore. Ye, as the mother of me godchildren, are now responsible tae entertain me. Blame yer offsprin'. Come with me now before wicked wee Bessie returns tae ruin me plans.' He stared deeply into my eyes, causing me to tingle all over as I giggled. He rose in one graceful movement and took my hand in his, helping me to my feet. I followed him to his suite, and as soon as he closed the door behind us, he took me in his arms, kissing me passionately as he led me towards his bedchamber.

Much later, as we lay side-by-side naked in his bed, each lost in our own thoughts, he turned on his side, his gaze fixed on me, confusion in his large brown eyes.

'I dinnae know if I can do this,' he said quietly. I stared back at him, now feeling confused myself.

'What do you mean? Aren't you having fun?' I struggled to sit up, then turned to gaze down at him.

'Bein' with ye like this, then havin' tae pretend tae everyone else that we're only friends isn't goin' tae work fer me in the long term. I'm just bein' honest. Naw bein' allowed tae want more than this from ye isn't fair, Abigail. I cannae change how I feel about ye. I did it once before, an' I'll naw do it again. Ye cannae dictate tae me how I should feel or behave. I know ye think me stubborn. Pigheaded even, but that is how it is.' He lay unmoving, his hands behind his head as he stared up at the ceiling.

'Well, you cannot dictate to me either, or force me to tell anyone anything about us.' I grunted crossly as I lay down on my back, staring at the ceiling now, too.

'All that I want is tae hold ye, Abigail. I dinnae care who is around, unlike ye. I'll respect yer wishes. Fer now,' he murmured, turning to move a lock of hair from my face with his finger.

'Maybe we should stop what has passed between us. For this to work, you must only want to lay with me, and be able to go back to our friendship the rest of the time. If it's too hard, we can finish it now and stay friends as we have always been,' I said, staring into his beautiful brown eyes that looked back at me so intensely I felt I must look away.

'Naw now. Naw after havin' been with ye like this. Once ye've crossed the bridge, there's naw way tae uncross it.' Circling my nipple with his finger, he continued, his voice low. 'Ye know Aaron made me promise tae fight for ye an' tae marry ye?'

'No. Fight for me against whom? That doesn't make sense. When did he say that to you?' I asked, feeling choked up.

'The last time I saw him. He knew there'd be many suitors knockin' at yer door before he was even in the ground. He dinnae want the types o' men who'd be tryin' tae court a woman newly widowed an' grievin' around his bairns. He said when ye were ready, he wanted me tae court ye an' marry ye. He knew better than anyone how much I'd love ye like naw other an' take care o' ye an' the twins. I dinnae believe him at the time, thinkin' things had been over between us fer so long. It felt wrong tae agree tae be with yer mate's wife when he's the one doin' the askin'. I could naw do anythin' but give him me word as he dinnae leave me any other option. Naw that I would've refused him. Deep inside, I still loved ye. I just dinnae know it. He made me promise him a lot o' things that remain private between him an' me, but one day when the time's right, I'll tell ye.' He gently kissed my neck, sending chills through me.

'First of all, whatever agreements you made between yourselves about me are null and void. It's not for either of you to decide my future. I have told you, I won't marry again and will not be pressured or forced into it, either, so you can get that thought out of your head. Secondly, I will not allow any man to court me, including you,

Hamish. I have already told you what I am prepared and able to give. I cannot do any more than that. I do not want you ever saying in the future I wasn't honest with you,' I told him as he stroked my cheek with his finger.

'Ye'll feel different in time. I'll wait. I've already agreed with yer terms fer now, but I've also been honest with ye. I dinnae want ye thinkin' in the future I've misled ye tae believe I'll give up an' go away when I'm naw needed tae fulfil yer needs. I willnae let anyone else have ye, Abigail.'

'I need to go back and bear the brunt of Bessie's wrath before readying myself for dinner. It's probably better you don't come to the suite until it's time to leave. I cannot promise she will not harm you.' I giggled at the thought of my outspoken maid and dear friend as his face broke into a grin.

'Stay a wee bit longer? We have some time.' He sat up, encircling me in his arms before pulling me close to his chest and kissing me again.

'All right, but only for a bit,' I replied, kissing him back as I ran my fingers through his long, curly hair, soft as silk as it fell to his broad shoulders, and I let myself melt into his arms.

I quietly entered the suite, not knowing what to expect as I carefully closed the door behind me. Bessie and little Mary sat silently on the lounge, side-by-side sipping freshly made tea. I had been there only a matter of moments when Thomas and Emmy ran into the room behind me, their cheeks flushed, their breathing laboured.

'We're sorry we're late, Ma. We forgot the time, an' when we realised, we bolted all the way back from the other side of the ship,' Thomas panted, trying to catch his breath as he leaned on the dining table. I tousled his sandy blonde hair, then turned to kiss Emmy. Knowing full well I would be a hypocrite to chastise them, I smiled brightly, smoothing Emmy's unruly hair.

'Go wash and ready yourselves for dinner,' I said, and they nodded before hurrying to their room. Little Mary rose to her feet and made her way across the room to go and assist them, while Bessie followed me into my bedchamber. An exquisite gown of emerald green, the intricate beading draping over the silk in places, sparkling in the light, was already laid out on my bed. Next to the gown was a beaded hair piece resembling a necklace, leaving me confused as to how it would be attached. However, I had no doubt Bessie would know. She assisted me into the gown, muttering to herself as she expertly secured the tiny buttons at the back.

Once finished, I straightened up to study my reflection in the cheval mirror, admiring Catherine's fine handiwork. She instinctively knew what suited my overly tall frame and liked to dress me in styles that emphasised my bust, waist, and hips. I allowed it despite many of her ladies finding some of her designs far too risqué, but I trusted her completely. If she told me I carried it well and did not look foolish, I believed her and wore the dress with gratitude. Even though she was considered eccentric by her more conservative customers, I believed she was years ahead of her time and would soon be setting the standard for ladies fashion not only in Australia, but around the world. I took one last look at the bodice before sitting down at the dressing table, aware of Bessie's impatience as she waited to paint my face and style my hair. Still appearing far from happy, she took the powder in her hand, grunting to herself as she applied my new cosmetics—compliments of the ship—lightly to my face with a small velvet pad and several brushes. Over the last three decades, most women had come to call cosmetics *make-up*, referring to anything applied to the skin of a medicinal nature, and embellishments such as pastes, powders and paints. Rouge, or blush, came in cream or powder, and lip rouge had become acceptable for women to wear in public and was readily available from the pharmacist or through a doctor without the need to worry of being accused of hedge creeping. Although many of the wealthy ordered theirs abroad, there were versions made at home, some I had heard containing harmful substances, and even the lower classes were known to indulge. I preferred to be fresh-faced, finding my skin felt somehow heavier when forced to wear it, but Bessie insisted I go about looking like everyone else, pale as snow with a hint of blush on my cheeks and lips, while softly lining my eyes with a charcoal pencil. She always ensured she applied it sparingly, aware I did not feel comfortable wearing it at the best of times.

'What is going on between you and Hamish? Do you love him?' I was not surprised by her bluntness, and remained silent as I watched her run the silver brush through my hair, tugging and pulling roughly as she took her frustrations out on my head. I cleared my throat nervously before confiding in her, telling her the truth of what had passed between us as she listened silently, twisting sections of my hair up and pinning it to the crown of my head, while allowing parts to fall unrestrained, curling down to my waist. She gently fitted the headpiece and secured it efficiently, fussing with it far longer than she intended. After what seemed like hours, the silence heavy between us, Bessie sat down next to me in front of the mirror, her kind eyes fixed on mine. 'All I've ever wanted is for you to be happy, and I was witness to that for thirteen-years, Mistress. Then when you lost Mister Aaron, God rest him, I saw you at your worst for two long years. And worried myself sick you'd never recover or ever leave that room again. Aaron was a fine man, a good man, and he loved you well, but he is gone now. Hamish is also a good and decent man and he loves you very much. And that's why I don't believe this arrangement will work when you are not able to love him as he deserves. I *am* happy for you, and I approve to a point, but I think you will find you have unleashed a caged tiger that you will have no control over,' she warned, squeezing my hand. I embraced her tightly before kissing her on the cheek, promising I would take care as I stood to leave.

'I would be lost without you, my dear friend.'

'And I you, Mistress. I have never seen you look more beautiful than you do right now. And at nearly thirty-years of age when many are starting to look a wee bit haggard. Tonight, with them jewels in your hair and across your forehead, you remind me of an Indian princess I once saw in London. You still don't look a day over twenty, you lucky girl.' She smiled to herself, patted my waist, then turned away, nodding her head in silent permission, only then allowing me to leave.

Thomas and Emmy were frantic to get to the dining room to see their friends, both hurrying down the hallway ahead of us while Hamish and I followed, taking our time as we talked of Willow Grove.

'Ye look lovely again tonight. The gowns Catherine made look stunnin' on ye. You've the most beautiful body I've ever seen on a woman.' He glanced across, looking me up and down appreciatively as we continued on towards the dining room, the twins now out of our sight.

'Well, I would feel much sympathy for any man who favoured me in body or mind.' He threw back his head and howled with laughter while holding the door open, politely ushering me inside the elegant room where our new friends waited, while I giggled to myself.

We arrived at our table, receiving a warm welcome from all present. I lowered myself into the chair between Maggie and Hamish, while Ronald and Irene sat opposite to allow the children to dine together. We chatted and laughed all through the decadent meal, sharing stories, old and new, as we enjoyed our meal then relaxed afterwards, sipping wine while enjoying the company and ambience of the room.

'Every man in the room is staring at our table, whether he wants to or not.' Maggie sighed, her eyes shining, her voice low as she leaned closer to whisper in my ear. 'Lord Harrington has not taken his eyes from you since you first stepped into the dining room.' I discreetly glanced across the room to find Lord Harrington walking towards our table, my heart leaping into my throat. I realised immediately, panic rising in me, I must have a reasonable excuse if I were to refuse him, only I had no knowledge of what this surprising man may ask.

'Good evening, Mrs Cavanaugh. You are a vision of loveliness, and I can compare your beauty to no other. Would you do me the honour of walking the deck with me after dinner?' He raised my hand to his lips and kissed it for only a moment. I saw Hamish stiffen; however, he remained silent and straightened up in his chair, watching and listening intently without guilt or shame.

'I am sorry, Lord Harrington, but I am unfortunately confined to my cabin after dinner. I have the children with me onboard and cannot leave them unattended. Their Nanny is out for the evening.' I pointed to Thomas and Emmy, both deep in discussion with their friends at the other end of the table, apologising again as he smiled, nodding his head thoughtfully as he gazed down at them.

'I understand completely, so please make no further apologies. As long as you agree to accompany me another night, I promise to not take offence.' I nodded, his face lighting up for a moment. 'I will be back to ask for the first dance of the evening, if you would be so kind?' I accepted immediately, feeling drawn to this likable chap without reason, while Hamish stared after him as he strolled away, an easy manner to him and a confidence that couldn't be bought or sold.

'Now, Hamish, you cannot be doing that,' I reminded him gently, and a smirk touched his lips before his face broke into a wide grin.

'Aye, I know, but he irritates me far more than anyone I've met in recent times.'

'He irritates you because he is handsome, charming and appears to be a very nice man. Stop behaving so badly or I will move away from you,' I warned as he grimaced, quickly lifting his glass to take a deep drink of whisky. Soon after, the music began, and Lord Harrington crossed the room immediately and took my hand, leading me to the front of the room as the musicians smiled down at us.

'I have been unable to take my eyes from you this evening, Mrs Cavanaugh. I believed last night you were the most beautiful woman I had ever seen, but I was wrong. Here you are again tonight, a vision of loveliness, and you have far exceeded all my expectations.' His deep voice, far deeper this evening than I remembered, calmed me as he spoke in hushed tones while we danced, despite Hamish's stare as he watched my every movement.

'Best not to have expectations, then you will never find yourself disappointed.' He stared down at me, his eyebrow arched as he swept me around the floor. I felt my face start to flush, and swallowed hard, paying no mind to several couples dancing around us. 'Thank you for your kind words, Lord Harrington; however, they are not warranted.' We glided slowly around the floor as more passengers stood up to dance, relief washing over me when I noticed the attention had shifted away from us.

'Not warranted? A beautiful woman needs to be told so every day, and is something to be treasured and cherished, particularly when she has been blessed with intelligence and common sense.' He smiled again, talking comfortably between us while we danced. I enjoyed his company. I found him to be extremely engaging, clever, and he had a kindness about him often absent in many of his class. He had obviously been well educated, sent to all the best boarding schools in England, I assumed. A real gentleman. A Duke who knew how to behave in society, and what was expected of him. Unlike me.

I was well aware every single woman on the ship was making every attempt to gain his favour and attention; however, he had shown no interest. Both nights onboard, he had only danced with me. I certainly found him attractive, and wondered if I had made a mistake taking Hamish as a lover—the situation already proving to be complicated, when I could have invited this handsome stranger to my bed, then left him in England. No harm done. Lord Harrington was the same age as Aaron and Hamish; however, had never been married and had no children. I knew, given his position and title, I was not a suitable woman for him to court. I was a widow with two children and couldn't provide him with an heir. It could never become serious between us, and could only ever go as far as an affair, a temptation easily considered when he was holding me in his arms and whispering in my ear.

He escorted me back to the table, then bent down to kiss my hand in farewell as all present stared on in silence. He bid everyone a cheerful goodnight before returning to his table, often glancing across at me as I gossiped with my friends.

'Oh, Lord Harrington is clearly besotted with you, and how fortunate he is handsome and wealthy.' Maggie lowered her voice, leaning in close to me. 'I heard he gets treated like royalty wherever he goes, and his future wife shall expect, and be given, the same. They say his estates are so large, and his houses so grand, he has a full staff of servants at each residence ready to attend his every whim at all times.' Maggie was unaware how we lived or of the wealth I had inherited;

however, in comparison to Lord Harrington, Willow Grove was a humpy. Maggie seemed to know more about him as each day passed, which surprised me, as I never saw her gossiping with anyone.

'I do not need any of that, Maggie. He is a charming man who is interesting and pleasant to spend time with, but only as an acquaintance, possibly a friend in the future,' I replied, starting to doubt my own intentions.

'Every woman on this ship would cut off their right arm and sack their maids to be in your position, and you do not want him?' she asked incredulously.

'That's right. I'm happy as I am,' I said, sipping my wine.

The evening had come to an end, and we reluctantly stood to embrace before parting. Hamish and I walked the children back to the suite, both saying very little and yawning as we escorted them inside, where Bessie and little Mary were waiting for us, returning earlier in the evening after drinking and dancing with their new friends in steerage. The twins kissed them all goodnight, and I led them into their room and readied them for bed, tucking them in before laying down between them to read a chapter of *Rebecca of Sunnybrook Farm*, a story they seemed to enjoy and only published in 1903. My dear mother-in-law had found the book in Melbourne recently, and purchased it as a gift for them to read on the voyage, the sweet woman—always thinking of others before herself in every situation. Once finished, I kissed them until they drifted off to sleep, exhausted from the adventures of the day. I returned to the sitting room; however, paused in the doorway, watching Hamish.

'How was yer night, ladies?' He sat down opposite Mary and Bessie on the lounge, while both stared at him suspiciously before Bessie caught his eye.

'Better if you would bugger off and go to bed in your own suite. I feel as if I've been transported back fifteen-years to a time when I worried myself sick day and night about what you were all up to. Forced to stay awake half the night while listening for doors opening and closing, preparing myself to catch you in the act. Oh, it was akin to being trapped in a nightmare you can't awaken from,' she complained, sighing deeply as he chuckled.

'But ye never did, did ye? Och, we only did that once.' Her eyes went wide, and I cringed, deciding not to join them on the lounge, sitting instead at the dining table as I listened.

'You wee mongrel. Are you telling me you had relations with my Abigail before she married Mr Aaron?' Little Mary blushed bright red as she glanced over at me before quickly looking away, while Bessie appeared ready to erupt like a volcano—just as angry as Mount Pelee when it destroyed Saint-Pierre in Martinique on the 8th of May 1902, causing the death of 33,000 innocent souls—although I was certain Bessie was far more fierce. It was said there had been only a single survivor left in the town, a prisoner held in an underground cell. There were others who lived on the outskirts of the city and some who had escaped by sea, but again, I found Bessie far more frightening. I could hear Hamish laughing loudly, and fought the overwhelming urge that came upon me to strangle him with my bare hands.

'That's naw what I'm sayin' at all, Bessie. I admitted tae sleepin' in her bedchamber only the once, an' nought about relations o' any sort, ye dirty minded wee deviant. Trust ye tae think about fornicatin' constantly. Yer worse than Leo, turnin' every conversation back tae what should only be spoken o' in private. Ye wanton wee trollop,' he teased, his eyes sparkling mischievously as she stared back at him, her mouth opening and closing, not a sound escaping from her lips.

'Bessie, it was all very innocent, so you can take that look from your face before the wind changes and you are stuck looking sour for the rest of your days. It was sweet and pure compared to what we're doing now. He is just teasing you,' I called out, rolling my eyes while Hamish continued to laugh uproariously.

'Ohhh, you shite. Stop misbehaving. I thought I would be getting a rest, but I think you have been spending far too much time in the kitchen with that wicked Leo and he's rubbed off on you. Now you are just as irritating. Stop walking about like the cat that got the cream just because you finally bedded her. You should hang your head in shame. Everyone that looks at you together will know. And with you meant to be her brother-in-law and all. It's disgusting is what it is. I'm warning you now, if anyone finds out what you two are doing in secret, there will be a scandal. I won't put up with it. The Mistress has been through enough, having her private life again spread out all over the papers for everyone to see and gossip about. She is known now by strangers, and I would hate for anything further to be printed of her private life. Especially now with you in her bed.' She sighed deeply as she struggled to her feet then made her way towards me, leaving Hamish and little Mary together.

Within moments, little Mary had excused herself and gone to bed, clearly mortified by the conversation. She had been waiting for an opportunity to retreat to her room since Hamish first opened his mouth, and found it as soon as Bessie left the room. He made himself comfortable on the lounge as Bessie glared across at him through the archway connecting the two rooms, before fixing me with a stare; her hands yet again on her hips. I rolled my eyes and sighed deeply, preparing myself to hear how wicked and sinful I was.

'I think it's time, Mistress. Hamish needs to retire to his own suite and allow me to ready you for bed. I have drawn your bath, and unless he plans to come in with us to wash your back, I can't see the point in him staying any longer. You are still my responsibility, even more so now Mr Aaron is gone. Until you find another husband, and from what you tell me, that will never happen, you are stuck with me. Are you going to ask your secret lover to leave, or will I?' She stood her ground, her eyes locked with mine, silently challenging me to disobey her. I could hear Hamish chuckling as he stood, then hurried to my side, wrapping his arm around Bessie's neck in a surprise attack. She tried to get away, but he held her tightly and pulled her towards him, bending down to kiss her on the top of her head where she stood, an entire foot shorter than he. I laughed as she muttered under her breath before he released her. She playfully smacked his arm before moving towards my bedchamber door.

'I'll leave ye tae bathe. Dinnae be long as yer secret lover will be waitin' in the other room. A room Bessie has naw jurisdiction over,' he called out, teasing her before kissing me gently on the lips. Bidding her goodnight, he took his leave and headed to his own suite. There was no point hiding our affair in front of them now given Bessie and little Mary knew. I had sworn them to secrecy, and they had given me their word they would not tell a soul.

I followed Bessie into my room, then stood for her as she helped me undress and took the pins from my hair, brushing the tangles out before leading me into the bathroom. Shortly after, I emerged from my warm bath dressed in my nightwear and dressing gown, my wet hair wrapped in a towel.

Kissing her goodnight, I stepped out into the empty hallway, then silently made my way to Hamish's suite. He had left the door unlocked, and I crept inside unnoticed before hurrying to his room and slipping into bed beside him.

Later, as I lay naked on my side of the bed, I drifted off into a deep sleep, dreaming of a tunnel, Aaron and an echidna.

Chapter Ten

TIME HAD PASSED QUICKLY, and after a fortnight on the ship, I had found my sea legs and was thoroughly enjoying the journey. Thomas and Emmy had made firm friends with the Delaforce children and Mark, Maggie's boy, and were far too busy to entertain their mother. I believed we were destined to meet, and felt it almost serendipitous to have been seated with them our first night onboard the ship, and strong friendships had formed. We all got along famously, and felt as if we had known each other for years, drawing us even closer given our children were around the same age.

Hamish and I had continued our secret trysts, and fell into bed together at every opportunity, often several times a day. Given the twins had jumped from the nest and seemed to have flown away, only reappearing for sustenance when it was time to eat or sleep, we had more than enough hours to fill. They would rise each morning, take breakfast with us, then disappear until midday. Returning only to partake in the decadent luncheon in the dining room as a family, with their new friends in tow, they'd soon disappear the moment they finished eating. Gone for the rest of the afternoon, they would return briefly to the suite to ready themselves for dinner. I was thrilled they were having such an exciting time, and had found a little independence being free to roam the ship as they wished.

Hamish had proven himself to be an enthusiastic and capable lover, who was more than eager to learn. It had taken us some time to get into rhythm with the other, but I was presently having sex that made me sweat and burn, and I felt like a woman again. Hamish had restored in me a confidence that I had lost, although there were times when he would break the rules, often resulting in me pushing him away and causing hurt feelings. I knew he was a jealous man, and he often became upset when I would dance with other men after dinner, but as Bessie had explained to him after becoming tired of his constant complaints, I was forced to keep up appearances to protect my reputation. If anyone knew of our affair, I would be disgraced. It would become even more of a scandal since most believed him to be my brother-in-law.

The children and I would meet Maggie and Irene and their children every afternoon for tea, and the three of us had become great friends. Our children had become close, spending their days together having fun wherever they went on the ship. I was certain they were getting up to mischief, as six young ones left without supervision were prone to do, but had no evidence of it yet, and no one had come to me with any complaints.

I shifted in my chair at the table, the balcony quite chilly this morning while waiting to start breakfast. Within moments, Hamish strode in, bending down to kiss Emmy on the top of her head before tousling Thomas's sandy blonde hair, then as he walked past me, he discreetly placed his hand on my shoulder and squeezed gently.

'Good mornin'. What's on yer busy social calendar taeday?' Hamish grinned down at the twins before seating himself down next to me and serving himself from the platters.

'We've all been talkin', Uncle Hamish, an' we've a favour to ask of ya,' Thomas said, his expression serious as he looked up at his godfather.

'Aye, go ahead, lad. I'll help ye if I can,' Hamish replied, shoving a large forkful of Spanish omelette in his mouth, then chewing thoughtfully as he waited.

'We were all talkin' last night at dinner when we were watchin' ya dance with Maggie, an' Ma was dancin' with that rich bloke. I remembered how Ma told us a long time ago when she met ya on the ship she couldn't dance for quids, an' ya taught her. Now she's a beaut dancer, an' we were wonderin' if ya could give us lessons so we can dance together, too?' Thomas continued to stare up at him, while Emmy pleaded with her godfather. Hamish sat unmoving and silent, while pretending to think long and hard about their proposal.

'I'd usually agree tae it, but alas, I've naw partner tae dance with meself. I'm unable tae help ye despite wantin' tae.' His face fell in exaggerated sadness, his eyes twinkling as I silently groaned.

'What about Mummy? Oh please, Mummy, would you do it so we can all learn how to dance as well as you and Uncle Hamish? Please, please, Mummy, we will love you forever,' Emmy begged, and Hamish smiled. How could I say no now and disappoint six little people? And he knew it, the devious bastard.

'Of course I will. I would just adore it.' I smiled brightly at them, then gave Hamish a look often passed only between a husband and wife, infuriating me as a wicked smirk touched his lips.

'Aye, it's agreed then. We'll start taeday an' meet ye in the music room after mornin' tea,' Hamish told them, his brown eyes twinkling.

'Thomas only wants to do it so he can hold Hannah in his arms and make ga-ga eyes at her,' Emmy piped up, making kissing noises on her arm while Thomas blushed.

'Don't tease your brother. It's unkind and does not become you, Emmy.' I gave her a stern stare before turning to gaze at my son, who was becoming more and more like his father each day. Emmy chose to continue eating her breakfast in silence, and I silently agreed with her wise choice. The moment they finished, they hurried to my side to kiss me and Hamish before running out the door, leaving us alone. Bessie and little Mary had taken their breakfast earlier, and were nowhere to be found. He leaned back in his chair, appearing proud as he stared after them, a gentle breeze coming off the ocean touching my skin.

'Sounds like wee Thomas has caught some feelin's fer the lass,' Hamish remarked. He smiled sympathetically and I smiled back, feeling mixed emotions start to well up inside, hurting my chest.

'Oh, I wish Aaron were here to talk to him and give advice on how to treat girls respectfully. The last thing I want is for Thomas to turn out to be one of *those* men who use women for their own purpose, then discard them without thought or concern. No offence meant to you. I want him to be with someone for love and love alone, and to be a good and decent man in every aspect of his life.' I raised my hand and placed it over my heart, wishing for the millionth time Aaron was here with us and experiencing all the cherished moments as his children grew into adulthood. To be here to guide them as only he could.

'Dinnae be sad, Abigail. Here, in this present moment, is the time tae be happy an' enjoy the journey. Remember that feelin' when we first met? The excitement an' innocence o' yer first love? I'll talk tae him if ye like? I know what Aaron would say if he were here right now?' he offered kindly as I continued to eat.

'Thank you, Hamish. That would be special, and very much appreciated. I cannot talk to him like a man would. I know he is close to me and tells me a great deal more than other boys his age; however, it's not the same as having a father. Or a godfather to talk of subjects he may be too shy to discuss with me.' I placed my hand on his as he gazed down into my eyes, a loud thump startling me as Emmy burst through the door and ran back out onto the balcony.

'I forgot my coat,' she said breathlessly, making her way across the room to find it hanging on the back of the chair where she left it. Suspicion crossed her face as she looked from Hamish to me, then back again, noticing immediately how close he was. I wanted to kick him under the table as I slipped my hand away from his and picked up my coffee. 'What are your plans for the morning? Please don't get caught up doing other things and forgetting about our dance lesson,' she called out over her shoulder as she turned to leave, coat in hand.

'Nothin' planned, Emmy, so ye dinnae have tae fash about me forgettin', lass. We'll be there,' Hamish promised, and she turned back for a moment to beam at him, her eyes shining.

'Well, I hope you find something fun to do. And thank you, Uncle Hamish. You are always there for us and we love you more than chocolate,' she sang sweetly before running out the door.

'It's an honour an' a privilege. An' I'm sure we will, Emmy,' Hamish called after her before rising to his feet and taking my hand, his face breaking into a beautiful smile as he led me to his cabin.

We were greeted by six over excited young souls the moment we stepped into the music room, their cheering floating out onto the deck. All the memories from when I was fifteen came flooding back as I gazed around the room, not so different from the one we had danced in on our journey over to Australia. I had not known then what awaited me, and did not realise at the time Aaron was waiting on shore and would turn out to be the only man for me—or he was the only soul who could ever have stolen my heart from Hamish. I had believed without doubt I would be with Hamish forever, and we would marry once we had settled in our new homeland. Life had certainly not gone the way I expected it to in so many ways. Now I was alone again and returning to the place I had left behind so long ago, and I was convinced I would find no joy or contentment in the future. I felt I had already lived a lifetime of happiness that was now over, blessed beyond measure to have enjoyed a loving and blissful union with a man whom I adored. A man I loved more than life itself and could no longer have.

Hamish decided to teach them the waltz first, just as he had done with me all those years ago. I sat down on the lounge beside them as they all waited to begin, several fidgeting and unable to hide their excitement. They seemed to have forgotten we required music, and groaned when told to be patient while we waited for the pianist Hamish had requested to arrive. Hamish made himself comfortable on the chair next to Thomas, Hannah sitting quietly beside him. I could see why my son was drawn to her as she was a sweet girl, and extremely pretty, her golden blonde hair and petite figure attracting a great deal of attention from the young boys on board.

The pianist strolled through the door, then paused in surprise and threw back his head and laughed, as did I—my arms open wide as I crossed the room to embrace him. He remembered me immediately and embraced me back warmly, before Hamish shook his hand, speaking with him in some detail of what had occurred since we had seen him last, albeit very briefly. The young ones were becoming agitated, watching us idly gossiping with him while they remained on the lounges, their impatience obvious.

'How is me dear Bessie? Is she still in service with you, Miss Delmont?' he asked politely, his weathered face breaking into a toothless grin. He had aged dramatically in the fifteen-years since we had last seen him, and time had not been kind; however, much of that had been self-inflicted from what I could tell, his nose bright red and his breath still stinking of rum at this hour of the morning.

'Oh, it's Abigail Cavanaugh now, Jimmy. And Bessie is well. Of course she is still with me.' I smiled at the thought of her before continuing. 'Even if no longer in my employ, dear Bessie would still be my close friend and live nearby. She is actually here with us on the ship.' His eyes widened, as did his grin, while I heard several impatient grunts coming from the corner of the room where my offspring sat rolling their eyes with their friends.

'I would very much like to see her. Do you mind asking her to meet me in steerage this evening?' He nodded politely before slowly making his way over to the piano to take his place, the sudden outbursts of cheers and clapping startling me for a moment as the young ones jumped to their feet.

'It would be my pleasure. I know she will be delighted to see you again. We often wondered what became of you, and spoke of you from time to time over the years. The last we knew, you planned to jump ship in Melbourne and settle in Geelong,' I reminded him, and he shook his head, a gentle smile touching his lips as he reminisced.

'I had every intention of taking that road, Mrs Cavanaugh. When Bessie announced the night before we arrived that she was choosing Danny, I felt I'd be wasting me time.' His face fell and sadness crossed his eyes, while I swallowed hard, unsure if I should change the subject or continue until he broke down in tears in front of the children.

'Well, I hope the road you did choose led to much happiness.' He shook his head again, his shoulders slumped as he prepared to play, his withered fingers tinkering at the keys.

'I've stayed on the path I was on doing what I know. There's some happiness in it, I suppose. I have a warm bed and food in me stomach each night, with a small wage to spend when in port. It's enough for me 'till I meet another Bessie.' He smiled weakly, dismissing me with his hand, and I felt dreadfully sorry for him. His life would have turned out so very differently had Bessie not decided on Danny, who I still believed was the better choice. He made Bessie happy every single day since they first met, and loved her well, and they were still deeply in love.

We soon started the lesson, with Hamish showing the boys how to hold their partner by taking me in his arms, teaching them where their hands should be and the appropriate distance they must maintain to avoid a scandal. I smiled to myself as he held me at a respectable distance for the first time since we had been on the ship.

Jimmy started to play, while Hamish held me in his arms and we slowly demonstrated the steps. They copied us to much hilarity, stepping on each other's feet multiple times, but within half-an-hour, several had perfected the waltz. Emmy was a natural, and danced with Ronald Junior, who was nearly as good, while Thomas was doing quite well, although he was a bit stiff, leaving me pondering if his awkwardness was because he was not naturally gifted or a result of Hannah being so close. Mark and Marianne were struggling to keep up with the others, missing steps and standing on each other's feet. Hamish noticed and called them over to dance next to us. He patiently went over the steps again, slower this time, and persevered until they were able to dance adequately enough. Hamish finished the lesson soon after, and they thanked Jimmy before huddling together out on the deck, preparing to go to luncheon in the dining room. We followed along behind them, talking as we went.

'They did well fer their first lesson. Emmy is the spit o' ye, Abigail. She only has tae watch fer a few moments an' knows the steps by heart, naw tae mention she's been blessed with the same ease o' movement. God help us all when the local louts start knockin' on the door. They'll have tae deal with me as her godfather, an' thank the Lord above they dinnae have her father here as well. He'd be far more ferocious than I. 'Tis obvious Thomas is besotted with wee Hannah. Ye can tell by the way the poor lad looks at her. Similar tae how I look at his mother.' He chuckled to himself as he walked beside me, now a respectable distance between us so as to not give us away to those who believed him to be my brother-in-law.

The children had already run ahead to the table before we even stepped into the dining room. We made our way across the room to where they waited for us with our new friends, a hundred different conversations going on around us. The room was one of the most extravagant I had ever dined in, the chandeliers above sparkling down over the expansive room filled with expensive furniture only seen in the grandest of homes. The heavy drapes were now parted, letting in the sunshine, while candles lit every table in the evenings, filling the room with a romantic ambience not often found even in the finest of hotels. I lowered myself into the chair between Irene and Maggie they had saved especially, noticing immediately both appeared relieved to see me.

'We heard a rumour this morning that you need to know about.' Maggie leaned closer and lowered her voice, while Irene glanced around the room suspiciously to ensure they were not overheard. 'We were walking on deck and passed by a group of young ladies taking morning tea while gossiping loudly. They were complaining and whining, but it was only when we heard your name mentioned that we took the table next to them and sat down to listen.' I nodded, waiting for Maggie to continue; however, she picked up her glass and took a long sip of wine. Irene smiled before lowering her voice.

'It seems they are all in a tizzy because Lord Harrington has made his intentions clear. He has firmly stated several times while in the company of the gentlemen on board that he is not interested in seeking female attention. Other than yours. Apparently, he has every intention of inviting you to his estate once we arrive in England. There is even some talk that he is determined to make you his wife,' Irene interjected, her face glowing, her eyes glinting mischievously. I swallowed hard, my cheeks becoming warm. I noticed Hamish grimace while he served himself green beans from the dish the footman standing by his side offered, before politely moving on to Ronald.

'Mind you, all the available women on this ship despise you intensely now. Even the married ones are keeping their husbands close when you walk by. I don't believe you will be making many friends on this voyage, Abigail,' Maggie teased, a smirk touching my lips as Hamish grimaced again.

'Oh, pay it no mind, dear friend. You will always have us,' Irene said, louder than necessary, clearly not bothered by what anyone thought of me at all. I had become close to both of them, confident since we first met I would disembark in London alongside two very dear friends I could trust and confide in without fear of judgement or betrayal.

We enjoyed our luncheon, chatting companionably while our children excitedly discussed their plans to get up after dinner tonight with the adults and dance. I remembered the first time I waltzed with Hamish in the dining room, and how nervous I had been. He had held me so formally, just as nervous as me, I had found out years later. I wondered if Emmy and Thomas would experience that same feeling tonight, and I smiled to myself.

'I must go, but I will see you both at afternoon tea,' Irene promised as she stood, bidding us farewell before hurrying away, leaving her children at the table to spend their afternoon as they wished.

'I love Irene dearly, but I cannot speak openly in front of her about the subjects you and I sometimes discuss, Abigail. Not about what happens in the bedchamber.' Maggie blushed, and I placed my hand on hers.

'That's only because you do not know her well enough yet. She is a very open-minded woman and possesses a wicked sense of humour that is so unexpected. It takes time to build trust with new friends, but that sorts itself out in time. It will happen.' Her face deepened to a mottled purple, and I patted her hand, uncertain if she was unwell.

'Yes, I suppose everything takes time.' She rolled her eyes before continuing. 'I am in need of your advice, and am seeking your opinion on the matter. I'm considering inviting Hamish into my bed. What do you think, as you know him best?' she blurted, startling me for a moment. I was unsure how to respond; however, I was acutely aware I had no claim to him, just as he had nought on me.

'I think you should do what feels right to you.' Hamish was big enough and ugly enough to make up his own mind on what he wanted to do once she approached him, and I closed my mouth given it was none of my business.

'I find him to be the most striking man on the ship, and far more handsome than the men I have seen in the magazines, but Lord Harrington comes close. Hamish is such a gentleman, and so charming when we dance together in the evening. I'm considering whether to ask him to walk on deck with me tonight so I can declare my intentions, or wait until he asks me.' I nodded, watching him closely as he spoke with Ron about the price of Australian wool.

'If that is what you want, Maggie, then that is what you should do.' I turned my attention back to her, then picked up my glass to take a deep drink of ruby red wine.

She talked of Hamish for a time, as dreamy eyed as Polly had once been, while noting his finer qualities, all of which I was more than aware of since our first night on board. Our luncheon had come to an end, and the guests had started to leave the dining room, while our children had already run off to explore the ship. Hamish and I stood to take our leave, bidding Maggie and Ron farewell and promising to continue our conversation this evening.

Hamish and I took our time as we made our way through the hallways and back to my suite, talking companionably, although he stayed far too close for my liking or comfort.

'Did ye see how nervous Thomas was today with Hannah? It reminded me o' what I meself was like the first time we danced. I thought fer certain ye could feel me hands shakin' when I held ye fer the first time. Ye were the most beautiful girl I'd ever seen in me life. Ye still are,' he said softly as we passed several other first-class passengers near the stairwell, paying them no mind.

'Please stop, Hamish. Someone may hear you speaking all sweet to me. When you talk to Thomas, would you please remember to tell him that girls are just as nervous as boys? I worry he doesn't realise that, given we are expected to raise our boys to only show the strong side of themselves. They are expected to know what to do when it comes to love but they are just as clueless as us. Girls feel just as shy and nervous, not to mention awkward and embarrassed. Always worrying they will make a fool of themselves or say the wrong thing,' I remarked as we arrived at the door of my suite.

'Are they really?' He seemed surprised as we stepped inside and made ourselves comfortable on the lounge, his arm soon around my shoulders. He kissed me gently on the forehead before taking my hand in his.

'I was, and I still get nervous when I dance with someone new,' I replied, smiling as he gazed down at me.

'Aye, ye've been doin' a lot o' that lately. I heard a rumour taeday about yer Lord Harrington.'

'I have already been told, so there is no need to go on,' I replied sharply, his grip around my shoulders tightening protectively.

'I'll naw allow another man tae court ye like I did with Aaron. I'll never make that mistake again. O' course I get jealous, Abigail. I know there are far better men than me out there who are seekin' yer attention. He's a Duke, fer Christ's sake. How am I meant tae compete with a man who owns half o' England an' has every woman in Australia seekin' him out fer marriage?' His voice shook with emotion as he placed his finger under my chin, raising my face to look at him before he kissed me. In the exact manner I had warned him not to. I pulled away after a time, settling my head back onto his shoulder.

'Oh, Hamish. Pay it no mind. You have nought to worry about given I have all the money I will ever need. I'm happy with how things are now. The last thing I'm looking for is marriage. Or to catch feelings for any man. I want to concentrate on getting my life back in order and on my children's happiness. I have no intention of marrying Lord Harrington. Or anyone else in this lifetime. I love you as my friend. Now we are lovers, I feel even closer to you. I have no intention of being with another, at this time. If that is what bothers you.' Taking his hand in mine as he stared down at me, he narrowed his gaze before grimacing as if in physical pain.

'At this time, Abigail? Ye ask a lot o' me, I'm tellin' ye. I'll wait however long it takes fer ye tae let me back in tae yer heart, but ye'll marry me one day. I'll naw stand fer ye sleepin' with other men, so get that idea out o' yer head. I dinnae care how much time must pass before I have ye as me wife. I'll naw risk losin' ye again tae another bloke.' I saw the hurt in his eyes and stood to lead him by the hand into his suite, hoping to reassure him once again of my feelings, and this time ensure he believed me.

Chapter Eleven

I HAD JUST RETURNED to my bedchamber when Bessie burst in, appearing flustered as she dashed around the room.

'You're late again. You must return earlier than this, or I end up in a bother. I understand Hamish races you off every chance he gets, but he is throwing out my day because of his filthy urges. I am in a routine and he has messed it up every single day since we came onboard with his late afternoon demands of you. You need to speak to him before I do if you do not wish me to say my piece,' she warned before helping me undress, then assisting me into a sparkling brown evening gown.

'And since when has that ever stopped you? It's not all his fault. It was late, and I fell asleep. I will make sure I am back from now on when you ask me to be,' I replied apologetically. She smiled affectionately at me before sitting me down at the dressing table to fix my hair, telling me of a new style she had learnt from another ladies maid and planned to practice on me tonight. I told her about our encounter with Jimmy earlier in the day, leaving her stunned when I informed her of his invitation.

'I would like to see him, but only if you come with me,' she replied, and I enthusiastically agreed. I had adored steerage the first time, no doubt I would enjoy it again. I knew for certain accompanying her to a part of the ship where first class passengers were not welcome would ease my homesickness for Willow Grove—the people and the music similar to the pub in the village. 'Many of the servants onboard tell me their Mistresses are green with envy over your wardrobe and the way the men look at you, and the married ones are enraged you have caught the attention of their husbands. I'm sorry. Mistress, but you are not well liked by any of the ladies on the ship. They infuriate me, and I feel like booting them all up the backside. If they only knew how sweet and lovely you are instead of focusing on how you look, they would realise they had nothing to fear from you. I have never seen you behave inappropriately towards another woman's man. Well, not with any men as you married Mister Aaron so young.' She applied lip rouge, and once satisfied my face was perfectly painted, picked up the brush and started on my hair.

'Please do not fash, Bessie. It does not upset me, nor should it you. These people are strangers to us, and will likely remain that way given how nasty they are.' She nodded, then touched the back of my head, indicating she had finished. I stood, embracing her before stepping into the sitting room where Hamish and the twins waited for me.

'Oh, your hair looks beautiful, Mummy. I adore how Bessie makes you look when she dresses you up in Aunty Catherine's creations,' Emmy called out from where she sat next to her brother. I smothered a smile at her reference to Catherine's dresses. She idolised her godmother and Catherine could do no wrong in her eyes. Emmy admired her strength and independence while appreciating her kindness very much. Often speaking of how her godmother was an inspiration to her who encouraged and supported her own creativity, her face lit up when in the company of my dear friend.

'When you are older, you will have help to style your hair, too, Emmy,' I said as she beamed up at me. I planned to employ little Mary as Emmy's ladies' maid once the twins turned sixteen. They were becoming too old and independent to have a Nannie, but they loved little Mary so—and her them—and I did not have the heart to take her away from them.

We crossed the dining room, quickly finding our seats at the table and greeting our friends. Hamish chose to sit in the chair next to mine, surprising given it was his usual habit to take the chair opposite and allow Maggie and Irene to sit beside me. Tonight, they huddled together to the right of me, both waiting to speak further of the gossip aboard the ship. Clearly still excited about Lord Harrington, they stared across at his table, the elegant ladies seated with him trying everything in their power to gain his attention. He caught me looking over at him and grinned broadly, ignoring his dining companions. Rolling his eyes, he feigned boredom while discreetly pulling faces at me. He was certainly a handsome man, and he had a way about him I found extremely attractive. Highly intelligent, warm and friendly, with a quiet confidence I admired. I smiled back at him and waved discreetly, and he raised his hand and bowed his head in acknowledgement, appearing delighted.

'Are you going to accept his invitation?' Irene asked, bringing my attention back to those seated with me.

'No, I don't believe I will. I am very busy throughout our stay in London, and then we must leave for Scotland soon after. I would be reluctant to accept even if we did have the time. I certainly do not wish to string him along or give the impression I would consider an offer of marriage, or even courtship, if I were to be honest.' I felt the tension leave Hamish, his shoulders relaxing as he exhaled, then turned to watch him as he picked up his silver cutlery and began to eat.

'But you cannot decline, Abigail. It would be the height of rudeness and almost unforgivable,' Maggie said, appearing mortified as she shook her head in disbelief.

'Aren't you interested in going, just to see the house alone?' Irene asked, her perfectly shaped eyebrow arched in curiosity as I smothered a smile. 'If he invited me, I would probably accept his marriage proposal and be condemned forever as a bigamist,' Irene continued, and all present at the table erupted in loud laughter—all bar Hamish, who was clearly unimpressed by anything to do with Lord Harrington.

We spoke throughout the meal, just as we usually did, despite the disapproving stares we received from the other passengers, something we had all become accustomed to and now ignored. No sooner had the dirty dishes been cleared away, Lord Harrington approached our table and pulled up a chair, placing himself between me and Hamish, much to Hamish's chagrin.

'How are you this evening, Mrs Cavanaugh?' he asked warmly before greeting my dinner companions and the children.

'Is it true, Lord Harrington, that you own many grand estates in England?' Maggie enquired, and I cringed. He leaned back comfortably in his seat, his hand on the back of my chair as he chuckled.

'I will not deny that particular rumour. I am hoping Mrs Cavanaugh will be my guest at Montfordly Abby while in England.' He gazed across at me awaiting my reply, while Hamish rolled his eyes, trying to get my attention.

'It would be my privilege, but unfortunately I have a great deal of business in London, then we must travel to Edinburgh to visit my mother. Sadly, I fear I will not have the time,' I replied apologetically. He held my gaze, his lovely blue eyes, the colour of the ocean, almost pleading with me.

'May I enquire where you are staying in Edinburgh?' he asked politely, his gaze so intense I was forced to look away for a moment to compose myself.

'I have not arranged our accommodation as yet, but I'm certain we will find somewhere comfortable. I am planning to rent a cottage close to where my mother resides and stay for a week or so.' I raised the palms of my hands to my cheeks for a moment in an attempt to cool them, finding it futile before placing them back in my lap.

'No, that will not do at all, Mrs Cavanaugh. I refuse to allow a lady such as yourself to travel to Scotland without knowing where you will stay, or be at the mercy of a landlord. You must all be my guests at my estate, Merinda Manor, which is just out of Edinburgh. I will not accept no for an answer this time, Mrs Cavanaugh, as that is a word I hear far too often from your sweet lips,' he said kindly, the children staring at him in wonderment. They were old enough to have heard the gossip on board, and believed him to be a member of the royal family, my children now having visions of living at Buckingham Palace and wearing gold crowns on their little heads.

'Well then, the matter appears to be settled, it seems.' I had given up trying to put this stubborn man off, and I did not wish to make a fool of myself, or him, in front of strangers, many listening in from nearby tables. He nodded his head, appearing pleased before he turned to speak with Hamish, wanting to know all about his role at Willow Grove. Hamish glanced at me, his face like thunder as I shrugged my shoulders. I had tried to refuse him; however, he would not hear me and had insisted. Despite the fact I had upset Hamish, I felt a small bubble of excitement start to well up inside me. I certainly enjoyed this man's company and was secretly looking forward to getting to know him better in his own environment.

The music started and Lord Harrington stood and took my hand, leading me over to the dance floor. I could feel everyone in the room watching us, keenly aware they had no doubt heard the rumours, too.

'Would you ever relocate back to England in the future, now that your husband has passed away?' His voice, gentle and kind, comforted me as he held me in his arms, much closer than he had before, his breath on my ear as he quietly spoke to me, sending shivers through my body.

'No, I would not. In fact, I could not, and have no desire to return. There is nothing there for me, and never really was. I started my life when I turned fifteen and I chose to do that halfway across the world, away from Scotland and the life I had known, creating a new one in my adopted homeland, which I now consider my own. Nearly all our friends and family are in Australia, and that's where my children's lives will be. They are little Aussies through and through, and we love our country and couldn't live anywhere else. They are used to the fresh air and the wide-open spaces in a place that is familiar to them. We buried my husband and twin sons at our property, and I could never leave them there with no one to take fresh flowers and visit them.'

'In my experience, Mrs Cavanaugh, there is never a problem that cannot be fixed. I too love Australia, and have seen no other place in the world like it. It has everything, as you say; however, I find it a much more relaxed society than you will find in England. Despite many of the wealthy bringing their traditions and money with them, even their households are far more casual than what you find in a grand house in the countryside in England. I could see myself becoming accustomed to that lifestyle, feeling quite partial to wanting to live that way.' His handsome face broke into a wide grin. He held me closer, much to the disgust of the women in the room, all gossiping madly while he murmured in my ear. I noticed Hamish, still seated at the table, not taking his eyes from us for a moment as he glared at Lord Harrington.

We chatted for a time about our lives and how different they were, given the restraints that came with his title, and his envy of the freedom of my lifestyle. Maggie and Hamish were soon dancing close to us, and I could see Maggie whispering in his ear. I smiled up at Lord Harrington, admiring his handsome features and dark hair, muscular frame and clean-shaven face. He was nowhere near the size of Aaron or Hamish in height or width; however, he was extremely well built and stood at six feet tall. I was no longer forced to strain my neck to look up at him, despite him being slightly taller than me. I liked him and enjoyed talking and dancing with him each night.

There was something about him I felt drawn to, and although surrounded by the golden glow like so many in my life, the pull towards him felt even stronger. I did not care for his title or money; it went deeper than that. I liked the man and felt good spending time with him. An intelligent businessman, he had impressed me with his strength of character. He was honest and kind, being far from materialistic and shallow, and was everything but what I had expected the first night he approached me. He had caught me off guard, turning out to be someone completely unexpected who I admired.

'I understand why you are reluctant to leave Willow Grove. The place sounds far too good to be true. I would enjoy it very much to visit this property of yours one day and see it with my own eyes when I return to Melbourne.'

'And you are very welcome; however, I'm sure it is humble compared to what you are used to,' I replied as we continued to dance.

'I have no doubt your home would be very comfortable. With you there, how could it not be a delightful experience?' He smiled as the music stopped and he escorted me back to my table, all eyes on us as several women seated nearby whispered behind their hands. Relieved I could now sit in peace, and the attention would turn back to Lord

Harrington's table, I relaxed back into my chair. He kissed my hand before we parted, sending tingles up my arm.

I told my friends what he had said, and they giggled while Maggie clapped her hands.

'That would make you a Dutchess, wouldn't it?' she asked, appearing confused. Not one of us had any understanding of titles, and we laughed loudly at our ignorance.

A waltz started, and Hamish rose to his feet, taking my hand. A jolt ran up my arm, different from when I danced with Lord Harrington, and although thrilling, it was not the same. Hamish's touch swept through my body like fire, leaving no part unscathed, just as Aaron had affected me in the same way. I was uncertain what it was about Aaron and Hamish that awoke such fierce desire compared to other men, and although some roused a yearning in me, it was nowhere near as intense as what I experienced with Aaron, and I now felt with Hamish.

We made our way over to the dance floor, the young ones following close behind. They watched as Hamish embraced me, and they followed his lead and began to dance. After a time, Hamish relaxed, observing them as they moved away and no longer followed our steps, and pulled me in close to him.

'Aye, so now we're stayin' at the Lord's estate? Will he be there, or are we stayin' there by ourselves?' Lord Harrington watched closely as I pushed Hamish away, trying to be discreet but aware how many were staring at us. He held me closer than I wanted; however, at a much more respectable distance.

'I am uncertain, and he said neither way. Does it really matter? He is a really nice man, and you haven't given him a chance at all. I have seen him try to talk to you many times, and you say only a few words, then ignore him. You are being rude, Hamish. You would like him very much if you took the time to get to know him,' I said far too loudly, my face becoming warm once again.

'Dinnae expect me tae be mates with someone who wants tae bed ye, Abigail. I'm bein' as patient as I'm able with ye an' doin' everythin' yer way, but dinnae expect that tae last long. 'Tis too much. I saw how he held ye taenight, an' ye responded tae him. Feels tae me I must compete fer ye all over again,' he whispered in my ear. I pulled back and looked up at him, narrowing my gaze.

'Well, you don't as there is nothing to compete over. I've told you my feelings about love and marriage. I am not looking for anything beyond an affair,' I reminded him, and he grunted, grimacing in frustration.

'Aye, dinnae I know it.' He leaned down and kissed my forehead before I angrily shoved him away.

'Hamish, it's bad enough you dance so close to me, but I'm warning you. Kiss me like that in public, and you will be unable to kiss anything or anyone again.' I turned on my heel and marched back to our table, leaving him alone on the dance floor, appearing bemused as he slowly followed me and sat back down.

I sat down with my friends, and we watched our offspring dance for the first time in public, remarking proudly how adorable they were. I grimaced when Hamish joined us moments later, as though nothing had passed between us only minutes before.

'You did a splendid job of it, Hamish. Look at them after only one lesson,' Maggie complimented him, her dainty hand on the sleeve of his dinner jacket. He smiled broadly, then placed his hand on the back of my chair. 'How did you become so good with children when you live as a bachelor?' she asked, batting her eyelashes at him.

'Aye.' He nodded, and I rolled my eyes, thinking him conceited. 'Weel, I've always had Thomas an' Emmy, an' then there is me nephew an' niece, who're of the same age. The bairns think me far less borin' than their parents.' He had always been a natural with children and they immediately loved him and followed him around, wanting his attention. All the children at Willow Grove loved him and any child that looked as if they were going down the wrong path, Hamish would take under his wing and guide them back in the right direction.

The children returned to the table, their faces glowing. They appeared exhausted, but oh so proud, and I thought them ready for bed. I excused myself before rising to my feet, nodding at Thomas and Emmy, who did the same.

'I cannae come,' Hamish said quietly, still seated.

'Well, that's not a good thing, Hamish,' I teased as he shook his head in disbelief, clearly shocked I would say anything even slightly provocative in front of strangers. I knew they had not an inkling of what I was referring to.

'Abigail, be serious. I promised Maggie I'd walk on deck with her. I tried tae think o' every excuse, but she willnae have it,' he said grimly as I smothered a smile.

'That's all right, because I have to go with Bessie to steerage tonight to see Jimmy. You don't have to spend all your time with me, you know? There are other women on the boat who have their eye on you. You are free to sleep with whomever you like,' I told him quietly, not giving him the chance to respond. I wished everyone a final goodnight, took my children by the hand, and guided them out of the room before they could nag me to stay.

Thomas and Emmy went to get ready themselves for bed as I poured myself a glass of wine, then sat down on the lounge to wait for them to call me. Two glasses later, I made my way into their room and lay down between them, taking the book Thomas had chosen to read tonight in both hands—*Hamlet* by William Shakespeare. I was well aware they were finding it difficult to understand; however, they insisted I keep reading it until they did. Within half-an-hour, their eyelids were heavy, and I placed the book down on the side table and kissed them goodnight.

'Mummy, I think you should marry Uncle Hamish,' Emmy murmured, startling me.

'And why would you think that?' I sat back down on the bed and held her hand in mine, lowering my voice so as to not wake Thomas, who snored softly beside her then turned over and farted loudly, and moments later, snored again.

'Ew, I hate sleeping beside a bugle arse like his. It's just plain filthy, is what it is. I'm never going to get married. You would have to be a halfwit to put yourself in that position for the rest of your days, tied by the ankle to a pig with no manners.' I collapsed into giggles as she wrinkled her nose in disdain, reminding me of her uncle Leo, before she rolled her eyes and continued. 'Now, about Uncle Hamish, Mummy. Going by the way he looks at you lately, I think he is in love with you. He is only ever *really* happy when you're with us, and can't stop grinning. And he looks after all of us. He already loves Thomas and me with all his heart. I know that for certain, Mummy. I think he would make a good husband for you, and would love you with his whole heart like he loves us, which is most important,' she said, yawning widely without even attempting to cover her mouth. 'First, though, you will need to find out if he blows it out his backside as much as my brother. I do not want more of them around making our private home smell like a thunderbox without any shame or apologies. What is even more hideous is that they believe themselves to be funny and highly entertaining, proud of letting one rip when you're standing beside them in the kitchen. If you find uncle Hamish is one of them when he isn't around me and Thomas, you will need to choose another husband as I'm not standing for it.' It took me several moments to compose myself, my stomach now paining me and my face tear-stained.

'Emmy, I do not need or want another husband. As your Daddy would often point out to me, I have enough on me plate looking after you nippers, and that alone keeps me busy enough. A husband can be like raising an extra five ill mannered bairns, something you seem to be well aware of.' I tickled her stomach, making her giggle before kissing her goodnight, crossing the small room and silently closing the door behind me.

I knocked at Bessie's door and asked if she could help me change into a simpler dress to accompany her. Once in my bedchamber, she had me stripped in no time, assisting me into a simple, brown house dress most efficiently, the bodice tight, the skirt plain. I sat for a moment while she unpinned my hair, allowing it to fall loose to my waist without even a grunt of displeasure, and within minutes we were ready to leave.

We descended the many stairs, and a kind officer allowed us through the gate placed there to prevent those travelling in steerage entry to the first and second class areas of the ship. I followed Bessie through the narrow hallways until we stepped into a large room filled with tables and chairs, while several passengers played musical instruments in the corner, a large group of people gathered around them singing uproariously. Others danced, sang and laughed as they talked and drank their ale or wine, while others nursed cups filled with strong spirits smuggled aboard by the passengers who could ill afford to pay the exorbitant prices the ship charged. I felt as if I had been transported back to 1890—the room filled with excitement, gaiety and high-spirited larrikins.

We found Jimmy at a table, and he and Bessie embraced before he went to get us an ale. I made myself comfortable across from Bessie, while she gazed around the room, appearing just as happy as I was to be back.

'He looks so old and frail, Mistress. I certainly made the right choice with my darlin' Danny. He has been a steadfast and true husband, bringing me happiness I thought I would never find. I imagined I would see out my days as your ladies maid, then hoped you would take pity on me and look after me in my old age. That is how life is for so many in service. They don't work on a property run as Willow Grove is, or get such comfortable accommodation provided. If you work in a grand house in England, they may have one or two married quarters at most, so many are unable to marry 'cause they don't have a home to raise a family, only a shared room with other servants. My life turned out very different to what I expected when we left London so long ago,' she said, her face glowing, her eyes sparkling with happiness, warming my heart.

'As did mine, Bessie; however, we have no choice in the matter and are expected to be thankful for whatever toil and trouble some higher power decides you deserve,' I replied, my eyes widening as she abruptly turned to me, appearing mortified.

'I'm so sorry, Mistress. Flaunting my happiness in your face about married life when you have lost your husband. I hate myself more than I despise Leonardo when I say such scaffy without thinking.' She apologised again, her head bowed as I took her hand across the table and smiled reassuringly.

'Bessie, you have every right to be happy. Danny is a wonderful man; however, he is also lucky to have you. I don't want you to feel you cannot talk about your life just because mine suddenly turned into an immense pile of pig shit. I am getting along much better than I was, and at least I'm out of bed and my backside is pointing to the ground,' I teased, her lovely face breaking into a half-hearted smile.

'Well, that's not all true, Mistress. You certainly have spent a lot of time in bed during this voyage.' She collapsed into giggles, her eyes sparkling.

'Maybe so, but in my defence, I no longer sleep the day away despite being in bed.' I laughed aloud as Jimmy returned to the table, handing me an ale, then placing another large glass in front of Bessie. He sat down next to her and they began to talk while I gazed around the room. It was certainly different from the dining room in first class. I felt comfortable and not out of place, despite my dress being far too plain to wear to dinner in first class, and far too extravagant for steerage. Most of the women wore plain skirts in serviceable cloth, and fitted shirts tucked into the band of their skirts, while some of the matrons wore plain house dresses that had seen better days. I gazed around the room, stopping to stare at several passengers while wondering why they were returning to England. The journey by sea was an expensive voyage to take, and it was never a decision taken lightly or made in haste. I knew a number of families who had immigrated to Australia around the same time we had, and they hated the place, finding the weather extreme and the people rough compared to their refined English cousins.

Bessie and Jimmy sat together, catching up on all the years. Suddenly, a large man sat down next to me, picked up my beer and drank it. I looked up to find Hamish staring down at me, his eyes glazed. He belched loudly, then shook his head several times as if to clear his mind, a look of disbelief on his face.

'What are you doing here? And why are you here so quickly? What's wrong with you, anyway? You look like a stunned mullet, Hamish.' I wanted to know everything at once, but he only sighed, then reached for the cup of whisky he had brought with him to the table.

'I just got propositioned by Maggie. What is it with women of the twentieth century? Och, it used tae be a man's place tae pursue the lassies, but now it's the other way around. I'm startin' tae feel like a deer bein' chased by a pack of starvin' hyenas.' He was clearly mortified, and I laughed aloud.

'Oh, stop being prudish. I see Maggie told you of her feelings?' His eyes widened, while his handsome cheeks resembled a plum I had eaten only this afternoon.

'Did ye know about this, Abigail?' He reached across and picked up a jug, then poured us both an ale.

'Yes, I did. She asked for my opinion,' I replied, smothering a smile. He was behaving as if she had violated him, and he was finding no humour in it.

'Why did ye naw discourage her or say somethin' about us, instead o' puttin' me through the embarrassment o' tryin' tae think up excuses? Ye could've warned me. Why did ye naw warn me? She kissed me, ye know? I was naw prepared for that.' He gazed across at a group of young men dancing a jig, the sound of their feet hitting the floor, and their howls of laughter louder than the music itself.

'Hamish, you are a grown man, and you are free to do as you please. I have no plans to put myself between you and other women.' His head snapped around to glare at me, his eyes glinting dangerously.

'Aye, so I'm free tae see whomever I please, am I? I suppose so ye can do the same?' He angrily rose to his feet and made his way to the other side of the room to buy another round of drinks before I had a chance to respond. I sighed deeply, knowing I had released the caged tiger Bessie had warned me of, and I had taken no notice. He returned soon after, appearing calmer, another bottle of whisky and two cups for Bessie and Jimmy in his hand, a jug of beer in the other. He poured a whisky for each of us, and I took mine and drank it in one swallow, feeling it burn my throat as it made its way down to my belly. 'It's certainly naw the same quality we're used tae,' Hamish remarked grimly, mirroring my thoughts exactly as I sipped my beer.

'Yes, but it does the same job.' I closed my eyes for a moment, the warm fire in the pit of my stomach spreading through my body, and he chuckled.

'Abigail, I know ye'll naw let me talk o' love or how I feel about ye, but I cannae stop meself sometimes. I could naw love ye any more than I do, an' I'll wait as long as I have tae fer ye tae fall back in love with me like ye once were. I'm naw interested in any other woman on this earth an' never will be, even if it was the princess herself. Yer are all I see. Thoughts o' ye fill me mind night an' day. Dinnae think fer a moment I view meself as an available man, or that I'd seek the affections o' anyone other than ye,' he murmured, staring deeply into my eyes.

I looked back into his, always reminding me of melted chocolate, and felt my heart soften ever so slightly. I returned his smile before turning my attention back to the crowd of inebriated dancers. As the time passed, we talked of other things, both noticing Bessie and Jimmy had settled back into their comfortable friendship lost so many years before. Hamish and I drank several more drams of whisky before he pulled me up onto my feet with both hands to dance.

'Oh, I just adore it here. I feel we are back at Willow Grove in our own rambunctious pub.' He guided me towards the front of the room where a young man sang a song from his homeland, while several others played musical instruments too precious to leave behind, his hand on my shoulder to steady me.

'Aye.'tis bonny 'cause I can hold ye close an' whisper in yer ear the things I'm goin' tae do tae ye later, an' naw one here pays us any mind.' He held me close, his heart pounding against my ear as we danced slowly to the music, a heartbreaking love song of loss that brought tears to my eyes. 'Ye look like a free-spirited wench in that dress, an' I'm usin' all me strength not tae tear it off ye in front o' witnesses.' His hand dropped from my waist to my backside, and he left it there for all to see. I glanced around to find he was right. Not a soul present seemed to care what anyone else was doing, and they were having a wonderful time. 'I think that's what I'll call ye. Me wee wench.' He bent down and kissed my neck, sending tingles through my body.

I was breathless when we sat back down to drink more whisky and replenish our bodies with ale. It was lovely being here with Hamish—and not one man had bothered me with requests to dance or invitations to walk the decks. I was truly enjoying myself for the first time since losing Aaron, and the jovial atmosphere along with all the wonderful people I was meeting on the ship had brought a glimmer of hope my life would one day be recognisable to me again.

Hamish and I chatted with others at the table who we hadn't met before tonight, finding them friendly and interesting.

Joe Irish, a farmer who had come to Australia five-years ago, was the friendliest of all, despite what he had endured. His wife, Louise, had recently died in childbirth, and a drought that had settled on Queensland had wiped out his crops and sent him broke. And toward Melbourne six-months ago. Having walked away from his farm and all he had owned, he found nothing in Victoria to keep him there, and decided to return to England to the bosom of his family. I found so many of their story's heart-wrenching. It seemed most onboard, no matter what their class, recognised me from the papers and wanted to talk of Aaron, and I talked openly for a time about my beloved husband, then listened to them talk of their own thoughts of him and his case with tears in my eyes.

By the time Bessie was ready to leave, Hamish and I had shared two bottles of whisky, and I was confident I had consumed far more than he.

'Looks like someone will be sick in the morning,' Bessie remarked, glancing at me as she rose to her feet and smiled, bidding Jimmy and her new friends goodnight. 'Let's get you back to the suite, Mistress.' She came to my side and touched my cheek affectionately, before taking me by the shoulders and lifting me up onto my feet. Hamish was soon standing beside us and slipped his arm around my waist to support me before I staggered out, unable to see anything around me—the ship moving far more than usual under my feet. Bessie followed us through the hallways and up the stairs, then bid us a goodnight before closing the door of our suite behind her.

Hamish carried me into his suite and soon after, placed me down on his bed. He chuckled to himself as he turned me over, unbuttoned my dress, then slipped it off me before gently placing me under the covers in my shift. Within moments, I felt the warmth of his body beside me before he wrapped his broad arms around me—an act of affection he was well aware he did not have my permission to do, yet I was far too drunk to argue as I let my body relax into him.

'I love ye, Abigail. Always have. I dinnae realise how much 'till a year ago. When I knew fer certain, ye were still grievin' deeply, havin' only lost Aaron a year before. I could naw tell ye 'till ye asked me tae

bed ye. I love ye with every part of me heart, me mind, and me soul.'
He gently kissed my face, then my lips, the room spinning around
me.

'Oh, stop, Hamish. You need to find yourself a good woman,' I
slurred, my eyes heavy while my stomach churned.

'Shhh, I've already found one.' He placed his lips on my forehead,
his arms still firmly around me as I drifted off into a tormented
sleep—where demons and angels called out to me as I descended into
the fiery pits of hell—before I woke in a haze, then vomited all over
the bed.

Chapter Twelve

W E WOULD ARRIVE IN London tomorrow, if all went to plan. Mr Malcolm had sent word to the ship he intended to meet us at the docks, and I was beyond excited. I had enjoyed every single day aboard, but I was ready to place my feet on solid ground again and get my business affairs in order. I had kept close to Maggie and Irene, and made no effort to make friends with others given their animosity towards me, and had enjoyed every moment with them.

Lord Harrington still directed all of his attention toward me, but had been a true gentleman in every way and never broached the subject of love. Not once had he been inappropriate, always holding me at a respectable distance when we danced, and he was careful not to ruin my reputation whenever I was near. The other gentlemen who had asked me to dance in the first week had given up when hearing of Lord Harrington's intentions, leaving me in his sole custody after dinner each night. He would dance with only me, and ask me to walk the deck with him afterwards, something I occasionally agreed to. I had come to know him quite well, and we had built the foundations of a friendship I hoped very much would continue. I held some romantic feelings towards him, and although I thought him attractive and felt quite close to him, he did not arouse unrestrained passion within me I had found so easily unleashed with Hamish.

Hamish had calmed the jealous beast within him and would make jokes about Lord Harrington now, often laughing at what a fool he made of himself over me. We still spent as much time as we could in his suite, or more accurately, in his bed. Hamish was starting to talk less of love, after finding I would become annoyed and irritated with him, as he didn't want to argue with me, which was a relief, as I hated feeling pressured. Having sex with him was exciting and passionate, not better than being with Aaron but different, which I liked, and I was comfortable with.

I lay next to him, listening to his soft breathing. I should have been getting back to my own bed, but I was comfortable and warm here. Ten-minutes more, I promised myself, and relaxed back into the pillows. I felt his hand creep across my waist and remain there. I took his arm and slid it off me as I looked across at him suspiciously.

'Och, yer awake,' he murmured sleepily, then yawned widely. 'Good mornin'. What are ye still doin' here? Ye never stay.' He seemed surprised as rubbed the sleep from his eyes, then turned on his side to gaze at me.

'I fell asleep and only just woke now to find you were trying to cuddle me again,' I said, narrowing my gaze as he stared into my eyes.

'Ye cannae blame a man fer tryin'. I thought ye were still sound-asleep.' He laughed as I smiled at him. 'Naw that I dinnae love that yer still here,' he said, pulling me into his arms and kissing me deeply.

Afterwards, as I lay on my back under the quilt, I stared up at the ceiling, uncertain if I should speak of it, swallowing hard before deciding I would.

'Hamish, there is something I have never told you, and it was the only thing I ever kept from Aaron.' I hesitated, swallowing hard again as he turned on his side to look at me.

'Sounds serious, Abigail. Are ye goin' tae tell me what it is?' He reached out, running his finger across my lips, my throat constricting further.

'Yes. Remember the night of Polly and Angus's wedding?' My voice shook as he nodded once and turned away, resting back against his pillow.

'How could I ever ferget? Which part? When I made a fool o' meself at the reception, or when ye found me in bed with Charlotte?'

He stared up at the ceiling, his handsome cheeks starting to flush before he turned back and held my gaze.

'The second one. I was on my way to your room that night to tell you I would accept your marriage proposal.' He stared at me for the longest time, silence hanging heavily over the elegant room. After what seemed like an eternity, he took my hand and entwined his fingers around mine, then placed it on his broad chest.

'There are two ways I can look at it, I suppose. The first is tae get all bitter an' hateful that the one mistake I made when it came tae ye ruined what could've been a lifetime o' happiness fer us. An' took away me chance tae have bairns with ye. Or I can take the second option.' He stared out of the large porthole, ten times the size of what the second and third-class passengers were privileged to have in their tiny cabins, while holding my hand tightly against his chest, his heartbeat strong against my palm.

'Which is?'

'Weel, had we married back then, neither o' us would've known Aaron an' come tae love him as we did. He loved ye weel fer a long time, but he also taught ye how tae love deeply an' how tae display affection. Ye weren't like that when I met ye. Ye were never cold, ye just dinnae know how tae show love 'cause ye had so very little o' it shown tae ye. Other than yer Sister Josephine, o' course. He gave ye two beautiful bairns I'd never wish away. They're part o' me, an' I love 'em. He became as close as a brother tae me, an' I treasured the friendship we had, an' if I could bring him back, I would. Even though it would mean I'd lose ye again. I know what I'd choose. Would ye have given all that up? Regret is a useless emotion, Abigail. Even though I wish that night never happened, I dinnae regret how it turned out in the end. I'd naw change anythin' tae do with our situation.' He squeezed my hand as he brought it to his lips, then gently kissed my fingers one by one.

'That is the loveliest thing to say, and the most beautiful way to look at it.' I felt tears prick my eyes as he turned back to me, kissing my lips for a moment before he pulled away, a broad grin on his own.

'Can ye stay a wee bit longer?'

'I can stay a lot longer.'

Thomas and Emmy were still sound asleep when I arrived back at our suite. I believed they had come to suspect something had changed between me and Hamish—when he brushed my hand with his, or looked at me a certain way now, they would glance at each other and smile. Before we stepped aboard the ship, Hamish would touch me in passing in front of the twins in a friendly manner, and they took no notice, but lately they watched us like hawks whenever we were together. I knew they loved Hamish, and I didn't want them believing a romance or marriage would eventuate between us.

I wandered over to the table in the small dining room to find a pot of coffee and freshly squeezed orange juice on a tray. Assuming it had just been delivered by the maid, I poured myself a glass of juice, then a cup of coffee, and stepped back into the sitting room to wait for my children to wake. Bessie and little Mary joined me soon after, pouring themselves a drink before sitting down beside me.

'So, I see you just got home, Mistress. You never stay with that boy for more than two-hours at a time. Why are you back so late? And have you lost your mind? Who wanders around a grand ship such as this half-naked in their nightclothes at this hour? No lady I've ever heard of,' Bessie snapped, a disapproving glint in her eye as little Mary glanced away.

'Does it really matter? As long as I am here when my children wake, I cannot see how I am hurting anyone.' I yawned loudly before relaxing back on the lounge, ensuring my dressing gown covered whatever part of me she was offended by.

'What if someone seen you coming into the cabin like that at this time of the morning? We would all be disgraced,' Bessie snapped again, shaking her head at me. I lay back on the cushions and stretched, luxuriating in the still warm glow I felt.

'Don't fash, Bessie. We would only be shamed for one day and won't see any of them again after tomorrow. Who cares what these strangers think?' I stifled another yawn with my hand.

'I do, and it's your good name I've been protecting all these years because you don't listen to anyone. You are rebellious, and you say what's on your mind far too often, even in polite society, you little shite.' She put her empty cup on the small table beside her, then crossed her arms against her chest, narrowing her gaze at me.

'I'm sorry, my dear friend. I know you worry for me, and I apologise for my tardiness. I fell asleep.' Poor Bessie. She was right. I had been a pain in her arse ever since she met me, not wanting to do things proper or behave in the way expected of a woman in my position.

'The problem with you, child, is you have a wild streak in you no one can tame. Although you are an angel itself, it is extremely hard to manage you sometimes.' Bessie gently touched my cheek, and I smothered a smile.

'I know, and I'm sorry for it,' I replied as she smiled back. Thomas and Emmy stumbled out of their room in their pyjamas, still half-asleep as they made their way to my side and kissed me, wishing me a good morning.

'Mummy, your hair is all messy,' Emmy remarked, running her fingers through my hair in an attempt to tidy it.

'Thank you, Emmy. That's much better,' I said as Bessie smirked at me knowingly. 'Do you mind if I skip breakfast and go back to bed? Uncle Hamish will be here to eat with you.' I felt exhausted in body and mind, and was finding it difficult to keep my eyes open.

'Are ya not well, Ma?' Thomas asked, his forehead creased in concern.

'It's not that, Thomas. I'm just overtired. I feel I need an uninterrupted sleep so I'm refreshed for tomorrow. It will be a big day, seeing everyone again.' They nodded, excusing me as I kissed them both before making my way to my room. I took off my dressing gown and slid between the sheets, then relaxed into the soft bed, the weight of the quilt laying heavy on me. I wanted to sleep on my own for as long as my body needed to, and I closed my eyes, sighing deeply.

I had been looking for the signs Aaron had promised to send since he died, and still there was nothing. I had started to lose hope it was possible he continued on in spirit, kept from my sight only by the thin veil separating the living and the dead. Or he really was sleeping peacefully until judgement day, just as the Catholics believed. Maybe

Aaron coming to me in my dreams was the sign, as it always felt so real. I could smell him and I would wake with tears pouring down my face, knowing he had just been with me.

My favourite time of the day was when I was asleep. He would always come to me in my dreams, and had done so every night since he passed. It felt like he was back with me again. I would talk to him of the children as he kissed and held me like he used to, the whispers of love flowing back and forth between us until I reluctantly woke. I relaxed my body to allow sleep to overtake me so I could once again see my Aaron and be in his presence. As I drifted off, I dreamed of langoustines, Aaron, and the hands of Big Ben striking midnight.

Bessie hurried in and opened the heavy drapes, filling the cabin with light. 'You must wake, Mistress. I have brought you a nice cup of tea, since you haven't eaten all day. It's nearly time to dress for dinner. You have slept all day, and I've had Hamish haranguing me to wake you every half-hour. I told him to stop bothering me or he'd be walking around without that appendage between his legs he was wanting me to wake you so desperately to pay attention to,' she said, and I laughed.

'What did he say?' I tried to smother a smile as she came to my side.

'Well, he never did come back after that,' she said thoughtfully.

'Goodness, Bessie. I wonder why? You threaten his manhood, knowing full well he has always feared you, no doubt thinking you will carry out your threats on him one day.'

She smiled, a wicked glint in her eyes. 'Ah, well. That won't hurt to have on his mind. It may be a good thing he's scared of me. You are my responsibility, and now he is following you around like one of them dingoes. And the way he picks you up off your feet and carries you off to his suite reminds me of them cavemen you told me about from your books. Well, he better be worried is all I'll say on the matter.'

She hurried off to my dressing room to choose an evening gown for my last night. I was glad to be getting off the ship, if only to not have to change clothes so often. I was forced to wear elaborate gowns every day and ensure my hair was styled and face painted. I appreciated living at Willow Grove more than I ever had. I could rise in the morning at any hour, put on one of my comfortable plain dresses, and go about my business with no one caring how I looked—or if I wore shoes in the garden, something I rarely did anymore.

I struggled out of bed and made my way over to Bessie. She swiftly dressed me in the most magnificent gown I had ever seen, the colours running through the cloth reminding me of a rainbow lorikeet—just one of the native birds I had come to admire since arriving in Australia—the style whimsical, feminine and far too snug across my breasts. Catherine had made a matching headpiece with small feathers on the band to be fitted into my hair, and I adored it. I sat down at the dressing table and watched intently as Bessie styled my hair, then fitted the elaborate headpiece, nodding her head in satisfaction before touching the back of my head. I stood and thanked her, kissed her goodbye, then stepped into the sitting room.

'Ahhh, the dead has arisen,' Hamish remarked, his handsome face breaking into a grin as he looked me over from my head to my feet. 'I thought ye were never goin' tae wake.' My irritated maid grunted as she crossed the room, rolling her eyes as I returned his smile.

We bid farewell to Bessie and little Mary, and walked side-by-side companionably to the dining room for the very last time, quickly finding our seats at the table. Ronald and Irene, along with Maggie and the children, were already seated and appeared as glum as I felt. I would miss my new friends dreadfully, but I was more than happy they lived nearby and our children had become close, leaving me confident we would visit each other often once we returned home.

'I feel so terribly sad that tomorrow we will part,' Maggie said, staring back and forth at me and Irene, and we solemnly nodded our heads in agreement. We enjoyed our last meal together, talking of the things we would do in England. We had only finished dessert when the music began, and I noticed Lord Harrington walking towards our table. Hamish also noticed him, and screwed up his face in disdain as he approached.

'Good evening, Mrs Cavanaugh. May I have this first dance on our last night aboard?' He was always so very polite—far too polite to challenge any hostility directed at him. It was clear he noticed, but chose to ignore, being the gentleman he was raised to be. I gave him my hand, glaring at Hamish for a moment as he rolled his eyes, and accompanied him to the front of the room, the candelabras casting a romantic light on his handsome face. 'May I say, you look particularly beautiful tonight? Have you been saving this gown for our final night aboard?' He held me firmly in his arms, a number of couples joining us as the music continued to play.

'No. My dear friend and ladies' maid, Bessie, decides what I wear. She is of the firm belief I cannot be trusted and knows full well I would wear a plain house dress every day to every occasion if I could get away with it.' I laughed as his face broke into a wide grin.

'Well then, your maid has superb taste. You must be so kind to pass on my compliments and thank her.' He stared down at my gown, nodding appreciatively before gazing back into my eyes.

'Thank her for what?' I asked, confusion crossing my face for a moment.

'For adorning such a beautiful woman with objects that only accentuate that beauty. It would matter not what you wore, Mrs Cavanaugh. You are the most exquisite women I have ever set my eyes and my mind upon,' he whispered, sending chills through me. Hamish stared at us from across the room, his displeasure obvious for all to see. Lord Harrington's lips were so close to my ear as he spoke of romance and love, I felt uncomfortable, wishing to return to my table as soon as the opportunity presented itself. 'I will wait to receive your telegram to confirm the dates you wish to stay at my estate in Scotland, and have the house opened for you.' I felt this was such an imposition for him; however, he would hear none of it, and I had given up, defeated by his persistence.

'Thank you, Lord Harrington. We appreciate your kindness and the generosity you have shown to me and my family.'

'My actions are purely selfish, I can assure you.' The music stopped, overwhelming relief settling on me as I stepped away from him. He escorted me back to the table, wishing me well and bidding everyone goodnight.

The children got up all at once from the table to dance, and I watched on proudly. They had taken lessons from Hamish the entire journey across the sea—while I was aware I was only there as a dance partner—and not one of them had ever missed a day. They were now familiar with most of the steps, and were able to dance alongside the most gifted of dancers without shame. And they did, having lots of fun in the process. It thrilled me to see them all enjoying themselves so much. Hamish soon stood and made his way to my side to sit with me, while my friends watched their offspring with as much pride as I.

'I missed ye taeday,' he said, his voice low as I turned and looked up at him.

'Do not go getting all dependent on me, Hamish. There will soon come a time when we will have to return to normal life at Willow Grove. You work long hours, and my days are busy. You will not see me as often as you do now.' His face fell for a moment, and he looked away. It was obvious I had hurt him, and it was the last thing I wanted to do. I only said what was on my mind, but I could see how this would be hurtful to him. Aaron and I had spent a lot of time together during the day, work or not. It was clear he was unable or unwilling to understand I would never again have what Aaron and I shared with anyone else, nor would he accept I would never fall in love again after being loved so well. There was no one walking the earth who could love me better than Aaron, or make me as happy. Of that I was certain.

We said our goodnights and took our leave, dragging Thomas and Emmy away from their friends, their complaints continuing until we reached the door of our suite. They reluctantly followed us in, then said their goodnights to Hamish before stepping into their room to ready for bed. I made my way into their bedchamber soon after, settling in beside them to read before tucking them in for the night. They had matured years in less than two-months, and it made my heart hurt for a moment. I kissed them both goodnight before joining Hamish in the sitting room.

'They have had the most wonderful time on the ship. They both seem to have matured and grown in such a short time,' I complained, while Hamish nodded. I made myself comfortable beside him, chatting over a bottle of wine until little Mary returned to stay with them. I stood and crossed the room to check on my babies, both sound asleep now and snoring softly, allowing us to retreat to Hamish's suite.

As we lay in his bed much later, he turned to look at me, placing his head on his hand exactly like Aaron used to do, only making my heart ache again for my husband.

'Will ye stay the night with me? Who knows when we'll get the chance again?' he whispered while gently stroking my face with his finger. I nodded before moving closer to kiss him.

Soon after, as I fell asleep on my side of the bed, I dreamed of a cottage by a river, Sister Josephine, and a girl named Freya.

Chapter Thirteen

S ITTING OUTSIDE ON THE private balcony to eat our last breakfast on the ship, I closed my eyes, the sea breeze gently touching my skin and reminding me of home. We had always taken our breakfast out here since stepping on board in Melbourne, as it was so lovely to look out over the ocean—the fresh air so very crisp and invigorating first thing in the morning. The large dining table was far less elaborate than the one indoors, but just as lovely.

Bessie and little Mary were more than happy to be disembarking today, as they too were at their wits end and tired of being cooped up like our chickens at home, no matter how extravagant and beautiful they found the ship. Thomas and Emmy were down in the mouth about leaving their new friends, but I could feel the excitement from all the adults the closer we came to shore. Well, except for Hamish.

He had enjoyed the privacy we had shared on the ship, and was not enthusiastic to stay with the Malcolms, recognising before we even arrived it would be impossible to get me alone for more than a few moments. I had made him aware there would be a scandal should I be found in his bed—a risk I was unwilling to take. We would not be alone again until we travelled to Scotland, and would be forced to refrain from sleeping together until then. Hamish was unhappy, and had asked to see me in his room after breakfast.

'So, wee Emmy an' Thomas. Ye appear tae have had an enjoyable time aboard the ship?' Hamish remarked, more a statement of fact than a question. Their faces lit up as they nodded, gazing up at him.

'Oh yes, Uncle Hamish. It was a wonderful journey. We are going to see our friends as soon as we arrive back home, and to know how to dance now is even more wonderful. I adore dancing more than anything in the world,' Emmy replied dreamily, and I again thought how much like me she was.

'And you dance beautifully, Emmy. I have snuck into the dining room on several occasions just to watch you an' Thomas dance with your friends. You made me so proud, I shed a few tears,' little Mary interjected, gazing lovingly at her.

'That's because you are soft and sweet and love us. I love you just as much as you love me,' Emmy told her sweetly, while the adults exchanged fond glances.

'She's like her mother, that's what she is. Even moves the same way, growing more and more alike each day. Let's hope she doesn't give you the same grief her mother gives me when you're her ladies maid,' Bessie warned little Mary as Hamish snorted in amusement.

'What about ye, Thomas? Yer quiet this mornin',' Hamish remarked as Thomas turned his head abruptly to meet his gaze, startled from his thoughts.

'I've had a fine time, Uncle Hamish, but there's somethin' I need to talk to ya about in private. If that's all right?' he asked, appearing perplexed.

'Aye, o' course, Thomas. We can go an' speak inside as soon as yer done with yer breakfast,' Hamish replied, hurrying himself along. I was not offended Thomas would go to Hamish over me. He was at that age now where he needed a trusted male to confide in.

'I have everything packed, and they have just come now to take the trunks down to the docks,' Bessie said, sitting back down to eat.

'Thank you, Bessie. I could not live without you.' I smiled at her and she smiled back.

'No, you bloody well couldn't! As you would say with your crude mouth.' Giggling quietly to herself, she raised a spoon to her mouth filled with porridge. 'Who would be there to boss you around and keep you in line? You don't listen to anyone else. At least you listen to me half the time. You wouldn't last a week without me.' She laughed again, as did Hamish, before concentrating on her meal.

His attitude to servants had changed completely during the years he spent at Willow Grove, witnessing first-hand how loyal and hard-working our staff were because we treated them well and valued them immensely. The wealthy, snobbish young man who spoke in a near perfect English accent I had met so long ago had disappeared. He had become friendlier and far more relaxed in the company of all classes, a quality I believed had always been there, along with his kindness and thoughtfulness. He continued to be judged harshly for his past mistakes and was still considered a womaniser by many, despite not behaving in that manner for many years now.

Hamish and Thomas stood together, retreating inside the suite, while I stayed and drank my coffee with the others.

'Are you excited, Mistress?' Little Mary asked as she finished her toast.

'I do not know how to feel at the moment,' I replied, memories of my life before Australia filling my mind.

'Is that because Daddy isn't here with us? I know you're sad, Mummy. I can see it in your eyes, but Daddy is here. We can't see him, but he whispered his feelings in my ear the last time I saw him at the gaol. He told me nothing could ever keep him away from us. Not ever. He will always be nearby. We only have to think of him, and he will come and sit beside us until we don't feel sad anymore,' Emmy told us as I broke down sobbing. I knew as soon as I thought of him, I would lose all control and be unable to hide my grief. Facing life without him was far too much to bear. Emmy continued eating and chatting with the others, becoming so used to my tears over the last two-years, she barely noticed.

It was the anniversary of his death in three-day's time. The mere thought of *that* day made everything even harder than it already was. I constantly wished I could turn back time, if only to see him one last time and say the things I forgot to tell him. Whenever I had news, good or bad, my first thought was always to find Aaron to tell him, before I would realise we would never speak again. I woke every single morning expecting to see him beside me before the realisation he was gone forever would dawn on me once fully awake, always leaving me broken-hearted and sobbing. The only place I was able to grieve in private since stepping onto the ship was in my own bed, where I could sob without affecting others. I knew it upset them to see me cry, and I did everything in my power to avoid it; however, this morning, the dam wall had burst.

'There, there. I know how hard it is for you to take this trip without him, and none of us can take his place, but we're here to support you and try to make things as easy as we can for you while you tend to your business affairs here. At least it will be all done and set in motion well before you turn thirty, and I will be by your side the entire time to ease the burden as much as I can,' Bessie reassured me as she stood behind me, her hands resting gently on my shoulders as I wept.

We would be on a ship heading home on my thirtieth birthday, after spending several months seeing England, Scotland, Paris and New York. We had not planned to spend more than a week or two in any one place; it was all the travelling in between that took the most time. It was fortunate my children did not suffer seasickness, having been taken out on their grandfather's fishing boats since they were small. They adored the ocean, and travelling by boat, which was one less worry for me to concern myself with while away.

'I know you are, and I appreciate it more than words can express. I am trying my best to appear happy and not weep anymore, but sometimes it just overtakes me and I cannot control myself,' I said through my tears as she wiped my face with her handkerchief.

'That's all right, sweetheart. We all understand you're finding everything a bit overwhelming at the moment. Emmy is right, you know? Sometimes I feel like Mr Aaron is standing next to you when I'm doing your hair at that dressing table in your bedchamber. He always liked watching you have your hair styled and arguing with me about it.' She smiled with tears in her own eyes as Thomas and Hamish returned to the table. They both appeared startled, having left me completely composed to now finding me sobbing uncontrollably for my sweet, darling husband, so brutally taken from us all. They both took their seats without speaking a word; however, Hamish sat next to me, moving his seat closer than usual. I felt his hand on my leg, discreetly attempting to console me without success.

'Mummy, please don't cry anymore. You can sob until you're eighty-five and Daddy won't come back. Not how you want him to. He told me he can never come back, but he can look after the people he loves, and see us whenever he likes. He is invisible now, that's all. Daddy is still the same person inside, and loves us no different. I know everything about the matter, because he told me in his whispers that day. He made me promise to never forget, and I haven't, not one word. He's probably sitting here at this table right now shaking his head at you, by the way, as he hated it when you cried,' Emmy told me as I tried to compose myself. Hamish stared across at me in silence, concern flickering in his eyes. Saying not a word as he sipped his coffee, his hand remained firmly on my upper thigh.

'I know, and I'm sorry for it. This should be a happy day. We're finally here and you will get to see Uncle Henry and Aunty Jenny and their family, who you haven't met yet. Richard has two brothers who have children about the same age as you,' I explained as I dried my tears and took a long drink of water.

'And then there is Sister. She always sends us lovely birthday cards an' knitted things, which are great 'cause our birthday is in autumn when it starts to get a bit chilly again,' Thomas said practically and I smiled. They loved the scarves, hats and gloves, along with the thick socks Sister would make for them and send for their birthdays. Always dark and conservative colours for Thomas, and bright and eclectic for Emmy, who hated anything plain.

'Yes. You're right. Then there is Sister,' I replied, sighing deeply. I couldn't wait to wrap my arms around her and look into her eyes again. She had brought me so much comfort over the years without even knowing it. I wouldn't have survived without her letters every second day, bringing me words to ease my mind and mend my broken heart.

'Ma, we have to go. We promised we'd see everyone before we got off the ship,' Thomas told me, still slightly flushed after his private talk with Hamish.

'That's fine, my love. As long as everything has been done. I want you both to go and check the suite in case you have left anything behind,' I called after them as they jumped up from the table, quickly kissed me and ran inside the suite. They left soon after to say their goodbyes to their friends, leaving us for the few hours that remained.

Hamish stood, saying farewell to Bessie and little Mary, and I followed to see what he wanted to talk to me about. Once in his cabin, I went and sat on the lounge, waiting for him to join me. He looked extremely serious as he came and sat down opposite, leaning forward as he rested his elbows on his knees.

'I dinnae want tae be introduced as yer brother-in-law, tae anyone from now on. That way, should I touch ye or look at ye in a way someone notices, they'll naw think I'm a mongrel out tae seduce me own brother's wife. I'd rather ye say I was Aaron's best mate.' His voice firm, I rolled my eyes in frustration.

'Hamish, I don't want any wee accidents. Or looks that would give us away. Surely you can keep yourself in check for this short time?' I replied, just as firmly.

'Aye, now ye finally asked me feelin's on the matter. Naw, I cannae an' I dinnae want tae keep meself in check. Seems convenient fer ye tae have me in secret, then go about yer life just as before. As if nought has passed between us. But I can naw be like ye. I want tae hold yer hand an' be able tae kiss ye when I like naw matter who's around.' His handsome cheeks started to flush as I glared back at him.

'That wasn't our agreement, and you know it. Like I have told you many times, we can stop this now if you cannot cope. I have given you many opportunities to walk away so if it makes you this unhappy, we will stop.' Angry with him for changing the rules when we would meet the Malcolm's in a few hours, I turned away from him to stare out the porthole at the ocean.

'That's the problem, Abigail. I cannae walk away from ye an' have never been able tae. I love ye more than I've loved anythin' or anyone. I'm naw goin' tae stop just 'cause ye demand it o' me. I'm naw sayin' I'll naw do it. I'm tellin' ye I dinnae know if I *can* do it. The fact o' the matter is, I dinnae want tae even try, but I'll respect yer wishes fer as long as I can bear it. That's all I'll promise.' He rose to his feet, gathered me in his arms, and without another word, carried me to his bedchamber.

We had arrived only an hour before, the smell of rotting fish wafting up my nose and causing my stomach to clench. As I gazed down at the docks, a place I had last seen fifteen-years ago, memories flooded my mind. Some comforting, others frightening. Only this time, I was no longer a girl kept behind orphanage walls and thrust out into a world I was unfamiliar with. I had brought my Australian children with me to see where I came from and to meet the people who were important to me they had only heard about. Little Mary and Bessie walked down the platform first to prevent the twins from running ahead, while Hamish and I followed, keeping a watchful eye on them. We were no sooner on the ground when I heard Jenny calling out, catching sight of her as she ran towards us.

'Oh, Abigail. We have missed you so.' Her arms embraced me tightly, then kissing my face several times, she pulled away. Taking me by both arms, she held me away from her so she could take in all of me at once. 'I still cannot believe it when I see you. You don't look a day over twenty. And still so lovely after all you have been through, my poor darling.' Tears filled her eyes as she pulled me close, embracing me once again. Bessie and little Mary stood off to the side as the Malcolm's hugged and kissed Thomas and Emmy, before greeting Hamish. Mr Malcolm came over to me, beaming as he took me in a warm embrace and kissed me on the forehead.

'It's so good to see you again, Abigail. Here you are looking so well. I must confess, this was not what we were expecting after receiving your letters after losing Aaron. They made Jenny cry every week when she read them out loud to us, and sometimes, I would hear her sobbing in the night for you. The pain you are experiencing, well, it just broke our hearts.' He patted me gently on the back as I tried to smile as brightly as I could, despite wanting to break down and cry.

'I appreciated every one of Jenny's letters that she returned. You will never know how they truly were a ray of light in a very dark storm for me.' Tears in my eyes, I embraced him a little tighter.

'There, there. We have plenty of time together now to talk about it all,' he said soothingly. I introduced them to everyone again, as it had been several years now since we had seen them when they stayed with Richard, and they led us to the waiting carriages. We approached the first carriage, the one behind full with our trunks, the docks just as busy as I remembered it. I looked up to find Mr Millar sitting in the driver's seat, just as I always remembered him.

'Oh, Mr Millar. It's so good to see you again,' I shouted up to him.

'And me you, Mistress Abigail.' He beamed at me as I shifted from foot to foot, my arms outstretched.

'Get down here and give your old friend a kiss. What kind of welcome home party is this with you sitting up there as though we are strangers? Come on, get you wee backside down here,' I called, his eyes going wide for a moment. He got down, quickly looking around to see if anyone was watching before allowing me to embrace, his work calloused hand tentatively patting my back several times before pulling away. He had aged significantly, his hair silver hair now, a number of deep lines to his face that weren't there before, but he was still the same Mr Millar to me. He assisted me up into the carriage where the Malcolms, Hamish, and the children waited. Bessie and little Mary were forced to sit up front with Mr Millar, as the Malcolms liked to do everything the proper way, and that included not travelling with their servants.

'An old friend o' yers?' Hamish asked, a smirk touching his lips.

'Oh yes, and very dear to me. He helped me so much when I first came to London all alone and without any idea about the world,' I said joyously, beaming at everyone. I hadn't felt this happy since losing Aaron, despite feeling so very grief stricken when I woke this morning. Dana had been right, and although the pain lay heavy on me, I felt I was taking the first steps towards a future, and there was a glimmer of hope I may be able to get on with my life and take whatever happiness I could find. I would endure the aching of my heart and cope for my children's sake, and because that was what Aaron had wanted for me.

We arrived at the Malcolms home, finding it exactly as I remembered. I watched the other carriage go down the driveway to unload our luggage, while we stopped out the front of the neat, double story house. I could hear Mr Miller helping Bessie and little Mary down before Hamish chivalrously jumped out, helping Thomas and Emmy, then Jenny, before taking my hand in his and assisting me down to prevent me falling on my face, a common occurrence when it came to me getting in and out of carriages. Mr Malcolm jumped down after me and led us along the path to the house, the front door wide open and their housekeeper waiting to greet us.

We nodded politely as we passed by, following him into the sitting room where everyone made themselves comfortable. Bessie and little Mary had gone around the back of the house with Mr Miller, and I hadn't seen them since. Hamish ensured he sat next to me, a little too close, causing me to discreetly move away moments later. Jenny beamed at me as she asked her housekeeper to bring morning tea, her hand on mine soon after.

'We are absolutely delighted to have you all here. I must say, after being at Willow Grove, we apologise that we are unable to accommodate you in the same way; however, I know for certain that makes no difference to any of you,' Jenny teased as Hamish and Mr Malcolm chuckled. We enjoyed our afternoon tea immensely, while chatting casually about everything but Aaron, only making me feel more lonely for him. He should have been here eating scones and drinking endless cups of tea with our dear friends who he considered my family.

Soon after, Jenny showed us to our rooms, opening a large door to an even larger bedchamber she had selected for me alone. Explaining she now had six empty bedchambers upstairs, she teased how her boys had flown the nest long ago and now she could open a guesthouse. Hamish had been shown to his bedchamber at the back of the house by Mr Malcolm, his large window overlooking the manicured garden I had explored many times with Polly and Richard all those years ago. To ensure my reputation was not tarnished, I had been placed in the grandest room they had away from him, Thomas and Emmy's room beside me, while the Malcolms slept just down the hall.

Bessie and Mary had been shown to the servants' quarters, then introduced to the staff. Now consisting of a housekeeper, two maids, a cook, and a young scullery maid to assist her. There was also a lad who maintained the gardens and carried out any heavy work associated with running a house such as this. Along with Mr Miller. Bessie and Little Mary were not allowed into the main house unless attending to me or the children. It was an impressive staff they had acquired since my first dinner at their home so long ago. I knew Mr Malcolm's law firm was thriving; however, I had not known to what extent until now.

Little Mary had come into the sitting room not long after we had arrived downstairs to take the children to the park, the thoughtful soul wanting them to feel the grass under their feet again. They had dragged little Mary away by the hand, their excited laughter filling my ears long after they were out of sight, while we relaxed in each other's company, sipping our tea and eating freshly baked scones straight from the oven the poor maid had just delivered for the third time. It was nearing luncheon; however, I could not refuse another, the sweet raisins dotted through the still warm scone delighting me.

'Well, Hamish. I know you were Aaron's best friend, as he told me himself many a time when I was at Willow Grove. It is splendid to see you again. The last time we spoke, I was visiting Aaron under the house to say our goodbyes before returning to London, and you were there. It is good of you to accompany Abigail and the children on this voyage, as a rich widow could be seen as easy prey. I feel far more at ease knowing you will take care of them, especially given how fragile Abigail is. I would hate to see a man take advantage of her in that way,' Mr Malcolm said, smiling across at Hamish, who smiled back warmly. They had liked each other very much upon meeting years ago, and I knew Mr Malcolm thought Hamish a good and decent man.

'Aye. It hasn't been a chore, an' I've enjoyed meself very much on the journey here, Mr Malcolm,' Hamish replied, his gaze fixed on me.

'Please, call me Henry. It is only Abigail who calls me Sir or Mr Malcolm, despite me trying to get her to stop and refer to me by my Christian name years ago. We hear, from Abigail's letters, you have been the manager of Willow Grove for a while now, and have been doing a fine job of it. The fact you have been a steadfast and loyal friend throughout her suffering eased our minds. We appreciated she had people with her who cared and were looking after her and the children. It gave Jenny some comfort,' Mr Malcolm said, the log on the fire crackling for a moment, startling me. Hamish appeared embarrassed, nodding his head while drinking his fourth cup of tea, silent as Jenny stared at me, tears in her eyes.

'My heart is truly broken for you, Thomas and Emmy. He was a good and decent man who loved you very much, sweetheart. He talked to Henry and myself of his love of family, and how that was the only thing preventing him walking into the Geelong police station to give himself up. He talked of this visit, only then he planned to come along too. Oh, if we could only turn back the clock and take him far from Australia, how different things could have been.' She sniffed delicately, wiping her eyes with a lace handkerchief before turning back to me. 'Oh, I must stop talking. I can see I am upsetting you, my dear. I feel our daughter has been returned to us having you back in our home,' she said, slipping her arm around my shoulder. I patted her hand, then kissed her on the cheek, Hamish and Mr Malcolm in deep discussion regarding the increasing number of cars on the city streets, and how for the first time, they had introduced licence plates. I was pleased to hear the powers that be had introduced a speed limit of twenty miles an hour, given many drove so fast I was frightened to even stand next to the road.

'I feel the same way,' I replied, a weak smile touching my lips as she nodded, then leaned forward to pass me a fresh cup of tea the young maid had so kindly poured, bowing politely before she backed out of the room, leaving us to our privacy.

Chapter Fourteen

M R MALCOLM HAD REQUESTED I join him in his library to speak in private after luncheon. He had set up an office in there when his children were small, a quiet place away from his growing family that was considered his and his alone, where he would continue to work in peace long after his daytime office had closed. I followed him down the wide hallway and into his private room, the logs in the hearth burning bright red, the room cosy and warm. He poured me a brandy while I sat down in a comfortable leather seat next to the fire. I couldn't help but stare into the flames, memories filling my mind of the last time I was in here—no more than a child expected to behave as a woman with little preparation to enter such a complicated world. Mr Malcolm passed me the glass, then sat opposite, making himself comfortable before fixing his kind brown eyes on mine.

'Well, Abigail, the time has come for me to play my final part in this long and very interesting saga.' He smiled fondly at me as he sipped his brandy thoughtfully. 'And I'm actually feeling quite sad about it, I must admit.' I smiled to myself, inhaling sandalwood and the scent of books hundreds-of-years-old while staring back at his still handsome face, the firelight dancing in his eyes. 'First of all, I must inform you of the balance of your trust fund.' He cleared his throat, then opened a notebook, showing me the amount available to me in my account, my hand going to my throat as I gasped aloud.

'That is more than a thousand people could spend in a lifetime, and that's only if they lived ostentatiously. I will never use it, and I wouldn't know what to do with it. I suspect the trust fund did not have anything near that figure in it fifteen-years ago, despite you refusing then to tell me the amount left to me.'

'That is true, Abigail. Due to the income the three Delmont Hotels generate, it has made the original inheritance appear small, I must agree. This does make you one of the richest women in all of Europe, and with that comes enormous power. I don't think you realise just how much this will change your life. It's all yours now to do with as you please.' He grinned at me across the small table that sat between us. I tried to compose myself, my mind racing. I slowed my breathing, my thoughts clearer the longer I sat staring into the fire, pondering for a time what this would mean for me and my children.

'Mr Malcolm, would you consider staying on as my lawyer here, and managing the fund and my business as you have done so very competently for so long now?' I asked, feeling it an imposition given he would soon want to retire now he had made his money, and his family were grown.

'Of course I will, my dear. I am getting on in age, but Jonathon and George know your business as well as I do. I am happy to continue to look after your interests here until your instructions change. The boys will take over when the time comes in the future, should you wish to continue with the same arrangements?' He smiled as he took my hand in his. We talked of the orphanage, and how he had increased their allowance as the cost of living increased, just as we had agreed before I left London. He believed I would be more than impressed with the changes that had occurred over the years at Emiliani House.

'Given what I have exceeds what I need, I would like you to double the amount they receive each year.' His eyes widened before clearing his throat again.

'Are you certain, Abigail? That is a great deal of money when what they receive now is adequate to meet the children's needs far above what even you requested. I do not believe giving them even more would be of any benefit.' He clearly did not approve, narrowing his gaze as I rolled my eyes in his direction.

'Of course I am certain. What they have may be adequate, but I want them to live well and have luxuries they are probably going without. Yes. I am certain that's what I want.' I was defiant, and he knew it, signing deeply before closing his eyes for a moment.

'Fine. I give up trying to talk sense to you, young lady. I know you have a lot of money; however, you never know what the future holds. As you wish, although I doubt the Sisters would know what to do with luxuries. I am *certain* they are not allowed to have them. Despite my thoughts on the matter, I will carry out your instructions.' I smiled brightly at him, relaxing back into my chair, while he shook his head at my stubbornness. 'There is another matter I must bring up with you. I do not know if Richard, or your previous lawyer, Mr McPhee, has any knowledge of this; however, it has recently come to my attention that an island in Fiji was left to you. Apparently, your great-aunt bought it many years before I met her when she was travelling the world. She came across it by accident, and thought it the most beautiful place on earth, going on in later years to purchase it from the natives who reside there. My understanding is that it is actually two islands. A large island that is uninhabited, and a smaller island next to it where the natives live. At low tide you can walk from one island to the other, I am told. I do not know the name of the island or the tribe, but I know your great-aunt was friendly with them and went to stay when she could, spending months at a time living with them and learning their customs. She paid them a lot of money for the island, when they would have accepted practically nothing. She was never one to take advantage of others, despite their ignorance. She ensured they were looked after—I am told they are the wealthiest tribe in Fiji as a direct result. I am uncertain what you will do with it, or if you ever intend to visit the place, but it's not something you will be forced to decide now or in the near future. The island takes care of itself, and costs you nothing to keep. One day, you may decide to do something with it, so do not give it away to anyone,' he teased as I shook my head in disbelief. It was shocking to me that there were things I was still finding out about great-aunt Isabelle, and what she had left me. How an Englishwoman who spent some time living in Australia was able to travel around the world as a single woman still astounded me for the times she lived in. She also intrigued me, as everything about her was so mysterious. 'One day you may get sick of Willow Grove and decide to go and live in paradise,' he said cheerfully as I smiled, my eyes fixed on the fire in the hearth, startling me on occasion when the wood would crackle and spit when the sap was touched by the flame.

'Never.'

'Now I want to ask you. How are you really coping with the loss of Aaron? I know you loved him deeply.' He settled himself back in his chair and made himself comfortable for a long chat between friends.

'And still do,' I replied, bursting into tears immediately. He looked at me with such pity, then handed me a fresh handkerchief from his breast pocket before encouraging me to continue. 'It feels like my heart has turned to ice since he left me. I still carry a heavy burden and am in immeasurable pain, but now I try to keep my grief private, and only allow myself to break down when I am alone, or someone brings him up.' I sobbed as he leaned over and took my hand in his again, comforting me greatly.

'I am so very sorry, my dear Abigail. I am deeply grieved you lost him, especially in the way you did. It is a cruel God to take a husband from his wife, and a father from such young children who still need him. It was all a very sad and sorry state of affairs. I do wish I had been in Geelong at the time he was captured. I am not saying I could have done any better than Richard; however, I do believe if I had him sit as my chair and we worked the case together...' He paused for a moment, swallowing hard several times before continuing. 'Well, I suppose there is no point thinking like that now. What I meant was two heads are always better than one, and we may have had a different outcome. They rushed him to trial so quickly, then ten -days from sentencing he was executed. Someone was intent on having Aaron dead, from what I have read in the papers, and from Richard's letters. He still blames himself over two-years later, poor boy. For the moment, I'm worried about you, young lady. You have lost that sparkle in your eyes that always twinkled when you laughed or said something cheeky. My wish is that one day it will be restored, and you will find some peace and happiness in your future. These things take time, longer for some than others, and you have all the time in the world. You are still young, and you are fortunate to have your children to keep living for. I know what has happened to you is one of the most grievous things in the world, and your pain is unbearable, but you must start looking forward, not back, as those days are now past and can never be retrieved. You could have any man you so choose in the future, when you are ready.'

'I do not have the strength to even care for myself some days, Mr Malcolm, let alone another man. It is exhausting trying to get through each day without him. My heart is so filled with pain, and too heavy to bear. I miss him, and it will not matter who I meet in the future.' He patted me on the back, my body wracked with sobs. 'My life will never be the same. I plan to stay by myself and take lovers, when I am ready,' I added, suddenly remembering who I was speaking to, and felt my face flush. For a moment, I thought I was with Richard. He had his father's eyes, and I had let my guard down. Mr Malcome stared at me in silence, clearly amused as he poured us another drink then sat back down.

'I personally am not here to judge you, nor do I believe there is anything wrong with that; however, do not tell Jenny or she will faint dead away at your lack of morality.' He smirked at me as I giggled without meaning to. 'Did you know that Aaron has become famous over here, known as a fighter for the underdog, a man who did what he believed in and stood up to those who abuse their power? The papers ran all the stories on the trial, and the subsequent uproar about his unjust execution. The biggest mystery is where he hid for all that time. Not one person who knows the truth has opened their mouths, including that strange chef you have in your employ. I must remember to tell you of an extremely confusing conversation I had with that young man.' I cringed at the thought of what Leo could have said to him, and quickly changed the subject, preferring not to know.

'Yes, I am aware. I have received thousands of letters from England. People still write to me two-years later, and visit our home in the hope of seeing Aaron's grave, something I will never allow. I have kept his resting place a secret, as it is private to me,' I replied as I wiped tears from my face.

'And so it should be. You should be proud, as Aaron did not die in vain. There has been an investigation into police conduct and members of the judicial system, with many sacked or stood down from their positions or pushed into carrying out menial tasks until they quit. People admire Aaron and have turned him into a hero because he stood up against a system that was unjust, and from beyond the grave changes did come. I know he was the sacrificial lamb; however, it is important you know that he was, and is, important to many people. The love you had for each other leapt off the pages as I read the news articles, as I'm sure it did to others. Many were sympathetic towards his cause—seeking vengeance on your behalf. Not many find a love like that in their lifetime, Abigail, and you are the lucky one for having been loved by him. You do not have to forget him, but you do need to move on with your life. You are strong and brave, and I know if anyone can do this, it's you,' he reassured me, then rose to his feet, indicating our meeting was over and the time had come for me to leave. I thanked him, then embraced him warmly before hurrying out into the hallway to find my children, while leaving him to his business as he closed the door behind me.

Bessie had only just finished dressing me for dinner when the twins came in, throwing themselves down on the bed. They liked to watch me get ready, often picking out my dress for the day or evening, and then Emmy would help Bessie with my hair while chatting incessantly in an attempt to keep me occupied.

Hamish had confided in me only hours before, Thomas had experienced his first kiss. Not that it sounded as if he had much choice in the matter. From the little he told me, Hannah had marched up to Thomas the last night aboard the ship and dragged him out onto the deck, telling him firmly they wouldn't see each other for a time and she felt they needed to say a proper goodbye, before putting her arms around his neck and kissing him on the mouth. He was quite taken aback by it all and had asked Hamish if it was usual for girls to be the first to kiss a boy, as he always believed it the other way around.

Hamish sympathised deeply with him, far more than I felt necessary, before going on about how women had changed in the twentieth century and had become predators of the male species, leaving Thomas in fits of laughter. Hamish had gone on to explain that some women, if a bloke was lucky enough, did indeed pursue men, especially if they were handsome and wealthy, proudly tousling his sandy blonde hair. They had talked further, but Hamish had kept that between him and Thomas, and I asked no further questions as I respected their privacy and the bond they shared.

Bessie and Emmy continued styling my hair, deciding to put all of it up as they stared into the mirror at my reflection while twisting and pinning every strand into place.

'You look so very lovely, Mummy. Everyone says you are the most beautiful woman they have ever laid eyes on—except for Uncle Leo. He says you're unfortunate looking and need to wear a bag over your head so you don't destroy his vision permanently,' Emmy said, twisting and pinning in the last curl.

'I'm glad you think so, Emmy. You favour me very much they say, so I hope you always know how beautiful *you* are. You know not to listen to anything Uncle Leo says,' I said, kissing her cute nose. Hamish knocked on the door, and I stood then crossed the room to greet him, as did the twins, bidding Bessie farewell. We made our way downstairs, chatting jovially, then stepped into the dining room to find George and Georgina, along with Jonathon and Isabelle, already seated at the table with Mr Malcolm and Jenny.

The room was large and formal; however, not as grand as I remembered when I attended my first dinner here as a wide-eyed, naive fifteen-year-old. Nor was it as extravagant as Willow Grove, and that suited me well. Jenny had insisted only her best crystal and serving-ware was laid on the table, while the silver candelabra flickered, casting a romantic light over the proceedings. Jenny led me to my seat in between Jonathon and Mr Malcolm, while Hamish was seated down at the other end of the table between Isabelle and Georgina.

'It is wonderful to see you again, Abigail. You look far lovelier than I remember,' Jonathon said, kissing my hand as I smiled at him. We talked between ourselves as we sipped our wine, Jonathon sharing with me how his father's law practice had expanded, and of his own life. 'Between you and me, Abigail, I've been dreadfully unhappy for many, many years now. I fear I made an unwise decision in my choice of wife. She is a vindictive, cold woman, who shows not the slightest bit of compassion or kindness to anyone, including myself. Once the children are grown, I hope to live separately from Isabelle, as I cannot bear to look at her.' I patted his hand, and he took mine in his own, then squeezed it for a moment, his eyes fixed on mine. Despair and loneliness stared back at me, and I felt desperately sorry for him. I hated to see anyone unhappy, but with someone I considered family, it was heartbreaking to witness.

We talked of Willow Grove, and the life we had made there. He appeared quite impressed, promising when he finally took the long awaited journey to visit his brother, he would be privileged to call on me and view the property.

'You have changed very little over the years, Abigail. Tell us your secret as it would benefit Georgina immensely. As you can see, she has let herself go since having the children, and has ended up the size of a whale. I'm sure she would appreciate anything you could do to help her, as would her husband George,' Isabelle remarked, my head jolting around abruptly before I fixed her with a glare. She hadn't evolved from the spoiled, nasty young woman I had met only a handful of times, disappointing and angering me as I attempted to bite my tongue.

'No secret, Isabelle. I don't believe Georgina needs any help at all. She still looks as lovely as the day I met her.' I smiled across at Georgina, who smiled back, her cheeks flushed while her hands trembled slightly. 'And the fact she has such a generous heart, and the kindest eyes I've ever seen, makes her one of the most beautiful people I know.' Hamish raised his eyebrows in amusement, while Isabelle glared back at me before throwing her napkin down on the table.

'You still believe you're better than everyone else because of how you look, and have always taken great pleasure flaunting yourself to ensure every man in the room takes notice of your every movement. You were no different at fifteen, and always had that air about you. We are all very much aware *you* are of the opinion *this* family is beneath you, given my father-in-law is in your employ and is treated as your own personal servant.' Her voice cold as ice, silence hung heavy over the room as everyone present stared at her, wide-eyed and in apparent disbelief. I swallowed hard, turning my attention to the grey sky outside the window. The day dim and cold, the bare branches of the trees appeared to shiver, while the fire in the hearth burned warmly. As did my cheeks.

'Have you gone mad since I last saw you, Isabelle? Did I hear you say I looked down my nose at you all those years ago? I was a child and I did not have a clue what I was doing. Nor did I understand anything about the way of the world and had not a drop of confidence whatsoever in me. I felt terrible about myself back then. I was completely overwhelmed by you all, and this house, having never experienced anything like it. You were the machete mouthed bitch who sat through family lunch as if you were sitting on the royal throne itself, all the while putting Georgina down at every opportunity,' I spat, causing Jenny to gasp aloud, her hand going to her throat, while the Malcolm men shifted in their seats and appeared mortified. A smirk touched Hamish's lips for a moment as he glanced across at Thomas and Emmy, both appearing quite amused.

'Enough! We ask you to respect our home and when seated at our table, there will be no arguments. We have come together as family, and shall treat each other as such. I include you all in this.' Mr Malcolm interupted, placing his hand gently on my forearm just as I was about to stand and rip her fucking head off. He gave Isabelle a hard stare and she lowered her gaze to avoid him. 'Are we all ready to eat?' Mr Malcolm called out cheerfully and we nodded in unison, much to his relief. He motioned for his servants to begin service, allowing me several moments to compose myself before starting the meal, the food just as delicious as I remembered.

I took a long sip of wine. After the soup, my children were served a large portion of lamb, then requested more roasted vegetables before polishing their plates. The maid seemed fascinated as she watched them devour their dessert soon after, her eyes wide while muttering to herself when they asked for a second helping while she cleared away their dishes.

'Is Mrs Shank still in your employ? She wanders through my mind on occasion and stops to linger a while.'

'Yes, of course she is still here. I'm aware she is quite eager to see you, my dear. She still talks fondly of you quite often, and never fails to point out to me how you are the only guest we have ever had who prefers to eat in her kitchen rather than in the dining room,' Jenny said, her mouth twitching as I smiled, while Hamish chuckled to himself.

Once every dish had been cleared away, Jonathon poured two whiskies from the crystal decanter before passing me a glass. We had not even raised the amber liquid to our lips before I heard a shrill voice, reminding me of two barn cats in a hessian bag fighting to the death.

'I hope you are not considering drinking that, Jonathon?' Isabelle warned, her eyes glinting dangerously as I turned away and rolled my eyes at the fireplace, unable to hide my displeasure.

'I am only having a small nip, Isabelle. This is a celebration, given Abigail has been safely returned to us.' His voice low and steady; however, it was clear he felt defeated, leaving my stomach in knots while my heart broke for him. I never understood why, once married, people were expected to stay together until they took their last breath—even after finding, as time went on, they were incompatible and terribly unhappy. It made absolutely no sense to me at all. I could not bear to stay with a man I despised, no matter what my circumstances; of that I was certain.

'You can put that glass down right now, Jonathon! You know you are not *allowed* to drink hard liquor,' Isabelle shouted across the table. A hush fell over the room as all present stared at her, then at Jonathon, with much sympathy in their eyes. He remained silent, rising to his feet before striding out of the room without another word towards the kitchen, his footsteps heavy. We remained still in the silence, hearing no more until the back door slammed in the distance. 'I could not have picked a more hopeless husband if I tried. Do you see what I have to put up with? He cannot think for himself even if his life depended on it. Are all men as useless as my Jonathon, or am I just the unlucky one?' Widening her eyes to make her point, Isabelle nodded smugly several times to herself, strongly implying that anyone who dared disagree would be considered a lunatic. I watched Hamish grimace as if he were in physical pain and realised he may have been thinking of his own situation—the women in his past who had behaved in a similar manner to Isabelle. Only he had been in the direct line of fire. Jenny stood, her face a mottled red, while her hands trembled, tears filling her pretty eyes. Mr Malcolm rose to his feet, gently placing his large hand on her shoulder to steady her.

'It's time we all retire to the sitting room.' Mr Malcolm wrapped his arm around Jenny's shoulder before guiding her out of the room. All present followed obediently. All but me. I picked up the decanter and filled both glasses before placing them on a small tray and hurrying out of the room to find Jonathon.

Jonathon sat on a bench in the garden, not far from the back door, his shoulders slumped. I pulled my cloak closer against the frigid air as I approached him, his woollen coat in my hand, the tray in the other.

'Here.' I passed him the glass before making myself comfortable beside him. He gratefully took his coat and slipped it over his shoulders. 'Drink it and be damned with the consequences.' I laughed aloud, trying to cheer him; however, my laughter rang empty through the manicured garden. It was lovely outside despite the cold. The weak autumn sun, unable to break through the heavy clouds most of the day, was low in the sky, bringing on the night. I gazed around in amusement, not surprised in the least that nothing had changed out here at all. He picked up his glass from where he had set it on the bench beside him and drank it in one swallow. 'Does Isabelle often attack you in that manner, Jonathon? I am the last person who should stick their nose into someone else's marriage but what passed between you was difficult to witness. Why would you not stand up for yourself? You cannot let her disrespect you in such a manner. Or shame you like this in front of everyone. I am not suggesting you strike her or use violence but you must put her back in her place.' I knew full well my advice was only making the situation worse. He affectionately slipped his arm around my shoulder, reminding me of dear Richard as we sat side-by-side in silence admiring the turn of the light. I handed him my own glass, sensing he needed it far more than I.

'It is difficult, Abigail. If I say too much, she only gets worse. I read about what it was like between you and your husband in the papers, and what I heard in conversation through my parents and Richard's letters. I've never had a relationship that is respectful and loving. Well, not with a woman. I accepted Isabelle only because my parents believed she would make a steadfast wife and we would make a good match. They are deeply regretful and have wished for years now they never pushed me into this union with such an unsuitable woman.' His mouth twitched in amusement as he glanced at me before fixing his gaze on the stables at the back of the property. A lamp burned brightly in the loft window, and I smiled affectionately at the thought of my old friend.

'I am not the best person to seek advice or an opinion from. My dear friend, Leo, tells all who will listen that I always say the wrong thing in every situation. Says I'm best to go against my instinct and take the opposite choice. Only then will I be right.' A weak smile touched his lips, although his eyes were filled with sadness. He had aged, his handsome face lined with worry, his frown lines deep. I understood from the little I knew of Isabelle, she came from a middle-class family and that they were good people. How they had spawned such an entitled and cruel woman was a mystery to all who knew them.

'Thanks for trying to cheer me, Abigail. I suppose we should get back inside before we are missed.' He rose to his feet, and I stood with him. He took a few steps towards the house before turning back, abruptly taking me by the shoulders, startling me. 'Come stay with me at the Delmont. I have wanted you since the very first day I met you, but you were far too young. I was newly married, hoping things would improve between me and Isabelle. You are the sweetest woman I know, and I do feel like I know you intimately. Despite having only met twice. You are a beloved member of our family, thought of often, and only spoken of with love and affection.'

'As you pointed out, we've met twice. You do not know me, Jonathon, but I do understand you have lost your head after that shameful display from Isabelle. I feel a great deal of sympathy for you, but your affections are misplaced.' He roughly grabbed my hands in his and as he stared down at me, I shook my head. I completely understood why he felt his happiness lay with anyone other than Isabelle, but I was unable to help him anymore than his family could—and I was aware they had tried. Kindly offering for him to return to the family home, they had been clear he had their blessing to divorce. No matter what scandal was likely to follow, they would support him in every way. From the little I had heard on the matter, he had quietly rejected all offers of help for reasons he refused to disclose. He raised his dark eyebrows, my hands trapped in his.

'I know exactly who you are, and that is why I am so very drawn to you. It's not only the way you look, although you are truly exquisite. More importantly, you are sweet and gentle, and I cannot imagine an ugly word coming from your mouth. I feel an unbearable need to be close to you. To draw some comfort and happiness for myself before the opportunity disappears. Come to me in secret and I will do anything you ask of me, now and in the future.' His desperation to escape his situation was evident as he shifted from foot to foot, the garden silent around us, all except for the sound of a car slowly travelling down a street somewhere in the distance.

'Oh, Jonathon. I am sorry, but I cannot do any such thing. You are a married man, and I will play no part in any affair, no matter what I think of your wife. Although it is tempting. If only to teach her a lesson for being such an awful human being.' I smiled up at him as he sniggered, the awkwardness between us now gone as I slipped my hands from his. 'You really do not know me at all. If you did, you would know ugly words come out of my mouth all the time. I have to remind myself constantly when in the company of your parents to watch my tongue and not say words that would make your mother reach for the smelling salts.' His eyes twinkled in amusement, his warm hands holding me by both arms as he stared down at me. He was only a few inches taller than me, but his frame was strong and stocky. If I had not considered him as kin, I might have been frightened by his determination.

'I am married only on paper, and you are now a free woman. Please meet me at the hotel. I will give the excuse that I was called to York on business for a few days. No one ever needs to know.' I heard voices drifting out of the sitting room alongside the house; the merriment of the evening gone since dinner, their voices low.

'I would know. I cannot consider anything of the sort, Jonathon. I apologise and I do hope you resolve these issues and find happiness.' I tried to swallow the lump in my throat while feeling extremely sorry for him. He was lonely and desperately needed someone to love him; however, refused to believe it was not going to be me.

He pulled me towards him, then placed his mouth on mine, kissing me deeply while holding me tight against his chest, probing my lips with his tongue and demanding I respond. He slipped his arms around me, his hands on my waist, and I allowed myself to melt into him. Only wanting to ease his pain and provide comfort, I returned his kiss, my Catholic conscience screaming at me no matter how much I screamed back my justifications. He raised one hand to my face and gently stroked his fingers along my jawbone, his kiss tender now. After the longest time, I heard a cough behind us and quickly pulled away. Expecting to see Isabelle as I turned around, my breath fast, my heart racing, I raised my hand to smooth my hair in an attempt to compose myself.

'They're servin' drinks in the sittin' room an' people are startin' tae wonder where ye are.' Hamish loomed large in the doorway, his voice calm while his eyes glinted dangerously. He gave a nod in our direction before turning on his heel and stepping back inside, his footsteps fading away as he strode down the hallway towards the kitchen. Jonathon stared after him, his handsome face thoughtful.

'You want to know something strange, Abigail? I do not care if he goes back inside and tells Isabelle.' I gasped in horror and grabbed his hand in mine, pulling him urgently towards the back door.

'Well, I do. Let's forget what passed between us and return inside to the warmth. And our dear family.' I squeezed his hand kindly, and he nodded, allowing his arm to fall to his side before I turned away and stepped through the door, Jonathon following close behind.

Chapter Fifteen

I STROLLED INTO THE sitting room, hoping no one would notice, while Jonathon had stopped in the kitchen to take a swig of brandy from the larder. Thomas and Emmy sat near the fire playing noughts and crosses on a wooden board, and had saved me a seat between them. Jonathon ambled in soon after and went to join his family on the lounges, sitting down next to Isabelle while I greeted my children with kisses. Lowering myself onto the tapestry seat only when they moved the board away, their smiles wide as Emmy placed it down on the floor, they welcomed me back.

'Did you drink that whisky? I can smell it on your breath. Do not think about lying to me, Jonathon, as I'm fed up with your deceptions. All you do is deny, deny, deny. Mind you, that is why you make such an excellent barrister and the only reasons I consented to this marriage. You do earn respectable wages and that's about all the good of you,' Isabelle snapped.

'It's brandy,' was all Jonathon could say, lowering his head. I watched his cheeks flush while his right hand twitched on his lap, his anger palpable as silence once again settled over the room. The urge to stand up and strike the woman dead welled up in me for a moment, until I saw Mr Malcom raise his hand, his palm pointed towards his daughter-in-law.

'Silence! That is quite enough for tonight, Isabelle. I kindly ask you to control your mouth when under my roof. Jonathon has taken only a small quantity of spirits yet he is not drunk; therefore, we shall have no more of this tonight. It is a celebration and a time of great joy to be in the company of those we love.' He fixed his daughter-in-law with a stare, relief washing over me his wrath was not cast in my direction. I loved Mr Malcolm dearly and was well aware he was a conservative man who had raised his boys with a firm hand. He demanded respect when not freely given. I had been told he was the spit of his grandfather, a highly regarded barrister who was familiar with my great-aunt when she was a young woman. Mr Malcolm refused to confide in me the true nature of their relationship other than he once acted on her behalf. I firmly believed he knew far more than he had told me.

'Of course, you are right, father. If my husband chooses to linger at the tavern by the docks, consorting with the sots who slumber in the doorways of the Molly Houses, it is his prerogative and reflects not on me,' Isabelle replied, her voice dripping with venom. We ignored her, while I enquired about Mr Malcolm and Jenny's grandchildren, all nearing adulthood in the next few years. George and Georgina insisted we speak more of Willow Grove. A place they were enchanted by after listening to Mr Malcolm and Jenny talk of their time there, along with the letters they received from Richard and Jasmin.

The hours passed quickly, and when I noticed Emmy yawn for the third time, I excused myself for the evening. Citing the children were overtired from the journey and I must put them to bed, our hosts graciously nodded. Saying our goodnights before I guided the twins up to their bedchamber and helped them into their nightclothes, I was relieved to shut the door behind me. Climbing onto the bed, I picked up the book I had placed on the table only hours before, the lantern in the corner flickering gently, while casting a romantic glow over the elaborate room.

'There was movement at the station,' I murmured, smiling to myself as I flicked through the pages for a moment.

'For the word had passed around,' Thomas chimed in, his eyes fixed on the ceiling, his hands behind his head as he waited for me to start.

'Oh, I just love this book. It reminds me of home,' Emmy whispered as I settled myself in between them, the book resting on my stomach.

I had selected the tome from Mr Malcolm's library, an entire shelf dedicated to Australian literature I had sent him over the years. He had become a dedicated reader of Andrew 'Banjo' Patterson—a lawyer by trade and a journalist by profession—soon after I immigrated, with *Clancy of the Overflow* and *Saltbush Bill* amongst his favourites.

The Man from Snowy River and Other Verses had swept the colonies when first published on the 17th of October, 1895—and I was one of the first to purchase a copy to send back to London to my dear friend. The book sold 7,000 copies in the first few months, the first edition selling out completely in the first week of publication.

'It reminds me of home, too, sweetheart. And your Daddy.' Thomas turned to face us, his eyes lighting up.

'Me too, Ma. He loved *Waltzin' Matilda* more than all of 'em. I would hear him whistlin' that tune when I'd find him in the stables workin' when me school day was done.' I turned and kissed his cheek, my heart heavy in the knowledge of just how much he missed his father. Emmy picked up the book and placed it in my hands, encouraging me to hurry up and read.

'Well, this book doesn't have that one in it, but I know the poem by heart if you would like me to recite it,' I teased, knowing full well he could do the same in his sleep.

This particular collection had been received with enthusiasm—not only in his homeland, but in England—and had resulted in Paterson's identity as 'The Banjo' finally being revealed, bringing him fame almost overnight throughout the land and beyond the shores of Australia.

Even I had heard the rumours that still continued almost a decade later, claiming that several months after the Shearers Strike of 1894, Paterson had visited the squatter family, Macpherson, who had settled at Dagworth Station. Making the long and arduous journey to Winton in Queensland with his fiancée, Sarah Riley, by his side; they had travelled at the invitation of her school friend, Christina Macpherson, and her brother, Bob, who managed the vast property.

I had met Sarah several times at the General Store when she visited Willow Grove to stay with Amelia. They had been close friends and confidants over the last twelve-years, however; she had remained aloof towards me, her disinterest in becoming anything more than acquaintances clear.

Amelia had told me, as relayed to her in letters by Sarah's own hand, while riding in a carriage to Dagworth that they noticed a swagman walking along the dusty road. Bob had made comment, *'that's what they call Waltzing the Matilda.'* A term Sarah was unfamiliar with, she felt the need to discuss this with her dear friend, going into great detail about her time spent at the station.

She had shared how Bob and Paterson had become firm friends and frequently went for long rides around the property, leaving her to her own devices for hours at a time, and she had tired of it.

During a tour of Dagworth, they stopped by the Combo Waterhole, finding a hide from a freshly killed sheep, while assuming the slaughter to be at the hand of a passing swagman. Sitting down to rest by the billabong, Bob told Paterson a story of a German shearer, Samuel 'Frenchy' Hoffmeister, a union leader who, along with a dozen other angry shearers, fired their pistols and burnt down a shed on the property during the strike only months before, killing over a hundred and forty lambs.

Bob, along with three constables, gave chase to Hoffmeister, who they believed responsible for starting the fire while leading the others in the violent uprising. Failing to catch up with Hoffmeister, he was found dead the following day at Four-Mile Billabong. Reports at the time said Hoffmeister shot himself in the mouth to avoid capture, but some suspected he was *caught up with* after all, and murdered in cold blood.

Amelia did tell me over afternoon tea only recently when discussing the origins of the poem, there had been a story doing the rounds at the time about a group of constables on the lookout for a man named Harry Wood. Accused of beating a native boy to death, the police had been unable to locate him for quite some time. During yet another search, they stumbled across a hapless swagman camped by Como Billabong who took fright at the sight of them, jumped in, and tragically drowned.

Amelia was of the opinion it was from this story, Paterson wrote *Waltzing Matilda*, and believed Bob's sister, Christina, helped him put the poem to music. Playing a tune one evening on her zither, Paterson had asked what it was, believing it would fit his words and create an uplifting, light-hearted ditty for the evening's entertainment. She explained she had heard *The Craiglee March* at the Warrnambool Steeplechase when she travelled to Victoria only months before, and proudly announced how she could now play it by ear.

It was on a visit to Winton township, Paterson and Christina used a piano in the parlour of the North Gregory Hotel to polish and finalise *Waltzing Matilda*, and soon after, it was performed at The Post Office Hotel by the Macpherson's neighbour, Herbert Ramsey who hailed from Oondooroo Station, and was said to be one of the best tenors in the district—the song soon spreading throughout the locality and beyond through word of mouth alone.

'I'm not sure if you know, the original song is quite different to the one you hear for Billy Tea,' I remarked, the tune now stuck in my head as I turned several more pages before deciding where to start. Emmy giggled, her arm tightening around me, her head on my shoulder, while Thomas chuckled to himself.

Paterson had sold the song in 1900, along with several other works combined into a bundle, to Angus & Robertson for five quid—if the rumours were to be believed—and the rights were bought in 1902 by James Inglis & Company, an importer of tea. They sold over a million-and-a-half-pounds of tea a year under the trademark Billy Tea, and were a favourite at Willow Grove from the staff right through to myself.

Marie Cowan, a gifted musician and wife of an accountant working for James Inglis & Company, had been given the task of improving the original song in 1903, changing some of the lyrics to fit the melody. It did not take long for the song to gain popularity after the sheet music and lyrics were printed, then wrapped around tins of Billy Tea.

'Aunty Amelia doesn't like Banjo. She says he's a cheat and a fornicator of the worst kind. And his beautiful prose does not reflect his blackened soul. Or the diseased old fella dangling between his legs he's forced to carry around,' Emmy murmured, her eyes heavy before I even began. Saliva caught in my throat and I choked, coughing uncontrollably for a moment before trying to compose myself.

There were whispers that Andrew 'Banjo' Paterson started a love triangle of his own during that time. That triangle included Christina and his extremely tolerant fiancee; however, no one really knew for certain. Except those involved—and Amelia.

What was common knowledge was Paterson had been kicked out of the Macpherson home shortly after writing the song, and the supposed affair left both women spurned and humiliated. Sarah soon called off the engagement and moved to London, and from what I knew through her correspondence with Amelia, neither woman had married. Christina never again entertained Paterson at Dagworth where she remained to this day, nor did she correspond with him. The last I had heard on the matter was, on the 8th of April, 1903, Paterson had married Alice Emily, the daughter of Mr Walker of Tenterfield Station. They settled soon after at Woollahra, and Amelia had confided their daughter, Grace, had been born to them earlier this year—and from all reports, all was well.

'That is not for us to judge, Emmy. We do not know the man, or his heart, and must refrain from wagging our tongues without thought. No matter what we hear. Best to keep our nose out of their business and away from gossip. No more nasty talk of things you are too young to speak of,' I warned her, a soft snore coming from her lips, while Thomas slept deeply beside her.

They often fell asleep in my arms when I would read them his work aloud, tales of the outback and wild bushmen filling their dreams, and tonight was no different. Only I had not read a word.

I kissed their sleeping faces before finding my way to my own bedchamber to discover Bessie waiting patiently for me. She assisted me out of my dress and had me in my nightclothes within minutes before sitting me down at the dressing table to brush my hair.

'Did you enjoy yourself today, Mistress?' Her voice low and gentle, she started to unwind my hair, soon picking up the silver brush while placing the pins in the pocket of her apron.

'Yes, I did, Bessie. It was a very nice night. Seeing all the Malcolms again has made me feel I have come home to the bosom of my family. They have always meant so very much to me. I will never forget they were the first people I met when I left the orphanage who showed me unconditional kindness. They had no obligation to embrace me as one of their own, but they did. I will always appreciate them for that act alone.' Relief washed over her, her shoulders visibly relaxing as she plaited my hair in an attempt to make her task easier in the morning.

I knew she had worried herself sick that I would fall in a heap as soon as we arrived due to Aaron's absence. I believed I had coped reasonably well, all considering, finding I had only broken down a few times during the day. She smiled down fondly at me, touching the back of my head before bidding me goodnight. I climbed into bed and pulled the covers over me, still feeling Bessie's gentle kiss on my cheek.

Tucked up under the heavy quilt and sleeping peacefully, I heard the door open, startling me awake from a dream I couldn't quite remember—although Aaron had been there—my eyes filled with tears at the thought of him.

'What the bloody hell do you think you're doing? Have you lost your mind?' I hissed loudly, his enormous frame looming in the doorway, a lamp in his hand lighting the bedchamber as he stepped inside. Closing the door silently behind him, he walked towards me.

'I have tae speak tae ye. It cannae wait.' He lowered himself onto the end of the bed, his tone controlled yet his anger obvious. I sat up and arranged my pillows before leaning back, preparing myself to be chastised. 'I heard an' saw everythin' between ye an' Jonathon this evenin'. Seems every time I look 'round, there's another man tryin' tae charm ye or wantin' tae take ye tae his bed. Or both. Tonight, I find ye in the embrace o' another man. An' kissin' him fer Christ's sake. How do ye expect me tae feel when ye know how much I love ye? Must I fight fer ye constantly against others fer the rest o' me life? When are ye goin' tae realise I'm the only man yer meant tae be with?' He lowered his head into his hands and grunted as I narrowed my gaze, the room bright thanks to his lantern.

'Hamish, I do not have to explain myself to you. You are a single man and I, a single woman. We are both free to do as we choose.

Since you heard *everything*, then you would have heard me refuse him?' I snapped. How dare he treat me as though I were his and his alone? I had been clear to him from the beginning that I wanted no attachment in any shape or form to another man. He raised his head to glare at me while crossing his arms against his broad chest, rage in his brown eyes, always reminding me of melted chocolate, no matter his mood.

'Ye only refused him 'cause he's married. If he'd been an available man, ye would've bedded him. I could see it between ye,' he spat as I returned his furious stare.

'And if I did, it's none of your fucking business. Get yourself out of my bedchamber now,' I hissed again, my hand going to a pillow. Launching it across the room with all my strength, although aiming for his head, the missile unfortunately landed near his feet as he crossed the room. Kicking it out of the way before turning the doorknob, he turned back to glare at me.

'Fuck ye, Abigail,' he growled before promptly walking out.

'And fuck you a hundred thousand times more,' I whispered hoarsely as the door clicked shut behind him.

Hamish and the children spent the week out and about in London, visiting several royal palaces, Saint Paul's Cathedral, and the Zoological Society at Regent's Park, to name only a few. I was unable to bring myself to join them or visit any of the places Aaron and I had talked of seeing together, feeling I would suffer a nervous collapse and take to my bed again.

I had spent my days with Jenny, shopping and visiting Georgina while the men worked. Jenny had wisely chosen not to visit Isabelle's home in Notting Hill while I was present, and I had formed the belief she suspected what had passed between Jonathon and myself. I was thrilled, and vowed to remain as far away from Isabelle as possible. After witnessing with my own eyes how she demeaned her husband in front of people, displaying no regard for his feelings or concern for the shame she caused him, I believed poor Jonathon was suffering far worse in private than any of us first thought. Hamish had been right. If Jonathon had not been married, I would have shared my bed with him out of sympathy without a second thought.

Hamish had not spoken a word to me since that night in my bed-chamber. Only being civil in front of Thomas and Emmy, he limited his conversation with me to only what he needed to ask regarding the twins. I was well aware his coldness towards me was only to force me into submission, therefore, I did what most sensible women did and ignored him. He was unable to comprehend or accept I had nothing to give him—my heart still belonged to Aaron. I was unable to give him the love he wanted, and very much deserves, or the affection he craved so desperately from me. I had been honest with him from the start, holding nothing back, and felt he was responsible for his own feelings, as I was for mine. I felt beyond angry with him for moving the goalposts in the middle of a game—breaking every rule he could along the way.

We were leaving today on the late train to Scotland, and had decided to travel overnight in a private compartment to ensure we arrived by morning and had the full day to settle in at Lord Harrington's estate. I was uncertain if Lord Harrington would be in residence or if he had delegated the task of hosting us to his servants in his absence. He was a busy man and it was unlikely he would find the time to travel to Scotland given he had only arrived back in London after a month in Australia. I hoped deep down he was in residence during our time there as I enjoyed his company and very much looked forward to seeing him in his own environment.

Staring down at my bairns, both snuggled into me on each side, Thomas snoring softly just like his Daddy. Emmy had been the first to come to me only an hour after I had fallen asleep, while Thomas joined us several hours later, the moon still high in the sky. It was clear to anyone who knew them just how deeply they missed their father; however, I suspected they were more concerned about me sleeping alone without him. Bringing me such comfort, my children were the only reason left that forced me to rise from my bed day after day. If not for them, I would have followed Aaron soon after. Despite being unable to function for the best part of two-years, they had religiously come to my side throughout the day to check on my welfare, then slept with me each night—my friends and family taking care of their physical wants and needs, while supporting them in their sorrow. A role I was unable to manage until recently.

'Good morning, Mummy,' Emmy chirped, her eyes flickering open as I gazed across at her sweet little face.

'Good morning to you, dear Emmy. And a glorious one it is at that.' I stared out the arched window, the sun just starting to rise, revealing a pale blue sky without a cloud in sight, indicating fine weather despite the frost covering the manicured lawn out the front of the elegant home. I sat up against my pillows, noticing a carriage driver rugged up in a blanket as he slowly guided the horses down the street, startling me when a horn sounded down below from the impatient driver of a flashy new car behind him.

I had overheard Hamish discussing this very car with Mr Malcolm only last night, speaking of Henry Ford, an American who had finally achieved his dream early last year when he set up the Ford Mack Avenue Plant in a rented wooden building in Detroit. Apparently, the production of the Model A Ford had saved him financially, producing 1,750 cars from 1903-1904—and from what I had witnessed on the streets of London, most of those had been imported to England. There was talk of the two-cylinder, two-seater runabout being released as a four-seater variant with a roof to keep out the weather in the near future, and it was said the eight-horsepower produced in this model that allowed the car to reach speeds of twenty-eight-miles per hour would be increased. I would never understand why, when the coppers enforced a limit of twenty-miles an hour on the streets of England—and I was glad of it, finding these horseless carriages even more frightening than I found the horses that drew them when arriving in London as a lass.

I snuggled back in between my children, ignoring the argument that had ensued outside—the car owner now standing next to the carriage, his fist waving madly in the air, his angry shouts disturbing the birds nesting in the tree above them.

'It's our last day here in London before we leave to see Sister. Is there anything you would like to do that you haven't gotten around to given how busy you have been?' I turned to kiss her face, while

Thomas continued snoring softly beside me as he lay on his back, his hands placed flat on his chest.

'Uncle Hamish has a surprise planned for us. He told me to tell you we are leaving before breakfast, and will not return until dark. Why isn't he speaking with you directly? You both keep passing messages to the other through me and Thomas. Don't think we haven't noticed, Mummy. Have you had an argument?' I sighed deeply and nodded, her eyes fixed on mine.

'Only a small disagreement. I'm sure it will blow over. I *am* glad you are having one last adventure, but we are returning here after Scotland to stay a little longer and say a proper goodbye.' The scullery maid silently entered the room to attend to the fire, and we greeted her warmly before leaving her to her work.

'That makes me so happy, Mummy. I love Uncle Richard's family. They treat us with such kindness,' she remarked as Bessie came hurrying in, quickly greeting the maid in passing as she gathered her work tools, rose to her feet, and was gone as quick as she came, the fire now burning warmly in the hearth.

'Sorry I'm late, Mistress. I can bring your breakfast trays here, allowing you to take your meal in bed, if you like?' She crossed the room to select a dress for me to wear, then hung the gown over a peg near the dressing table. I was aware she intended to spend the day packing our trunks, while organising the new acquisitions collected during the many shopping adventures I had shared with Jenny, along with what Hamish and the twins purchased in the many shops they had visited.

'No thank you, dear Bessie. The children and I will eat in the kitchen this morning before they leave to go on an adventure.' She nodded before turning on her heel and making her way to the bathroom.

'Hurry up, Thomas. Every minute you sleep, you lose another from a splendid experience out there in the world. And Uncle Hamish has the biggest surprise for us. Get up,' she bellowed in his ear while shaking him by the shoulder. He yawned widely, and they soon rose to their feet, kissing me on the cheek before returning to their bedchamber to prepare themselves for the day. I dragged myself out of bed, stumbling across the room to Bessie's side—who had me trussed up and in my dress within minutes. I sat down at the dressing table, ready to have my hair styled. I wanted to leave my hair loose today, having become tired of wearing it up. Feeling obligated to dress every day as if I were attending a gala event appeared to be the price I was forced to pay when accompanying Jenny all over London to meet her sophisticated women friends.

I had enjoyed every minute I spent with her, finding her company distracted me from the frequent thoughts and memories of Aaron that settled on me without warning. She had become a mother figure to me when I first met her; the years only deepened the love and sense of belonging the Malcoms provided me. I knew I would see her when we returned before leaving for Paris, and we would meet again in the future. The Malcolms would visit Australia in the coming years to see their son and grandchildren, but that did not take away the sorrow I felt at the thought of parting. Even for such a short time. Although distance did not matter when it came to the bond we shared, being in each other's company was such a special time. We were as close as if we lived down the street from each other through our weekly letters, but I missed their company so very much. Jenny treated me as a daughter; however, she was also a very close friend and confidante, whom I would always love dearly and keep close to my heart.

I strolled into the warm kitchen to find the twins sitting up at the sturdy wooden table, chatting animatedly with Mrs Shanks, telling her of our own kitchen at Willow Grove and the characters who worked within its walls. Her eyes lit up at the sight of me as she came to embrace me warmly—her usual habit each morning when I arrived, often ravenous and begging to be fed.

'You look lovely, my dear. Oh, your children are such a blessing and a delight. The way they go on, I would think they're twenty and five, not thirteen. You have raised them well, dear Abigail.' She guided me over to the table before turning on her heel to return to her work. 'They make me laugh so hard with the stories they tell of all the people who live at Willow Grove. Especially your chef, who they say they call Uncle?' She raised a curious eyebrow in my direction as I laughed aloud before lowering myself into a chair between the twins, Mrs Shanks giggling to herself as she stood over by the stove stirring our porridge.

'Leo is their godfather and my closest friend. His role as chef comes secondary to that, or he would have lasted no more than a week in our employ.' She giggled to herself again as I continued. 'I'm aware some of the stories surrounding Leonardo may sound too fantastic to believe; however, I assure you, they are all true.' She turned to face us, a lock of silver hair escaping her bonnet, the saucepan in her hand as she slowly made her way back to the table.

'Oh, I don't disbelieve them for a moment. When the Mister and Mistress returned from Australia, all they could talk about was a strange Italian cook who behaved like no one they had ever met before. Jenny told me he acts as if he is *your* employer and you *his* servant. Goes as far as bossing you around, throwing tantrums, and refusing to cook for you, if what the Mistress says is true. Mr Malcolm said they witnessed him threatening to taint your food because you wouldn't let him wear one of your diamond necklaces for the day. If I did that here, I'd be thrown out the door quick as a flash. I heard the family discussing over dinner one night how he says what he likes, doesn't care who he offends, and behaves how he pleases without conscience. It sounds to me he isn't a servant's backside, 'scuse me language.' She shook her head in disbelief, while the twins roared with laughter at the thought of Leo ever being considered a servant, and, no doubt, what his reaction to this conversation would be.

Mrs Shanks served our breakfast, placing steaming bowls filled with smooth, sweet, creamy porridge in front of us. Not stopping there, she continued to cook, moving back and forth between the stove and the table to place trays of bacon, eggs, sausages, black pudding, and toast. I avoided the black pudding; however, helped myself to the rest after serving the children. She made fresh coffee on the stovetop as we chatted about her life and what she had been doing since I was last in London. I found it sad that Bessie had been right when telling me of life in service. How many chose not to marry—the expectations and living arrangements for the working class making it almost impossible to do both. They were completely tied down to the job from the time they woke until the time they closed their eyes late at night. Their bodies exhausted, they lay in their rickety beds for mere hours—some sharing a room with up to five others—before rising to their feet in the early hours to repeat the day before.

I was beyond grateful to Great-Aunt Isabelle for building a village for her workers. She planned and prepared Willow Grove so competently and thoroughly that when I took over the property, all that was left to do was hire the staff to fill the terraces. I would never have thought of something so wonderful, and would always appreciate her foresight in creating such an extraordinary estate that we were able to expand and finish what she had started decades before.

Hamish marched into the kitchen, grinning widely at the children before joining us at the table. He wished everyone a good morning, then kissed the twins on the tops of their heads before sitting down.

'Are ye so excited tae go out today ye could wet yerself?' Hamish asked as Mrs Shanks gasped, her hand flying up to her throat. Hamish started to flush, while the children collapsed into fits of giggles. He often forgot where we were and would, at times, say the most inappropriate things to Thomas and Emmy—not unlike Leonardo himself. He had also become far too comfortable with the laid-back lifestyle of Willow Grove, making it difficult when mixing with those who held themselves to higher standards in social situations. 'I must apologise, Mrs Shanks. That slipped out o' me mouth without me considerin' who was present in the room. I'm startin' tae remind meself o' someone who irritates the...' He paused for a moment, collecting his thoughts. 'What I mean tae say is I know someone who is similarly ill-mannered, an' I think I may have been spendin' far tae much time in his company before we left Australia.' I snorted with laughter, while Mrs Shanks regained her composure. He glanced at me darkly as he began to eat, his handsome cheeks still quite red.

'I accept your apology, Mr Makenzie. I understand you're a man used to talking rough with other men, but the children are so young, and I fear you will have a negative impact on them if this is how you speak when they are present.' She narrowed her gaze at him, her disapproval clear as he turned a deeper shade of red, grimacing across at me as the twins continued to laugh. I sipped my coffee in silence, watching on in amusement, when Jonathon strode into the kitchen.

My stomach dropped to the floor as Hamish turned abruptly and glowered at him, then me, turning back to him before grunting to himself.

'Oh, good morning, my darling boy. Have you come home for breakfast? That wife of yours is a slovenly, controlling, vindictive young woman who couldn't be bothered to look after my boy as he deserves. I have no doubt she is still lazing the day away in bed while your poor housekeeper, Merle, must deal with her unreasonable demands. I wish you had listened to me, Jonathon. I told you back then she wasn't the right match for you and would make you a miserable life. And here we stand in that exact predicament. How are your beautiful children? They are growing up so fast now,' she remarked as she embraced him, patting him on the back for the longest time. He sat down next to Hamish after a short discussion with Mrs Shanks and began helping himself to the food.

'How are you this fine morning, Abigail? You look lovely with your hair down like that,' Jonathon remarked, smiling across at me. His eyes fixed on mine, I averted my gaze as the twins began to chat with him. Here and there, Mrs Shanks would stop and put in her own penny before resuming her work at the stove, the smell of pancakes filling my nose.

Jonathon would visit with his mother at least once a day since we arrived and always asked after me. I had feigned a headache each time, worrying Jenny so much she wanted to call a doctor to attend me by the third time I took to my bed. I liked Jonathon a great deal, finding him very much like Richard in looks and character; however, I wasn't attracted to him in a romantic way. I knew how downtrodden he was, how badly he was treated in his marriage, and the torment he was suffering. All I wanted was to be his friend and offer support; however, I could give him no more than that.

'What are your plans today, Hamish?' Jonathon asked cheerfully, while Hamish stared back at him in silence, suspicion in his eyes.

'I'm takin' Thomas an' Emmy out fer the day. There's some places their father wanted 'em taken tae that we've naw managed tae get tae yet. As it's our final day, I thought we could finish the list Aaron wrote me o' what he wanted them tae see. Once we've returned from Scotland, I'll take 'em tae places I'd like 'em tae see,' Hamish replied, speaking directly to the twins, his thoughtfulness touching my heart. He had ensured Thomas and Emmy had been to all the places Aaron and I had spoken of, silently ticking each one off as he completed what he set out to do—carry out his mate's last wishes for his children after he was gone. I knew it was taking it out of him, and affecting him in mind and body. Some mornings he looked as though he hadn't slept a wink, and there were times his eyes were red-rimmed as though he had wept all night. I did not wish to argue with him; however, I was not going to be bossed around either.

'That sounds wonderful. You two are very lucky to have such a good godfather. I hear your godmother is just as devoted to you,' Jonathon said, smiling down at them, and they beamed back at him.

'Oh yes, Aunt Catherine would do anything for us. She makes all our clothes exactly how we like them, and all for free. I don't have to pay for a thing even when I'm old and in my thirties,' Emmy explained as he chuckled, then tousled her hair. Hamish rolled his eyes, grunted to himself, and shifted in his chair while I ignored him and continued with my breakfast.

'Well, you are very lucky. Are you taking your mummy with you?' He glanced across at me, lust in his eyes, while I squirmed in my chair, feeling uncomfortable.

'Nah. It's too difficult for Ma to go to all the places that we're seein' without our father with her. We understand, though. The last thing we want is for her to get sad an' sob, especially in public when so many of 'em recognise her,' Thomas told him matter-of-factly, impressing Jonathon with his maturity and sensibility.

'They recognise us too, Mummy. A lady told us yesterday she saw a photograph in the paper of Uncle Hamish carrying me, and you were walking beside him holding Thomas's hand. She has cut out every newspaper article they ever printed about Daddy and keeps them in a book. She was crying so much Uncle Hamish had to calm the poor woman down. They act as though they know us, and that's a little frightening,' Emmy admitted, while we all nodded in sympathy. Hamish was dragging his feet, reluctant to leave Jonathon alone with me. They had all finished eating, yet he remained where he was, slowly sipping the last of his coffee. Although the twins were starting to become impatient, out of respect neither Thomas nor Emmy would speak up or hurry him along, yet they fidgeted and wiggled in their seats as if bull ants had crawled into their undergarments.

'They do mean well, Emmy. I also found it difficult to understand, but your daddy explained it to me in the most sensible way. He told me that people are generally very kind, and when they see someone suffering, their natural instinct is to try to help in some way. They tried by writing letters and protesting, and despite their efforts failing, the most important thing to remember is that they tried. Now when they approach us, they want to help by providing words of comfort. Not everyone is kind, but most are, which is something you must always keep in mind,' I told her, and she nodded before turning to Hamish and gently kicking the leg of his chair. Hamish appeared as if he wanted to speak to me; however, his pride rendered him silent. I had no intention of playing games with him and kept my thoughts to myself, enjoying the last of my own coffee.

'Excuse me, Uncle Hamish. I do not wish to be rude, but you told us you wanted to leave early. We finished our breakfast half-an-hour ago, and if I eat or drink another thing, I will be running to the thunderbox praying not to piss or shit myself. Are you nearly ready to go?' Emmy asked, a gasp coming from Mrs Shanks direction, while Hamish and Jonathon chuckled. I sighed deeply, shaking my head in resignation.

'Emmy! Please do not speak that way. We are in polite company. If Mary or, God forbid, Bessie heard you talk like that they would take a strap to you.' I was firm in my tone despite wanting to collapse into giggles. Hamish's time supervising Jonathon and I was coming to an end. He reluctantly stood, the twins springing to their feet moments later, before coming to my side to embrace me. They took his hand, while Jonathon called out to bid them farewell and wish them wonderful adventures, before Hamish walked out without another word.

I settled back comfortably in my chair, confident Jonathon would behave in front of his beloved Mrs Shanks. He hadn't taken his eyes from me since the children left and relaxed back in his chair opposite me. Such a handsome man, he could have his pick of any wife—leaving me confused and questioning why he had chosen such an awful woman to be the mother of his children. So kind and gentle, he loved to talk, and not just about the weather.

Highly intelligent and a wonderful barrister, from what I had heard, he had represented many high-profile defendants and was often in the newspapers himself. The camera loved him, enhancing his dark eyes and features, along with his muscular frame. He could find himself a mistress within minutes if he so wished; however, he had set his sights on me, much to my discomfort and embarrassment.

'Are you looking forward to Scotland, Abigail? We will all miss you; however, it is nice to know you will return for a time before you leave.' His voice kind, I nodded, telling him of Sister. He listened in silence until I had finished, then reached over and took my hand in his. 'You are a good woman, Abigail. I'm aware of just how much you do for Emiliani House. Not because you've said anything, but because I help manage your fund. I will be taking it over when my father retires; however, he is likely to work until he is ninety.' He chuckled as my mouth twitched, then I laughed aloud. Mrs Shanks hurried past and into her pantry, leaving us alone, the room silent except for a sparrow chirping on the windowsill. 'Have you given any more consideration to my proposal?' His tone, so soft I could barely hear him, held a hint of impatience, while he nervously glanced around the room to ensure we were alone.

'No, and I have no intention of doing so. Let's leave it in the past and move forward as friends,' I told him as he shook his head.

'Do not ask that of me, Abigail. I have no control over how I feel. You constantly fill my mind, and I can no longer bear to even look at Isabelle now I know what is missing in my life. I won't...' he trailed off as Mrs Shanks stepped back into the room, a broad grin on her face.

'Jonathon. I cannot even consider it,' I said, confident Mrs Shanks would have no clue what we spoke of. He held my stare, his face falling and deep sadness settling on him. All I could hope for was that he would meet a kindhearted woman in the future who would love him well and help fill the emptiness within him.

'Abigail?' I rose to my feet, nodding at him politely before smiling weakly across at Mrs Shanks.

'I do apologise. I must retreat to my room. I feel a headache coming on. Thank you for the delicious breakfast, Mrs Shanks, and for your wonderful company. Jonathon, it was lovely to visit with you this morning. I wish you all the best. We will not have the opportunity to see you again before we depart. This is goodbye for now; however, I have no doubt we will speak upon my return.' I nodded again, then smiled as kindly as I could, bending slightly to smooth down my skirt with my hand before hurrying out of the kitchen and back upstairs to the protection of my bedchamber.

I gazed out the window of Mr Malcolm's office, the late afternoon more miserable than the morning. The icy wind had picked up speed—the trees shaking to and fro, several appearing to be at risk of losing branches or being swept away completely. We gathered together to sip whisky and spend the remaining moments talking by the hearth, the logs crackling and spitting as it warmed the room. Due to leave in only a few hours, I wanted to spend as much time as possible with Mr Malcolm before departing. His days were filled with work, often leaving before the sun rose and not arriving home until well after dark. Since our arrival, I had only seen him briefly in the evenings. I appreciated and admired his work ethic, and again thanked my great-aunt Isabelle for leaving her estate in such trust-worthy hands. He had taken care of me over the years in a way many in his position would not, and always went above and beyond what his obligations were to me as my lawyer. I loved him deeply and looked to him as a father, as I did with Mr Cavanaugh. Despite the fact we shared no blood. We were connected just as closely as any father and daughter I knew, and I was grateful for it. Although I had been tempted to stop in York and travel to Castle Howard during this journey, I trusted great-aunt Isabelle and took her at her word no good would come of it. Deciding to focus my time and attention on Sister and the orphanage instead—family to me in every sense of the word and where my heart would always be—I was at peace with the choice I had made.

'I know it has been extremely difficult returning here, Abigail. I wanted you to know how proud you have made me showing such strength and courage. At least financially, you have nothing to burden your mind. By the time you turn thirty and are sailing home, your instructions will be carried out. I will remain on to manage all aspects of your international businesses, while Richard will concentrate on your business interests in Australia. He and I are in regular contact, just as I will continue to be with you. If only to reassure you all is well. I believe what you and I discussed last night was a very wise decision for the children and their futures. I have added it to the list I have kept since you arrived and documented everything we discussed when meeting here each night. No matter how brief our time together, I've enjoyed every moment.' He patted my hand before lighting his cigar, a kind glance in my direction causing me to smile as I inhaled deeply. I detested the things myself, but enjoyed the smell of others smoking in my presence.

'I appreciate all you have done to make my life easier. And all you continue to do. As my lawyer *and* my friend. I trust you will keep my instructions private, even from your sons? I wish for them to be given only the information required to manage my funds efficiently. No more than that.' He nodded only once, then took my hand in his—the fire in the hearth blazing as the chilly afternoon turned into an even chillier evening.

'Abigail, I know this is none of my business, yet I am forced to ask given Jenny's incessant haranguing of me from the moment I wake until I lay my head each night. I cannot understand why my wife refuses to ask you herself; however, I am still waiting for the day to meet a man who understands a thing regarding how the mind of a woman works.' A smirk touched his lips, amusement in his eyes as I rolled my own in his direction.

Leaning forward, I took a deep drink of whisky from the crystal glass, a set of six he only brought out when entertaining important businessmen in his home. A warmth settled in the pit of my belly, somehow bringing comfort. As did his company and conversation.

It was in this very office he had brought Frederick Henry Royce and Charles Stewart Rolls together in secret, months before their official meeting at the Midland Hotel in Manchester in May of this year. Charles was a close friend of Mr Malcolm's son, George, and had met only three-years ago in a gentlemen's club in Highgate. Charles had done well for himself and operated a London dealership for Panhard, a French motoring company, and Mr Malcolm had only recently placed an order with him to buy his very first motorised vehicle.

Mostly by coincidence, but perhaps by serendipity, Mr Malcolm was related by marriage to Frederick, who established and ran his own electrical and mechanical business for the last two-decades. Several years before, Fredrick decided to build a horseless carriage of his own, feeling completely and utterly dissatisfied with the performance of the Voiturelle—a small, three-seater, two-cylinder, with a gasoline engine—that he had regretfully purchased from Decauville and imported from France.

He was soon successful in building his own two-cylinder, ten-horsepower car, naming it the *Royce 10*. Quickly becoming known for its near silent engine and smooth ride, and only finished this year—January 1904, to be exact—by March, he had caught the attention of Charles, who requested an introduction from his mate's old man and contacted Mr Malcolm.

During the clandestine meeting in Mr Malcolm's office, Frederick's determination impressed Charles. As did many of the creative ideas he shared over a bottle of brandy that night, discussing the possibility of combining their talents and expertise in the future before parting in the wee hours of the morning to stagger home to their respective beds.

Although Charles had a predilection for three-and-four-cylinder cars, it was only when they met in Manchester, he advised Fredrick how impressed he truly was and agreed to buy as many of the *Royce 10* as Fredrick could make. Later that evening, they reached an agreement that allowed four different models to be produced and all would bear the newly formed name of Rolls-Royce, agreeing they would be sold exclusively by Charles in London at his dealership.

Mr Malcolm proudly informed me they planned to present the first Rolls-Royce, two-cylinder motor car at the Paris Salon by the end of the year, and that was rolling around fast with only eight-weeks left before we would celebrate Christmas.

'You can ask anything of me, my dear friend, and I will answer as truthfully as I am able—but only if your question, or my answer, does not embarrass either one of us.'

He threw back his head and howled with laughter, while the maid outside in the hallway, vigorously sweeping the carpets, became silent, immediately ceasing her work to listen at the door, no doubt.

He cleared his throat, shifting uncomfortably in his seat before fixing me with his gaze. 'Well, Jenny insists on knowing why you will not allow Hamish to court you. She goes on and on about how obvious it is to anyone with eyes that he is deeply in love. With you. I must agree with my wife this time. His manner towards you has changed dramatically in comparison to when Aaron was alive. The way he looks at you these days, even in passing, exposes the truth in his heart every time. The poor boy. I say this from a man's perspective, Abigail, and do not feel obligated to answer. I would prefer you did not, if the truth be told. From my own observations, it appears you and Hamish have become more than friends. In secret. I see the tension between you, and I suspect there was an argument between you before you arrived here. It's obvious to me when a man has seen a woman naked. That's all I'll say on the matter.' He cleared his throat, his cheeks slightly flushed as he picked up his glass and lifted it to his lips, finishing the whisky in one swallow before pouring another for both of us, then handed me my glass with a smile. 'I spoke with Hamish last night after you retired, and he confirmed my suspicions.' I choked on my whisky, coughing and spluttering while Mr Malcolm thumped me on the back before handing me a clean handkerchief from his breast pocket. 'Not directly. He is certainly discreet. You must remember, to this day, I come face to face with many a man called to stand in the witness box before me who has attempted to hide the truth. Needless to say, Hamish is as honest as the day is long, and after prodding him along for a few minutes, he told me the truth of the matter and confided how deep his love truly is for you. I must say, I admire his integrity. To have hidden his feelings for the last year out of respect given you were still grieving deeply is the act of a gentleman,' he remarked, rising to his feet to place several logs in the hearth, the bright red embers catching the logs almost immediately.

'That's the point, Mr Malcolm. I will grieve Aaron until the day I join him. I have nothing to give another man and would only make Hamish miserable. Who else could live up to the man I was blessed to call mine? Not one that I know, or have ever met. My time of love and living a life of bliss is now over and I intend to focus my attention on Thomas and Emmy.' I finished the last of the whisky in my glass, then stretched out my arm for another. He smiled to himself as he topped up both glasses again, then made himself comfortable in his large leather chair next to mine facing the fireplace.

'In my opinion, Hamish is a kind and decent man, just as Aaron was. Although they are completely different, in body and character, they hold the same values and morals regarding what is important. Including love of family. You have yourself a good man there, Abigail. He adores you and the twins with his whole heart. I have never seen a man as lost as I witnessed last night. He only wants what's best for you all; however, he doesn't know how to help you through your grief. Hamish understands why you are pushing him away, yet it was obvious how deeply that wounds not only his heart, but his soul.' I felt tears sting my eyes, and I sniffed, willing them away before taking a long swallow of whisky. 'He is a strong-minded man, Abigail, and I sense that once he sets his mind to something, he generally succeeds. Even if it takes longer than he wants or expects, as in your case. I cannot tell you what to do or how to feel; however, I will say that I hope, in time, you will give him a chance. He may surprise you. The last thing you want or need is another man exactly like Aaron—an impossibility given no two men are alike. At least with Hamish, you already share a solid foundation of friendship. Not all unions are based on love, at least at the start, as you well know. Love grows when nurtured with respect, honesty, and tenderness. I know this for certain, Hamish would care for you like no other and protect you with his body in every circumstance. Thomas and Emmy are of an age where they need a father, Abigail. It's time you start thinking of them and put their needs before your own.' His tone was gentle, his face full of sympathy, yet I felt my stomach knot up. The urge to argue rose up in me. Wanting to force him to hear me and needing him to understand, I was rendered speechless and took a deep breath to gather my thoughts.

I knew he meant well, but the fact he was of the opinion my children were not at the forefront of every decision I made since Aaron was taken from us offended me deeply. Everything I did was for them. Should I feel in the future they did need a man around the house as a father figure, it was something I was prepared to consider. I failed to understand how remarrying and replacing Aaron would benefit me, or Thomas and Emmy. He was irreplaceable in every way to every single person who knew and loved him—but to us, he was everything. I forced a smile and nodded, my hands trembling slightly in my lap.

'Thank you for always being here for me. I must excuse myself and retire to my bedchamber. Only for an hour to rest before readying myself for the journey. I feel lightheaded after all that whisky, but I do want you to know before we part that you are very important to me. And I love you.' I struggled to my feet as he rose, placing his hand on my shoulder to steady me. I stepped forward and slipped my arms around him, placing my cheek on his chest, his heartbeat strong against my ear. He affectionately patted my back before guiding me out into the hallway. Handing me over to a servant, who assured him she would return me to my bedchamber safe, he bid me a cheery farewell. The strongly built maid placed her sturdy arm around my waist and gently led me up the stairs to my room, just as she promised. She deposited me on the bed before leaving without another word, the room spinning slightly and forcing me to close my eyes.

I soon crawled under the covers, fully dressed, and within moments had fallen into a drunken sleep—tobacco leaves, a sky filled with pink diamonds, and Aaron filling my dreams. He spent the entire time sliding in and out of my mind, all the while attempting to convince me to let him go when at my most vulnerable—unconscious and unable to wake to advise him I would never, never replace him.

Chapter Sixteen

I SAT AS STRAIGHT as an arrow at the dressing table. Not by choice. The corset Bessie demanded I wear pulled so tight I could barely breathe. She stood behind me, styling my hair to perfection while insisting I dress as a lady, given I was stepping out in public. Although we were travelling overnight on the train to Edinburgh, she did not care a fig that most of the passengers would sleep the entire journey. Wanting me to look my best should Lord Harrington be present when we arrived in the morning, she had carefully selected my gown without consulting me.

'I must say, Mistress, I'm beyond excited to see Scotland. It's been an experience staying with the Malcolms, where the staff, although treated kindly, are really only servants and regarded as such. I feel we have hardly seen you and the children, given we were not allowed in the main house unless you called for us. I'm telling you now, if this was how Willow Grove was run, you wouldn't have any of your original staff left.' She smiled at me in the oval mirror, then glanced outside at the moonless night, the fog thick. 'It's so impersonal, and divides people by class, unlike at home where everyone gets along, no matter who they are or where they come from. Not that I'm complainin', by the way. I appreciate coming on this voyage and being able to stay here and visit London again. I've had a wonderful time seeing old friends, and I could only do that 'cause me and Mary barely had to work.' She beamed down at me, then touched the back of my head. I rose to my feet and made my way over to the cheval mirror, while Bessie finished tidying the room.

I resented being forced back into my elaborate gowns rather than the plain and comfortable dresses I had worn while staying with the Malcolms. I was uncertain if Lord Harrington would be in residence, or if we would be left in the company of his servants, and I did not wish to offend him by taking no care with my appearance as Bessie had so bluntly reminded me when I had initially refused to wear the gown she selected. I was hoping he would be too busy in London to travel, leaving me free to concentrate on the orphanage and spend all my time with Sister Josephine, while staying out of Hamish's way.

I quietly made my way into the twins' bedchamber, bending down with great difficulty to kiss their sleeping faces, as they too had fallen asleep after dinner. Their eyes sprang open, and both quickly jumped out of the enormous bed just as little Mary hurried in, their clothing hung over her arm.

'Is it tomorrow or the day after tomorrow that we get to see where you grew up, Mummy?' Emmy asked for the hundredth time. She had been counting down the days until she met Sister, telling me often how she felt she knew her, given they exchanged letters occasionally now Emmy was older.

'Well, it is nearly tomorrow now. We will travel to Emiliani House the day after, only so we have time to settle in at Merinda Manor. It would be rude to leave our trunks there and disappear as soon as we arrive. I'm thrilled you and Thomas will finally see Sister Josephine, who, as you know, is very special to me. I'm aware how desperately you have wanted to meet her, especially after all the knitted presents she sends you.' Little Mary had them both dressed and ready within minutes, their hair brushed and faces washed. I smiled at her as she gathered their belongings and tidied the room before we thanked her, then made our way downstairs to join our hosts for a cup of tea before we were forced to depart. Our trunks had already been taken to the station earlier in the evening by Mr Miller, leaving us with a carpet-bag or two to carry with us. He had assured me our belongings were safely loaded onto the train, aware of a gang of petty thieves targeting train carriages holding trunks and items for transport, their aim being to steal the unsuspecting passengers' possessions. We stepped into the sitting room to find Mr and Mrs Malcolm waiting for us, their bodies close as they sat side-by-side, holding hands. Thomas and Emmy ran into their warm embrace before sitting down opposite, leaving a space for me between them.

'It's nice to see you so excited. Your faces are shining. Even yours, Abigail. I would bet a hundred quid it has something to do with a lady named Sister Josephine,' Mr Malcolm remarked, the children nodding frantically. He chuckled before fixing his gaze on me. 'I do keep a close eye on your Sister when I visit each month. She has a sweet tooth, so I take chocolate and sweets to her in secret. Of which she hides under her bed and tells not a soul. I must say, Abigail, your Sister can really be quite wicked in a wonderful way. I like her very much, especially her sparkling eyes and words of wisdom. She has been extremely worried for you and would only recently have received your letter advising of your impending visit. Just as we, too, had very little warning of your arrival. I've not had the opportunity to visit Emiliani to inform her before your arrival, yet I'm certain she is aware. I cannot imagine how she is feeling, as you are all she talks of. She has every photograph you have ever sent to her pinned up on her bedchamber wall so she can look at you all when she says her prayers morning and night. She is a sweet and gentle woman, and I understand why you love her so deeply. I have no doubt you will be surprised at how fat she has become since the quality of food improved.' He wiggled his eyebrows at the children, chuckling to himself as they collapsed into giggles while Jenny shook her head at him, amusement in her eyes. It mattered not how fat she became—I would still get my arms around her and never let her go.

Mrs Shanks greeted us warmly as she carried a large tray holding a teapot, several glasses of milk, and freshly baked raisin biscuits. She smiled to herself as she placed the elaborate tray down on the table, encouraging Thomas and Emmy to help themselves while handing them large glasses of warm milk—reminding me of Aaron. He would make mine with sugar and cinnamon when I couldn't sleep; the thought of him bringing tears to my eyes. Before composing myself, several tears escaped, making their way down my cheeks as I quickly brushed them away with the back of my hand before anyone took notice.

'Sister is the loveliest woman I know, As are you, dear Jenny.' I smiled across at her, and she returned my smile just as Hamish entered the room. Freshly bathed, his still damp black hair gleaming and neatly tied at the nape of his neck, his curls fell several inches down his back. He looked striking in his new shirt, his pants fitting snugly across his backside, the fabric complementing his vest. I averted my gaze as he placed his woollen coat over the back of a chair. Sitting himself down next to Thomas, Jenny poured the tea into her best china cups left to her by her great-grandmother.

'Are you looking forward to returning to Scotland, Hamish? I understand that is where you were born. I see you still speak the brogue after fifteen-years.' Mr Malcolm remarked as Hamish nodded, ignoring my presence completely.

'Aye, I am. Although I lived there when I was a bairn, me parents schooled us in England an' raised us on an estate our mother inherited from an uncle o' hers just out o' London. I still have kin in Scotland, but I'm naw close tae 'em, bein' on me paternal side an' all. We lived near the village o' Strathpeffer.' Mr Malcolm's eyes lit up, and he nodded as Hamish chewed thoughtfully.

'Oh, you must be speaking of Castle Leod being a Makenzie. I know it well. Sits to the east of Ross-shire, up in the Highlands.' Now it was Hamish's turn to nod as Jenny caught my eye and smiled affectionately.

'Aye, 'tis one an' the same. 'Twas where I spent the first few years o' me life. We travelled back tae Castle Leod after we moved tae England several times a year 'till me grandfather passed, but I've naw plans tae visit this time. Me childhood was naw a happy one.' Mr Malcolm nodded while Jenny sipped her tea, her eyes glistening. The twins gazed across at Hamish in silence, appearing enthralled by these new revelations from their godfather. 'Our governess was more o' a parent tae me than either o' me own. Me poor mother wanted tae be more involved with Angus an' meself, but me father'd naw allow it. Said it'd make us soft an' turn us in tae dandies. Or worse.' Hamish took a long sip of tea, his eyes twinkling. 'O' course I now know that's naw the case when it comes tae raisin' bairns an' I resent me father very much fer it. He wanted *his* sons tae behave an' speak like English gentlemen. An' I did as the man wanted 'till we arrived in

Australia. 'Twas really only after he disowned me, I made a point tae blatantly go out o' me way tae speak the way of me ancestors. More so tae irritate him.' Mr Malcolm threw back his head and howled with laughter while Hamish smirked wickedly, the twins laughing along with Mr Malcolm. 'The only good deed the old man ever did was force us tae immigrate tae Australia. An' fer that I thank him. I've made lifelong friends who've become family tae me. Closer than me own blood.' I sipped my tea, tears pricking my eyes. Hamish continued to ignore me, fixing his attention on the Malcolms. 'I must seem like a terrible person given I've naw intention o' makin' contact with me Makenzie kin, but there are some old friends I'd like tae see.' Hamish was never this vocal or honest regarding his childhood with anyone, nor did he ever express his true feelings on the matter. He had not told me he had no intention of making contact with his many aunts and uncles, not to mention his Makenzie cousins, of whom he often spoke of with affection.

'Family business can be complicated, and we do not judge you, Hamish. It sounds to me you would struggle to visit anyone given how busy you will all be once there. It is our good fortune you have agreed to return to our home for a time before we lose you again,' Mr Malcolm replied, winking at the children. Emmy's top lip, coated in milk, resembled a moustache as I reached out and wiped it away with my handkerchief.

We reluctantly finished the last of the tea and biscuits, the twins devouring most of the first batch and nearly all from the second plate brought out soon after, still hot from the oven. Thomas and Emmy took my hands in theirs and pulled me to my feet, the Malcolms ushering us out of the sitting room and towards the front entrance with Hamish close behind. Stepping out onto the front porch, the frigid air stung my cheeks as we hurried towards the carriage where Mr Millar waited atop his seat. Bessie and little Mary sat beside him, both wrapped up warmly in their woollen coats, gloves, and thick knitted hats covering their heads, along with several scarves wrapped around their necks. He jumped down to assist Jenny, then helped me up, turning back to guide Emmy and Thomas in after me. Mr Malcolm and Hamish followed, the door clicking shut behind them before they made themselves comfortable. Mr Miller promptly returned to his seat and within moments the carriage jolted forward.

'It's not goodbye. We will see you when you return; therefore, it's not a sad day at all,' Jenny said, tears in her eyes stating the opposite. I smiled affectionately at her, thanking them both for everything they had done for us.

'You are our family, Abigail, and you always will be,' Mr Malcolm said, his voice full of emotion. I nodded, unable to speak as the carriage travelled at great speed through the empty streets, the roads slick, the air frosty. We soon arrived at Deptford Station and said our goodbyes, for now, before quietly boarding the train. A conductor led us to the first-class carriage, then politely showed us to our private compartment. I made myself comfortable by the window where Aaron used to sit when we travelled to Melbourne. Turning to the window to gaze out into the night while the children seated themselves next to Hamish, Bessie and little Mary chose to sit with me. The train started to move, and I watched the twinkling lights of London slowly fade. We soon reached open fields, scattered houses and farms passing in a blur under the dim moonlight as we barrelled past.

I closed my eyes, listening to the lively chatter from all around me, the children enthusiastically talking of all the wonderful things we would do once in Scotland. Aaron was constantly in my thoughts, the only relief from memories of him found when I shared a bed with Hamish. We had not spoken for an entire week now, and it upset me deeply. I refused to apologise for my feelings on the matter, and he obviously felt the same way. Neither would yield—and I felt my stubbornness was justified.

I had not felt Aaron beside me as I expected I would, leaving me increasingly distressed as the days passed. Being so far away from Willow Grove had left me feeling disconnected from him. It was something I was unable to explain even to those dearest to me why I felt closer to my husband after visiting the island and spending time talking to him and our boys. Aaron had always looked forward to seeing where I grew up with his own eyes, and finally meeting Sister Josephine—telling me only months before he died how he wanted to embrace and thank her for loving me so well. And now, we were here without him. I felt tears trickle down my face and discreetly wiped them away with the back of my hand without opening my eyes, hoping no one noticed.

After several hours had passed, a cheerful woman stopped outside our compartment, her trolley filled with hot and cold beverages, sandwiches, and a selection of cakes parked in the doorway. Bessie and little Mary were still bright-eyed and bushy-tailed, while the children and Hamish were deep in conversation. It appeared I would not get a wink of sleep due to my travelling companions' excitement, although my heart sped up slightly at the sight of the woman before me.

'Good evenin', one an' all. Could I tempt ye with a nice cup o' tea tae warm ye belly?' All accepted with great enthusiasm as I stared up at her and she smiled. She had barely changed since we first met on the train from Edinburgh to London fifteen-years ago. I slowly sipped the tea handed to me while the others filled their bellies and drank their fill. Bidding us farewell, her trolley rattled as she continued on down the carriage, cheerfully going from compartment to compartment, offering weary travellers a late supper. Soon after, the talk slowed, and Emmy swapped places with Bessie to be next to me. I gazed out the window at the farms and towns passing in a blur, while wondering how I would cope without him by my side when it came time to return to Emiliani House.

I took a blanket from a rack above and snuggled up close to Emmy, hoping sleep would find me. Hamish continued to play word games with Thomas and Emmy, their laughter filling my ears, while Bessie and little Mary spoke between themselves in whispers. Sleep did eventually find me, though much later than I had hoped—my dreams filled with a ship named Freedom Angel, a knife, and a lass called Lotte.

I slowly followed Hamish along the platform, Bessie and little Mary behind me holding onto Thomas and Emmy, while another train pulled in. The loud horn startled me before it released a crowd of weary travellers eager to get where they were going. I grunted to myself, ducking and weaving through the many tired and impatient passengers, the smell of sweat and unwashed bodies filling my nostrils. Finally, descending the stairs leading back up to *Waverley Station*, I sighed in relief as I stepped down onto Princes Street, my bag over my arm. I bent forward to straighten my gown, breathing easier since loosening my corset only an hour into the journey. The busy terminus lay between the old town and the new, and sat next to Edinburgh Castle and the Princes Street Gardens. Rebuilt only two-years ago, an impressive dome had been added, only exaggerating the grandness of the building.

'Are you all right, then, Mistress?' Bessie asked as she adjusted her bonnet, little Mary still holding on tight to Thomas and Emmy, while Hamish stood alone gazing across at Edinburgh Castle.

'I am, dear Bessie, and thank you for asking. I do hope *that* contraption over there has not been sent for us.' I rolled my eyes and pointed to the street, then laughed when she turned to look, her hand going to her mouth as she gasped aloud.

Nearby stood one of the largest and most ostentatious carriages I had ever seen. Six Martarino horses were harnessed to it, solidly built and calm in nature, their ebony coats glimmering like wet silk. All they were missing were feathers in their bridles, a member or two from the royal family, and people lining the streets for the parade that was bound to occur at the sight of such extravagance. A second carriage, far more practical, waited patiently behind the first, only with four Arabian greys harnessed to it, along with a large cart sitting near the corner pulled by two majestic chestnut stallions—our trunks loaded high and tied securely to the tray.

A man wearing a dark brown uniform came towards us, his black hair neatly brushed, his blue eyes shining, and a wide grin on his homely face as he cheerfully greeted us.

'Weel, guid mornin' tae ye all. Ye are Mrs Cavanaugh, are ye naw?' I nodded, a smile touching my lips as he took the bag from my arm, then guided us over to the largest carriage. 'I had yer trunks loaded as soon as ye train pulled in. Me Master provided a fair an' accurate description of ye, Mistress.' I heard Hamish snigger somewhere in the distance as this pleasant man—standing no taller than I, and no more than a decade older than me—helped Thomas and Emmy inside, kindly settling them next to each other before tousling Thomas's sandy blonde hair. He soon turned around to lead little Mary and Bessie around to the back of the carriage. They climbed up to the bench seat with his assistance, and sat down where the servants were expected to travel—rain, hail or shine—when fortunate enough to be given a seat and not be forced to walk alongside. Returning to my side within moments, he gently placed my carpet bag inside the carriage under the seat before assisting me up. 'Me name's Archie Campbell, an' I'm Lord Harrington's personal driver. He sent me this mornin' tae see ye safe back tae Merinda Manor.' He nodded politely at Hamish, already making himself comfortable inside the palatial compartment of this extraordinary carriage, Thomas squirming excitedly beside him. Archie grinned at me before closing the door, the carriage rocking several times as he climbed up to his seat.

'Mummy, why is it called Waverley Station and not the Edinburgh Terminus?' Emmy asked, her eyes fixed on the grand buildings.

'Well, you know of Walter Scott, sweetheart?' She nodded while Thomas's eyes lit up. The carriage jolted slightly as the horses moved forward, soon rocking gently as they trotted down the cobblestone streets towards the edge of the new town.

'Of course, Ma. He was a genius of a writer, an' the most prolific Scot of his time,' Thomas remarked, while Hamish looked down at him with pride. I nodded as he continued. 'Ya should know why the Terminus is called what it is, Emmy. You've read the books a hundred times.' Emmy glared at her brother as I raised my hands, attempting to placate them before an argument ensued.

'You are right, Thomas. By inserting fictional characters into actual events, he created the historical novel as we know it now, and that has influenced every single writer who followed him. Prolific is the most wonderful word to use regarding such talent.' They both nodded in my direction, their eyes fixed on the eclectic mix of people bustling through the streets, their tongues silent for the first time since leaving London last night. 'Do you know that only a few streets away from where we are now sits the Assembly Rooms?' Emmy shook her head, confusion crossing her face, while Thomas nodded, his cheeks flushed with excitement. 'That's where, in 1837, Mr Scott revealed he was *The Great Unknown* and the author of the *Waverley Novels*,' Thomas interjected, Emmy shaking her head in disagreement.

'That's not right, Mummy. I know it's not because he was dead by 1832,' she whispered, Hamish now in deep discussion with Thomas over their shared love of one of Scott's earlier novels, *Rob Roy*. Also, a favourite of Aaron's.

'1827 is the year, but everything else your brother said is correct,' I whispered back, and she smiled, her face like sunshine.

' I understand why they named the Terminus Waverley Station now, but just so you know, the best novels he ever wrote were *The Chronicles of Canongate*.' She laid her head on my shoulder, staring out at the overcast, grey day. The sun had been up for only an hour or so; however, it made very little difference. The gloomy, damp weather was just as I remembered, but I had come prepared—my thick woollen cloak pulled tight around me, the fur-lined hood resting back on the seat. Catherine had made the pale green cloak especially for me to wear in the freezing temperatures of Scotland, ensuring it was lined in several layers of thick wool. The cloak, elegant and warm, dropped to my ankles, hiding my calf-high, laced leather boots, which I had swapped during the night for the uncomfortable high-heeled shoes Bessie had insisted I wear under my elaborate gown. I had ensured before we took ship, the children, along with Hamish, were fitted for coats made from the fleece of Australian merinos to keep them warm while away, having never forgotten just how brutal the winters. Or how cold it could get at this time of year in my homeland.

The horses continued on at great speed; the farms taking over the landscape, Edinburgh now behind us. I had never stayed at a grand estate before—not a real one like those found scattered throughout England, Scotland, and Wales. I looked forward to seeing Merinda Manor with my own eyes and exploring the rooms and grounds far more than I would admit. Even to myself. Hamish was the only one out of the lot of us who knew what it was to live on a grand estate surrounded by hundreds of years of history—and strangely, unlike us, he showed no signs of excitement. I gazed around the interior of the magnificent carriage, acutely aware that if Aaron had been here, the first thing he would have done was purchase one similar and have it sent to Australia. It was truly beautiful, the wood paneling stained to perfection, the heavy velvet drapes matching the sapphire blue upholstered velvet seats, the carriage designed to hold eight, or even ten, passengers in comfort.

The horses slowed, and I turned to look out the window. The part-Gothic, part-Tudor building I assumed to be Merinda Manor loomed large, visible from the road. Nestled at the end of what appeared to be a mile-long driveway, Archie guided the horses in through the twelve-foot gates, azaleas and rhododendrons lining each side of the private driveway. Most planted at the base of the enormous oak trees, the bare branches appeared to wave in greeting as the carriage meandered towards the Manor, a thick fog hanging low across the paddocks.

The stone building was three-stories high in places, the central block even higher with its projecting tower, while the slate roof and freestone dressings were charming. The porte-cochere was flanked by several two-story wings, the corner turrets and arrow-loops giving it the air of a castle rather than a manor. It was certainly not what I had expected, and by the expressions on my children's faces, nor had they. There were several towers, some round while others square, one with a bell-cote and clock, while the building seamlessly went from single story to double, then back again, some wings standing up to four-stories high from what I could tell from where I sat. The arched windows were enormous in places, while smaller pane-sash windows were prominent on the lower levels. There were several covered walkways, and I assumed a number of walled gardens within, given the size of the place.

The carriage came to an abrupt halt at what appeared to be only one of several entrances to the manor; however, this appeared to be the main entrance, being central and much larger than the others we had passed.

I heard Bessie and little Mary jump down from their seats as Archie opened the door and assisted me and the children down, leaving Hamish to sort himself out. I stood off to the side with Bessie, surprised to see the servants lined up on either side of the imposing front doors. All immaculate in their black and white uniforms, Lord

Harrington stood proudly in the entrance between them, waiting to greet us.

'Ooh, it's so exciting to finally be here. See? I told you that your Duke would be waiting. I would have bet my right arm he wouldn't miss the chance to see you again, especially after all the rumours on the boat his valet spread to keep those slovenly trollops from catching him,' Bessie remarked, her voice low as my eyes went wide.

'How do you discover these things? I wondered where the talk was coming from. I knew I had not said a word to anyone but you, and I was certain he was not indiscreet. He obviously trusts his valet as much as I trust you, only his friend and employee appears to have a very large mouth,' I whispered loudly to her, while Hamish snorted sarcastically behind us. I turned abruptly and fixed him with a glare. He quickly looked away, concentrating on the highland cattle he had noticed as we passed their paddock earlier.

'You hit the nail on the head, Mistress. Alisdair Campbell possesses a mouth larger than your idjit friend, Leonardo, but it seems in this instance, he had gained his Master's permission. I gather he didn't mind Alisdair spreading his wishes around that he be left alone,' she murmured, and I nodded. As far as I was aware, nothing Lord Harrington and I had discussed in private had been repeated or gossiped about; therefore, I was fairly confident he could be trusted—and I did trust him.

Lord Harrington stepped forward as we walked towards him, our heels clicking on the grey cobblestones lining the driveway and front courtyard leading to the entrance of the grand Manor, his arms stretched out wide.

'Welcome, my dear, dear friends. It is such an honour and a privilege to have you here as my guests. To have the pleasure of your company, Mrs Cavanaugh, is more than I deserve in this lifetime,' he announced grandly as we stood shoulder-to-shoulder in front of him in a straight line, not unlike his servants flanking each side of him. He reached out and gently removed my glove then lifted my hand to his mouth, brushing his lips over my knuckles for only the briefest moment; however, long enough to send pleasant shivers throughout my body. 'And to you, my dear Mrs Cavanaugh. It brings me great pleasure to see you again.' He released my hand, allowing it to fall gently back to my side before he bowed low and ever so formally, Hamish grunting in annoyance beside me.

'It is wonderful to see you again, Lord Harrington, and we are delighted to accept your generous invitation.' I curtsied slightly, feeling ridiculous, when Bessie snorted in amusement, causing me to lose my footing and stumble. Lord Harrington reached out to steady me by the shoulder, my face flushed as I thanked him before shrugging him off as politely as possible. His servants were introduced one by one then quickly dispersed to carry our trunks to the guestrooms, Bessie and little Mary following behind to organise them.

'Welcome to my home. Please, come with me,' Lord Harrington announced, graciously taking my arm and placing it through his, while Hamish and the twins followed. We stepped into the reception room, the panelled walls exquisite, the wide staircase sweeping up four floors, the carved handrail over barley-twist balusters with carved tread ends immediately catching the eye. A chandelier hung above, only slightly smaller than a motorised car, the coffered covered ceiling enhanced with garlanded corners and a central rose, scalloped hoods on every door. The logs burned brightly in the hearth, the grand marble fireplace surrounded by timber carved with figureheads of Raleigh and Shakespeare, while garlands were carved in others, the room impressive, but more importantly, warm.

He led us through a door opening into an elaborate drawing room, the panelled ceiling bordered by guilloche and fret patterns complimenting each other, the bay window covered with traceried shutters. Furnished in blue and white, it was obvious a woman had taken great care in decorating this room, and it appeared well used.

We followed him through endless hallways, a beautiful domed roof above. Most of the doors to the rooms we passed were tightly shut. Until he stopped at the bottom of another staircase, this one not quite as grand.

'These stairs lead up to the bedchambers. It was once the family wing, but now used to house my guests.' Pointing up, he smiled before continuing on. He truly did live in a beautiful building, the high-vaulted ceilings and slit windows throughout only adding to its grandeur, while allowing a great deal of light in when the sun did manage to shine. Lord Harrington led us past another drawing room, this one smaller but no less grand than the first. Decorated in a soft peach and cream with gilded furniture cluttering the room, the floor to ceiling windows looked out over an enormous glasshouse to the left of the building—or conservatory as many called them.

'It is lovely, my Lord,' Emmy called out, her hand in mine as he turned back and smiled.

'If you like what you've seen so far, Emmy, what splendor you will encounter while exploring the grounds. We have a boat house on the loch. A summerhouse—not that we have much use for it here—a tennis court, and a swimming pool. Again, it is rarely used.' His voice apologetic, Emmy beamed up at him.

'Oh, do not feel bad, Mister Lord. We also have a swimming pool no one ever uses. Most living at Willow Grove prefer to swim in the rivers running through the place. Or they venture out to the ocean when the weather gets really hot and they want to risk their lives as shark bait,' Emmy reassured him cheerfully. Lord Harrington threw back his head and howled with laughter while Hamish grunted again somewhere behind me, Thomas by his side.

'There are five cottages here that sit alongside the river down by the woodland and a farmhouse you are welcome to explore. They haven't been used for decades now. Not since my grandmother passed.' His voice was steady, although a sadness seemed to settle on him for a moment. 'With ten bedchambers for guests alone, there is a great deal for you to explore. We have four reception rooms, an underground cellar, alongside another where I keep my wine. A billiard room *and* the largest conservatory in Scotland and all of England—if not for Castle Howard.' Emmy nodded, remaining silent as he walked us though two of the grandest rooms I had ever seen—the ballroom and the great hall. Leading us into a sitting room, I looked up to find a chandelier made of antlers added a fascinating touch. Several logs burned in the hearth, while the room was half the size of most others I had witnessed during his guided, and very thorough, tour of his castle. I lowered myself down onto the armchair he offered by the fire, the mantle carved from wood and not a speck of marble to be found anywhere, while Hamish, Thomas, and Emmy sat down politely on a wide settee. Lord Harrington called for his butler, pulling on a long rope near the drapes before taking a seat opposite me. Soon after, his stern looking butler appeared with a tray of refreshments, several maids following behind carrying silver trays filled with cakes and sandwiches. They spoke not a word, placing their trays down on the low-lying table before hurrying out of the room, the butler closing the door behind them.

'So, what ya do here, me Lord, to fill ya time?' Thomas asked, biting into a cucumber sandwich, then wrinkling his nose.

'Ah, well, there's fishing, and pheasant shooting, and deer stalking to start. You can ride the horses over the two-hundred-thousand acres the estate comprises, then back again,' he teased, both Thomas and Emmy collapsing into giggles.

'Willow Grove is two-thousand acres, but it's more than enough for us,' Emmy chimed in through her laughter. He nodded at her, grinning widely before fixing his gaze on Hamish.

'I have organised a valet for you, Hamish. I am aware you do not travel with one. Clyde may be getting on in age, but he will take great care of you, and treat you well,' he said kindly, and Hamish nodded then thanked him politely, much to my surprise. 'You must be famished after such a long journey, Mrs Cavanaugh. Sandwiches and cake are no replacement for a hearty meal. I do not know what my staff were thinking, but I will show you to your rooms personally to allow you to settle yourselves in while breakfast is prepared.' He smiled across at me, and I nodded, my stomach rumbling at the mere mention of a warm meal.

'Thank you, Lord Harrington. We really do appreciate your generosity. I must say I am quite overwhelmed by your home. I have never been in anything so palatial. I cannot believe you reside here alone. I understand your main residence is in the north of England,' I replied as he smiled, nodding once, his eyes fixed on mine.

'Yes, it is. You have an excellent memory, Mrs Cavanaugh. I believe I only mentioned that fact in passing on the first night we met. I also have a terrace home in Notting Hill, where I stay when in London. I am considering purchasing a property in Melbourne for when I am there on business. I have tired of staying in the hotels, although you will get no finer accommodations or service than at *The Delmont* in Swanston Street. I've even tried several of the boarding houses over

the last year, thinking they would feel more homely. It is not the case.'
He held my gaze, behaving as if there was no one else in the room.

'You are always welcome to stay at Willow Grove. I have more guest rooms than I could ever fill. You can consider and treat one of them as your own. It seems such a waste to have a property you only visit two to three times a year sitting empty.' I smiled brightly before raising my china cup to my lips and taking a long sip of milky tea, now cold, his teeth perfect as a boyish grin settled on his handsome face.

'I thank you for your kind invitation, Mrs Cavanaugh. I accept with great delight, and will rely on your hospitality the next time I travel there.' Hamish glared across at me, the twins in deep discussion about what part of the estate to explore first, while Lord Harrington smiled across at them. I narrowed my gaze at Hamish, then grunted while raising my eyebrows questioningly. Who I invited into my home had nothing to do with him, and had no effect on him, given he lived with Polly and Angus, and he knew it well.

'I do not wish to be rude, but may I ask where you purchased your Martarinos?' I settled back in my chair, the children stopping their argument to listen, while I prepared myself to hear the name Howard more than once or twice during our stay here.

'The Harrington's have purchased these magnificent beasts from an estate down near York for generations now. They are the only family I know who still breed them to this day—other than you.' He appeared delighted I had noticed, his attention now on my children. 'Well, then, Thomas and Emmy. Do you like horses?' Their faces lit up, their eyes going from Lord Harrington to Hamish and back again.

'We love them, Mr Lord, and we have our own at home, Majestic and Rainbow, who we ride most every day. They're twins too,' Emmy sang, her face shining at the thought of home, and all that was dear to us.

He nodded, then glanced out the window for a moment. 'How about we take your mother down to the stables before lunch today, and you can all choose your own mount to make your own during your stay? I will show you around the grounds of Merinda Manor, and we can have a picnic down by the lake.' Thomas and Emmy whooped in excitement before I tried to hush them. They had not been on a horse for months, and it was clear they missed them very much, while a flash of jealousy crossed Hamish's face for only a moment. I suspected he was far more upset over Lord Harrington attempting to win Thomas and Emmy's favour than my own.

'Thank you, Sir Lord. We would enjoy it very much,' Thomas replied, while Emmy nodded fervently beside him.

'It is agreed, then. If you would like to follow me, I will show you to your accommodations.' Lord Harrington rose elegantly to his feet, then guided us out of the room and back to the second staircase, the wood polished so highly, I could see my own reflection in the balustrade as I followed behind him. Leading us to Hamish's bedchamber, we were politely introduced to his valet, who waited patiently by the window. Clyde—an elderly man who was seventy if he were a day—appeared familiar; the golden glow surrounding him almost blinding me and forcing me to hurry from the room, much to Hamish's irritation. He had always detested the idea of a valet, just as Aaron had. Mr Makenzie never went anywhere without his manservant, and had done so ever since Hamish could remember. Hamish found it ridiculous a grown man would not only allow, but request, another man to dress him and wipe his arse in the mornings when summoned.

When I married Aaron, Mr Masters had already interviewed and hired a valet for him—without our consent. He had assumed it was something we would want, as it was the proper and right way of it for a man who ran an estate such as Willow Grove. Aaron had politely refused and found employment for the man with Dana and Martin soon after. Poor Martin had not wanted a valet either; however, he had no choice in the matter when it came to obeying his strong-willed wife.

Lord Harrington led us to a beautiful bedchamber overlooking a walled garden, a large fireplace in the corner, two double canopy beds sitting side-by-side in the middle of the spacious room, decorated in greens and yellows, the heavy quilts covering the beds made from the finest cloth I had seen in recent times, the silk trim the softest I had touched.

'I understand you carry out the majority of the practical tasks and care of your children, so I have gone ahead and placed their

Nanny downstairs in the servants' quarters. I'm aware that if they need anything during the night, they go to you. Are these arrangements satisfactory to you, Mrs Cavanaugh?' I stepped away from the window and smiled across at him; Thomas and Emmy now wrestling on the bed, his pale-green eyes sparkling mischievously. It appeared he wished to join in the fun, and I laughed aloud, my hand on his forearm as I stopped beside him where he waited near the door.

'Yes, they are. Thank you, Lord Harrington. Thomas and Emmy are of an age where they rarely wake during the night, but there are times they do come to me, even now. They have been good sleepers since they were born.' I watched them jumping on their new beds, Lord Harrington smiling on fondly as they laughed and teased each other.

'I must say, they are well-behaved, Mrs Cavanaugh, and you should be proud of yourself for the way you have raised them. Most children of privilege are spoiled, and I cannot stand to be around them myself, but Thomas and Emmy are respectful, well mannered, and just about the happiest children I have had the good fortune to meet.' He took my arm in his, and we left the children to their fun, stepping back out into the wide hallway before he led me into the room next door. I followed him into the enormous bedchamber and gasped aloud. Bigger than the children's room, mine was far more elaborate. Decorated in tones of lilac trimmed in gold, with heavy purple drapes and an oversized canopied bed surrounded by fine velvet curtains tied at each post. I strolled into the room, crossing over to the window seat upholstered in lilac, small stems of lavender printed on the cloth, while Lord Harrington remained at the door, appearing pleased with himself.

'How lovely,' I murmured to myself.

'I do hope you will be comfortable here, Mrs Cavanaugh—no matter how long you choose to remain as my guest. I will not stay, and it would be rude to enter a lady's bedchamber unless otherwise invited. I would not refuse you if you did, by the way; however, I must leave you now and see to breakfast. I will send your maid to assist you to freshen up, and will see you down in the dining room shortly.' He stepped back from the door, his face flushed, the reality of his words uttered without thought settling on him before he turned on his heel and marched away. I stared down the hallway after him, my mouth twitching as I tried not to smile at how shy and lovely he truly was.

I returned to the window seat, the enormous glass conservatory to the right, a man I assumed to be the gardener carrying a hessian sack filled with manure on his shoulder. He dropped it at the door, returning to pick up another before catching sight of me, his eyes going wide, while the blood drained from his face. My heart raced as I quickly ducked out of sight and hurried over to the bed, Bessie arriving shortly after, out of breath but deliriously happy.

'I've never seen such a house in my life, Mistress. It makes your own grand home look like a cottage, doesn't it?' She pulled me to my feet, leading me into the bathroom to wash, a jug of warm water already waiting on the stand. Stripping me of my uncomfortable gown and corset, she scrubbed me from neck to knee with orange-blossom soap, then dried me off before helping me into a far simpler dress.

'Yes, very much so. It is far grander than anything I have seen up close.' I stretched out my arm, sweeping it around the room, Bessie nodding, while clearly feeling quite overwhelmed by the wealth on display. The artifacts within Marinda Manor's walls had obviously been handed down over generations, while paintings of the Harrington ancestors going back centuries hung in every room. It felt strange, yet familiar, strolling the hallways, the oversized portraits on every wall appearing to come alive, the eyes fixed wherever you stood, the echo of my footsteps no different than they would have sounded hundreds of years before. Far too large and extravagant for someone like me, who preferred my world to be as simple as possible, the thought of getting lost here made my heart race before I had even left the bedchamber.

'Well, let's get you downstairs to that dining room. I don't like your chances of finding it alone.' She took my hand, leading me to the door, then stopped to look me over one last time, a self-satisfied smile settling on her lips.

'I will require your assistance after breakfast, if you don't mind, please, Bessie? Lord Harrington is taking us riding, then for a picnic lunch. I am so very relieved I insisted you pack my riding habit. I had a feeling I would need it, but never imagined anything like this.'

Her eyes went wide as she nodded, leading me out the door and into the wide hallway, a portrait of a young woman sitting by a river, her blonde head bent close to a girl who looked like me, catching my eye for a moment.

'Oh, isn't he lovely? Taking the children along with you, when he clearly wants to be alone with you and have your full attention. Bloody men,' she grunted, leading me down the stairs. 'They expect you to drop everything to listen to their shite. Lord Harrington's not like that at all. I find him to be a very kind-hearted and considerate man. He would make you a good husband, Mistress. I know he would propose immediately if he even thought for a moment you might accept. His valet has been heard to say he had never seen his master act this way over a woman, and often boasts of just how many women are seeking that man's attention. I don't think you realise just what a wonderful catch you have yourself here. I understand Mister Aaron was indeed a fine-looking man; however, you must open your eyes now to others. It's good this one is different. There is nothing casual or relaxed about him, but I believe in time, especially if he spends more of it with you, that stick up his backside may loosen a little. Oh, that's terrible of me. I sound like that idiot, Leonardo.' Her cheeks burned red, my laughter echoing through the halls as we approached another staircase.

'You are right. I do compare everyone to Aaron, and I cannot stop. I don't believe there is a man strong enough to put up with the cart load of shit I drag behind me.' I followed her down a flight of stairs, then along another hallway until we reached the stairs near the front entrance.

'All right. Enough memories of Mister Aaron. You are going to go down and enjoy a lovely breakfast with a very nice gentleman, who not only wants to spend time with you, but with your children as well. There aren't many men, especially of high breeding like Lord Harrington, who would accept another man's child. They want the woman, and then pack the bairns off to boarding school. I don't believe he is like that at all. You need to count your blessings where you find them, my dear girl.' She took my hand in hers and led me down the last flight of stairs, nodding her head in the direction I was to take, the dining room several rooms away. Little Mary and the children stepped out of a doorway, surprising and delighting me at the same moment, leading me through the hallway and soon arriving breathless at the entrance to the dining room, the smell of bacon filling my nose, a feeling of happiness settling over me for far longer than I expected. But I was grateful.

Chapter Seventeen

WE HAD EATEN AN exceptional breakfast, Lord Harrington's butler, under butler, and several footmen serving us an eight-course meal in the very formal dining room. Hamish had hardly uttered a word throughout, although polite to all present, bar me.

I had excused myself to change into my riding habit, the only outfit I wore at home these days when out and about on the property on Delly. I rarely rode in dresses or skirts anymore, as everyone around me had once insisted, and I certainly never rode side-saddle. Emmy had demanded Catherine make her riding habit the same, the cream-coloured trousers fitted snugly to her legs, a brown velvet jacket tailored in at the waist, three buttons at the front, the coat stopping atop her thighs, her crisply ironed shirt tucked in, a brown necktie secured neatly around her collar. I wore the same trousers in black, an emerald green jacket only just covering my backside—a request Aaron made years ago of Catherine for all that was good and decent.

I felt tears prick my eyes as I did up the last button of the jacket, then sat down at the dressing table to wait for Bessie. She crossed the room, muttering to herself, her hands on my shoulders before she picked up the silver brush, her eyes fixed on mine in the looking glass.

'That valet attending to Hamish seems to rule the roost around here, Mistress. Best you be careful.' She swept all my hair up, securing it into a long braid before allowing it to fall to my waist, a sympathetic smile touching her lips as I brushed away my tears, then sniffed loudly.

'Oh?' I leaned forward and pulled on the long boots, panting for breath when I straightened up in my seat.

'He's a mouthy wee bugger. Was born here on the estate some seventy-five years ago to a ladies maid in service to Lady Charlotte. Gretal, I think he said her name was. I'm guessing she had some power here by the way the servants look up to the man, and she only recently passed from what I can tell. She's spoken of with great affection, and some sadness over her absence. Must have been close to a hundred and fifteen when she finally went to God, poor dear. If I got me sums right. Heard the old goat say she was forty when blessed with him.' I sighed deeply, my brows arched as she rolled her eyes. 'I'm only saying it 'cause he has a bee in his bonnet about you, and everyone takes what comes out of his mouth as gospel itself. He announced not a quarter of an hour ago down in the kitchen that you're Isabelle Delmont returned from the dead. He looked upon her as an aunt, and from what I could tell, he loved her—but he's not so fond of you, and could bring trouble to your door. It's fortunate for you that the Archbishop is away from the parish and they cannot call him to conduct an exorcism to free you from evil, going by what old Clyde is sayin'.'

She touched me on the back of the head, and I stood, sniggering to myself before thanking her, then calling out a cheery farewell. I hurried towards the children's room, pausing at the doorway for only a moment before they saw me and rushed into my open arms, embracing me tightly.

'Mummy. Why is Uncle Hamish so upset? He is in a mood and refuses to tell us why. Do you think Thomas and I have done something to make him angry?' I held her hand, Thomas in front of us, eager to get to the stables, his excitement palpable as he led us into the hallway and towards the stairs.

'Some use their bad mood as an excuse to punish others. Your uncle is not above that type of behaviour,' I mumbled, the urge to smack him taking hold of me for a moment.

'It's because the Lord looks at Ma with lust in his eye,' Thomas teased, glancing over his shoulder as I shook my head at him, while he tried not to smile. He nodded once before leading us down the stairs and into the front reception room where Lord Harrington waited by the fire, his eyes widening when he caught sight of what Emmy and I wore. I was well aware that there were a number of women in his circle who joined the men fishing and hunting on these estates, and their riding habits were no different from ours. It was clear he expected me to wear a gown from morning 'till night as I had done on board the ship; his standards high, the risk his expectations of me were about to be shattered even higher.

'Well, Thomas. You look dapper in your jacket there, and don't you look comfortable, Emmy?' He placed his hand on Thomas's shoulder, cheerfully guiding us through the manor and out a door into a garden. Following a path leading down to the stables, we talked animatedly with Lord Harrington about Willow Grove and our life in Australia; the branches of the oak trees above bare, the sky grey, the air crisp. Looking up at the two-level building, the stables made from grey stone like so many on the grounds of Merinda Manor, this appeared to be a recent addition. The smaller and much older stables sat off to its left, although no longer in use. 'All right, Thomas and Emmy. Let's go and choose you a horse.' They cheered as we entered the stables, and I stopped to take a deep breath, the sweet smell of hay mixed with horse manure mingling in my nostrils and reminding me of home. I watched on in amusement as Lord Harrington took them from stall to stall, introducing them to the beasts and telling us the history of each. Impressing me in both word and deed when in the company of my children, he did not appear intimidated by them or nervous while in their presence. Nor did he pressure them to like him. Although they clearly did. All three soon settled on the horses we would ride, amidst much clapping and laughter. Lord Harrington had chosen my mount after I confided I was not a natural horsewoman—a young stable hand soon leading her over to me, then handing me the reins before I led her outside to wait for the others.

'Are we ready?' Lord Harrington called out, Thomas and Emmy behind him leading their own mounts as I swung up on mine, the mare aptly named Lady. Lord Harrington had not taken his eyes from my backside until he noticed I returned his stare. Mounting the large gelding, he kicked him forward, and we obediently followed. Men were still strangely fascinated by the sight and shape of a woman's ankle or calf if not hidden under heavy skirts, despite being just as decently dressed as they were and possessing a similar one of their own. I often looked at their backsides with no choice in the matter, and if their trousers were fitted too close or they had outgrown them, not one seemed to care if they offended me when forced to gaze upon their balls and bat, as Leo would say, and I certainly found no thrill in it.

Lord Harrington led the way, recounting myths and legends as he showed us around the estate, often stopping to point out a place or an object as he spoke of the history or recalled a fascinating story told to him by his ancestors. I found him charming, and the longer I spent with him, the more I liked the man and felt comfortable in his presence. He was kind to my children, and they seemed to like him, only increasing my feelings of affection towards him. Guiding us down to the village of *Merinda na Monadh*, the horses trudged the well-worn road with a practiced ease; the river running alongside the main street, the waterfalls the town so well known for further down where the hills began to meet the fields of Merinda Manor. From the little I knew, the village stood on Harrington land; however, not all who lived there were directly in his employ. Unlike his forefathers, Lord Harrington had no jurisdiction over the residents unless they were considered a tenant, with some families renting land from the Harrington's for generations still living here, often in a small residence they built with their own hands on land they would never own.

The children had gone ahead, leaving me far behind, my gaze fixed on the shopfronts as I slowly walked Lady down the main street of the charming little village. Already passing two churches, a multitude of interesting shopkeepers plying their trade from the doorways, and an impressive tavern on the corner, I came upon a small hospital; the residences surrounding the business district built in a similar fashion, some lovely, some derelict. Lord Harrington had told me Merinda Manor had been in his family for over six-hundred-years, and I struggled to comprehend the enormity of that act in itself. To know the history of those who came before, while sharing the same blood and an inexplicable connection with anyone other than my children was something I would only ever dream of, and Lord Harrington had not a clue how truly privileged he was.

Lord Harrington pulled his horse up in front of a small tearoom, its walls made from stone the colour of sand, the exposed beams above painted black, the shingles on the roof the same. Lace curtains fluttered in the open windows, while well-crafted tables and chairs sat inside and out, all cheerfully painted in pink, yellow, and green; vases of dried heather sat in the centre of each. The smell of freshly baked bread wafted over from the shop next door, filling my nostrils and causing my stomach to rumble, the baker singing to himself out back as he stoked the fire, then placed a dozen tins filled with dough in the oven, one after another.

'I am aware of your great love of coffee, and anything made from the roasted beans, Mrs Cavanaugh. After such a long morning, I thought you may appreciate a stop here to have a cup before we decide where to take our picnic luncheon.' He politely helped me dismount, his hands firmly around my waist as he put me back down on my feet, a thousand butterflies set loose in my stomach at his touch. I enjoyed his company, and he allowed me to live in the moment, never once demanding I speak of the future or make promises I could not keep. He placed no pressure on me at all, and I had learned quickly that he was not a man to use force or manipulation to get his way. I knew well that if I told him to leave me be, he would, and I was uncertain how I felt about the matter.

'Thank you, Lord Harrington. You are very kind, and I appreciate your thoughtfulness.' I stared up at him and smiled, his hands still on my waist, while several women stopped outside the shop to watch, their baskets over their arms as they gossipped in hushed tones, their inquisitive glances friendly. He allowed his hands to fall to his sides, a wide grin on his face as he offered me his arm. I accepted, stepping up onto the footpath before he left me there amongst the women, turning back to tether the horses to a post. Thomas and Emmy had already dismounted a short distance away out the front of the sweet shop. A smile touched my lips as I watched them lean into the window, wide-eyed at all the sweets beckoning them inside.

'I have noticed the twins possess a love of all food, not unlike their mother,' he teased, placing my arm through his again before guiding me down the street towards Thomas and Emmy. 'I still must hide my surprise when I dine with you, my dear. I have never met a woman who eats as much as I have witnessed you consume, yet remains so slender. Not undernourished, as is the fashion of late.' He chuckled to himself, his mouth near my ear as he lowered his voice to a whisper. 'These trousers you wear hide nothing. You have been blessed with a beautiful body. One I would like to get my hands on in the near future if you would let me.' My heart went to my throat, my cheeks flushing pink in the frigid air as I avoided his gaze, a bright smile on my face as I stepped towards the children and embraced them. I could take him to my bed without a drop of guilt or regret; however, I knew he was looking for a wife, not a lover, and certainly not one who would leave the country soon. The regret would be all his; of that I was certain. 'I assume you would both like some sweeties to eat after lunch?' Lord Harrington enquired, their enthusiastic screams filling my ears and causing several more people to stop and stare. He had a natural affinity with children, and although he was yet to have his own, he was sensible in his interactions with mine, and it was clear to every observer he would make a wonderful father.

'Oh, yes, please, Mr Lord. You don't have a clue just how much Thomas and I adore chocolates, and lollies, as we call them back home. Our Uncle Leo says we would suck the sugar out of an anthill if we could—whatever that means.' Emmy shook her head, appearing confused for a moment. 'Our Daddy used to feed us melted chocolate on his fingertip before we could even sit up.' Lord Harrington smiled down at her, then glanced across at me, his eyebrow raised inquisitively as I began to laugh to myself, memories of Aaron filling my mind.

'Yes, it is all true. Their father spoiled them from the moment they were born. He started feeding them things he shouldn't when they were only a few weeks old, the cheeky bugger.' I smiled sadly as he moved his body closer to mine, his eyes fixed on mine before slipping his arm gently around my shoulders. Thomas and Emmy, both distracted by what they would buy, hadn't noticed at all, leaving us alone on the street after disappearing into the shop.

'He sounds like a wonderful father and a very good man, Mrs Cavanaugh. It's clear in your eyes how much you loved and adored him. They light up when you speak of him, ever so proudly. Reminding me of emeralds sparkling in the firelight, your eyes are the most exquisite I have ever seen in my life. I would not normally confide this, but the first time I stared into them, I felt my heart stop for a moment. The fact that they belong to such a beautiful woman, inside and out, makes me question how I could be so fortunate to have met a lady such as you.' His voice was low as I discreetly shook him off and stepped towards the window to take a closer look at the toffee apples. 'That moment when you are in deep discussion and realise Aaron is no longer here with you, I see the pain in your eyes. I wish there were some way I could ease you of it; however, I am helpless as to what to say. There is nothing I can think of that would not appear insincere or exacerbate the grief you carry. I cannot begin to understand the pain you attempt to hide, and I cannot pretend to. What I will say, Mrs Cavanaugh, is that I consider you a friend, no matter what the future holds for either of us, separately or together. I do hope you will allow me to become closer to you during your stay here at Merinda Manor.' I bent down to look at the bottom shelf of sweeties displayed in the window, my cheeks burning as I stared at long straps of red and black licorice.

'Are you asking me to take you to my bed?' I blurted far too loudly, a small man scurrying by choking on his own saliva, his eyes as wide as Lord Harrington's, who turned to face me, both hands grasping my shoulders as I held his gaze.

'I am not, Mrs Cavanaugh. I respect you immensely and would never risk your reputation by asking such a thing. I was only hoping we could relax some formalities between us. Please call me Reg, just as my friends do. As I have mentioned, I consider you at least that.' I nodded slightly, feeling the same.

'Thank you, Reg. To be fair, you must call me Abigail. Everyone else does, including many in my employ.' He chuckled to himself, crouching down to study the lower shelves, baskets and baskets of sweets overflowing, the colours almost blinding me.

'I imagine they would. You are a delight to behold in a world of mundane traditions and unachievable expectations. Speaking of these, I must go in and pay the shopkeeper. It's about all their elders are good for at their age.' He laughed aloud before chastely kissing my cheek, his eyes sparkling as he stepped into the shop to be greeted enthusiastically by the children, seemingly the only young ones in the village today under the age of two and five.

I stood alone, an icy chill in the wind starting to whip up around me as I waited for them, while soon taking notice of how many had stopped and were gossiping quietly between themselves up and down both sides of the street. It appeared *Merinda na Monadh* was no different from any other small village in any country throughout the world when it came to curiosity regarding another's private business.

I imagined Lord Harrington's life was the cause of much speculation, being such a powerful figure, only exacerbated by the strong relationships he had formed with residents of the town. Many had resided there for generations, and most had been in the employ of his ancestors at one time or another. Some still worked up at 'the big house', as they referred to Merinda Manor; however, others laboured in their own businesses, or farmed the land around the estate. He had shared so much about the property with me while onboard the ship. Seeing the place with my own eyes had left me feeling I had spent time here before; many of the shops and their vendors were impossibly familiar to me.

I strolled back up the street to the little shop Reg had brought to my attention, and soon made myself comfortable at a table outside, the smell of coffee wafting up my nose and making me heady as I waited for them to emerge from the sweet shop, an old song coming to mind called the *Coffee Cantata*, composed by Johann Bach in the 1730s, pleading the case of a young woman begging her disapproving father to give his blessings on the newfangled fashion of coffee drinking—and her devotion to it—much like me.

'Oh! How sweet coffee does taste. Better than a thousand kisses, milder than muscat wine. Coffee, coffee, I've got to have it, and if someone wants to perk me up, oh, just give me a cup of coffee!'

The children seemed to be taking an extraordinary amount of time, and I continued humming to myself, only quieting when I heard someone sitting at the table behind me mention my name, my ears pricking up immediately as I tried to listen in to their conversation.

'Ye do know who she is, Harold? Aaron Cavanaugh's widow. Did ye naw see Lord Harrington with her an' the bairns? Oh, he looks like a real family man, God bless him. Reminds me of when the Dowager used tae bring him here tae buy sweeties when he was a laddy. The way he held his arm around the poor widow, no different than if she were a fragile wee bird needin' protectin' was the sweetest thing I've seen in the last week. An' she's such a beauty fer a matron. They look so handsome together, dinnae they?' The woman nudged her husband—Harold, I assumed—in the ribs with her elbow, demanding an answer.

'I dinnae know, Peggy. How's it our business what they do? I know it now who she is when I look at her—an' aye, she's a stunnin' woman. I would have tae say the most beautiful lass I've seen in the last year, except fer ye, me sweet darlin'. Much prettier than the papers showed her tae be. I can only feel sorry fer the poor woman after what she's been through, an' now havin' tae raise those poor bairns without a father is a terrible burden tae carry,' I heard him reply, tears welling in my eyes as I stared out over the road at the river flowing alongside. I refused to allow myself to cry in front of strangers, and sniffed loudly, brushing a tear away with the back of my hand as they continued to talk, still no sign of my children—or Reg, as I had agreed to address him.

'It may naw burden her fer long. Did ye naw see the way Lord Harrington looked at her? He has eyes fer nae other. I've seen him around many o' the women his parents tried tae match him tae over the years, an' naw once have I witnessed the lad lookin' happy. Naw like this, anyway. He's always been a joyful soul since he was a bairn, but 'till now he's had naw luck in meetin' the right woman. Can ye imagine, Harold? We'd have *the* famous Mrs Abigail Cavanaugh livin' in the big house with Aaron's bairns. Look, there they are now. See how fatherly he is with 'em already, buyin' 'em sweeties an' makin' 'em laugh? Oh aye, Lord Harrington appears genuinely happy fer the first time in me memory when in the company o' a lady. The Dowager, God rest her, would be somersaultin' in her grave tae see him so content,' the woman cackled, the children catching sight of me and running in my direction, a large, wrapped parcel under each of their arms, Reg following along behind chuckling to himself. I embraced them as those at the table behind watched closely while listening to every word spoken between us.

'Now all that's left to do is get you a cup of that black liquid you appear unable to live without.' Reg smiled across at me as I slipped an arm around each of my children, guiding them to a seat and encouraging them to make themselves comfortable at the table. He made his way inside to order from the young woman who appeared to be in charge, while I left Thomas and Emmy to eat from the small bag of sweets they held between them, their packages now placed safely on the table. I tousled their hair before following him into the quaint shop, the aroma of coffee and freshly baked cinnamon cake filling my nostrils. He stood at the counter ordering two cups with milk and sugar, along with lemonade for the children.

'So, Reg. Do you mind my asking what is in the packages?' I hurried to his side, the shop empty, other than the two women standing behind the counter, and they both appeared to work there.

'Not at all. They chose a few sweets to take back to the manor. I let them have a small bag to share now, and the rest is for afterwards,' he replied, his green eyes widening in mock horror. I snorted in amusement, the shopkeeper laughing quietly to herself as she carried two bowls of coffee towards me. I returned her smile, finding comfort in the old ways and traditions they still insisted on here in this charming village.

'I see they have already manipulated and tricked you without your consent or knowledge. What made you change your mind about waiting until after luncheon?' I accepted the bowls and waited for her to bring the tray holding the lemonade, while he gazed down at me, his eyes twinkling in amusement.

'I felt some sympathy for them, given they did not complain or beg. I am very aware I'm at risk of appearing to buy their affection; however, I am not responsible for their love of sugar, nor will I be blamed for the ease in bribing them or purchasing their loyalty.' He chuckled as he raised his hand and caressed my cheek for a moment with his finger, sending tingles through me as I took the tray, thanking the women profusely before turning to make my way back to the children.

He politely held the door open, soon relieving me of my burden, before strolling out to the table and placing the refreshments down in front of them. The chatter had ceased at the sight of him, not only from my children but from everyone around us, and I wondered if he noticed. Or he chose not to. I was uncertain, but I admired his fortitude and his stubborn refusal to allow the actions or words of others around him to dictate his mood. I lowered myself down next to Emmy while Thomas sat across from me. Reg soon joined us, making himself comfortable next to my son.

'Mr Lord? We can see you are sweet on our mother, but we do have some questions for you,' Emmy announced, and I choked on my coffee while he grinned at her. She glanced at Thomas, his face blank as he stared back at her, before she elbowed him hard in the ribs. 'Go on. You promised you were going to say it, and now you're as wobbly as the Aspic Uncle Leo prides himself on,' she prompted, while Thomas grimaced as if in pain, his face flushed as he turned to stare up at Reg, but not before glaring at his sister.

'All right, Emmy. Get off me back, would ya? You're just like Uncle Leo. A whinin' nagger. Youse hound us all into the ground 'till ya get ya own way.' He shook his head at her before turning his attention back to Reg. 'Mr Lord? Me sister an' I were talkin' before we came on this ride with ya. We've heard the gossip on the ship sayin' you're plannin' to court our mother. We'd like to know ya intentions 'cause whatever decisions ya make'll affect us directly. We don't wanna leave our home, even if it is to live in a palace. We have our family an' friends there, an' then there's our horses, Majestic an' Rainbow. We could never leave 'em, but we know you're a very important man, an' would expect our mother to live here,' Thomas told him bravely, and I felt my heart melt. Trying to assume responsibility for me and his sister now his father was no longer here to care for us, I was about to answer and relieve him of a burden that was not his to carry; however, Reg responded before I was able, a lump now lodged in my throat.

'Thomas, I would never ask or expect you to give up your home. It is true. I like your mother very much, and enjoy her company a great deal. We have struck up a friendship, and if she should allow me to court her one day in the future, then I would consider myself privileged. Until then, everything will remain as it is,' he assured them, relief crossing Thomas's face, while Emmy relaxed, a smile spreading across her own.

'So, if you did marry our Mummy, would you move to Willow Grove and give up all your castles?' Emmy asked, her eyes wide as he ruffled her hair.

'Aye, I would, wee Emmy, and that's the truth of the matter. I couldn't think of anything better than calling you all family,' he told her, and I cringed inside, forcing a smile in his direction. Why did he have to go and ruin what had been a lovely day with talk of marriage? Especially when he was well aware it was the last subject I wished to discuss or hear about from any man. I sipped the coffee from the clay bowl, thoroughly enjoying every drop as I watched the three of them interact with each other as though they were old friends. This man certainly had a way with people, and to win the twins over so quickly proved his gift. It was not the sweets alone that endeared him to my children—they had their own money in their pockets and were free to spend it as they wished. No, they appeared to like the man because he treated them well, and he was always interested in what they had been doing with their time, or of their opinions on a subject they were discussing. He did remind me of Aaron at times, not only in his mannerisms, but in the way he spoke to the children—the last thing I needed clouding my judgement regarding the matter.

He rose to his feet and moved around the table to my side, Thomas and Emmy in deep discussion about our future, questioning if they would hold our wedding in England at Westminster Abbey, or at Willow Grove. Reg sat down next to me, his eyes flickering in amusement as he listened to them.

'I meant every word I said to them, Abigail. I would give all this up in a heartbeat if you ever allowed a romantic love to develop and grow between us.' I looked away, glancing across at the table behind me, those sitting around it silent, although, every ear cocked in our direction, several other groups now filling the tables and chairs around us. 'If these are what women wear in the outback of Australia when riding, I would be more than content to move there,' he whispered, pointing to my trousers as I blushed furiously.

'This is not what most wear at all. Only the clever ones, like the Suffragettes. And I do not live in the outback for the hundredth time. We are from Geelong, and it is hardly different from the city of Melbourne,' I whispered back, a smile touching my lips, a smirk touching his. He was so damned attractive; however, he had made himself clear. If he were to have me, it would be in the context of marriage—and I was having none of it, aware our friendship would become even more complicated. I gathered the empty bowls and cups together, placing them back on the tray.

'Rightio. Let me take you out to the loch where I used to fish as a lad,' he said, his voice low, 'and I still swim there when the weather becomes warm enough. I often go out there when I need time alone, or must make an important decision, and I would enjoy it immensely if you would allow me to show you the most beautiful part of the estate. Once there, I will unpack the luncheon, which I understand you both had some influence over.' I rose to my feet, confusion on my face for a moment as I straightened my skirt, while Thomas and Emmy jumped to theirs, beaming up at him as we crossed over to where the horses waited, mine drinking from one of the water troughs dotted up and down the street.

'Oh, yes, our Lord, we were asked for our opinion. I told your cook we are used to regular food, no different from them, and we like larger helpings. We were worried they would send that fancy scaffy they like to serve to impress everyone, and that always leaves us starving,' Emmy complained, while accepting his kind offer to help her mount her steed.

'Ya won't be goin' without today, Sir Harrington. We've just about everythin' ya could want in that basket. We even have a full puddin' in there with clotted cream for dessert—an' now, sweeties for afters,' Thomas called out, reining in his mount behind Reg, who turned and offered me his hand, the other holding the mare steady by her bridle.

'Oh, what a fabulous day it truly is,' Emmy sang, sounding very much like her Uncle Leo for a moment. I smiled, glancing across at her affectionately as she pulled her horse up next to Thomas, both appearing so small in comparison to the beasts underneath them.

I lifted my foot up and placed the toe of my boot in the stirrup, the eyes of the entire village now on my backside as I swung up onto my borrowed horse, loud gasps and exclamations coming from the small crowd that had gathered along the street. Reg chose to ignore their whispers—just as I did—his sensibility in every situation delighting me as I followed along behind him through the village. The undulating hills soon disappeared, opening up into wide fields, and we kicked the horses into a canter, my children beside me, the sound of hooves pounding on the wet ground, the laboured breath of the beasts filling my ears. I would not have chosen to be anywhere but here at this very moment, of that I was certain.

Chapter Eighteen

'HAVE YOU GIVEN ANY thought to what you will wear this evening, Mistress?' Bessie enquired, her hands on her hips as I languished on the bed. 'You need to make haste. It's strict here,' she warned, raising her finger to wave it at me. 'You must be in the drawing room not a minute later than seven-thirty to be called by the butler at eight for dinner once the first course is set out on the table. It's going on seven now, and you're still in your undergarments.'

'You are welcome to choose for yourself. Maybe something I haven't worn during the latter part of this journey? I doubt very much he will remember or even notice he's seen it before.' She nodded before hurrying to the dressing room where she had unpacked my trunks and organised my wardrobe earlier. Returning soon after, an emerald green gown over her arm, I struggled to my feet, groaning loudly as I crossed the room. Within minutes, she had me dressed, then taking me by the shoulders, she guided me over to the dressing table, pushing me down onto the seat to style my hair. Pulling and twisting the top half up into curls at the crown, she pinned it securely before placing the matching hairpiece over my forehead—in my opinion, so very closely resembling a gemstone necklace—her practiced fingers expertly weaving it into my hair within moments.

'Your great-aunt was well known here, Mistress,' she remarked, touching the back of my head. I stood and strolled across the room to the window, the light almost gone as the afternoon slipped into the evening.

'That woman has been such an enigma to me. And still is,' I murmured, gazing down over the conservatory, several lanterns burning brightly while lighting the way of the interconnecting covered walkways. Bessie stood behind me as I carefully lowered myself onto the window seat.

'It may do you good to spend some time with the staff here. Only for your own peace of mind, I suppose. It's not a bad thing to go searching to find where you come from, and I know you well. You won't rest easy until you do.' I nodded, remaining silent, my eyes fixed on a kitchen maid meeting with the gardener I had frightened earlier, it seemed, in secret. 'I know you refuse to have anything to do with your parents, and you know where they are, but this appears to be a way to guard your heart and mind while still finding the answers you seek.'

'I do not know where the woman who gave birth to me is. I've never known where she went. Only her name. Mary Campbell.' My voice, barely above a whisper, faltered for a moment, a lump lodged in my throat. She rested her hand on my shoulder, her reflection in the window staring back at me, her eyes filling with tears.

'Oh, Mistress. I've already been told the story of her and her sister, Anna. My heart leapt to my throat when I heard the housekeeper discussing them with Archie, knowing the little I know about your mother, most being only her name and the look of her. I kept my mouth shut, as I'm aware it's not something you like to speak of.' She sat down beside me for a moment, gently taking my hand in hers.

'Lord Harrington's driver?' She nodded, a sympathetic smile on her lips.

'He is your uncle, if what I heard was the truth. So is that big mouthed valet, Alisdair.' I sighed deeply, tears stinging my eyes. She nodded to herself, her hand trembling slightly as she passed me a clean handkerchief. 'I questioned him further, Mistress, if only for my own piece of mind. I know you are likely to want nought to do with it all, but should your children have questions one day, I may hold the answers they are seeking if you direct them to me.' I turned towards her and nodded, embracing her for the longest time.

'It's nice to know my mother has two brothers and a sister who love her, no matter where in the world she may be.' She patted my back one last time before releasing me and rising to her feet, turning to help me to mine as a loud knock on the door startled me.

'Sisters. There are two more. I know you won't believe me, Mistress, as I barely believe it myself, but our Maisie is one of them.' I gasped aloud as Hamish and the children stepped into my room, all dressed smartly in their evening wear. Greeting them warmly, I managed to compose myself and push everything other than the thought of dinner to the back of my mind. Hamish avoided my gaze, strolling over to the chair near the fireplace and settling himself down comfortably to wait. He still had not uttered a word to me in well over a week, leaving me questioning why he had agreed to come at all.

'Oh, Mummy. You look extra beautiful tonight. I remember when you wore this gown on the ship, and I have adored it ever since. May I have it when I'm older?' Emmy asked, her body pressed in close beside me near the door, her hand running up and down the fine fabric as I prepared to leave.

'Thank you, Emmy, and you look even more beautiful than I ever could, sweetheart. You are welcome to choose anything from my wardrobe as soon as you are of a similar size, and that will not be long, now.' I reached down and squeezed her waist, and she collapsed into giggles, Thomas striding out of the room to wait in the hallway after losing all patience with us.

'I hope my boosies will be as large as yours,' she remarked as Bessie's head snapped around towards her, my determined maid soon shooing her out into the hallway with her brother.

I bid Bessie farewell and followed Hamish out to join the children, my stomach growling. Emmy held Hamish's hand, chatting animatedly as she led him towards the stairs, Thomas behind them. I cringed as they told him of the day and how we had spent much of it with Reg. Still feeling full from the decadent luncheon we had enjoyed by the magnificent loch, I belched, covering my mouth after the fact, aware if the children had not been there with us today, it would have been terribly romantic. They hurried ahead of me, waiting at the foot of the stairs before accompanying me to the drawing room, the butler hurrying in before us and announcing dinner before we even stepped in the door, much to my chagrin. A stern-looking man in his sixties, and dressed immaculately in his black uniform, a crisp white shirt underneath, he escorted us to the dining room and across to the ornate table, quickly seating me next to Reg where he relaxed at the head of it all, Hamish shown to the chair directly across from me to Reg's left. Emmy made herself comfortable next to Hamish, while Thomas sat down to my right, a wide grin on his face. Despite how large and extravagant the room, it felt strangely intimate and cosy seated down one end together like this. Almost like family.

'My dear, you look even more beautiful in that gown this evening than you did on the second night of our voyage. An impossible task you seamlessly achieved,' Reg remarked, personally pouring a glass of wine for me, the ruby red liquid deep and lush, the candelabras lighting the room in a soft glow. The footmen served us from the sideboard, carrying the platters and bowls from person to person, rather than leaving it on the table, allowing common sense to prevail and us to serve ourselves without bothering them.

'Thank you, Reg. I was hoping you would not remember.' I nodded politely, not wanting Hamish to know the truth of the matter. Or the fact I was enjoying the time I was spending with Reg immensely, aware just how jealous he could be despite having no claim to me.

'I forget nothing when it comes to you, Abigail.' He stared down into my eyes, my children exchanging knowing glances while Hamish glared at his plate, appearing angry at the roasted pheasant in particular, the Gratin Dauphinoise coming off second best.

I was not surprised by the number of servants he had in his keep, going by what I had heard on the ship. Observing at the very least ten fold the staff I employed in my own house, they sounded far less, all being far more formal and quieter than anyone who worked for me. The servants in service at Merinda Manor did not speak, most even when spoken to, only providing a brief response when left with no other choice. Except for the butler, and although far more confident, he only spoke when spoken to—while all avoided eye contact with anyone they, or society, deemed to be above them. This was not a way in which I myself would choose to live—I would hate every part of it, in fact. It came as no surprise to me that the man was lonely, and I could not imagine him taking his dinner in the kitchen surrounded by servants in an attempt to remedy that, no matter how alone or melancholy. I imagined all his evenings were this formal, whether he had guests or not. It was no wonder he craved a wife and a family of his own, the poor man. Although, tonight, Hamish appeared to be the only one at the table who was not satisfied with his lot in life.

We had no sooner finished our dessert, a decadent pavlova topped with cream and stewed rhubarb and nectarine, made in our honour and a favourite Reg had discovered at the Delmont Hotel, when little Mary hesitantly stepped into the room to collect Thomas and Emmy. They would bathe in the evening and Mary still helped them ready themselves for bed, often sitting to tell them stories she had once heard their father tell, now committed to her memory. They embraced me before bidding us all a good night, their footsteps fading down the hallways as Reg turned to me, a smile on his lips, his green eyes twinkling.

'I would enjoy it very much if you would allow me to show you the gardens by moonlight. They are quite beautiful, and out of all the women I am acquainted with, it is you I believe will appreciate the sheer magic of it all the most.' He placed his hand over mine, and surprisingly, I did not move it away.

'I would be delighted to accompany you, Reg. I have admired the grounds at every opportunity since arriving.' I picked up my glass and raised it to my lips, avoiding Hamish's glare, the wine sweeter than I was used to. It was not my intention to enrage Hamish, or make him jealous, nor was I attempting to pay him back for withdrawing his friendship; however, I was more than aware he would disagree with me. I genuinely enjoyed Reg's company, even more so after spending an idyllic day with him and the children. Being near him cheered me immensely, and why would I choose a future filled with misery and melancholy knowing happiness could find me again?

Without any hesitation or delay, Reg rose to his feet and took two steps towards me, offering me his arm.

'Good night, Hamish. It is a pleasure having you here at Merinda Manor as my guest. I will call for Clive to attend to you. Rest well.' Reg nodded politely, while Hamish returned his friendly stare, nodding his head back at him before asking the footman to pour him another whisky as I was guided out of the silent room and into the darkened hallway to find my cloak.

The gardens were truly magnificent and seemed to stretch on forever around the mansion.

'This here was commissioned for my grandmother, Charlotte, soon after she arrived here to marry my grandfather. She came here *from* Australia, can you believe? Wasn't born there, though.' He swept his arm wide over an extensive walled garden comprising three very separate enclosures, all covered with romantic trellises, hornbeam hedges and herbaceous borders filled with the scent of old rose petals, a sheltered paradise of colours and intoxicating perfume amongst a mass of what must have been thousands of rose bushes, all distinctive and different from the next. He stopped by a small fountain, a cherub pouring the crystal clear liquid from a jug perched on his shoulder into a pot at his feet, the sound of running water distracting me for a moment as I stopped beside him, a pile of leaves someone had forgotten to collect nearby. 'I find Merinda Manor such a comforting place to be. My hope is to spend more time here in the future. Around April, the daffodils cover many of the gardens around the estate in various shades of yellow, which is then replaced by the azaleas and rhododendrons with their white, pink and vibrant red blooms, the heather washing the fields in all shades of purple. The place is more than a building to me. It reflects everything I am, and those who came before me who made this possible.' His voice, barely above a whisper, had grown husky, and he glanced down at the ground, layer upon layer of dead leaves like crumpled paper beneath his boots.

'It is truly grand and like nothing I have seen before. Well, not a private house,' I replied, pulling my cloak tighter around my neck.

'Could you see yourself living here, Abigail? Or in a home similar in Australia?' He reached for my hand, then gently pulled me closer, taking my breath away while barely touching me.

'The truth is, I could not. The circles you mix in and the lifestyle you lead are far too formal and fancy for the likes of me. I could never leave my home. Not forever. I have my children to consider,' I replied, his face so close to mine, his warm breath tickled my ear.

'May I be direct with you?'

'I thought you already were after our interactions today,' I answered softly, and he pressed his cheek against mine for a moment.

'We have known each other long enough to form a familiar bond and a fond attachment built on friendship. I want more than that and would like to kiss you, Abigail, if you would be kind enough to consent?' he whispered in my ear, sending tingles through me. All I could do was nod before he swiftly placed his lips on mine, kissing me deeply, my arms circling his neck. I found it much easier kissing a man who was not as tall or as wide as Aaron or Hamish. Although muscular and strongly-built, Reg was nowhere near the size of either of them. The thought of Aaron made me pull away, gasping for a moment as I struggled to regain my breath. He smiled down at me before taking my hand in his and leading me through the garden, the moon beaming silver and softly illuminating the cobblestone path, a heavy mist hanging low. 'You captured my attention the very moment I saw you, and you still have all of it. Dancing with you in my arms every night was the most enjoyable aspect of the journey, along with walking the decks and getting to know who you are. My initial curiosity and admiration has turned into something unexpected, and I have formed a strong attachment to you, Abigail. I would like to court you, if you would allow it?' His voice faltered, and he appeared nervous for the first time in my company since we met. He offered me a seat near the kitchen garden by a back entrance, and I accepted, patting my hand on the polished wood beside me as an invitation. He lowered himself down next to me and smiled, remaining silent as I gazed up, not a star in sight. Always so quietly confident, I had never witnessed any awkwardness in his manner or seen him unnerved, and I swallowed hard, a thousand thoughts running through my mind as I tried to consider my response.

'You pay me such a great compliment, Lord Harrington,' I began, stopping to clear my throat, his eyes fixed on mine.

'Please, call me Reg,' he reminded me, and I turned away, unable to return his stare. He had such lovely eyes, so honest and kind.

'I'm sorry, Reg. I still mourn my husband deeply, and I fear you would give your time and attention to me in folly. I could never return to England as I have told you before. I have no interest in marrying again, and I am unable to provide you with children of your own blood, and that would be unfair. To you most of all. I would like to continue our friendship, but I can give you no more than that.' He held my hand in his, a deep sigh coming from him, his eyes now fixed on an owl overhead on a branch of the oak tree above.

'I understand your position being so recently widowed, but I ask you to give me the upcoming week to change your mind. I will not place pressure on you, or use force; however, if you allow me that, I believe I will succeed in gaining your affections.' He had such a comforting smile, a smile that gained trust immediately, and I almost recounted. Almost.

'I wouldn't put my money on it, but I will give you the time you have asked for.' He nodded as he rose to his feet, offering me his arm again before escorting me back to my bedchamber, raising my hand to his lips in farewell as we stood in the doorway.

'Goodnight, Abigail. Sleep well.' He bowed deeply, then straightened up without another word and strode away, leaving me standing in the hallway outside my door feeling confused.

I stepped inside to find Bessie waiting for me. 'How was your walk with the Duke?' she asked inquisitively as I crossed the room, slipped off my coat then sat down at the dressing table. I told her what he had said to me as her eyes went wide.

'He wants to court me.' I took the warm face cloth she passed me and began to wipe the paint from my face, her hands working swiftly to brush and plait my hair.

'Oh, Mistress. There are far worse things that could happen,' she teased, then touched the back of my head, smiling to herself. She went to my wardrobe, then helped me ready for bed. Crossing the large room, she pulled back the heavy quilts, and I climbed up into the bed. She wished me goodnight before extinguishing all but one lamp and quietly leaving the room to find her own bed. I lay unmoving, my eyes fixed on the shadows outside my window thinking of poor Lord Harrington. So very lonely, he was prepared to take on a widow well past her prime when he could find a nice young woman willing and able to do his bidding—and bear him a child when I could not.

I soon fell into a deep sleep, but was startled awake within the hour, my eyes fluttering open to find Hamish standing by my bed. gazed down at me, the room silent as he slipped his shirt over his head then slid in beside me, his body on mine, pinning me down under him.

'I love ye an' I miss ye.' His voice, husky and low, broke before his lips were on mine, his kiss passionate. Without warning, he was inside me, leaving me gasping for air as he groaned then started to thrust hard and fast. I returned his kiss, my hands running up and down his muscular stomach, his eyes on mine. Slipping my nightgown off over my head, he lifted my legs, circling his waist as I tightened my muscles around him. He thrust faster and deeper inside me, his hands on my hips, pleasure exploding through every part of my body as he groaned, his body shuddering before collapsing on me. He gazed at me in silence, his head on my shoulder, his breathing slowing. Without saying another word, he kissed me for the longest time, then rose from the bed and collected his shirt before striding across the room without making another sound, closing the door quietly behind him.

Seven words he had spoken the entire time he was here, clearly out of character, yet I believed he and I were friends once more. Closing my eyes, I drifted off into a deep sleep, dreaming of Aaron, two sisters—one dark, the other fiery red—and a lonely wee laddie with hair the colour of wheat tormenting me until the early hours.

Chapter Nineteen

I STRETCHED, TENSING EVERY muscle, my eyes still closed as I yawned loudly. I turned to find Emmy in my bed, and assumed she came in through the night and I hadn't heard her, or woken once since. I stared across at her perfect wee features as she softly snored like her father, her head on the pillow where he would have been had he still been with us. Thoughts of him filled my mind, and how different this journey would have been had he been allowed to stay. I would not be fending off suitors, that I knew for certain. He made me feel safe and loved from the moment I met him until the final moment we shared. I was still loved by those around me, a different love altogether, but the romantic attention from other men was unwanted, and always had been. As for feeling safe, I felt as lost as I ever had been, and so very alone.

I understood now I was officially out of mourning, I was expected to keep up appearances for the sake of those around me. Especially the children. And I was doing a good job of it all; however, inside I was screaming. I moved closer to Aaron's side of the bed where our child lay, shaking my head at myself given he had never been here. I wished with all I had in me he was beside me now, watching his daughter sleep. Tears slipped down my cheeks as I stared up at the ceiling, waiting for Emmy to wake. Soon after, Bessie hurried in, her eyes lighting up when she noticed Emmy.

'Good morning, my sleeping beauties,' she called out cheerfully, fresh towels under her arm, a jug of hot water in her hand. Emmy turned slightly, screwing up her face before she yawned, her eyes still firmly shut, her arms outstretched. She raised her head, peering up at her through heavy eyelids, her hair tied up in rags from the night before thanks to little Mary. 'Mary is looking for you, sleepy head,' Bessie told her before busying herself around the room, tidying what was already tidy.

Emmy cuddled into me, taking her time to fully awaken before kissing me and rising to her feet to go find her beloved little Mary. I quickly followed, excitement starting to bubble up inside me for the first time in years. Bessie knew I wanted to look my best today, for I was finally going to return to where I grew up and introduce my children to one of the most important people in the entire world to me.

Bessie hurried into the dressing room, selecting a lovely gown made from a bronze fabric with a flattering boat neckline, the sleeves falling elegantly past my wrists, the golden lace curling into wispy tendrils fluttering below my hands. Made from a heavy fabric underneath that would keep me warm, along with my green woollen cape with its fur-trimmed hood and pockets, I stared into the cheval mirror, my nose wrinkled in disdain.

'Do you think this one reveals too much? They are nuns, Bessie, and I have no doubt I will be expected to remove my coat when inside,' I reminded her as I studied my reflection, then glanced back at her standing behind me, her hands on her hips. Although respectable enough to wear out during the day under any other circumstance, the neckline exposed the top of my shoulders, the fabric crossing over at the front just above my breasts, joining at the embroidered bodice. She looked me up and down, nodding her head approvingly.

'I wouldn't send you to the nuns unless you looked like a proper lady, and you do, Mistress. While on the subject, I wish you would wear the corsets without complaint. I don't like some of the new undergarments Catherine is making you. They wouldn't support an apple, let alone anything the size of your breasts. At least the dresses are made with a fair hand and the structured bodices keep everything in place, I suppose. Not the same as a corset, though,' she said, staring at my chest with a critical eye before taking me by the shoulders and guiding me over to the dressing table.

'Corsets were invented by a man, of that I am certain, and if forced to wear them, they would be redesigned into something far more comfortable. If they had to carry and bear children, the human race would have died out before it even got started.'

I stared out of the window next to me, wondering what Sister Josephine was feeling right at this very moment, hoping she would still love me the same after fifteen-years of separation. I was returning not as I left, and the triumphs and tragedies of life had changed me. I turned back to the mirror as Bessie started to twist my curls, then pinned each one to the back of my head, some strands left loose to frame my face.

'You look lovely, Mistress. Just as you did before all that sorry business, but your eyes still hold such pain and sadness. I'm hoping that by seeing your Sister Mary Josephine again, the light may start to shine in them again.' She placed her hand on my shoulder, and I lifted mine, placing it firmly over the top of hers.

'Thank you, Bessie. I cannot wait to be reunited with her. It took all my strength not to summon Archie yesterday and ask him to bring the carriage to take us there unannounced; however, I know that would be considered rude. They are expecting us today, and I did not want to impose on them.' I rose to my feet and turned to embrace her before crossing the room to collect my cloak, slipping it over my arm then promptly making my way downstairs, a smile on my lips and joy filling my heart.

Waiting for me at the bottom of the staircase, Thomas and Emmy took my hand and led me through the large hallways and majestic rooms, only stopping once we entered the dining room. I would have to live in this house for at least a year before I was confident to find my way around the place without getting lost. I could not imagine the rooms here were ever really filled to overflowing, even if hosting a party for a thousand people.

Crossing the room and making our way to the table, Reg and Hamish rose to their feet to greet us. They had been in deep discussion for the first time since they had met, surprising me greatly. I sat down next to Reg, my children returning to the chairs they had been seated in the day before. I made myself comfortable while the butler and footmen served Emmy and Thomas their breakfast. Picking up the silver pot, I poured my own coffee—much to their astonishment, it seemed, going by their side glances and exaggerated eye rolling when they thought we weren't paying attention.

'How did you sleep, Abigail?' Reg asked, his grin wide as he turned his attention to me. Hamish abruptly stopped eating, also turning to me, his eyebrow raised, silently challenging me.

'I slept well, thank you, Reg. I was most comfortable.' I ignored the smirk on Hamish's lips and smiled before fixing my attention on the food before me.

'Och, aye. I slept like the dead fer the first time in over a week,' Hamish interjected, despite no one asking for his thoughts or opinions on the matter. I lightly kicked him under the table, connecting with his shin, although he did not flinch, his face giving nothing away as he focused his attention on Reg.

'I'm pleased, Hamish. I am unhappy when my guests are unhappy.' Reg nodded politely at him before turning to me. 'I understand you are visiting an orphanage today, Abigail. What a kind and charitable act to carry out while you are here,' Reg remarked, admiration in his eyes.

'I am returning there, if the truth be told. That orphanage is where I grew up.' Surprising even myself how comfortable I felt sharing such a private part of me, he seemed curious as I settled back in my seat and smiled at him.

'You were raised there? You must have fallen on good times since, dear Abigail, as I would never have known,' Lord Harrington remarked kindly, his face softening further as I told him briefly of my first fifteen-years at Emiliani House, and what had occurred when the wooden box arrived. He stared at me in silence, his eyes widening at different times, Hamish and the twins not uttering a word, their gaze fixed on me. As I finished, deciding I had said far too much, I explained the purpose of my visit coinciding with my thirtieth birthday, while Reg relaxed back in his chair, his handsome face thoughtful.

'Abigail, I thought highly of you before, but now my admiration is immeasurable. It is rare I am left speechless, no matter what the subject. You are an incredibly brave woman to have lived the life you have, and still have that lovely smile on your face. After hearing what led you here, I see your life really has been divided into three separate and distinct parts,' Reg remarked, while I raised my eyebrows enquiringly. 'Oh, you are not aware?' I shook my head in confusion before he continued. 'The first part of your life started at the orphanage, where you were given limited opportunities. Then, serendipitously, your life changed for the better, and you began the second part of your life with Aaron, living happily for many years until you lost him. Now, you have the opportunity to create whatever you desire, and live the rest of your life however you would like that to be. You will find love again, Abigail, as you are far too lovely to waste away alone. Deep down within me, I am certain you will one day find the happiness you once had.' He placed his hand on mine encouragingly, the children and Hamish still silent as they continued to eat. He was such a kind man, and so very handsome. I hoped he found a woman who deserved him, and he did not end up bound to someone like Isabelle Malcolm, only one of thousands looking to marry for money and power while hiding a cold and vindictive streak.

I gave a thought to poor Jonathon, and his unwanted visits to me while in London—his determination to convince me to take him to my bed reaching a point where even Jenny suspected there was something amiss. I had begged him to stop seeking me out; however, he refused to listen, turning up unannounced at his parents home at least once a day. Hamish had been outwardly cold towards him, resulting in Jenny becoming suspicious of all three of us. She did not know what had occurred—all she knew was something had passed between us but had not broached the subject directly with me, therefore, I never confided in her.

'That is such a sensible, and very comforting, way to look at it,' I replied as I smiled across at Reg, his hand gently squeezing mine. Hamish watched on in silence, not uttering a word as he raised his glass of apple juice to his lips and drank deeply. Thomas soon noticed Reg's hand on mine, and nudged Emmy under the table, his eyebrows raised as he nodded his head to her in our direction, their eyes twinkling in amusement, while my cheeks became warm under their stare.

'Thank you for trusting me, Abigail. I have no doubt it was difficult growing up in that situation, and I can only imagine the pain you would feel speaking of it, no matter how long ago. My father was an unofficial benefactor to Emiliani House since the time I myself was a small bairn. He was forced to help privately for reasons he refused to discuss right up until his death—other than my grandmother forbade it. He would take me along when he would visit with Sister Mary Monica in secret to leave his monthly contribution to their good work. You would have been there then, which does ease me knowing he helped you, even if only to prevent you starving, which I've been told was the likely outcome way back when you were first taken there.' He stared into my eyes with something resembling pride, a flash of memory of a man favouring him with a young lad beside him coming to mind. There were many who came and went through the hallways of Emiliani House while I was there, and I had paid no attention to most. Including the man who I now knew to be his father, a powerful figure with a powerful presence who never once uttered a word when he passed by any of us, nor did I pay attention to the boy always by his side, only ever seeing them for a brief moment if scrubbing the floors when he marched past.

'Thank you, Reg. It touches my heart to hear of the people around the district—oh, I am sorry, I should say parish—who have provided charity to the Sisters and bairns over the years.' It seemed his father held strong values, along with a generous heart, just as he did. He settled back comfortably and took a sip of his coffee, gazing into my eyes, a smile touching his lips.

'I offered to continue the financial contributions in his place when I took over the estate after his death, but they politely declined. I later heard rumours they have an extremely generous benefactor who ensures their needs are provided for well above how most souls live. Are you aware of that, Abigail? I heard whispers that no one actually knows who has put such a significant amount of money into the rebuilding and renovations of the mansion, not including the ongoing maintenance of such a grand building. Rumour has it, some women leave their daughters there at birth because of the wealth the Order now has.' He shook his head in disbelief, leaving me wondering if I had indeed done the right thing for those involved—past, present and future. 'The standard of living provided to the children is in many cases much higher than the majority of working-class parents can provide. I am unsure if you have been told by your Sister Mary Josephine how much the place has changed since you left. I have been there myself regarding employment opportunities for the young lassies about to leave, as we have always done here at Merinda Manor for those less fortunate than ourselves. To know you were once living there when it was such an impoverished institution disturbs me greatly; however, it has only strengthened my admiration and respect for you. I feel very privileged, and I have to say moved by your history, Abigail, and the fact you chose to share something so personal with me is appreciated greatly. It is now clear to me why you became the person you did, and how thrilling that is for those of us around you.' His voice, full of emotion, faltered as I slipped my hand out from under his and continued with my breakfast.

'There are some who don't like our Ma 'cause she came from an orphanage. As if she had any control over that. They talk like she's a vagrant 'cause of it, an' look down on her. It makes me wanna snap their necks with me bare hands,' Thomas growled menacingly, Hamish and Reg turning to him in surprise, the look in his eye causing my stomach to drop—no different from his father.

'Who says these things about yer mother, Thomas?' Hamish asked, his voice steady; however, he was unable to hide the anger in his eyes.

'The ones from Makenzie Station, Uncle Hamish. It's your father and sister, Jemima, talking that way. The housekeeper's children, well, they go to school with us, and they have heard it all. And tell us about it at the first opportunity. They like Mummy very much, and do not agree with your Da at all that she's a slovenly trollop who grew up in the gutter, no different from a dunny rat,' Emmy interrupted before Thomas could answer. I choked on my coffee, coughing and spluttering as Thomas turned and patted me on the back until I caught my breath. Hamish appeared furious—at whom

I was uncertain. Reg sat back in his seat, astounded by what had just come from my daughter's sweet lips, his eyes full of sympathy.

'Emmy, your mother is certainly not what these people say she is. It is a terrible slur against her reputation to be spoken of in that way. If I ever hear anyone speak such terrible words about your mother, they will have me to face,' Reg told her kindly, her face lighting up in a grateful smile.

'Thank you, Mr Lord. Now that our Mummy doesn't have a husband, she has no one to stand up for her. They only say terrible things about her now because our Daddy isn't here to punch their faces in. He would do that, you know? If anyone did anything to Mummy, he would cut off their...' she went to say before I quickly clamped my hand across her mouth and smiled brightly at Reg, who smirked back at me. Hamish looked set to explode as he finished his breakfast, wiping his mouth with his napkin before he stood abruptly.

'I apologise fer draggin' Abigail away from ye, Lord Harrington, but the time has come fer us tae depart,' Hamish said, nodding politely before glancing down at me expectantly. Thomas and Emmy obediently rose to their feet, their excitement obvious, before shaking Reg's hand as he smiled at them fondly.

'Have a wonderful day, Thomas and Emmy. I look forward to hearing of all your adventures on your return,' he told them, and I noticed Hamish grimace. I stood, as did Reg, who reached out and took my hand in his before kissing it gently and wishing me well. He escorted us out, while Hamish followed close behind, making no effort to disguise his irritation.

Everyone had taken great care with their appearance today, even Hamish, who looked handsome in his new shirt and trousers. The pants were fitted a little too snugly, showing off his backside to perfection, unable to avert my eyes as I followed him out to the carriage. He assisted us in one-by-one, this carriage being far smaller than the other and drawn by only two horses, and soon climbed in and shut the door behind him. He sat down next to me, Thomas and Emmy opposite, talking quietly between themselves.

'How are ye feelin' about today, Abigail?'

'Nervous, excited, scared. I'm feeling too many things to be able to put into words,' I replied, sitting back and trying to calm myself. He took my hand in his and placed it in his lap, sending warm tingles up my arm.

'I want tae apologise fer what me father an' shite o' a sister have been sayin'. I dinnae know, an' that's the honest truth of it. I'll be confrontin' the both of 'em when we arrive home.' I stared out the window as we hurtled down the driveway, the horses going at great speed. 'Somethin' has changed between ye an' Lord Harrington. I'm naw blind or stupid. Have ye taken him tae yer bed?' His voice so low, I could barely hear him, and I turned abruptly, narrowing my gaze.

'How dare you say that! No, I have not. You would have noticed last night when you came to my room if he was in bed with us,' I hissed, his face flinching as Thomas and Emmy stopped talking for a moment, glancing across at us curiously, before turning back to each other and resuming their conversation as if we weren't in the carriage.

'Aye, all right. I know I'm actin' jealous, but I meant what I told ye. I willnae let another man have ye, Abigail. Just keep pushin' me, an' you'll see,' he whispered calmly as I inwardly fumed at him. He refused to let go of my hand, despite my attempts to pull away from him, leaving me no choice but to remain how we were if I did not want my children to notice the argument between us. He was perfectly calm and pleasant in his manner since his visit to my bedchambers; however, I was feeling far from the same toward him. Behaving as though he owned me—typical of every married man I knew who kept his wife close—was something I abhorred.

Aaron had tried the same throughout our marriage on many occasions, never with intent to cause me harm; however, most boys were raised with the expectation that once grown and ready to start their own family, their wife would be subservient to him as the master of the house in all manner of ways. It was true once married; you did in fact become your husband's property to do with as he pleased.

Anything you owned automatically became his, unless you had a legal contract drawn up between you, as in my case. It was only if the man used excessive force or was considered cruel towards his wife could a woman go into hiding and be seen as justified in her actions seeking a separation and, or, divorce; however, the law was reluctant to become involved in what they called a 'private domestic matter'. Aaron had respected, loved and protected me, and always listened to my opinion, unlike many men I knew who did as they pleased; however, he was still a bloody man and wanted to be in charge of everything, and I would fight and obstruct him as best I could every time. We always came to some resolution in the end, generally after a heated 'discussion', each of us as stubborn as the other.

Hamish did not differ much from Aaron had been, with only one detail of variance—he had no claim to me. I had no intention of allowing him to strong-arm me into anything I was not comfortable with. Reg was completely different. He did not pressure me, only attempting to gently convince me I had nothing to lose by getting to know him better, and I did not disagree. I had not wanted to be with Aaron when I met him either; however, my feelings soon changed, and I was grateful for it when reflecting back.

We slowly descended a small hill, passing through the village I used to walk through to church as a bairn, my stomach starting to churn, the realisation we were close now laying heavy. Their faces pressed up against the carriage windows, Thomas and Emmy stared out the window, their eyes wide, their mouths open as we passed by the church and several taverns, the shops on both sides of the wide road bustling. They knew every building, as I had described this village to them many times over the years when I would put them to bed, when they would ask me to tell them stories from my childhood. I made sure my tales were not grim, not because I did not want them to know the uncomfortable childhood I had experienced, but because I did not want them to ever think I felt sorry for myself, as I did not even for a moment. I truly believed my life had been blessed with so much love and good fortune that I did not deserve, despite the tragedies I had endured.

The carriage passed through the elaborate front gates, and I saw Emiliani House for the first time in fifteen-years, a lump forming in my throat that I could not dislodge, no matter how hard I tried. I was stunned at how different the orphanage was now. No longer a dilapidated mansion that had fallen into disrepair like so many, it was now magnificent as it loomed before us, the walls and roof now repaired, the paint on the windows and trim fresh. Now no different from any grand house accommodating aristocrats, it felt wonderful to finally come home where I had left part of my heart with Sister Josephine, a place that had sheltered me despite my resentment whilst there, a place that would always remain within the depths of my heart and soul. Home.

Chapter Twenty

THE HORSES CAME TO an abrupt halt in front of the grand front stairs sweeping up to the entrance, the front verandah swept clean, the old wooden double doors now painted a deep green, the trims around the windows identical. Three stories in some places, the front of the two-level building had been rebuilt in places where walls once crumbled, threatening the integrity of the structure. Now, I was unable to distinguish if a wealthy family lived here or the building was in the hands of an institution, my thoughts interrupted by children of all ages running towards us from every direction to touch the carriage and stroke the horses, any assumptions I may have made if calling on them for the first time now clear.

'Finally, Mummy. Finally,' Emmy whispered, her face still pressed up against the carriage window, Thomas next to her staring out at a young girl smiling up at him, her blonde hair curlier than my own.

'Aye, Emmy. Finally,' Hamish murmured, a smile touching his lips as he patted my hand for a moment.

'I cannot believe it's the same place. Mr Potts worked hard here every single day, but he never kept the gardens like this,' I remarked, gazing out at the azaleas and rhododendrons planted under every window, not a weed to be seen in any of the garden beds.

'Is he still here?' Hamish asked, preparing to open the door, the children now surrounding the carriage, hooting and hollering, their excitement palpable.

'Well, he's here, but his backside no longer points to the ground. He passed a decade ago and is buried somewhere out back. Mr Malcolm wrote to me afterwards, telling me how Mr Potts had a morbid fear of being buried in consecrated ground—don't ask me why.' I placed my hand up to Emmy as she went to speak. 'I have no idea and no one has told me, but I will tell you this. He must have been a hundred and fifty when he went to God.' Thomas and Emmy collapsed into giggles as Hamish navigated his way past them, chuckling to himself. I heard cheerful banter, then loud laughter filling my ears as I looked up to see the Sisters pour out of the imposing door, many clapping their hands, while several approached the carriage, waving and shooing the girls away to allow room for us to get down. Hamish turned to help Thomas and Emmy, while Archie assisted the nuns in moving the children away. I hurriedly stepped down, refusing to waste another moment waiting for help, my heart racing at the thought of seeing Sister and wrapping my arms around her. Returning had overwhelmed me with emotion I had not expected, and I felt five-years-old again.

I stood at the bottom of the stairs gazing up at the Sisters who gathered together on the wide verandah running the length of the building, smiling at the familiar faces I found, while nodding and waving at the new, younger Sisters present calling out their welcomes to us. I searched among them, my eyes darting from face to face, until I saw Sister Josephine making her way through the middle of them and down the stairs towards me, her arms wide, her blue eyes sparkling with tears.

I broke down and sobbed as she gazed at us, tears of happiness sliding down my cheeks, while my heart felt it would burst with joy. I ran to her, and within moments, we were in each other's arms, our sobs rising above the ruckus. I had not seen her for what felt like an eternity, yet now we were together, it felt as if no time had passed at all.

'Mo luaidh. How I've prayed fer this day tae come. I feel I've been with ye every day since ye left through yer letters. I've experienced all yer joys an' all yer sorrows along with ye over these years we've been parted. An' I've laughed 'til I've cried as often as I've wanted tae comfort ye. I love ye, me dear lass. 'Tis bonny tae have ye back here with me, an' I thank the Lord above fer all o' it. Welcome home.' She held me close to her chest, while I clung to her, unable to release her if I wanted to.

'Oh, Sister. I love you, and I've missed you dreadfully. It was your letters that gave me hope in my darkest times. Sometimes, I felt you there beside me, and that comforted me greatly.' I cried softly, my head on her shoulder as she patted my back. We wiped each other's tears, then giggled as she directed her attention to Thomas and Emmy, both standing close beside me, while Hamish remained behind them, a broad grin on his face as he watched on in silence.

'An' why did ye bring this old man an' woman tae our door. Where are your bairns? she teased, glancing down at them, her eyes twinkling mischievously.

'We aren't old, Sister Josephine. We *are* her children,' Emmy insisted before throwing her arms around her, and they both collapsed into uproarious laughter. Thomas went to her, and she gazed up at him in silence while he hugged her tight, tears in her eyes. I knew she already adored them; she always had, right from the day she received my telegram telling her of their birth. Emmy already stood taller than Sister, while Thomas towered over her. She had put on some weight around the middle; however, appeared healthy and very happy, even more so now she was pleasantly plump. In her late forties now, yet she did not have a wrinkle on her lovely face, although, I could not tell if her hair had changed as it was covered with her wimple, the temptation to pull it off and expose the curly brown hair I knew was under it overwhelming me for a moment.

'Sister, I would like you to meet Hamish, a dear friend to our family, and uncle and godfather to the children.' He shifted from foot to foot as he stood beside me, clearly uncomfortable. Having been raised Catholic, he had developed a terrible fear of nuns during his childhood, he had once confided, and I smothered a smile as she gazed up at him, her eyes dancing.

'Weel, I know all aboot ye, Hamish, right back tae when my Abigail first met ye on the ship. You've been a very dear friend tae her an' Aaron, not tae mention what you've done fer the bairns. Abigail's mentioned ye many times over the years, leavin' me feelin' as if I already know ye. I must thank ye fer always bein' there an' takin' care o' 'em. I'd hate fer someone tae take advantage o' me, lass, an' I was relieved tae read ye would be accompanyin' 'em on the journey. I'm sorry tae say there are far tae many souls in the world who're naw always honest an' decent, an' the thought a man would be able tae take advantage o' a young, wealthy widow has been constantly on me mind. I know she's safe with ye watchin' o' her an' takin' care o' the bairns.' She beamed up at him, a weak smile touching his lips, while embarrassment mingled with guilt flickered in his eyes as she embraced him for the longest time.

We followed Sister Josephine up the stairs and through the door. The Sisters soon returned to their work, while the children wandered off, some in groups, others alone. Memories flooded my mind as I stepped into the parlour where I had sat so long ago with her on my last day here. Back then, it was a tired, neglected room that was rarely used; the furniture shabby and old, and there had been paint peeling from the walls. Now, it was bright and cheerful, carefully refurbished with comfortable furniture that was still practical, given there were children living here. She led us over to the lounge, where we soon made ourselves comfortable.

'First o' all, what would Thomas an' Emmy like tae do? Ye can stay here with us an' take tea like proper ladies an' gentlemen, or ye can go out tae the grounds an' play with the others?' Sister Josephine asked, smiling sweetly at them. They glanced at each other, quickly deciding they would rather be outside than shut indoors listening to conversations that bored them. 'Weel, come along with me, then, an' I'll introduce ye tae the others.' She rose to her feet and took them by the hand, crossing the room, my children giggling as she teased them. I watched her step out into the hallway and reflected on how little she had changed. Still short, something I had not expected to change, while her large blue eyes were just as lively as they ever were. She had barely aged, surprising me greatly, and the weight she had gained suited her. I wondered again if her hair was still brown, or if it had lightened to silver. I was well aware I was only fascinated with her hair because we could never see it.

'I feel like I'm at mass, an' am about tae be summoned in tae the confessional box,' Hamish whispered, squirming uncomfortably in his chair, while never once taking his eyes from the door.

'I noticed.' I smirked across at him, a small red-headed child sticking her nose through the door for a moment as he grinned sheepishly at me.

'Abigail, ye have nae idea how difficult this is fer me. I've a morbid fear o' any woman wearin' a habit an' carryin' rosary beads. History has shown me they also carry a rough, leather strap in there somewhere, ready tae belt ye with it fer the slightest misdemeanour. I know fer a fact there were nuns here who treated ye in the same manner. Why dinnae ye feel like runnin' from this room screamin'?' I smothered a smile, his face serious.

'Only because I wasn't born to be on the stage in a theatrical production like you so obviously were,' I teased, waving a hand dramatically. 'If they dared pull out that strap now, I would whip their backsides so quick, they would never have the nerve to try again.' I laughed aloud, visions of Sister Monica running from me in the hallway filling my head, while he chuckled to himself, taking my hand warmly in his.

'Thank ye fer bringin' me here, Abigail. I know this place is close tae yer heart, an' I feel privileged ye would think tae share it with me.' He smiled, squeezing my hand, and I squeezed back, screams of excitement floating up through the open sash window from the children in the driveway playing ball.

Relief washed over me. I was glad we had returned to how we once were, as I would always consider him my friend first before anything else. This change in attitude surprised me, even more so at breakfast when he did not react outwardly to Lord Harrington holding my hand, and had placed no pressure on me when he came to my bedchamber during the night to allow him to court me publicly, as was his usual habit. Nor had he complained about our agreement, something he also did regularly, irritating me no end. I was once again enjoying being around him and felt as if the old Hamish had suddenly returned without warning or explanation.

'You're a dear friend, Hamish, and we appreciate you being here more than you know.'

'Aye. I take it the place naw looked like this when ye lived here?' His eyes moved around the room, the walls now papered in sage green, cream and various shades of gold, the furniture of excellent quality. I relaxed back in my chair, telling him several stories, while explaining as best I could what it was like when Polly and I were growing up—right down to the food they tortured us with. 'I'm very much lookin' forward tae seein' the changes ye've brought about here, Abigail. I've never known anyone tae support a place like this all by 'emselves. I'm so proud of ye, lass. I want ye tae know that. I cannae even imagine how many lives you've changed over the last fifteen-years. What an amazin' transformation from what ye say it once was naw so long ago.' He winked at me, letting go of my hand, then swatting it away in a panic when the sound of footsteps coming down the grand hallway came closer.

Sister Josephine stepped back into the room, a tray carrying freshly baked cakes, a pot of tea, along with a jug of lemonade for the twins, in her hands. On seeing the chocolate cupcakes, I burst into a flood of tears, unable to compose myself no matter how hard I tried.

'Mo luaidh, what's happened tae ye?' Sister Josephine asked, appearing alarmed as she placed the tray down on the table in front of me then quickly came to my side. She lowered herself down next to me, her arm sliding around my shoulders firmly as I sobbed, telling her how Aaron would bring me a cupcake every month.

'And I haven't been able to look at or eat one since,' I wailed, collapsing back into her arms.

'Oh, aye, lass. I must be losin' me mind, forgettin' somethin' as important as that. O' course he did, the sweet laddie. Let me take this back tae the kitchen, an' I'll bring somethin' else.' She apologised again before whisking the plate away, promptly crossing the room and disappearing out the door, her footsteps fading to silence within moments. Hamish leaned over and kissed my tears away; however, he did not utter a word, knowing better than anyone how much I still missed Aaron. By the time Sister Josephine returned with a sponge cake, I had composed myself, my face wiped clean with my handkerchief, my hair smoothed back down with the comb in my bag. 'Dinnae fash, mo luaidh. I'm sorry fer it, an' dinnae think how a wee thing like cake would affect ye. Abigail, look at me.' I smiled weakly, her finger under my chin as she gently lifted my face towards her, her eyes locked with mine. 'Yer doin' everythin' Aaron asked of ye, an' I'm sure tryin' tae make up fer things in yer own mind that never bothered him when he was here. Yer up out o' bed an' raisin' yer bairns, an' yer participatin' in the world again, tryin' tae find some happiness, I hope. I've worried meself sick about ye, thinkin' ye would never recover, but here ye are, thank the Lord an' all the saints,' she murmured, her smile gentle as she stroked my face.

'I do not believe I will ever recover, Sister. Even if I lived a thousand lives.' I burst into tears again, Hamish watching on in silence, his concern for me obvious. She slipped her arms around me again while I sobbed for Aaron, her hand gently stroking my hair, while she whispered soothingly to me.

'Ye will have yer good days, along with others when ye feel you cannae go on, an' that's well an' good, mo luaidh, as long as ye dinnae ever, ever give up.' She held me until I calmed, then handed me a dainty china cup. 'Now, drink this, an' ye will feel much better. A cup o' tea can end a war.' She smiled, her kiss lingering on my cheek as I smiled back through my tears.

'Now we've finished an' the bairns have returned, I'll give ye a tour o' the house, if ye like?' Sister Josephine asked, her eyes flitting from one to another, pure love radiating from her pretty face. The twins jumped to their feet, both screaming enthusiastically, while Hamish quickly stood. 'Aye, I'll show ye the dormitories first, as I'm certain dear Abigail would wish tae see 'em given her interest in beds.' She wiggled her eyebrows teasingly as Hamish snorted in amusement, her footsteps quick and light as we followed her across the room.

She led us through the brightly lit hallways, then guided us to the dormitory I had slept in all those years ago. Gasping aloud as I entered, Thomas and Emmy gazed around the room, their eyes wide and mouths open for another reason. They had never witnessed a place where children did not have parents and slept in groups, sharing one large room among many. I had planned to take them to the orphanage in Geelong, where I had volunteered my time over the years, once they were old enough, but life had gotten in the way. I was not as active or invested as I was in Emiliani House; however,

I still provided a small financial contribution every month to help feed and educate the orphans in their care, and had every intention of continuing.

I stepped into the middle of the large room, noticing there were half the number of beds in the dormitory compared to when Polly and I lived here. Now containing ten, solid, well-made wooden beds, all covered in thick linen and quilts, they could be separated from the rest of the room by a curtain that surrounded each, allowing each girl their privacy, no different from having a small bedchamber all of their own. During the day, the curtains were all tied back, exposing the neatly made beds, a chest of drawers and a wardrobe, along with a side table next to the bed, a lamp sitting on top. I lowered myself down onto one of the beds, bouncing up and down gently to ensure they were comfortable before throwing myself flat then rolling from side to side. Hamish loomed over me, an odd expression on his handsome face, his eyes full of emotion I could not recognise.

'This was where yer Mummy used tae sleep when she was a wee lass, but 'twas very different back then. We had old beds that wobbled with only thin mattresses atop, an' one blanket fer each o' the weans nae matter what the weather. Scotland can be very cold, much colder than Australia.' She wrapped her arms around herself, pretending to shiver, her teeth chattering as Thomas and Emmy laughed. She bent down to them, lowering her voice, her hand cupping her mouth as if ready to tell a secret. 'Now the bairns have as many blankets as they ask fer. I know she keeps this a secret, but I do believe ye should know—an' be very proud of yer mother. It's her money that's paid fer all this, as well as feedin' an' dressin' every soul who lives within these walls. Yer Mummy has helped an enormous number o' lassies who were once just like her.' I struggled to sit up on the bed, my face starting to flush. Thomas turned abruptly to stare at me, while Emmy gasped, her small hand going to her lips, their eyes wide. To them, who had been given everything they ever needed without question, living this way was not something they had once considered, or been forced to think about during their own short lives. I hoped with everything in me this week would give them an appreciation of how privileged they truly were, while instilling compassion and empathy for those around them they would carry with them their entire lives.

'Oh, Mummy. You really are the richest woman in the world, just like Uncle Leo tells it,' Emmy exclaimed, taking my hand and leading me to the door, several steps behind Sister and Thomas. Hamish followed behind at a distance as we were shown through the remaining dormitories, of which there were many now, along with shared rooms where the older girls lived. There were game rooms, along with nooks and crannies where the children could relax and read a book or play a quiet game, and multiple classrooms where the children received their daily lessons; the decor so very well thought out and implemented.

I was most interested to see the library, and hurried down the hall behind Sister, excitement welling up in me. Sister allowed me to step inside first, my eyes widening as I stared up at the bookshelves to find thousands of tomes from floor to ceiling, placed neatly inside. She appeared to take great delight in my reaction, dancing around the room while pointing out some old manuscripts she had recently been sent from a family member. I strolled around the room, picking up book after book to find they were all well-used, which delighted me. Sister Josephine and the twins walked out hand-in-hand, and I reluctantly followed. As they wandered down the hallway ahead of us, Hamish placed his hand on my shoulder and turned to me, pausing for a moment longer to allow distance to grow between us.

'This is the happiest I've seen ye in a long time, Abigail. It's nice tae be here tae witness such a shift. Yer face is glowin'.' He gazed down at me, then slipped his arm around my waist and pinched my backside, his hand lingering there for a moment while he glanced around, checking several times that none of the Sisters were charging towards him, strap in hand and raised above their heads. I smiled up at him before we hurried ourselves along to catch up with the others. We found them near the kitchen door, the twins still holding tightly to Sister's hands as they chatted animatedly with her.

Sister invited us into the kitchen, proudly showing off the four industrial stoves, along with two tall ovens beside them and several iceboxes. An enormous workbench sat in the centre of the room where they carried out their meal preparations, just like we had at home, only three times as large. Good quality pots and pans hung overhead, the shelves along every surface holding everything from plates and cups to fine crystal glasses, and the room was wonderful-ly cheerful. The kitchen staff were already working hard preparing lunch, several young women shyly glancing across at us as they peeled and chopped the many and varied vegetables, while something was bubbling away on the stove in large pots, the smell wafting up my nose and making my mouth water as I glanced into the panty, joy filling me when I saw it was full.

We bid the staff farewell before Sister guided us into the dining room. I gasped again at the new tables and chairs; the room now more resembled a restaurant than an orphanage, its crisp linen tablecloths and fresh flowers set in lovely crystal vases impressing me no end. I was grateful to Mr Malcolm for insisting on quality when he was purchasing items on behalf of Emiliani House, and although far from extravagant, they had all they needed; it was homely and very comfortable. I wanted the girls to grow and blossom in a nurturing, safe environment; however, I could see no reason why it should not be just as lovely as anyone else's family home, with all the things that made it personal and special included. We were unable to give them what they craved most—their parents—but we could certainly ensure they had everything they required to start the best life they could when they left here to find them. Or not.

Sister Josephine hurried us out of the room and up the stairs towards her bedchamber, passing several closed doors along the way. She paused for a moment outside a door, tapping it gently with her finger before turning back to us.

'This here was Sister Mary Emeline's room. She was yer great-aunt Isabelle's daughter, an' a dear soul at that. Sweet as honey, she was. I've always been meanin' tae ask ye, but I'd forget me head if it was nae stuck tae me neck. Did ye name wee Emmy in honour o' her?' I swallowed hard, shaking my head as she continued on to the next room, the children beside her.

'No. That was purely a coincidence. A lovely one, given how highly you speak of her. I have heard whispers over the years from my groom, and what you yourself have told me, Sister, but the truth of the matter is, I know very little about my aunt, or her family.' She nodded sympathetically, then welcomed us into her bedchamber. I brushed past her, feeling like a small child allowed into her parents' room for the first time.

'We are grateful tae ye fer the new beds an' drawers ye bought fer each o' the Sisters. They came only two mornin's past, an' everyone is sleepin' better already.' She hurried in after us, the children choosing to sit on her double bed next to the wall, the thick quilt tucked over several pillows filled with goose down, while the new drawers matched the bedside table, the wardrobe, and the crafted dressing table I had insisted each Sister have. I sat down at the small table kept by the window where Sister liked to sit and write to me, a bird outside catching my attention as Hamish strolled in, the large room now suddenly quite small. I had recently discovered through Mr Malcolm quite by accident that throughout all the years I had supported Emiliani House—and despite having the money to do so—the Sisters still slept in their old beds, choosing to only use the money for the direct benefit of the children in their care. I had ordered replacements within a day of hearing of their plight, requesting they be delivered directly from London by train, and I was relieved to see with my own eyes they would rest comfortably now. I patted the seat next to me, asking Sister Josephine to join me, and I handed her a small, wrapped parcel when she did, much to her surprise.

'I wanted to buy you something to remember me by occasionally, but I know you are not allowed to own things. I'm hoping you can hide this under your habit, and no one will ever know you have it but us,' I said as she opened the box, gasping when she found the elegant gold cross, several tiny diamonds embedded, and a delicate gold chain to wear it around her lovely neck. She gazed across at me, tears in her eyes as her fingers caressed the necklace.

'Och, I dinnae know what tae say, mo luaidh. Thank ye, wee Abigail. I'll never take it off, an' I'll think of ye every time I touch it,' she whispered, leaning across to kiss my cheek, her hand stroking my head for a moment. 'I'm sure the heavenly Father will forgive this one wee act o' disobedience,' she remarked, turning to smile at me as I slipped it around her neck and secured the clasp. She swiftly raised her hand and tucked it under her habit, out of sight, a giggle of delight bursting from me without warning. It was wonderful to be back in her company, and I felt truly happy.

She showed me every letter I had ever sent her, bound up tightly in a bundle—thousands of them—all containing the best and worst times of my life. Every thought, every feeling I had ever experienced since we parted, it was all here in the millions of words poured from my heart out onto the paper.

'Aye, then. 'Tis about time fer yer meal, an' I can hear ye stomachs growlin' ferociously at me,' she teased Thomas and Emmy, taking their hands again in hers. 'Come away with me tae the dinin' room where we can eat our fill.' The children pulled her to her feet, laughing loudly as they dragged her towards the door, while Hamish and I followed, the passing Sisters smiling brightly as we stepped out into the wide hall.

Chapter Twenty One

I SAT BETWEEN EMMY and Thomas; the linen tablecloth crisp and clean, the sweet fragrance from the flowers placed on the table mingling with the smell of roasted meat wafting up my nose and causing my stomach to rumble. I smiled across at Sister Josephine, standing in line behind two others at the serving window, grunting to myself as I rose to my feet to help her. The children were delightful; several girls greeted me cheerfully as I crossed the room, the sounds of cutlery scraping plates and laughter filling my ears and lightening my heart.

'Here, mo luaidh.' Sister handed me a tray with two plates, along with a small pot filled with gravy, then turned back to pick up the other tray holding three oversized portions of roasted meats and vegetables, before leading me back to the table.

We placed Thomas and Emmy's luncheon down in front of them, doing the same for Hamish, then ourselves, before I returned the trays. Returning to the table, I sat back down between Sister and Emmy, feeling ravenous despite eating a hearty breakfast, along with an entire sponge cake filled with jam and cream between us.

I sighed in bliss as I tasted the lamb, tender and roasted to perfection, then smothered a crunchy potato in the dark gravy before lifting it to my lips and sighing again. The meat was no longer served resembling old boot leather, nor were the vegetables boiled until mushy, and I sat back in my chair while I chewed, a self-satisfied smile touching my lips as I gazed up at the high ceiling, the intricate stonework on the walls and floors exquisite now it had been brought back to its former glory.

'An' where are ye off tae in such a tizzy, Isla?' Sister enquired as a blonde girl of no more than five ran past the table, slipping as she tried to slow down. Sister reached out to steady her, affection in her eyes as the child tried to catch her breath.

'Oh, I'm sorry fer it, Sister. I'm so terribly hungry, an' me friends are eatin' their second helpin' an' I've nae had me first,' she gasped as Sister gently touched her cheek.

'Where've ye been, lass? 'Tis naw like ye tae be late when the bell rings.' She nodded frantically, a sweet smile spreading across her tiny face, her blue pinafore covered in grass stains, a smear of dirt across her petite nose.

'Och, weel, Sister.' She reached out her tiny hand to stroke Sister's cheek for a moment. 'Ye know out o' everyone how much I love me dancin'?' Sister nodded, the child moving closer to her side. Thomas and Emmy continued eating, their eyes fixed on her in friendly curiosity, while it was obvious to me, if no one else at the table, they saw her as a kindred spirit. 'I let meself get distracted practicin' me steps out on the lawn. Ruthie was meant tae remind me, but she buggered off. I found her fillin' her face over there, an' she nae gives a toss if I starve tae death. If there is a God, she'd strike her down dead before that fatty can even get tae the kitchen window tae ask fer dessert.' She pointed an accusing finger at a dark-haired girl not much older than herself—whom I assumed to be Ruth—sitting at a table in the far corner, the lass paying us, or Isla, no mind.

'Haud yer wheesht, ye wee fiend. Somebody may hear ye, an' 'tis naw only crude an' offensive, 'tis blasphemous.' Her eyes went wide as she stared up at Sister in silence, her face flushed pink. 'Ye know ye can eat 'till yer belly bursts here, Isla. Some days, ye are full o' the devil, an' others ye are like sunshine. Get on with ye, lass.' Sister ruffled her loose ringlets before Isla continued on, her steps fast, yet not considered a run from where I sat. I watched as several children followed Isla to the serving window to get more before turning back to my food.

'Why is Isla so terrified of going hungry? She's far too young to remember what it was once like here. Is she new, or have you run short of food in recent times?' I asked before taking another bite of potato as Sister smiled to herself.

'Naw, she's been here since the day she was born. Wee Isla is nae much different from what you once were, mo luaidh. She's spouted off since she could first talk that one day she'll be famous fer her dancin', an' I happen tae believe her. Once she fixes her mind tae somethin', there's naw man, woman, or bairn with the strength or fortitude tae stop her.' I narrowed my gaze, watching closely as she sipped a glass of barley water, her blue eyes sparkling, while the children at the next table rose to their feet all at once to collect their dessert, their chairs scraping loudly on the stone floor.

'Are you implying I'm prone to exaggerate? And I possess a vivid imagination and should be on the stage? Or that I'm determined?' She collapsed into giggles, Thomas and Emmy joining in, while Hamish chuckled to himself. I widened my eyes at all of them before picking up my cutlery again.

'Maybe Sister thinks you are the same because you both worry about starving to death,' Emmy remarked, collapsing into a fresh fit of giggles, the room even noisier now our table had joined in the cheerful ruckus.

'Or it could just be the filthy language spillin' out their mouths when they happen to open them,' Thomas added, their laughter filling the dining hall.

'Och, dinnae fash, dear Abigail. Wee Isla is cut from the same cloth as ye, no more or less meant by it. I see ye in her, an' it helps on the days when I'm missin' ye the most.' I swallowed hard, tears stinging my eyes as she reached across and patted my hand.

'Do you still have your old school pinafores, Mummy? I need a very small one to put on Delilah to remind me of our visit once we return home,' Emmy enquired, then turned to smile up at Sister, placing her small hand over ours.

'Weel, 'tis bonny o' ye tae think o' yer wee friend back home, Emeline. Yer mother will nae have anythin' o' the sort 'cause durin' her time here, the Order had very little money. Barely enough tae provide a dress or two a year for the poor bairns.' I nodded, scraping my plate clean, then discreetly reached over and picked up a slice of bread from the basket to mop up the gravy, Hamish following suit. 'The lassies are all dressed the same fer the moment, but that's only 'cause ye came tae call durin' their school hours. They've a selection o' clothin' tae wear when they're naw in class, an' naw longer have tae go about wearin' dresses made from the same cloth in the same style as every other lass livin' here as yer Mummy had tae do.' The twins appeared curious, Emmy wiping gravy from the corner of her mouth with her napkin before pushing her plate away, not a morsel left on it.

'Oh, Delilah is not my friend. She isn't even a real person. My friend, Beatrice, gave her to me as a going-away present the week before we got on the ship to come here,' Emmy informed her, and Sister nodded.

'Aye, she's a wee kitty or doggy, then?' Sister arched her eyebrows curiously, reaching out to discourage two young lasses from running past our table on their way out to the grounds.

'Oh, no, Sister. Don't be silly. Delilah is a doll. Stands nearly as tall as me. You would think, given Beatrice's sister is a renowned seamstress, she would have included a wardrobe for her, but of course not. She can be so cheap at times,' Emmy complained wearily, and I choked, coughing and sputtering while Thomas pounded me on the back.

'An' the most unfortunate lookin' one at that,' Thomas interrupted. 'Beatrice only gave that to ya 'cause she couldn't stand the ugly thing starin' at her across the room in her own bedchamber.'

'That's a lie, Thomas. Take it back now,' Emmy hissed, her tiny hands clenched into fists by her side. 'Take it back! Beatrice is like my older sister and is my best friend in this whole, entire, miserable, bloody shit of a world, and you will not accuse her of passing her rubbish on to me. She loves that doll, and she loves me, and that's why she sacrificed such a beautiful creation.'

'Ya just called her cheap! What kinda friend are ya? An' she's too old to be ya best friend. Ya could be that Isla's sister with the mouth on ya, though. An' I've heard ya say more than once Beatrice's parents are tighter than a fish's...' he went to say as my hand clamped around my son's mouth, his eyes widening as I straightened up in my chair, regaining my composure and allowing my hand to drop back to my lap once he was silent.

'Enough. You are behaving no differently from the urchins living in the alleyways of Little Lon. Apologise to Sister immediately for your poor manners and seek forgiveness for your lack of self-control.' I put my hand up between them, silence descending on the room and hanging heavy over our table.

'I'm so very sorry, Sister. I forgot where we were,' Emmy said, her cheeks bright red, while Thomas nodded in agreement and apologised, his blonde head lowered, avoiding my gaze.

'Ah, weel. Naw harm done. I'm certain yer wee doll is bonny, Emeline. Come with me now, an' we'll go order our dessert from Sister Mary Maude.' My children jumped to their feet, Emmy clapping her hands, while Thomas cheered. Several groups of children remained at the tables, lingering over their dessert, while most had gone outside as soon as they had eaten their fill. Sister did not have a clue how wrong she was, and I grimaced at the thought, my eyes following them strolling hand-in-hand towards the serving window. As their mother, I was aware I could not take sides; however, I was forced to agree with Thomas on this occasion. Delilah was not only unfortunate in appearance, when I first saw her in Emmy's room after Catherine and Beatrice called on us for tea, I had jumped in terror, the fact she wore not a stitch of clothing exacerbating my fear.

Sister returned to the table, a tray in her hand holding bowls filled with treacle pudding, a generous portion of thick custard in each, and a bowl of clotted cream we could add if we so chose. She placed them down in front of us, Thomas and Emmy's eyes lighting up when she slipped a wrapped sweetie into each of their bowls. Lowering herself down onto the chair beside me, she exhaled deeply, glancing at me for a moment, and smiled as she turned back to pick up her spoon.

'Do ye remember how ye were forced tae eat in silence here, or ye missed out altogether?' she asked, her voice low as she leaned in to me, our gaze on Thomas and Emmy, chatting animatedly with Hamish, the room still jovial despite the mass exodus.

'How could I forget?' She took my hand in hers and squeezed gently, while spooning her pudding into her mouth with the other.

I was satisfied with how they now ran Emiliani House, and impressed by their financial restraint, more so now since I had seen it for myself. I was thrilled that the girls living within its walls were no longer forced to spend their days carrying out menial chores and were receiving an education, allowing them the freedom to enjoy their childhood.

'Would ye like tae take a walk in the garden before I show ye yer favourite place, mo luaidh?' Sister asked as I finished my dessert, and I smiled, wiping my mouth with a napkin.

'I would enjoy that very much.' Hamish nodded with renewed enthusiasm, while the twins were already up out of their seats.

Sister Josephine guided us across the now nearly empty dining hall and through a door leading out to the verandah. I glanced up at the grey sky and sent a prayer of thanks above for holding off the rain, noticing when I looked back down there were now plenty of places for the children to play or sit outside, several beautifully carved wooden benches placed around the garden under the umbrella of several oaks, the blackbirds, robins and wrens perched up on the branches singing their afternoon chorus, while pigeons and pheasants roamed the property at will.

She led us towards the stone barn standing next to the abandoned milking shed at the back of the property, and on to an open field belonging to a neighbour when I had lived here, a generous amount of land now sectioned off as a vegetable garden, the hothouse in the corner only recently added to my knowledge standing amongst the numerous and varied fruit and nut trees. The paddocks beyond held cattle, another to the side accommodating only sheep, while several horses I assumed were used to pull their carriage grazed in a separate paddock by the restored stables, once ready to collapse on itself, the crumbling walls now repaired, the slate roof now watertight where no roof had been for decades. Reminding me of home, my stomach clenched, and for a moment I missed Willow Grove and all who lived there dreadfully, before staring across at Sister standing by the gate, the realisation settling on me that I did not wish to be anywhere else but here.

'See all this, mo luaidh?' Her arm swept out across the property and the paddocks beyond, then back again to the ground on which we stood and the nearby pigsty. I nodded as Hamish strolled across the grounds towards us, his hands on my shoulder as he paused behind me, his attention on the land Sister was showing us. 'We were able tae buy this plot fifteen-years ago an' plant most o' what's needed tae feed the bairns, along with raisin' our own meat. All o' this would never have been possible without ye, wee Abigail, an' I'm oh so very proud o' ye,' she said, her voice barely above a whisper as she raised my hand to her lips, kissing me gently before pressing it tightly to her breast. Hamish gave me a look I did not understand, a hint of admiration in his eyes as he listened to her speak, her voice so full of emotion. 'I dinnae think ye can truly appreciate the changes that've occurred here, Hamish, naw unless ye see it fer yerself with yer own eyes. If ye come along with me, I'll show ye some photographs o' the house from the time wee Abigail lived here.' He nodded once, towering over her as she led us back inside, hurrying us down the hallway to the parlour.

We made ourselves comfortable on the lounges as she bent down next to an elegant sideboard and took out a book, passing it to Hamish and the twins to look through before sitting down next to me, a small box in her hand.

'Oh, Mummy, this is positively awful. The house appears as if it is ready to fall down about your ears. It looks terribly frightening, and the children seem so very thin and sad, not like any children I have ever seen or met before,' Emmy remarked, her voice trembling, her face pale as they studied every photograph in the album. Their eyes widened every so often, both filled with sadness as they passed the loose photographs that Sister handed them back and forth, staring at each one for the longest time, the silence heavy between us. Hamish gazed across at me, his face like stone, a tear in his eye, before he looked back at the photograph in his hand. I had no interest in seeing them myself, preferring to leave the past in the past where it belonged.

'Look, there's a photo of Emmy,' Thomas said, confusion crossing his face as he looked across at his sister, back at the picture, then back at Emmy again, a frown creasing his brow. Sister Josephine rose to her feet to take a closer look, straightening up soon after, a smile on her lips as she tousled his sandy blonde hair.

'Och, naw, Thomas. 'Tis yer Mummy. Aye, Emmy does favour her at the same age.' She smiled at the memory, lifting the photograph to her lips before bringing it back to me. I took it with a trembling hand and glanced down at the black-and-white picture of a young girl, her long wavy hair plaited neatly, her large eyes filled with a sadness I had never seen in my daughter's. Emmy stared up at me, a smile on her face, although tears filled her eyes; the similarities between us were almost unsettling. Until this very moment, I had no recollection of how I looked as a bairn, only ever seeing the photograph Polly had stolen from Sister Mary Monica, and still kept to this day. 'Ye can keep that, mo luaidh. I'm sure ye dinnae have a picture o' yerself when ye were young, an' 'tis bonny fer yer bairns tae have,' Sister murmured, passing me another photograph. 'Weel, now it's time tae visit wee Abigail's most favourite place in the orphanage. I promise ye, I've saved the best 'till last.' I tucked the photographs into my bag as she rose to her feet, and we followed suit, soon stepping out into the hallway, her hand on my arm as she guided us into a wing off to the side of the mansion, while my great-aunt Isabelle came to mind, a vision of her sobbing against the door we just passed tearing at my heart and sending shivers up my spine—the image so real, I felt an overwhelming urge to reach out and touch her in comfort.

'It's bonny tae see ye back here after all this time, Abigail. We've missed yer help with the weans more than ye know. I've been fol-lowin' yer life through the letters Sister Mary Josephine receives from ye that she's so generous tae share with us.' Sister Mary Marion stopped abruptly, placing her hand on my shoulder in comfort. 'Ye dinnae need tae fash, or pull that face at me, ye wee fiend. Sister Josephine keeps yer confidence, an' I'm sure ye know that. O' course ye do, bein' so close an' all.' I tried to remember which eye I should look in when addressing her as she wove in and out between the rows of cots, swiftly making her way over to the enormous hearth, the elaborate fireplace running the entire length of the room. The weans room had always been the warmest and most inviting of all in the house, and had remained so despite nearly everything else at Emiliani House changing. 'I've read about ye in the papers. What an awful business it's been, ye poor lass. O' course it has, o' course it has,' she muttered, placing the kettle on the stove to boil. 'Weel, I feel as though I know ye far better now than when ye lived here under our roof. So much has been written, but ye know that. O' course ye do.'

Hamish strolled over to a cot and picked up a wean wrapped in a mohair blanket, her back hair thick under her cap. She blinked once; her muted blue eyes gazing up at him. The longing for his own black-haired, brown-eyed child was apparent as he lifted her to his chest, her tiny face nuzzling into his neck, and I prayed once again he had the opportunity to hold his own in the near future. It would not happen if he refused to consider stepping out with women other than me, and I had told him so on numerous occasions. I believed it was not too late for him to start a family of his own, despite Nellie throwing him over not long after Aaron was murdered. The gossip on the passionfruit vine of late was that she still loved him and would take him back in a heartbeat, and if he stopped being so stubborn, he would soon have the son he craved; of that I was certain. Still in his prime and handsome along with it, he could take his pick, and he knew it. He glanced up from the wean, a wide grin on his face.

'What? The poor lass looked helpless layin' there by herself. I'm naw takin' her home, just havin' a wee discussion.' He smirked, his large fingers stroking her cheek, while Emmy and Thomas stood beside him making cooing noises at the poor child. I moved around the mostly empty cots, the children on the floor a safe distance from the fireplace, some lying on thick carpets, others playing with toys under the Sisters' supervision. It seemed only the very young weans were sleeping or kicking away in their beds, waiting their turn to be held and fed. I lifted a tiny lass up into my arms, her small rosebud lips pursed, a whisper of blonde hair underneath her cap. I held her against my chest, her face peering down at my children over my shoulder.

'Please, can we take some home, Mummy?' Emmy asked, reaching up to stroke the wean's rosy cheek. I laughed aloud as she gazed up, her eyes pleading her case.

'Oh, Emmy. I have you and Thomas to care for, and would not be the best choice of mother for a babe so new to the world. And I'm widowed. Bairns are not like kittens. You cannot select the one you like most from the litter and take it home. All the children here are cared for well, and will have many opportunities as they grow, I promise.' I handed the wean to her, watching intently as she sat down on the carpet before settling her comfortably in the crook of her arm, leaning forward to kiss her forehead. Thomas sat near the hearth cross-legged, playing with the older babies, just as I once did sitting right where he was, the children screaming to get his attention as they climbed over him. He laughed at them, picking up a lass and holding her above his head as she giggled, her squeals of excitement piercing my ears. Feeling ever so proud of Emmy and Thomas, their behaviour when interacting with others impeccable since leaving Australia, I was grateful Aaron and I had been firm, insisting they used their manners and reminding them to treat others how they wished to be treated. Sister hurried about the room, gathering us up while returning the bairns to their beds.

We said our goodbyes to the children and the Sisters, and I promised Sister Mary Marion we would return tomorrow, much to their delight. They embraced us all with great affection before we obediently followed Sister down the grand hallway to the entrance of the orphanage.

'Thank you for having us here today, Sister, and for taking such good care of us. It has been the most wonderful day. A piece of my heart has been restored once again. Now I am back here with you,' I murmured in her ear as we embraced, the twins behind me waiting their turn.

'As is mine, mo luaidh.' She held me tightly to her chest, Hamish and the children looking on, their faces filled with love for her. She pulled away, turning to lead us to the carriage where Archie sat atop, waiting for our return. We had given him a time to collect us this afternoon, and he had arrived not a minute before or after, impressing me greatly, while only highlighting my embarrassment at keeping him waiting near on an hour.

'I was surprised not to see Sister Mary Monica here. Is she well?' I enquired, realising once the words left my mouth why our visit had been so pleasant. Sister Josephine looked away for a moment, her cheeks flushing pink before turning her attention back to me.

'Aye, she is bonny, an' 'tis kind o' ye tae ask. She was called away today on matters naw disclosed tae me, an' we're unsure when she'll return, but I'll pass on yer good wishes.' She embraced me again, and I lay my head on her shoulder as I once did. 'It has been one of the happiest days I've spent here on earth, seein' ye again. I thought the day would never come, an' ye were lost tae me forever. Ye must lay the heavy burden o' grief ye carry at the Master's feet, an' let him ease ye. I pray fer ye several times a day in the hope yer heart'll be healed, an' you'll find happiness once again.' She patted me gently on the back, my arms locked tightly around her.

'Thank you, Sister. It eases me knowing you are with me always in heart and mind.' I kissed her cheek in farewell, and she released me, turning to embrace Hamish, Thomas and Emmy as Archie assisted me up into the carriage. They followed me within moments, the children pressing their faces against the glass as the carriage pulled away, their shouts of farewell filling my ears, their hands waving a frantic last goodbye. Thomas and Emmy were soon deep in discussion about the orphanage and what they had learnt today, talking quietly of all they had seen.

'Abigail, what you've set out tae achieve here beggars belief. Aaron would be immensely proud of ye if he'd been able tae see it.' I burst into tears, startling him. Taking me in his arms, I sobbed against his chest while he gently stroked my hair, murmuring soothingly; the children so absorbed in their conversation, they barely glanced in our direction. 'I think ye have had enough fer now, lass. This journey has heightened yer emotions from the start, an' I know 'tis hard fer ye bein' here without Aaron, but we're all here fer ye. Ye even have yer new Lord,' he teased, tightening his grip around my shoulder for a moment. 'Ye need tae rest before returnin' there tomorrow, an' take dinner in yer room tonight.' He moved a loose strand of hair from my eyes with his finger, his eyes fixed on mine.

My body felt heavy with exhaustion, my mind scattered, and I contemplated whether he might be right. I was not confident I could sit through dinner tonight without bursting into tears and alarming those around me, and I had promised myself I would not cry or cause a scene in front of witnesses. At least in my bedchamber, even as a guest in this enormous castle, I could cry alone without upsetting another soul.

Stepping into the reception room of Merinda Manor, Thomas and Emmy ran off ahead of us to find little Mary, excited to tell her of their day. They had found out quickly where the kitchen was, and would go down there any chance they had to see what had just come out of the ovens. They would sit at the table with the house staff, often waiting for little Mary to find them, while they chatted away about anything and everything with anyone who would listen.

Reg had brought this to my attention only this morning, concerned I would be upset they were mixing with servants. I had explained how they had been raised in our kitchen at home, and I would allow it as long as they were not pestering his staff. I climbed the stairs, my bag over my arm, Hamish following close behind. Hurrying along the hallway, I glanced back over my shoulder to see him still behind me, soon stopping outside my door.

'Abigail, I need tae speak with ye.' He gently pushed me into my room, closing the door behind him, before stepping forward and taking me by the arms. Pulling me into his chest, he wrapped his arms around me, lowering his head to kiss my forehead.

'What do we need to talk about, Hamish? I am far too tired to argue.'

'I dinnae want tae talk about anythin', truth be told. I wanted tae get ye alone fer a moment.' He smirked, while all I wanted to do was sleep so I would be fresh for the morning. He held me in his arms for the longest time, his chin resting on top of my head. 'Aye, then, lass. I can see ye naw feel like talkin'. I'll go summon Bessie tae attend tae ye so ye can rest. I will return in the shadow o' darkness,' he teased, releasing me from his embrace before preparing to leave. 'Until then, I'll go an' entertain yer Lord Harrington. I dinnae like the fact he is tryin' tae ingratiate himself tae Thomas an' Emmy. Naw, dinnae say a word as I'm naw set tae argue with ye, either. I must get down there tae prevent 'em formin' an attachment tae the man.' He quickly kissed me again before hurrying away to rescue his godchildren from Reg, a smile lighting my face as I walked across the room, while running my finger over my tingling lips as I closed the door behind him.

Wishing for home, where we did not refer to our rooms by their proper names, or have a hundred staff roaming about the house, I strolled over to sit down on the bed, and jumped in fright when Bessie rushed into the room, appearing as if she had run up ten flights of stairs carrying a sack of grain.

'Are you unwell, Mistress? Hamish came down to the kitchens and told me you needed me.' Her brow creased in concern as I threw myself back on the bed, my legs dangling down over the side.

'No, Bessie. He should have said it wasn't urgent you come so quickly. I'm bone tired, and have decided to take a tray in here for dinner, is all. I only need your assistance to change from this into my nightgown, if you don't mind? And would you please pass on my apologies to Lord Harrington?' I yawned, closing my eyes for a moment.

'Of course, Mistress. I will go now.' She rushed out before I opened them again, leaving me on the bed fully dressed, my laughter filling the room. She was in such a tizzy, she forgot me. Certain she would realise and return flustered and apologetic, I laughed harder, my hands clutching my stomach, my feet on the floor as I stared up at the ceiling.

Hamish had been wonderful today, going out of his way to spend time alone with Sister, sitting with her on a bench under a tree while I walked the gardens, reminiscing about my days there for the longest time. Maybe the silence between us had done him good, and given him time to reflect on all the things I had tried to tell him over the last two-months. He had softened towards me, and seemed to now understand how I felt. Bessie rushed back into the room without warning, the door slamming behind her.

'I'm so sorry, Mistress. I don't know where my head is today, and to leave you here waiting to change and get into your bed is unforgivable. Please forgive me,' she gasped, running out of the little breath she had, before leaning down with her hands on her knees, trying to catch her breath. I laughed aloud as she straightened up, glaring across at me as if I had truly gone mad.

'Don't fash, Bessie. I was confident you would return.' I continued to giggle as I rose to my feet, breathing a sigh of relief when she loosened my corset and helped me strip off my gown, my gaze fixed on her as she hurried off to my wardrobe to select a fresh nightgown. Once free of my dress and in my nightclothes, my dressing gown tied tight around my waist, I sat for Bessie at the dressing table to attend to my hair.

'Lord Harrington sends his best regards, and wishes you good health. He would like to call on you to enquire how you are feeling; however, he feels it most improper to visit your bedchamber, and hopes to have your delightful company at breakfast. There, I think I said it right. He made me repeat it several times before he was satisfied.' She raised an eyebrow, her eyes fixed on mine as she looked at me in the mirror, her nimble fingers placing hair pins on the table as quick as she pulled them out.

'That sounds very much like Reg.'

'He would make you a good husband, Mistress. He is obviously interested in you, and he is good with Emmy and Thomas. Think of the opportunities they would have here with their stepfather, a Duke and all. The best schools, rubbing shoulders with all the important people in the world, and they would marry into the best families who all have estates like this.' She held my hairbrush mid-air, lost in a daydream as she stared out over the immaculate grounds.

'Oh, Bessie. I like him very much, but I will not marry again. This isn't the life for Thomas, Emmy, or me, and we would hate it. We are not interested in social connections, or I would have all that in Australia, and I choose not to. Can you see me wandering around a house like this when we don't even use all the rooms we have at home?' She stared back at me, her forehead wrinkling for a moment before straightening up and continuing with my hair, the brush moving swiftly.

'No. I suppose not. I'm only thinking of your future happiness,' she teased, and I laughed aloud again. She touched the back of my head, and I stood, bidding her farewell before crossing the room and climbing into bed, exhaling in relief as my body relaxed into the feathered mattress. I fell asleep before she even closed the door, and was woken by her only two-hours later, bringing my dinner on a tray. My eyes heavy as I ate, I noted the food, although not as good as Leo's, was delicious. Bessie took the tray once I had eaten my fill, and before she left, I called out my goodnights, requesting I not be disturbed until morning.

Falling back into a deep sleep almost immediately, I was woken by a tender kiss on my lips. Opening my eyes, my mouth curled up into a smile as I gently touched his face.

'You came back?' I murmured, his kiss passionate before he sat back up on the bed next to me.

'O' course I came back. I cannae keep away from ye. It was impossible fer me tae remain silent around ye fer so long.' He straightened his broad shoulders before removing his robe and sliding into bed, his naked body next to mine. 'Are ye all right, lass? I hate seein' ye so broken-hearted.' He stared into my eyes, his finger gently caressing my neck.

'Well, there's nought to be done about that, unfortunately,' I replied, resigned to the fact I would never have feelings for anyone but Aaron.

'I could if ye let me, but ye keep pushin' me away. I adore ye an' always have. Yer meant tae be with me now Aaron is gone. I know ye dinnae love me in the same way. That'll come in time, if ye would only give me the chance. Dinnae shut me out, is all I ask of ye.' He turned on his side to face me, resting his head on his enormous hand, his eyes fixed on mine intently.

'Please, Hamish. For the love of all that is good and holy, I cannot keep talking about the same thing over and over with you. I have explained myself many times and have always been truthful. I cannot do any more than that,' I replied, sick of the subject.

'Aye, lass, but this is the last thing I'll say on the matter. There will come a time when I'll openly court ye, an' I *will* marry ye, whether ye like it or naw. I told ye from the beginnin', I dinnae know how long I could do this in secret, so I've been just as honest with ye. If I'm good enough tae take tae yer bed, then I'm good enough tae be yer suitor an' considered a good match. There's naw point startin' anythin' between ye an' the Lord Harrington's of the world, as I will naw allow anyone else tae have ye. I'll say naw more than that.'

'Did you lock the door?' I whispered, aware nothing would be gained, whatever my response. No matter what I did, he refused to take me seriously.

'Aye, I'm naw soft in the head. I dinnae want Emmy or Thomas walkin' in here an' catchin' me with me bare arse in the air. I dinnae want what's between us tae be a secret, but I dinnae want it that public, either.'

I remained wrapped in his arms for several hours before I asked him to return to his own bed so I could sleep without interruption.

'I'll see ye in the mornin', me wee wench.'

I hugged him tightly before he left, kissing him goodnight before he quietly made his way back to his own room. Falling into a deep sleep soon after, I dreamt of a silver triangle, a woman named Lilith, and a ship full of soldiers sailing out to sea, never to return.

Chapter Twenty Two

WE HAD SPENT EVERY day since our arrival in Scotland at the orphanage with Sister Josephine, often staying from early morning until late into the evening. I had become familiar with the young girls living there, while spending all my time in her company. Today, we would be forced to part, and a sadness had settled on me at the thought, not knowing when we would see each other again. As the weeks passed and our time together drew near, I had not wanted to think of it and pushed the thought to the back of my mind, not wanting to even consider my life without her by my side.

I had walked in the garden each evening with Lord Harrington, as requested, and had thoroughly enjoyed his company. Feeling drawn to him from the first night we met, we had become firm friends over the following months, discovering in each other the qualities we felt were lacking within ourselves, going on to form a strong and warm friendship. Last night, he had professed his love for me and kissed me as he had never kissed me before. There was a passion in him I had not expected to find in someone brought up in such a conservative manner, especially when it came to love and duty.

I stepped into the dining room; the children greeted me loudly from the table. Hamish and Lord Harrington stood immediately as I made my way across the room to join them.

'And how is everyone this morning?' I enquired, lowering myself down onto the seat next to Reg, Emmy on my other side.

'Heartbroken you all leave tomorrow,' Reg said, pouring me a cup of coffee before the footman had time to put down his tray. 'However, you do look lovely today, Abigail.' He cast an approving eye over my green velvet gown, the trim made of gold ribbon, the lace neckline high. The small hat sitting to the side of my head and made of the same fabric, the feathers from a golden bird of some type stitched onto the band at the back, had already started to itch, and I regretted putting it on in the first place.

'Thank you, Reg. I will pass on your compliments to Bessie.' He threw back his head and laughed, while I served myself from the platter his footman politely offered.

'We barely got a wink of sleep last night thinkin' how we'll soon visit Paris an' New York, an' finally see for ourselves the things Daddy used to talk about,' Thomas said, his grin wide as he glanced up at Hamish, turning back to smile at me. My stomach dropped at the mention of Aaron; however, I summoned all my strength to hide the grief bubbling up inside me.

'It will be wonderful, Thomas,' I replied, smiling back while chewing my marmalade toast. I gazed out the window, avoiding Hamish's stare, finding the weather much improved; the sun fighting hard today to break free of the clouds that had obscured it the majority of the time we had been guests at Merinda Manor. Hamish had crept into my bedchamber every night since we had been here, and several arguments had ensued regarding the attention I allowed Reg to show me. As far as I was concerned, I was free to do as I pleased; however, in Hamish's eyes, I belonged to him. I refused to allow him to control me, and he refused to mind anything I said, and continued to do as he pleased and say whatever he liked, much to my chagrin.

'Please pass on my regards to Sister Mary Josephine today, Abigail. It was a privilege to have a woman as sweet as her as my guest. I certainly understand why you love her so deeply. You remind me of mothers and daughters everywhere in the world. It does not seem to matter if you bring them into the world yourself, or if they come to you from another. It would appear from my observations of you and Sister, the love between you is no different. I would hope Thomas and Emmy will be given the opportunity in future to have a father again,' Reg remarked, his brows drawn, while Hamish stiffened, his shoulders straightening as he sat back in his chair.

Reg had graciously invited Sister to dinner several nights before, and she had enthusiastically accepted. Returning with us in the late afternoon from the orphanage, Archie had slowed the carriage several times when we neared the estate for Sister to point out a number of places familiar to her. Although she had once written, telling me in the strictest of confidence that she herself had been born at Merinda Manor to the cook in service there at the time, we had never spoken of it since. Not in our written correspondence or in person. Still holding fond memories of growing up at the estate, she remembered Reg as a lad of five when she left to join the convent only months before her eighteenth birthday. Sadness overwhelming her, Sister spoke of her mother, Agnes, and told us how she never married, remaining at Merinda Manor until her death nearly twenty-five-years ago. Reg remembered Agnes with great affection, and they had gone on for hours afterwards talking of their memories of Merinda Manor and the people who roamed within its walls all those years ago, along with several who still did.

I had listened to her in silence and had been quite taken aback to hear her talk of things she had never spoken of before. To hear her mother had been unhappy with her choice to dedicate her life to God, Sister made the decision for herself and departed in the night, taking only a small bag, while leaving a letter for her mother to apologise. She travelled to Inverness the very next day to join the Sisters of Emiliani, accepting the offer of a ride on the back of his horse from a friend who agreed to keep her confidence, while trusting him implicitly, as he had also been born at the estate several years before her, a young groom at the time and a close friend since birth. Soon transferred to the orphanage in Edinburgh as a postulant, she found me on the doorstep only a week later.

Her mother's dear friend, Lady Isabelle Delmont, visited within days of her arrival at the orphanage, the excuse she gave at the time being to check on her welfare on behalf of the only parent she had. Upon finding her happy and committed to her chosen lifestyle, Lady Delmont promised to inform her mother and wished her well. Sister described what she called a strange conversation passing between them before they parted for the last time; however, she would not elaborate, only saying my great-aunt Isabelle died shortly afterwards at Merinda Manor in the guest cottage she had stayed in.

'We don't need another daddy, Mr Lord. We had the best one in the world, and he will always be our only father, even when we can't see him. It's our mummy we worry about. We would like her to have another husband now to look after her. Thomas and I are blessed, as we have many who care for us, but Mummy has no one once our Daddy was killed. Our Uncle Leo has been saying lately that he will have to marry her if no one else will have her, but we can't imagine it. They fight like two feral barn cats, and we know without a doubt one of them would be found dead in mysterious circumstances within a week. And he does not like women. He only shares his bed with men,' Emmy advised matter-of-factly. Reg's eyes lit up in amusement before he glanced at me enquiringly, and I nodded my head slightly.

'Well, Emmy, we are only here for a short time in the scheme of things, but it's far too long to live in misery. I am of the belief that men who hold romantic feelings for other men are born this way, and there's nothing to be done about it. I try not to make judgements one way or the other, given I was born to like women. That is the way I am. I have heard many stories since I met you and your mummy about your Uncle Leo. He sounds like an interesting man. Regarding your mother finding someone to look after her, I agree wholeheartedly, and I'm confident she will find that person in no time. As for your Uncle Leo, I must admit, I look forward very much to meeting him when I visit Willow Grove,' Reg replied, Emmy beaming up at him while Hamish and Thomas snorted in amusement.

'Interestin' isn't the word for him. Add boss gossiper an' chief whinger, an' he's spoiled, but he's a loyal friend to our Ma, so we choose to only take notice of his better qualities,' Thomas told him as he bit into his third piece of toast.

'That's a very generous way to look at it, Thomas,' Reg said, pouring himself a fresh cup of tea. His staff cleared the table of dirty dishes as Thomas smiled up at him.

'I will warn you now, sir. Our horses are much better than yours. You may wear a crown and own all this,' Emmy interrupted, sweeping her hand around the extravagant room, 'but ours are the best

Martarinos you will ever lay your eyes on. You will turn green with envy and drop to the ground.' Laughter filled the room, even Hamish finding some humour in the moment.

Anxious to leave, I wiped my mouth politely before standing, hurrying them along. Reg's well wishes still ringing in my ears, we moved quickly through the hallways, passing room after room until we stepped out the front door to find the carriage waiting, Archie smiling from his seat upfront. He jumped up, his heavy boots thudding on the cobblestones as we hurried down the stairs and towards him.

'Is Lord Harrington speakin' truth or fiction about comin' tae stay?' Hamish asked, his voice low as we watched Thomas refuse assistance from Archie and help Emmy inside, swiftly climbing in behind her.

'Truth. I enjoy his company and am not opposed to spending more time with him. I consider him a friend, and would like to see him again.' He offered me his hand, helping me up, soon following me inside and making himself comfortable beside me as he closed the door.

'I think yer leadin' him on. There's naw chance of anythin' startin' between ye 'cause I willnae allow it. Ye need tae tell him the truth o' the matter,' he whispered, and I turned to glare at him.

'What the bloody hell do you want me to tell him? That you share my bed sometimes? That's all it is, and all it ever will be. It's none of his business, or yours for that matter, what I do in my bedchamber. And I am not leading him on, you bastard. I have told him I will not marry again; therefore, will not allow him to court me. That does not change the fact we have become close friends and I like the man. I will be seeing him again, and it has nought to do with you,' I whispered back, his cheeks flushed in frustration, his gaze stony.

Thomas and Emmy chatted animatedly as the carriage wound its way down the roads and around the small hills; my eyes closed while listening to their melodious laughter. We were soon trotting down the main street of the small village, some of the shopkeepers still there from when I was a bairn, the cottages on small plots of land giving way to open pasture, while Emiliani House loomed in the distance.

'Don't be melancholy, Mummy. We will see Sister again. I feel it deep inside me,' Emmy reassured me, taking my hand in hers. I sniffed, nodding slightly as Hamish clapped his hands three times to get our attention.

'Naw tears or thinkin' o' anythin' today that'd make any o' us sad. Let's enjoy the time left with Sister, an' we can miss her tomorrow. How about we play *Key Tae The King's Garden*?' Thomas and Emmy stared back at him blankly, and he snorted. 'Aye, then. It's much like *Grandmother's Trunk*, only we cannae sit on the ground in a circle.' They shrugged their shoulders at him, and turning to me, Emmy rolled her eyes while Thomas appeared similarly unimpressed. 'Och, come away with it. I'll show ye an' start. *I sell ye the key tae the King's garden*, then I have tae point tae the person on me left or right, an' they have tae add tae it by sayin' somethin' like this, *I sell ye the rope that held the key o' the King's garden,* an' the next person says, *I sell ye the goat that wore the rope that held the key o' the King's garden.* Ye go round takin' it in turns 'till someone forgets tae repeat it back in the order 'twas said.' The carriage was silent, bar the clip-clopping of the horses' hooves, the children returning his stare.

'Borin' as eatin' brown paper for brekkie,' Thomas remarked, Hamish flinching for a moment.

'Or suffering through one of Uncle Leo's performances when he's given himself the starring role,' Emmy added, screwing up her nose in disdain. 'Someone other than Mummy needs to tell that man he cannot hold a tune, and remind him the kitchen is not a stage, or our home a theatre.' Emmy shook her head in disbelief before placing her hand on Hamish's sleeve. 'I will agree to play with you, Uncle Hamish, but only to distract myself until we arrive, and I do not wish to hurt your feelings. I love you more than chocolate.' His face softened, no different from the chocolate they spoke of melting in the sunlight. I closed my eyes, a peace settling on me, their voices fading as I drifted in and out of sleep.

The carriage came to an abrupt halt, jarring me awake. Bleary-eyed, I stared up at Emiliani House, the two Sisters sweeping the front verandah with their straw brooms, pausing to wave while several children scampered inside for their breakfast.

'Hurry up, Mummy. They may still be serving pancakes,' Emmy called out over her shoulder as she jumped down, Thomas close behind as Archie came to the door, a wide grin on his face.

'I've a soft spot fer this place, Mistress. The Sisters here are selfless, an' make a real difference fer the young ones.' I nodded, taking his hand as I stepped down from the carriage, Hamish tucking his newspaper up under his arm before following me.

'I know there are far worse places a child could be,' I said, and he smiled as I turned back to him, a sadness in his eyes.

'Och, an' dinnae I ken? I spent some years in the workhouse after me Ma died. Was fostered away from me brother an' sisters fer a time.' A lump lodged in my throat, and knowing now who he was and our connection, I avoided his stare and turned to climb the stairs. 'Dinnae be sad on me behalf, Mistress. It all worked out fer me in the end. An' me brother, an' me sisters. Weel, most o' me sisters.' I continued on, unable to speak for fear of making a spectacle of myself, while fighting an urge to turn back and run to him, to embrace my uncle before sitting him down to find out every detail he knew of my mother and her kin. Knowing it would come to no good, I continued on.

There was no one to be seen when we stepped inside; the hallway empty, our footsteps the only sound as we hurried to the dining hall. Finding the children eating breakfast, Thomas and Emmy sat down to a second breakfast with two of the older girls they had befriended during our time here.

Hamish and I left them with their friends, continuing on to find Sister Josephine. Making our way down the hallway towards the parlour where Sister often went to escape the chaos, we turned a corner, and I gasped, the wind knocked out of me, a Sister in far too much of a hurry colliding with me. Hamish reached out to steady me as I doubled over, gasping for breath while she slowly straightened up, her face a mottled red, her expression twisted in fury. She glared down at me; her shaking finger pointed in my face, her wooden rosary beads swinging by her side.

'Weel, here she is. The lady o' the manor has returned, nae doubt expectin' all tae bow down in her presence an' move out o' her way or risk bein' knocked down.' Her eyes passed over me several times, while a grey aura swirled around her like storm clouds. Swallowing hard, I raised my eyes to meet hers, smiling as brightly as I could as I straightened up in front of her, while summoning all my strength to keep my composure. Hamish stood silent beside me as he glared at her in disbelief.

'Good morning, Sister Mary Monica. I do apologise for being in such a hurry and bumping into you. It is splendid to see you in such good health. I understood you were called away?' Her knuckles white, the rosary beads gripped tight, an awkward silence hung above us.

'I've naw been anywhere. Just avoidin' ye, ye scabby bassa, yet here ye are, the famous Mrs Aaron Cavanaugh. I've nae doubt that ye' an' yer criminal o' a husband brought the whole mess tae yer own door, an' I've naw shed a single tear on yer behalf. As fer me health, ye wouldn't care one way or another if the truth be told on the matter. I never liked ye. Always such a rebellious waif with opinions far above yer station when yer worth nought. Nae one wanted ye here then, an' nae one wants ye here now. Tae have tae listen tae the talk, as if ye are the virgin mother herself, almost drove me tae the gin bottle many a night, but tae witness ye gettin' all this,' she snarled, her thick finger pointing at my gown, then my jewellery as I gasped, feeling sick to my stomach, my legs trembling. Hamish reached out and steadied me, his hand on my waist to prevent me crumpling to the ground, his face stony, his tongue silent. 'I cannae think o' anybody more undeservin' than ye tae be given such good fortune, but then o' course, I hear recently yer luck has changed fer the worst, an' I celebrated with a nip o' whisky in me room that night. I cannae think o' a better punishment sent down by the Almighty himself tae ensure ye suffer fer the sins ye continue tae commit. May yer husband rot in the pits o' hell as a result, Mrs Cavanaugh,' she hissed, mocking me in her tone and manner, widening her eyes as if challenging me. To what? I was uncertain, but I recognised hate when I saw it.

'Sister Mary Monica, you are a servant of God. You are not allowed to be this mean or hateful towards me,' I murmured, then promptly burst into tears, the urge to vomit overwhelming me.

'Aye, an' here are the tears just as I expected. There are nae journalists here, nor anybody tae run after ye tae take yer picture fer the papers with these pretend tears runnin' down yer face. Tae cry, ye must have feelin's, an' fer that, ye need a heart, somethin' ye dinnae possess, an' never have.' I remained where I was, my feet stuck to the floor, as did Hamish, Sister standing before us unmoving. 'Ye come from evil, Abigail, an' yer wicked. That I've always kent fer certain about ye. Since the day ye were left on the doorstep, ye have been like a stone in me shoe, rubbin' me wrong an' irritatin' me no end. I cannae look at ye without wantin' tae hurt ye, an' I have the overwhelmin' urge tae smack ye 'till yer perfect face bleeds all over the floor. Yer nought, Abigail. Nought. Ye came from nowhere, an' belonged tae no one. Even yer dead husband kent how fortunate he was tae escape the likes o' ye, even if forced tae do it by death. George Maslow is kin, me favourite first cousin tae be clear, an' I ken without doubt he would never do what ye have accused him o'. All lies! I hope yer sufferin' has only begun, an' every day from here on forth that ye draw breath 'till yer sent tae join yer outlaw husband in the fire where ye belong, is filled with the misery ye deserve,' she hissed, her face so close to mine I could smell porridge, her breath hot against my cheek. Hamish reached out and gently took her by the arm, moving her away from me, while I remained where I was, my head pounding as if it would explode, my legs threatening to give way, my heart shredded into a mess of confusion and hurt.

'That is quite enough, Sister. I fear openin' me mouth tae a servant o' God in this manner, but ye need tae hush now an' be silent. The words yer spittin' out yer mouth are vile an' untrue, an' I'll naw have anyone speakin' tae Abigail in this manner,' Hamish said, his voice steady, while his face resembled thunder. She glared at him, then at me, then back at Hamish, her eyes glinting dangerously.

'An' who may ye be? Her lover, I assume. Abigail has always been kent fer her loose morals an' low standards.' She paused, familiarity flickering across her face. 'Aye, I ken exactly who ye are. Ye were in the papers a few times. Yer her husband's best friend who manages Willow Grove fer her. 'Tis all makin' sense. She would've had ye in her bed long afore Aaron was sent directly tae hell tae await her arrival,' she spat, while Hamish shook his head in disbelief.

'Yer a wicked wee woman, aren't ye? Spittin' poison like this, let alone thinkin' this way, would have every good Catholic bayin' fer yer blood if they knew ye were responsible fer raisin' these bairns. What kind o' bride have ye made the Almighty? Goin' from what I've heard in the last few minutes, ye may need tae prepare fer a divorce. I've always known ye an' yer kind had threads o' evil runnin' through ye, an' yer as dangerous as a yellow-bellied snake, but 'tis naw often ye show yer venomous forked tongue in front o' witnesses. Ye should hang yer head in shame fer what ye have said tae Abigail,' He paused, her glare fixed on his handsome face, his voice low but steady. 'Everythin' around ye, includin' the clothes ye wear an' the food ye eat, is paid fer by this woman ye so obviously despise, far more than ye appreciate the comfortable life she's provided ye. I think that demands respect at the very least, dinnae ye, Sister?' His tone menacing, he took me by the arm and brushed past her, her mouth open as she remained where she was, staring after us. 'I'll be sure tae mention yer name when I'm next interviewed for the papers, Sister. I'm sure many will be interested in Mrs Cavanaugh's thoughts on how she was treated by ye when livin' here as a helpless waif. Cut that out an' put it in yer scrappy books.' I doubted anyone had ever spoken to her in this manner, or laid hands on her before today.

'Ye will have nought but trouble bein' involved with the likes o' her, Mr Makenzie. Far too many unsettlin' incidents occurred here around the time the imp was born. Mark me words, she's filled with an evil I cannae describe or put in tae words. I kent it the first time I laid eyes on her, an' I still feel it just standin' near her. It dinnae surprise me at all when I discovered she was related tae that witchin' hoore, Isabelle Delmont. Get away from her while ye still can,' she called after us, her face pinched. Hamish hurried me along down the hallway, his arm supporting my weight as I sobbed silently into my handkerchief. I had never understood why she detested me so intently, and today was no different.

Admitting often to those around me I had not been a perfect child, was headstrong, and known for getting up to mischief; however, I was far from the worst who had ever been dragged up within the walls of Emiliani House, of that I was certain. Most here seemed to like me well enough. Well, except for Sister Mary Monica, and to a lesser degree, Sister Mary Agnes—my relief when she went to God soon after her transfer back to the mother house, leaving me ashamed to this day. Sister Agnes did not like children, any of them; however, Sister Monica seemed to love all of them—except for me.

Chapter Twenty-Three

W E FOUND SISTER JOSEPHINE in the garden near the barn, her gaze fixed on the abandoned milking shed, her legs tucked up underneath the carved wooden bench where she seemed to be saying the rosary, her nimble fingers moving from one polished bead to the next, while her lips moved in silence. Hamish led me over, a goat bleating as she grazed in the herb garden, a young man I assumed to be the gardener running towards her after only realising she had escaped her enclosure. He sat me down next to Sister, and I broke down again as she slipped her arms around me in a tight embrace, appearing startled to find us here so early.

'Och, what has happened tae cause all this, mo luaidh?' My body trembled as I sobbed harder, her gentle hand on my cheek. Hamish lowered himself down beside her, and promptly informed her of what he had witnessed, her expression stony as she listened in silence, my head in her lap as she stroked my hair, my attempts to compose myself failing miserably. 'As ye would both understand, I'm naw allowed tae speak ill o' me own sisters in Christ, but I'm so very upset she's behaved in this way towards ye. I have faith the good Lord above will look upon me with grace, an' forgive me this one, wee sin.' She turned back to stare at the milking shed, the stone wall crumbling in places, a small section of the roof caved in—a stark contrast to the barn standing next to it, the walls and roof repaired, the livestock inside warm despite the frigid weather. I had been under the impression before arriving that all the out-buildings had been repaired a decade ago, and still felt slightly confused as to why this one had not; however, when asking a number of people on more than one occasion, every single one of them avoided answering. 'It was clear tae all o' us from the moment Sister Mary Monica set eyes on wee Abigail, she took a dislike tae her. I still tae this day cannae understand how a grown woman o' God could feel anythin' but love towards an innocent wean, especially one so bonny. She had these eyes that seemed tae be a hundred, an' a mass o' auburn hair when only hours old. She was blue from the cold when I found her, an' I could naw help but fall in love with the lass. If I were naw a woman o' faith, I'd admit 'twas as if she'd been here before, so bright an' alert, her emerald eyes starin' back at me as if she were tryin' tae communicate. As she grew, she'd babble away, as if talkin' tae someone who understood. She certainly knew what she was sayin'.' Hamish chuckled to himself, while Sister continued to stroke my hair, a smile touching her lips at the memory, while speaking only to him as I tried to calm myself. 'Once wee Abigail could strin' her words taegether, 'twas shockin' how she spoke. Naw like a Scottish lass at all, an' despite bein' raised here an' never settin' foot outside Scotland afore leavin', she sounded naw different than a well-bred English lass. Sister Mary Monica's dislike fer her increased the older she grew, an' I felt obligated tae stay here tae protect the wean 'till she was grown enough tae protect herself.'

'Aye, but wee Abigail is a woman now,' Hamish pointed out, his attention on the gardener wrestling with the goat, my sobs now silent tears, my head heavy in her lap as I stared up at the sturdy branches of the oak above sheltering a myriad of birds.

'Weel, now I stay 'cause I know I found me callin', an' while Sister Mary Monica remains the head o' the house, me place is here should another wee lass require me protection. I've never seen her act this way towards any bairn. Except wee Abigail, o' course. Sounds tae me, Hamish, ye handled the situation well. I'll naw be raisin' it with her, either, an' I doubt she'll be raisin' it with me. Sister Mary Monica knows me feelin's on the matter, an' rarely crosses me path these days, or causes me disruption.' Hamish nodded, while I sat up and blew my nose before wiping my face clean, her eyes on mine. 'She may appear tae be a terrifyin' an' powerful force tae, ye, Abigail, but nae go forettin' I've lived alongside the woman fer most o' me life. She knows me well, just as I know her, an' is reluctant tae upset me, an' that is all I'll say on the matter.' Hamish rose to his feet and wandered over to the fence to cast an experienced eye over the stallion craning his neck towards him, his soft whinny catching my attention. 'Ye do need tae know fer yer own self, I was naw aware at the time the bonny wean I found that dark night in the basket out front was connected in any way tae Isabelle Delmont. I suspected she was yer kin later, but wasnae 'till I received yer first letter after ye left us I knew it fer certain.' She gently wiped my face as I straightened up, sniffing again before forcing a weak smile.

'Thank you, Sister, for all you've done and continue to do for me. It matters not where I come from anymore, or those connected by blood.' She nodded as I glanced back at the mansion, my eyes darting from window to window then back at the grounds. I was well aware Sister Mary Monica would be delighted to look out over the garden to find me sobbing as though my heart was broken—and I refused to give the old mole the satisfaction. Sister took my hand in hers, while calling Hamish back to her side, placing her hand on his shoulder when he sat down heavily beside her.

'I apologise again fer what Sister Mary Monica said tae ye both. I've always tried me best tae shelter ye away from her, mo luaidh. That was why I lied, God forgive me fer it, an' told ye she was called away. I was hopin' ye would naw come face tae face durin' yer visit, an' did believe the heavenly father had answered me prayers, 'till now. I'll be spendin' all next year doin' me penance fer lyin', an' fer tryin' tae justify me actions tae meself an' all around me.' A smirk touched her lips, and I smiled as Hamish rose to his feet again, calling back over his shoulder he needed to speak to the gardener regarding the oversized vegetables growing all around us. Appearing calmer after talking with Sister, he wanted to give us time alone, my gaze fixed on him as he approached the young man at the door of the barn, the goat now secured by a rope around her neck and being dragged inside, clearly against her will, going by the noise.

'Ye ken he's in love with ye, dinnae ye, mo luaidh? He told me himself. I'm surprised a man like him, so strong an' handsome, has turned out tae have such a sensitive soul. He runs far deeper than I first thought, an' I never expected him tae talk tae me of ye. He's a different kettle o' fish compared tae yer Aaron, an' he forgets I know every soul livin' at Willow Grove as well as ye do through yer letters,' she said thoughtfully as we watched him from across the garden, deep in conversation with the gardener.

'I know he is, Sister, and I do not know what to do about it.' I felt ridiculous. I was a grown woman who already had a family. Why I could not get my life in order was frustrating the hell out of me.

'Yer tyin' yerself up in knots fer naw reason. Ye dinnae have tae do anythin' about it at all, wee Abigail. Take life one day at a time, an' address what dinnae serve ye when an' if it happens, that's all ye can do tae keep yer own sanity. Who knows what wonderful things may come tae ye? He's a good man, an' he loves Thomas an' Emmy very much an' would make a good husband tae ye, an' a good father tae them. Not today or tomorrow, not even next month or next year, but I dinnae think he'll give up on ye, an' I ken how determined ye can be. Yer likely tae muddle this along fer another ten-years.' She smiled to herself, patting my hand as I looked over at him again. I knew he was a good man and any woman would be lucky to have him. The problem was, I did not want any man to call my own other than Aaron. Not to marry, anyway.

'What do you mean by determined?' I asked, my brows arched suspiciously as I sniffed again, wiping the last of my tears away.

'Weel, ye have made up yer mind you'll never love or marry again. I know ye better than ye know yourself, wee Abigail. Once you make up your mind, 'tis almost impossible fer anyone tae change it. I worry fer ye, mo luaidh, an' dinnae want ye tae grow old alone. I know what that feels like. I know in me head I'm naw really alone, but it does feel that way sometimes. I've a husband ye cannae see, an' naw bairns tae leave any legacy tae, other than ye, mo luaidh.' A wry smile touched her lips, our hands entwined on my lap.

'I am also married to a man you cannot see, so I completely understand,' I teased, and she laughed aloud, the pigeons at our feet scattering in every direction, the smell of mint, parsley and lemon thyme wafting up my nose.

'He's a braw lad. I overheard several o' the postulants whispering about him last night, the sinful lassies. They were talkin' about the size o' him, an' how strikin' they find him tae be. If they're naw careful, they'll spend more time in confession with Father Appleby than out o' it.' She threw back her head and laughed again, her voice music to my ears. Casting a discreet glance in his direction, he towered over the gardener, his mood serious as he discussed new farming methods with the poor man, who clearly wanted to go about his work.

'He is handsome, and all you believe him to be, but you've not witnessed us argue. He is exasperating and never gives in, only wanting to control everything I do, and I will not have it. Not from him, or any other man. I do not need to be married, and I do not want to be now Aaron is gone. I have been forced to make all the decisions on my own now, and I could not go back to seeking a man's permission in relation to everything I do. I am slowly getting used to not having anyone to answer to for the first time in my life. I respected Aaron as the head of the household, and I was a good wife to him, and allowed him to be the boss, but I will not ever do that again. I was fortunate he was a kind and sensible man, and he never abused my trust and always consulted me about decisions that needed to be made, asking my thoughts on the matter. Although I tried to be submissive and agreeable, I used to argue terribly with him, too, now I think back.'

'They are the times we live in, mo luaidh, have always lived in, an' will continue tae live in while a man's pride is considered more important than a woman's right tae walk among 'em as an equal. Ye must be subservient tae yer husband, or ye will shame him, an' yerself. I cannae imagine ye were an easy wife tae control fer poor Aaron, God rest him, but I do know he loved ye well. 'Twas so very clear in yer letters durin' the time he was beside ye, but he's gone now, wee Abigail. Ye deserve tae be with a man who'll love ye just as deeply, an' I believe Hamish does. If ye would only let him knock down the walls ye have built around yer heart since losin' Aaron, ye would find happiness once again. A lass like ye was put on this earth tae love an' be loved. It hurts me heart tae think o' ye spendin' the rest of yer life alone.'

I stayed by her side the entire day, while Hamish helped with the chores outside, and Thomas and Emmy played on the manicured lawns with their new friends. Thrilled with the new Emiliani House, I surprisingly felt comfortable here for the first time. The Sisters, old and new, treated me like family—all except for Sister Mary Monica, who I had not laid eyes on since her vicious attack on me. Knowing she was a Maslow had cleared some of my confusion over her treatment of me now, but did not explain her treatment of the newborn wean I once was. Pushing it all to the back of my mind, I set out to enjoy my last day with Sister, not knowing when or if we would ever meet again in this lifetime.

I glanced out the window of the parlour, and satisfied the rain would hold off, turned back to finish the last of the afternoon tea. Thomas and Emmy sat opposite with several friends drinking warm cinnamon milk, their excited banter filling the room for the last quarter of an hour. Teresa and Martha only recently turned fourteen, and had lived at Emiliani House since being abandoned on the front steps only weeks apart. They were not related by blood as far as anyone knew, but had been like sisters since they could walk. My children liked them immediately, meeting the day we arrived when they kindly offered to show them around the mansion and grounds. Sticking together like overcooked rice everyday since, they had become firm friends, while Thomas and Emmy were impressed by their fortitude and cheerfulness considering they had no parents.

'Aye, is it true, then, Mrs Cavanaugh? That yer our benefactor? I'm only sayin' 'cause if ye are, I'd like tae thank ye fer helpin' us, an' fer givin' us such a wonderful life here. We've heard many stories from the Sisters about what it used tae be like. It only started tae change the year before we arrived,' Martha told me, my cheeks flushed. It was not a secret that I supported the orphanage; however, it was not something I spoke about in great detail to anyone other than Mr Malcolm and Sister. I was unsure how the children happened upon information my connection to the orphanage was more than that of a grateful waif returning home, given even Thomas and Emmy had no knowledge of the extent of my involvement when it came to Emiliani House prior to our visit.

'I do help out a little, Martha, and I'm thrilled to have heard from all of you how much you enjoy living here. I know it can be difficult when you are separated from kith and kin and are at the mercy of strangers. It eases me to know this place is comfortable, your bellies are full, and most importantly, you are safe and well cared for. Between the lessons you attend each day, and all the interesting things to be done around here keeping you all so very busy, I'm happy you have plenty of time to decide what you would like to do when you leave Emiliani House. For now, you can enjoy being young,' I replied, her face lighting up, while movement caught my eye near the open door. Isla scampered inside, soon followed by Ruthie, both gasping for air as they climbed up onto my lap and made themselves comfortable. Hamish and Sister sat companionable in their leather armchairs by the fire, a flicker of pride in Sister's eyes as she cast her gaze over the children sprawled on the lounges and perched cross-legged on the carpets, most eating their second slice of sponge cake, the raspberry jam made only this morning, the whipped cream sweetened with honey.

'Aye, I already ken what me callin' is, Mrs Cavanaugh. I plan tae join the Sisters here, an' help raise the bairns, while dedicatin' me life tae God an' doin' his service,' Theresa said, Sister's eyes fixed on her across the room. I could see her as a Sister of Emiliani one day in the near future. She was quiet and polite, and knew how to behave as a young woman should. Unlike me, she would suit them well.

'Aye, wee Teresa's been tellin' me this since she was a wean o' naw more than four, an' she's nae faltered once in her commitment. The next time ye visit me, mo luaidh, I've naw doubt ye will find 'tis Theresa greetin' ye at the front door. Only naw as a resident.' I sipped the last of my tea, nodding at Sister as she smiled across at me affectionately. It had come time for us to depart, and I had done everything in my power for the last half-hour to delay the inevitable.

'Mrs Cavanaugh?' Isla said, her face near mine as she stroked my cheek with her finger. Ruthie sat on my other knee, and not to be outdone, soon reached up to do the same.

'Yes, Isla?' She relaxed back against me, her eyes darting around the room as Hamish rose to his feet, reminding us again that we must depart if we were to arrive back at Merinda Manor at a respectable hour.

'Weel, Sister Maude has been on readin' duty o' late in our dormitory, an' we've finished The Wonderful Wizard of Oz only two nights past. If she weren't a slow an' borin' reader, we'd have finished a month o' Sundays ago.' She shook her head in disbelief, while I smothered a smile.

'You are fortunate to have that book, Isla. It was only published in 1900, and by January 1901, they finished printing the first edition and sold ten thousand copies, of which yours is one if you look at the date it was printed in the front. When I was living here, the only books I could find were so old they were not worth opening, and I would have cut off my...'

'Mrs Cavanaugh?' she interrupted. 'I know what I want tae be when I leave here, but Ruthie says I'm naw allowed.' She turned and gave her friend a dark stare, then scowled before sitting forward and grunting to herself.

'The way I heard it is you want to be a dancer.' I smiled down at her, encouraging her to continue, the twins busy gathering their things, Isla and Ruthie both sinking themselves deeper into my lap.

'Aye, there's that,' she said, nodding thoughtfully, 'but I want tae be Dorothy 'cause she's so splendid, but Ruthie says I'm more like the Scarecrow.' Ruthie rolled her eyes before slowly getting up from my lap and strolling across to the door, appearing to be in no rush. 'Yer that cowardly lion, Ruthie, an' I stand by it. If ye had o' let me choose Dorothy, I would've let ye be Toto,' she called out, Ruthie pausing to turn around in the doorway, her tiny eyebrows arched, her black hair plaited neatly down her back.

'Ye think far tae much o' yerself, Isla Ruth Naename. Ye will never make a Dorothy, an' ye dinnae deserve tae wear the ruby slippers. Ye cannae go a minute without shovin' food down that fat gob o' yers, an' yer face is uglier than the barn cats' backsides all put together,' Ruthie called back, her hand firm on the door jam, 'an' fer the love o' Jesus, Mary an' Joseph, at least I'm braw enough tae tell ye that ye cannae dance tae save yerself.' Isla gasped before jumping to her feet, startling me, her golden ringlets standing on end, her tiny hands curled up into fists, while Ruthie took off running down the hallway.

'Och, I'm goin' tae catch ye, Ruth Isla Naename, an' I'm goin' tae drag ye tae Sister Mary Monica's office by the lug meself fer tryin' tae destroy me dreams. An' fer stompin' on me heart,' Isla shrieked, already at the door, her tiny fist in the air as she disappeared around the corner, her footsteps surprisingly heavy as she chased after her friend—Ruthie now long gone, her calico bonnet catching my eye through the parlour window as she ran across the lawn towards the barn where her beloved cats lived. I smothered a smile as I leaned forward and collected the dirty cups, placing them on the tray, before gathering my things and rising to my feet. Sister came to my side carrying my cloak, and reached up to slip it over my shoulders, her blue eyes twinkling.

'You may have to separate those two for a time. Looks to me as if they dislike each other immensely.'

'Och, naw. They remind me o' ye an' Pollyanna at the same age. They're closer than most sisters, an' one would be lost without the other,' she remarked, her hand moving swiftly over the woollen cloak, brushing off a number of leaves picked up in the garden, along with several stray threads.

'I dread the thought of leaving you, Sister, and I do not know when I can come again. It now falls on my shoulders to ensure Willow Grove runs just as Aaron wanted.' She nodded, her hand on my shoulder. 'I feel a piece of my heart has been restored since arriving here; however, now we are forced to part, and I fear the sorrow it will bring not knowing when I will see you again. I wish you would reconsider leaving the Order and coming to live with us. We would care for you until you took your last breath, and you would be among family.' I felt tears sting my eyes, a smile touching her lips as she pulled me into a warm embrace. 'You have told me more than once you would have left had I not been here. Now is your opportunity. You are not even fifty, and could start a new life with us in Australia.' She pulled me closer, her voice barely above a whisper, her head on my shoulder.

'Aye, mo luaidh, I would like nothin' more, but I've an obligation tae the bairns here. I cannae leave 'em, despite wantin' tae pack me bag an' walk out o' here with ye now. Me life is here. I must finish what I started, naw matter what me own heart's desire may be. Ye go with all me love, an' I'm only a letter away. Whenever ye miss me an' want tae talk, sit down an' write me, as ye do. It'll ease yer mind, an' yer letters make me feel as if I am there beside ye when I read 'em.' I nodded, her hands cradling my face, her eyes shining as she gazed up at me. 'Remember all I have said tae ye 'till we meet again, an' I have faith we will soon enough. I pray daily fer us tae be reunited, an' I ask the Lord fer so much more fer ye, wee Abigail, but if all he does is keep ye safe an' happy enough with yer lot, I've done me job as yer caretaker.' She released me, and I straightened up, composing myself as best I could. She guided me to the door, where Hamish and my children stood waiting, Teresa and Martha embracing he and I both affectionately before walking us out. We stood on the verandah, Sister Josephine and I clinging to each other, while tears streamed down our cheeks. Thomas and Emmy continued down the stairs to say their goodbyes to the friends they had made, most now surrounding the carriage, all waiting to say their farewells and wish them luck.

'Would you visit me in Australia if I paid your fare? And promised not to keep you prisoner? And allow you to return here, if you must?' She smiled weakly, her eyes glistening as she took my hand in hers, swiftly leading me down the steps to where Hamish waited, the twins by his side. Crying tears of joy at meeting them, mingled with sadness at being forced to part so soon, Sister embraced Thomas, Emmy and Hamish in farewell, each shedding tears of their own. Hamish appeared just as sad as I felt as he helped Emmy up into the carriage, turning to wait for me as he watched Sister and I embrace again.

'I'd have tae get permission from Mother Mary Bernadette, but aye, nothin' would make me happier, mo luaidh.'

'Well, go and write your letter of request now, then.' I smiled down at her, kissing her on the cheek for what could be the last time.

'Safe travels, wee Abigail, an' remember what I tell ye. I only want ye tae be happy,' she called, sniffing loudly while wiping her face with her handkerchief. I climbed up into the carriage, my nose only inches from the window, my hand raised to wave her goodbye as she watched the horses pull away. It was not until we emerged from the driveway and turned onto the road leading back towards Edinburgh,

I broke down in heart wrenching sobs, my eyes closed tight, wishing it all away as Hamish pulled me into his arms.

Bessie stood behind me, her hands on my shoulders as I stared at my reflection in the oval mirror, the room lit up with more lanterns than usual, while several candelabras twinkled near the windows. She had only just finished styling my hair, pinning each curl to the nape of my neck, while I sat for her at the ornate dressing table in my undergarments, the corset she demanded I wear for the last dinner at Merinda Manor digging into my ribs and causing me some discomfort. She insisted I take extra care with my appearance tonight, wanting me to look nice for Lord Harrington, whom she liked a great deal, and would not loosen it a whisper no matter how much I pleaded, let alone allow me to disregard it all together.

'He kissed me differently last night. I am uncertain what that was about, but he seems to believe he's in love with me.' I sighed as her face lit up, several hair pins she held between her lips dropping to the floor.

'You heard that from his own lips, or was it gossip from the servants?' She raised an eyebrow suspiciously, and I nodded, her face lighting up again. 'What was it like? The kiss, I mean. Did you feel anything?' she probed before touching the back of my head, and I stood to finish dressing.

'It was nice. He has a way about him when it comes to romance, and he also appears to be quite experienced when it comes to the art of *rouler une pelle*.' I smiled to myself as she slipped my dress over my head, turning to secure the tiny buttons at the back, her face darkening for a moment.

'Are you thinking about taking him to your bed, Mistress? You know you can't be sleeping with Hamish and getting involved with another man while you're doing it? If anyone found out, you would be disgraced. I wish you would stop saying you won't marry again when you are clearly happy enough to accept one of the privileges of marriage. If you're going to allow a man into your bed, you *must* consider his offer of marriage. I won't have anyone thinking you are a woman of loose morals.' She grunted to herself before hurrying off to find my shoes, a smile touching my lips.

'Well, no one is going to find out unless you tell them. You're the only one who knows, so if my private business becomes common knowledge and my reputation is ruined, I will know who to blame,' I called out after her, the muffled grunts coming from my wardrobe making me smile. 'In all seriousness, Bessie, I no longer care what others think of me, nor will I base my decisions on anything other than what I believe is right for me and the children, or worry I could be gossiped about as a result. Aaron used to say that opinions are like arseh... Well, you know what he referred to, saying everyone has one and they should keep it to themselves, and I agree with him.'

'He had a crude mouth on him, that boy.' She returned to my side, kneeling down to slip my leather shoes on. 'You have your head firmly planted up your own backside if you think this isn't going to blow up in your face, Mistress. Lord Harrington is now in love with you, as is Hamish. Look at them. Both strong minded and intelligent, and far too used to getting what they want. Mark my words, Mistress. You are on dangerous ground.' She rose to her feet, and I bent down to kiss her forehead, the twins bursting into my bedchamber as she smiled up at me affectionately; however, continued shaking her head as I joined Hamish at the door and followed him out into the hall, Thomas and Emmy close behind.

'Good evening to you all,' Lord Harrington called out warmly, his arms spread wide in welcome as he turned around where he stood in the corner of the drawing room gazing out over the darkened sky, the sun now gone, the immaculate lawn sodden. 'I have ordered an exquisite banquet for your last night here with us, and I hope you enjoy every dish. The servants have been preparing since the wee hours, and as they like you all very much, have vowed to me they intend to make this evening particularly special.' He strolled across the room, meeting us near the fireplace just as his butler stepped inside and announced that dinner was served. I was aware we had been running late; however, it wasn't until I glanced across at the mantle, the huon pine clock quickly revealing the truth, I realised it had gone eight o'clock five-minutes before. He had been a wonderful host and treated us all as if we were related to the royal family itself, and tonight was no different as he ignored our tardiness and guided us to the dining room where we took our seats. One of the kindest people I had ever met, there was nothing I did not like about the man in word and deed, and the golden glow around him had drawn us closer.

The first course, steaming bowls of Cullen Skink, were already set out before us, while baskets of crusty warm bread had been placed within reach, the sherry that always accompanied the first course already poured into tiny crystal glasses. The thick and creamy fish soup was one of my favourites, the smoked haddock cooked to perfection with the leeks, onions and potatoes, while a mixture of high and low centrepieces ran the length of the table, the candles glowing gold as they twinkled, trails of creepers and flowers laying on the white linen tablecloth. A large bowl of exotic fruit sat in the very middle to accompany our dessert, and the children were encouraged by Reg at the end of every evening to take what they liked to their bedchamber should they wake hungry during the night. The second course soon followed, mackerel in a delicate sauce, the accompanying white wine fresh and crisp, as were the long green beans served with it.

'I heard the kitchen maids talking about your aunt, Mummy. They said you favour her, but she was a witch, no doubt about it,' Emmy announced, while Reg threw back his head and howled with laughter.

'Oh, dear Emmy. Lady Isabelle had no magic powers, nor was she maleficent. I remember her as a kind woman, and found she was always interested in what I was doing, no matter how trivial. She spent a great deal of time with me when she came to stay the last time at Merinda Manor after leaving for Australia that last time, well before I was born. Lady Isabelle left a long-lasting impression on me, and I have fond memories of her. You would have liked her very much, I promise,' Reg reassured her, and she nodded, her eyes fixed on the entrée of sweetbreads served with a glass of claret, followed by a vol-au-vent filled with salmon in a robust cheese sauce. Emmy turned her nose up at the sweetbreads before the footman politely offered her an extra pastry, pleasing her greatly given salmon was her favourite.

'In your staff's defense, I've heard much the same over the years. Well, not directly, but some have alluded to it,' I interjected, not wanting anyone to be reprimanded for speaking so freely in the presence of my children. The footmen carried in the relevé, the most substantial part of the banquet, the roasted joints of beef, lamb and poultry set down on the sideboard for Reg to carve, while they placed roasted potatoes and root vegetables down alongside boiled vegetables picked from their own gardens on the matching buffet. No sooner had we been served, the footmen carried in the next course of snipe, wild duck and pheasant served with game chips, so thinly sliced, you could see through the disc shaped potato, while I refused the glass of claret I was offered to compliment the meal, feeling light-headed already from all the wine and champagne. Next followed a series of entremêts, the dressed cauliflower sweet, while the savarin of apricots and cherry tart complimented the other. The conversation jovial and light from the time we arrived, the butler had cast several disapproving glances in our direction throughout the evening when the children became overexcited; however, I had chosen to ignore the mean spirited little man, and refused to meet his gaze when he placed the devilled sardines on the table in front of me alongside several wedges of cheese.

'I had a neighbour ask after you today, Abigail,' Reg said, shifting his chair back slightly from the table as the footmen cleared away the dirty dishes, a younger footman placing a clean set of wine glasses down, alongside dessert plates, an ice plate on top to set the finger-bowls, the silver cutlery polished to perfection. Another quickly set the finger-bowls to the left of each plate, while another entered with flavoured ices, serving them quickly, the room warm.

'Oh,' I said, shrugging my shoulders slightly, while picking up my spoon to eat the creamy gooseberry ice.

'Well, not really a neighbour as such.' He pointed in the direction of two grand estates bordering Merinda Manor, and I nodded, feeling curious despite the knots clenching in my stomach. 'They live down in Merinda na Monadh. I believe you are acquainted. Well, they tell me they are family friends. Mr and Mrs Appleby wanted me to remember them to you.' I sat back in my chair, my face warm, while he appeared puzzled. 'Have I offended you, Abigail?'

'Oh, no,' I said, shaking my head as the ice plate was whipped out from under my nose before I had finished, leaving the dessert plate underneath for the nuts and fresh fruit they offered, a glass of port of madeira placed in front of me despite my protests. 'The Appleby's are not friends of mine, nor have they ever been. I'm surprised they are still upright given they were old when I met them. Only on one occasion, mind you. When I first arrived in London. Please do not discuss me in their presence, Reg, as I am suspicious of their motives.' He nodded, appearing confused for a moment until I explained myself, albeit briefly, before he straightened his shoulders and raised his glass. 'Here's to friends, old and new, and those who so desperately want to be, but cannot.' I laughed aloud, as did he, Hamish finding no humour in it as Little Mary stepped into the dining room to take the children up to their rooms to help ready them for bed. They bid us goodnight, following her out obediently while we chatted of our day, along with Emiliani House, my stomach so full I thought I would burst. Reg placed his hand over mine, and turned to me, his expression sincere.

'I will miss you, my dearest Abigail, but I will ensure I make it a priority to travel to Australia in the following months after you are settled back home at Willow Grove. I am serious about courting you after you have had time to consider what we discussed last night.' Hamish slammed his hand down on the table hard, startling me, a gasp coming from my lips without warning, while Reg sat back in his chair suitably shocked, his eyebrows raised.

'Stop! I've had enough. Are ye goin' tae tell him the truth o' the matter, Abigail, or shall I?' He glared across at me, his eyes glinting dangerously, his voice low, while my hands trembled in my lap, hidden from view.

'Hamish, calm down. Please? We can discuss this in private instead of embarrassing our gracious host,' I said, my face flushing as he fixed me with his stare, while Reg looked on in silence, his face blank.

'I'm naw puttin' up with this anymore, Abigail. I love ye an' I'll naw allow another man tae court ye. I forbid it.' He slammed his fist down again, the remaining glasses threatening to spill the last of the madeira.

'But you are her brother-in-law,' Reg interrupted, his voice calm as he watched Hamish, his eyes fixed on his.

'Naw! I'm naw her brother-in-law!' Hamish roared, his handsome face twisted in rage. Reg leaned forward and poured him a whisky, kindly passing it over to him as Hamish calmed himself enough to tell him of our shared history, going right back from when we first met on the ship until this very day. I remained where I was, silent and unmoving, while grateful he did not reveal I had taken him to my bed in secret. Reg, too, remained silent, his eyes full of sympathy as he listened, nodding as Hamish told him of Aaron's last wish for us to be together.

'Hamish, I am not one to hurt another person with malicious intent; however, I too am in love with Abigail. I understand the situation, but I will not quietly bow out. In no way do I wish to make an enemy of you, but I will not withdraw my affection or attention unless Abigail makes that decision and asks me to. I think until that time comes; we leave it in her hands. I would like to remain friends with you both, as I like you, and I believe we could all be *mates,* as the Australians like to say. I very much want the same as you, Hamish. For Abigail to be happy once again.' Hamish nodded once, and Reg grinned, reaching out to shake his hand. I was aware he also enjoyed Reg's company and liked him as a person since getting to know him better during our stay.

'Aye, we'll leave it at that, then. I've nothin' against ye personally, Reg. I could even be mates with ye, as ye say, but I'll tell ye from man tae man right here where we sit. Abigail belongs tae me.' I grimaced, grunting to myself, fury rising in me as I listened to them go back and forth, albeit calmly and rationally. I had told them more than once, I had no intention of allowing anyone to court me, let alone marry me. And neither seemed to have heard me during the hundreds of times I had said it over the last few months. I abruptly rose to my feet, throwing my napkin on the table with some force, my glare passing between them and back again.

'I must excuse myself if I am to not lose my temper and make a fool of us all in front of your staff. I am tired and feeling wretched after today, and having to say goodbye to Sister is more than I can bear. At the moment, I would prefer not to be around either one of you,' I snapped, turning on my heel before marching to the door, while ignoring the curious glances from the butler and his men. Hurrying through the hallways and up the staircase, I arrived at my bedchamber door to find it open. Sighing deeply as I stepped inside, I locked it behind me with the key. Turning around to find Bessie waiting to help me ready for bed, relief washing over me at the sight of her.

'Why are you in such a tizzy?' She stepped towards me and took me by the shoulders, my body still trembling with rage. Infuriated, these two men seemed to see me as some prize to be won, both unwilling or unable to see I would never recover from the loss of my husband. To let any many court me when my heart would only ever belong to the one man I could never have again would be a betrayal. To him. To myself. To my children, and to my Aaron's memory and all we shared while he was here.

'Men are shit,' I spat, promptly collapsing into a flood of tears. Her face broke into a wide grin as she stared up at me, pressing a clean handkerchief into my hand.

'Oh, Mistress. Any woman with half a brain knows that. The important thing is to not let them get the best of you.'

Slowly and with much care, she guided me across the room, and after stripping off my gown and slipping my nightgown over my head, she gently pushed me down onto the chair in front of the dressing table.

'I am determined to get through this journey for the benefit of my children. I promised myself at least that before we left,' I murmured, more to myself than my friend and maid. She nodded silently, her hands moving quickly as she wiped the cosmetics from my face with Pond's cream, a favourite of hers. 'Thomas and Emmy need and deserve my full attention, not another man forcing his way in to save us from ourselves. They are all I have now. All Aaron has left here in this miserable, shit of a world to keep me breathing. Their happiness is my only priority.' Bessie nodded again, the silver brush in her hand gliding swiftly through my hair.

'And you are all they have now their beloved father is no longer with them, Mistress. Whatever choices you make will affect them.'

'I refuse to be pressured or manipulated by any man, and I include Hamish in this, despite how much I care for him,' I continued to rant, while she nodded sympathetically. 'Even though I've been honest with him from the beginning, I have come to realise I may have opened a door that would have been better left locked.' The left side of her mouth tucked up into a wry smile as she touched the back of my head and I stood, turning to embrace her.

'Ahhh, so now my words are ringing in your ears, you fiend.' She took me by the shoulder and led me towards the bed, my dressing gown over her arm.

'I know now I should have listened to you, and now I'm in a big mess,' I mumbled, my face warm, irritation with myself rising. Lowering myself down onto the bed, my bare feet on the carpet, she sat down next to me and took my hand in hers.

'All you need to be worrying yourself about is getting through this journey for the children's sake, and making sure they have wonderful memories so that when we return home, you can begin your lives again. That life looks different now, and while Aaron is no longer here in body, you can keep his memory and spirit alive for them. You made a solemn promise to Aaron, and it's a responsibility that is now yours to carry. I don't know what the future holds for you, Mistress, nor do I pretend to, but I do know as long as you are together, everything will eventually come good.' Placing my dressing gown on a hook beside the bed for the morning, she kissed me good-night. Bending forward, she pulled the heavy quilt back and helped me climb up onto the bed, covering me within moments. 'You lay your head now, Mistress, and sleep well. Stop worrying yourself over them boys, as fretting comes to nothing. They'll soon realise you say what you mean and mean what you say. I'll do my best to keep the suitors sniffing around at bay while you're away from home, and on our return, my sweet girl. It will all work out in the end, and why wouldn't it when you and the bairns have me to look after you for the rest of my life, no matter what happens?' A lump lodged in my throat as I stared up at her lovely face, her hand gently stroking my brow, her smile reassuring me I was not alone.

'Thank you, my darling Bessie. I honestly do not know what my life would be like without you in it. You are my best friend and confidante and I love you with all my heart,' I murmured, kissing her cheek as she kissed mine.

'Well, I love you, too, Mistress, but let's stop getting all sentimental. You just concentrate on what is important, and I will take care of the rest.' She straightened up, and patted my hand one last time before bidding me goodnight and quietly making her way to the door, extinguishing all but one lamp before she left.

As I lay under the covers with Bessie gone and the door securely shut, I drifted off to sleep—a river running through Willow Grove, a pink diamond, and a black rat invading my dreams and leaving me exhausted before the new day even dawned.

A Word from the Author

Thank you for taking the time to read my series 'Samsara-The First Season'.' It's been nearly a decade since I wrote the first sentence of Abigail's story, and it is a privilege to share it with you.

If you have a few moments, I would be deeply grateful if you left a review on your chosen platform or website. It will help other readers find books that they may never have discovered otherwise. Your feedback means the world to authors and we cannot thank you enough for your support! Thank you for investing your valuable time and money in this story and I hope you enjoyed reading it.

If this series was not for you, that's perfectly okay. We all have different tastes as readers and we can't please everyone all the time. Thank you again for your support and I wish you well in finding novels that bring you joy. Much love to all xx

To find out more,
go to www.jlmartinauthor.com

SAMSARA

THE FIRST SEASON

Letting Go
Volume One Book Seven

What if you could remember a past life?
Or worse, what if you couldn't?

*A*BIGAIL ATTEMPTS TO MEND *her broken heart by connecting to another, but questions if she truly has the ability to love again after losing Aaron.*

Strong friendships are formed during their time abroad, the most significant with a soothsayer, Lilith Arcadia. Opening a door to the afterlife Abigail never considered existed, she discovers her connection to Aaron is not broken, only invisible, and life does indeed go on. And on. And on.

Continue your journey with Abigail in the epic new Australian historical fiction series spanning a lifetime. Based in Geelong, this debut series by J L Martin spans a lifetime, from 1890 to 1968. Join thousands of readers accompanying this cast of characters through each decade, sharing their joy and sorrow, their triumphs and tragedies, while trying to find out the meaning of the golden glow. The first series of twelve full-length novels are available in ebook, audiobook and paperback from all good bookstores and on-line platforms, and the author's website.

www.jlmartinauthor.com